Twinning

Charles Kirk

Twinning

Vanguard Press

VANGUARD PAPERBACK

© Copyright 2024
Charles Kirk

The right of Charles Kirk to be identified as author of
this work has been asserted by him in accordance with the
Copyright, Designs and Patents Act 1988.

All Rights Reserved

No reproduction, copy or transmission of this publication
may be made without written permission.
No paragraph of this publication may be reproduced,
copied or transmitted save with the written permission of the publisher, or in accordance
with the provisions
of the Copyright Act 1956 (as amended).

Any person who commits any unauthorised act in relation to
this publication may be liable to criminal
prosecution and civil claims for damages.

A CIP catalogue record for this title is
available from the British Library.

ISBN 978 1 80016 964 7

This is a work of fiction. Names, characters, businesses, places, events and incidents are either the
product of the author's imagination or used in a fictitious manner. Any resemblance to actual persons,
living or dead, or actual events is purely coincidental.

Vanguard Press is an imprint of
Pegasus Elliot Mackenzie Publishers Ltd.
www.pegasuspublishers.com

First Published in 2024

Vanguard Press
Sheraton House Castle Park
Cambridge England

Printed & Bound in Great Britain

Acknowledgements

You may have an idea in your head, but everyone can be influenced by something they have seen, heard or done. If we all knew everything, then there would be no fun in life in having to learn something new.

"If you are the smartest person in the room, then you are in the wrong room." — Confucius

My sincere thanks go to the following for providing necessary help, usually in times of either panic or frustration. There is always someone out there to provide help, no matter how insignificant or trivial you think the problem may be.

Margaret's Florist in St. Annes, for expert advice on poppies.

Peter Sarstedt for great song titles.

Wikipedia just for being Wikipedia.

Everyone else for their encouragement.

Contents

Definitions	9
Appendices	10
A Little Introduction	13
Chapter 1	
Greetings and Meetings	15
Chapter 2	
The Dead See Scrolls	28
Chapter 3	
Time to go Home	50
Chapter 4	
A New Beginning	65
Chapter 5	
Far Better or Worse?	76
Chapter 6	
The Wedding Feats	93
Chapter 7	
The Mourning After	101
Chapter 8	
Schlock, Aleing and Watermelon	111
Chapter 9	
The Taming of the Shrewd	123
Chapter 10	
From Wags to Witches	132
Chapter 11	
Poetic Injustice	149
Chapter 12	
The Grapes of Ralph	155
Chapter 13	
Ducks and Drake	160
Chapter 14	
The Birds and the Bees	169
Chapter 15	
The Honey Trap	179

Chapter 16		
All Together Now		188
Chapter 17		
Sauces and Sources		194
Chapter 18		
Hooray Henry		204
Chapter 19		
Twinning		211
Chapter 20		
The Power and the Glory		229
Chapter 21		
The Power and the Gory		237
Chapter 22		
Little Feet		243
Chapter 23		
Big Foot		253
Chapter 24		
The Look of the Irish		261
Chapter 25		
The Storm Before the Calm		275
Chapter 26		
As Time Went By		281
Appendix 1		284
Appendix 2		285
About the Author		286

Definitions

Psionism

Ability to use psychic powers, manifesting itself through telepathy or special awareness.

Psychokinesis

The ability to move objects by mental effort alone.

Psychoanimatic Projection:

The ability to channel mental energy through an inanimate object to influence others.

Appendices

1 Places referenced with both their original and current name.

2 The First Arrivals.

Death makes you realise how short life is.

A Little Introduction

It was not so much a parish council that looked after the needs and welfare of the village, but more a group of slightly crafty, but well-meaning individuals who upheld standards, and maintained law and order; not that there was any crime, and generally catered for the wellbeing of every resident.

The small village of Stoleware had a population of around two hundred and fifty. However, no one had actually bothered to take an accurate headcount. It had always been on the list of things to do. Within the quiet rural village is a pub and brewery, a place of worship which was used as a social centre, meeting room and schoolroom, a general store from whence virtually anything could be obtained, a small but extremely well-equipped combined health centre and veterinary practice, a bakery, numerous other businesses and a number of extremely desirable, well-camouflaged, detached properties.

The village still generates its own power from an extremely efficient solar station. In fact, it's an idyllic haven where the annoying sound of a mobile ringtone is nowhere to be heard.

Just outside the village is a perfectly flat area of approximately two and a half thousand square metres. It is covered with a type of exceptionally smooth artificial grass, roughly ten centimetres in depth, on top of a cool, solid steel, retractable platform. There is a slight humming noise coming from below the surface. The purpose of this area will be explained later.

The village was totally self-sufficient, even down to all meats, vegetables, fuels, materials, utilities and general supplies. Nobody asked any questions and so no answers as to the initial legitimacy of the resources were ever necessary. There are only half a dozen well-maintained lanes within the confines of the village and one beautifully tarmacked, non-potholed road in and out of the village. Kenmore, in the Scottish Highlands, is the closest listed village being around twenty miles south-east of Stoleware. So Stoleware seems the perfect place that time has left alone.

The only professionally qualified resident was the doctor/surgeon who, when necessary, doubled as a vet. He had stumbled across the village, quite by accident, some years ago. It was not that he was kidnapped, more that he was delayed in his departure. Other residents were well-educated within the village to an extremely high degree and produced experts in the fields of information technology, energy, communications, construction, agriculture, engineering, chemistry, biology and any other subject you care to mention.

There is an abundance of extremely well-bred livestock, pedigree dogs and horses, the acquisition of such animals to be explained in time. There is also a high concentration of natural minerals within a one-hundred-mile circumference — copper, tin, coal, gold, silver and diamonds, and these have been carefully mined since the birth of the village some twelve hundred years ago, while still preserving the natural beauty and landscape of the surrounding area.

The nearest known river is the Tay and over the years, a number of channels have been cut to divert the clear, fast-flowing highland waters through the village. The Tay is still renowned for providing excellence in salmon and as fortune had it, our early fishermen accidentally discovered that salmon are attracted to light and therefore with an ingenious use of a sophisticated 'boxed beacon' as they called it, he lured the fish downstream towards Stoleware. More recently, solar-powered underground beams continued this extremely lucrative, yet highly illegal method of salmon fishing.

I sit relaxing in a perfectly secluded, unspoilt clearing in the woods, admiring the calming flow of the nearby stream. Suddenly a fully mature prime salmon leaps majestically, seemingly effortlessly, hardly disturbing the water's surface as it displays a perfect, almost acrobatic arc before returning gracefully to the clear water…

Chapter 1

Greetings and Meetings

"...that is mine!" yelled the burly Viking warrior as he struggled to land the slippery customer. "You lot find your own."

In the early part of the 840s, a large Norse fleet invaded the west coast of Scotland via the Isle of Mull, landing around Oban. A small scouting contingency of ten invaders slowly made their way east across the mainland and eventually found themselves by the River Tay. With it being rather late in the day, by the time they had found a safe and suitably secluded area near fresh water, they decided to set up camp.

Morning came and on waking, they were astonished at the surroundings to the extent that they, almost as one, decided to forego the fighting, even though the rape and pillage still had some appeal; and decided to settle, cultivate and develop the area as their newly found home. They had originally planned on going further north. However, they agreed that there were more than enough warriors available to fight any battles, and so made their own plans to explore lands to the east. There was not really much that ten scary looking fighters could contribute, should they meet a whole garrison of irate Scottish warriors seeking to slaughter the unwelcome visitors.

By chance, a scouting party of twenty battle-weary Scots had been travelling from the east along the shores of the River Tay and stumbled across our reluctant invaders nonchalantly taking time out, by now, being slightly intoxicated from the effects of traditional Viking mead. So, what do you do when the odds are two to one against? You are completely exhausted and the last thing you want is a violent and possibly avoidable confrontation.

As luck would have it, at about this time, Irish monks had started arriving in Scotland to establish a community and Christianise their Celtic brethren. Along with their good intentions, they brought with them a method of creating a stable alcoholic beverage by distilling heather ale.

Armed with some well-used weapons, the Scottish scouting party had also fortunately packed numerous corked bottles of this refreshment. Wary of their would be conquerors, the gallant, yet sociable scouting party, slowly approached the campsite. The Norsemen half-heartedly considered taking up arms but being slightly disorientated, quickly realised that common sense should prevail and were preparing to surrender. The surprised scouting party, after they had tried to intimidate the overseas warriors with a few perfunctory grunts and chants, on seeing no reaction, took this as an ideal opportunity to join in the time out and it was not long before an impromptu social was in full swing, drinks being freely exchanged. Language proved to be no barrier as no one could fully understand what the other was saying. It did not really matter. The Vikings had a slight knowledge of the English language; however, a broad Scottish accent was definitely beyond translation. Grunts and gestures sufficed. In no time at all, the whole thirty revellers were well gone, and the area was filled with the stench of alcohol and a scent of malodorous aromas emanating from a cacophony of personal wind instruments.

The following morning presented the pressing problem of nursing severe hangovers. Garmund, one of the Viking warriors, was familiar with natural remedies. Fortunately, the area had an abundance of centaury leaves, which when mixed with hot water calms the nerves and reduces the effect of such self-inflicted pain. It must have been quite amusing to watch the tenderness and caring displayed in administering medication to this group of over six-foot, sixteen stone plus warriors dressed in full traditional combat gear. Almost akin to trying to spoon feed a young child by saying, "Open wide, here comes the train."

Next on the agenda was breakfast. With such a large group of highly skilled warriors you would have imagined that trapping some of the local wildlife would be quite a simple task. Oh no. After approximately two hours, the results were in. There was: one warrior with a dislocated shoulder, three with concussion having run headfirst into trees while chasing rabbits, six black eyes, the result of tripping over colleagues sitting on logs suffering from diarrhoea and one from a spear in the foot, from a colleague's misdirected shot at a wild boar.

Luckily, not too far away was a handsome stag. It was not dead, just totally intoxicated from the night before, having entered the campsite while all were asleep and having quenched its thirst on whatever liquids were left over. It was quite sad trying to decide who would have the unenviable task of finally slaughtering the deer. Nobody had the heart.

Fortunately, the problem solved itself. The deer woke, startled, quickly stood, hardly majestically though; and started its escape, tripping over one of the Vikings who had just risen to his feet after his fourth case of the runs and impaled itself onto his upright hunting spear. Lunch was caught. A spit was hastily erected, dry wood collected and before long, a roaring fire was lit to roast the meal. Neither group could honestly complain — fresh salmon yesterday and venison today.

Both Scotsmen and Vikings were proud of their appearance and tried to maintain a high standard of dress. Both were familiar with the arts of weaving and dyeing and their catch of stray sheep served two and very occasionally three, extremely useful purposes. Unbelievably, our heroes were rather well domesticated. They were well skilled in crafting tools, weapons and jewellery from mined minerals and ores and demonstrated their arts in creating a comparatively modern environment of which they became, to a large extent so house-proud.

The language barrier was addressed and just like a schoolboy with his first dictionary, the more colourful words were the first to be learnt and as time went by, their building, hunting, communication and medicinal skills using old-fashioned herbal remedies began to improve and an unbreakable camaraderie began to unfold. There were arguments but mainly over which herb was best served with chicken and whether salmon be fried or poached. However these problems were soon resolved without too many tears. There was not really a leader at first. There was quite a diversity in the backgrounds of each of the settlers and democracy ruled. Life was great at first, partying every night, hunting, constructing dwellings and reconnoitring during the day but all good things must come to an end eventually.

Where were the women?

Life expectancy in the ninth century was around the thirty-five-to-forty-five-year mark, so, the need to maintain and progress with the new civilisation was discussed. So where should they be looking? Trips from Scotland to Scandinavia were quickly ruled out as being unnecessarily time consuming and too extravagant; so, it was decided that females should be acquired from south of the border so as not to offend the Scottish contingent.

How many should be acquired and what physical and mental attributes should be considered? The first round of suggestions, as expected, was an absolute farce. Requests ranged from the equivalent of a Russian shot-putter to a supermodel, which leaves quite a bit of leeway. Eventually a compromise was reached. Lots were drawn to select six individuals to be tasked with acquiring suitable females.

Three Vikings, Gerik, a level-headed individual, Enar and Asmund, who could be quite impetuous at times but also possessed good persuasive skills and three Scotsmen; Boyd, a diplomatic strategist, Alban, a rugged ex-farmer and Mungo, who displayed quite a saintly demeanour and was chosen as the leader for the mission.

They were all given strict orders not to sample the goods before they were delivered. They were all over six-foot, muscular and had seen much action in their lives. The Scotsmen sported long, dark hair and straggly beards and moustaches. The Vikings, on the other hand, had well-groomed beards and hair, and reddish skin. Gerik and Enar had dark hair and Asmund had blond hair. All looked extremely healthy and athletic.

It was estimated that the one hundred and seventy-five mile trip to Carlisle should take around three days, so the group was given ten days to achieve their mission which was basically to approach reasonably attractive, healthy, willing, quite intelligent, unattached females around the age of twenty years, appealing to their sense of adventure in populating a multi-national commune of young hard-working males, where peace and harmony would prevail and establish the foundations of an unrestricted society.

Well, that was basically the long-drawn-out idea, if anyone could have come up with such a mission statement.

This philosophy was to be the foundation to which future generations would adhere, with just a few minor alterations throughout the years. Those chosen were to be given the promise of a fresh start and the opportunity to be present at the birth (literally) of a new developing age, where women would have equal rights in determining the future. What minor detail was overlooked at first, was the fact that these women would be only ones in a group of around thirty sex-starved men. However, this potential problem would hopefully be addressed and settled by the time the scouting party returned.

As there was no chance whatsoever of any of the six fully remembering the list of requirements, their mission was condensed into; "Find six healthy young unattached women wanting to start a new life with a small group of hard-working and honest men."

In the village, trouble was brewing as to who would be selected to father the children. All that had been agreed initially, because of the current ratio, was there would be two Vikings and four Scotsmen. The problem was alleviated to some extent when fourteen ruled themselves out for various reasons; two for having just one eye, two who felt that they would better serve the community as ministers, six as they believed they had better things to do in the administration, development and safeguard of the village; one because he was just downright ugly, or so he was led to believe, and three as they had discovered that women were not their scene. So, that left sixteen eligible bachelors. The six villagers tasked with searching for females would be automatically considered for procreational services as they would have shown an ability to lie, cajole, bribe, communicate or just simply wear down potential candidates.

So, how would they decide who else would have the enviable task of ensuring the continuation of life within the village? It was not always the biggest (in all aspects) that would get the job. Fitness, intelligence, common sense and etiquette were to play a part in selecting the prospective fathers. However, the final decision would be left to the womenfolk on their return. It was a bit like a ninth century blind date.

Various tests and events were drawn up for the ten remaining competitors by the newly created administrators who were to referee the contests; in the hope that at least twelve villagers, including those on the outward-bound mission, would possess the requisite qualities. Contestants had to demonstrate their ability in construction, hunting, manners, singing, dancing and nature; as well as the more sporting events of accurate spear throwing, rock catching, running and jumping. This, as you may well imagine, did not go strictly to plan. It was the organiser's job to ensure fair play which is why two referees were chosen — one from each nationality.

Neither the Viking nor the Scottish warriors tended to know many ballads, and the traditional drinking and battle songs were not considered appropriate in trying to woo the attentions and affections of a prospective partner. Music appreciation and singing lessons were introduced. A not exactly even talent show reject standard, but at times highlighted an uncharacteristic ability to change pitch, akin to squeezing one part of the male anatomy. Most of the settlers had a better musical farting range than a vocal range.

Similar problems occurred with dancing. Arguments over who should take the lead were regular occurrences until the contestants were forced to use a crafted and camouflaged tree branch as a partner.

Sporting festivities eventually got underway. However, as there was still an abundance of alcohol remaining, while waiting for the opportunity to excel, the rules of some events happened to be accidentally on-purpose misinterpreted for the opposition. For a while, until the referees noticed, a couple of the sporting events somehow changed to rock throwing and spear catching. This slight miscommunication resulted in the disqualification of two of the Scottish competitors.

Eventually, by the fifth day, after much merriment and a great deal of cheating, six prospective fathers were chosen from the encampment — four Scotsmen and two Vikings. Five days of riotous behaviour was clearly visible. Much work had to be done to almost reconstruct some of the dwellings, dispose of empty drinking vessels and generally make the place presentable. It is quite easy to cause much destruction in just one day but the clearing and cleaning up tends to take a little longer.

So, based on the initial estimation of the scouting party being away for around ten days, which left five days to make the village presentable to the new arrivals, but to be on the safe side, they considered a maximum of four days would be better.

After a few miles hike on foot, the scouting party came across a small ranch. Ensuring there was nobody at home, they 'borrowed' six horses. There were over one hundred horses in the field so their assumption that six may not be missed seemed fairly reasonable or so they convinced themselves. A roughly one hundred- and seventy-five-mile trip, purely on foot was asking a little too much.

After a relatively uneventful three-day trip, our intrepid explorers had reached a small village a few miles from their destination.

Ponderton began life as a small settlement called Mullovium in around 55AD, situated approximately fifteen miles north-east of Carlisle. It was originally a wooden Roman fort, but over the next few hundred years became a thriving settlement with the extremely basic huts, being replaced by markets, industries and houses, some timbered with tiled roofs, floors and even heating. This would appear to be an ideal base from where to complete their objective. The village was to prove extremely significant in the future.

The Scots were well aware of the comparatively modern layout of the nearby city of Carlisle, having had ample opportunity to detail Roman activities from AD71 to AD213, but had not put all this theoretical knowledge into practice. The fourth century saw the decline of the Roman civilisation and unlike Carlisle, which by the end of the ninth century had been sacked by the Vikings, Ponderton was left very much intact and continued, almost unnoticed, to develop.

The Vikings first "official" visit to Carlisle was some five hundred and eighty years later when they overshot Scotland and managed to run amok on Lindisfarne. However, there is evidence that several stray Viking holiday cruises had surreptitiously landed within this time, on an information gathering basis, with the odd bit of rape and pillage thrown in.

If everything went to plan, they decided that it would take between three and four days to find six volunteers and another three days to return.

Carlisle was still under English control until the middle of the tenth century and was subject to frequent Danish invasions. So, the plan was to get the women, avoid the Danes and sneak out unnoticed back to their home.

They came across a disused barn in a wooded area just outside Ponderton, not far from the Carlisle city boundary. As it was getting quite dark, they decided to settle down there for the night.

The following morning, Mungo clarified the aims of their mission and then all were dispatched into the city. They agreed to meet back there within twenty-four hours. Gerik and Mungo remained in the barn, looking after the horses and preparing for a quick retreat should the need arise.

Unfortunately, our heroes had entered the city through the less affluent area and after independently making approaches soon mustered twelve prostitutes between them. All were more than eager to surrender to the needs of a group of six exceedingly masculine warriors. The problem now was whether to gently tell each of them they were not exactly suitable or just make a quick exit. The latter seemed the more prudent option even after one expeditionary party member had further sampled the local delights — four times!

Moving further north, they reached the more respectable area of the city and were astounded at the complexity of the technical innovations. Alban decided therefore, not only to complete their task, but also to press-gang, on a permanent basis, any suitable officials who were responsible for maintaining the infrastructure of the city.

In order to avoid any further confusion and upset, each member of the group was tasked with securing the services of one fair maiden. Poetry was suggested as the first attempt to woo the poor victims and Alban, one of the more eloquent and educated members of the raiding party, quickly scribed the following lines:

> "Oh, maiden fair of beauty and grace
> The time has come to break and chase.
> Thy servant who will take thy hand.
> In travelling to the promised land
> Be one with nature, clear and bright.
> Oh, be ma guide, ma star tonight.
> Travel through lands to a haven rest

In a place of peace that nature's blessed."

The greatest problem was not being fully conversant with the language differences and accents. Despite the fact that the poem was recited to the group many times, there still appeared to be a misinterpretation of the words to this Romantic ode, so believing it to be a traditional Scottish love poem and without even questioning the sense in these lyrics, the following lines became imprinted on some of the minds of the Viking suitors:

"Home made in far off Bute he agrees.
That I'm a scone to bake in cheese.
Thighs certain to awake thy man.
In travelling to the promised land
Beyond an itch, ye clean and bite
A beaming hide may stert tonight
To reveal true loins to a heaving breast
I'll place ma piece that nature's blessed."

The original version, when serenaded to prospective targets, was met with almost ridicule and derision as being rather condescending and patronising and failed to secure any young maidens, whereas the attempt by a Norseman, who's grasp of the English language was rather less limited, received high acclaim and Asmund actually succeeded in securing the services of two eager maidens.

Twin sisters Anna and Nesta, nineteen years of age, well-educated and fluent in French having mixed nationality parents. They were both slim built, just over five foot tall, with long blonde hair and Mediterranean looking. Their affluent parents were highly respected members of the community, the father being a goldsmith and the mother an owner of several French vineyards, who imported fine wines.

One of Nesta's best friends was Elen, whose father was the city's mayor. Elen was slightly taller than the twins, similarly, built but with black hair in a neat bob. She overheard Nesta and her sister discussing their recent encounter with Asmund and questioned them as to what he wanted. Nesta told Elen that Asmund and five of his friends had travelled from Scotland to find female companions to help start a community. She explained that the battle-weary Norseman wanted to make a new life away from the horrors of war.

This appealed to Elen. She had seen, first-hand, the misery caused during conflicts and the pressures of administration imposed on her father. It was the perfect opportunity to break away from a humdrum life. Elen had always dreamt of a quiet rural life. Even when she was very young, she used to walk to the edge of the city and look out onto the rolling hills, wondering if she would ever be lucky enough to see the outside world. She now had the chance.

The fourth victim literally fell into Boyd's arms. He was walking along a pathway, admiring the surroundings, when a young villager named Matilda, came running round a corner and bumped into him. The foods she was carrying spilt out and were well scattered.

"Sir," she said breathing quickly "I am so sorry, please forgive me." She hurriedly collected some of the provisions whilst looking nervously over her shoulder.

"What is worrying you?" asked Boyd.

Matilda looked up but said nothing. She hastily gathered what she could. Suddenly a group of irate market traders appeared.

"She is there," one of them yelled.

Boyd guessed what had happened and said to Matilda. "Quickly, jump over the hedge." Matilda obeyed, throwing her provisions over before she inelegantly dived through the hedge to the sound of a few painful cries. Boyd threw a few of the remaining items over the hedge hearing the odd "Ouch," as a large string of onions caught Matilda smack in the middle of her forehead, then he sat down on a pile of rocks.

The traders ran up to Boyd yelling. "Where is the thieving whore?" The warrior slowly raised his massive six-foot ten-inch frame, hands on his hips, looked down at the angry group and pointed to a large farmhouse some fifty yards away.

"She ran that way," he said in a booming voice. Nervously the group thanked him and quickly made their exit. Slowly a head appeared over the hedge.

"Sir, have they gone?"

Boyd looked round and said smilingly, "Who has been a naughty girl?"

An embarrassed Matilda, with a very noticeable bruise and numerous cuts from the prickly brambles, stood up fully, peered over the hedge to check her pursuers had disappeared out of sight, then turned back to Boyd and indignantly said, "I am not a whore." The tone of her voice then quietened, and she continued, "Thank you for saving me, I was starving. I have not eaten for three days and have no money. How can I ever repay you?"

Boyd was very tempted by the long blonde-haired, just over five foot beauty but remembering the orders, said, "It was my pleasure to save such a beautiful young maiden."

Boyd's cheeks reddened as he wondered how someone with normally such a gentle, reserved, introvert personality, could be so direct. He was acting like a love-struck teenager.

"Sir," continued Matilda, "I cannot stay here now. If I am caught, I will be flogged or maybe worse."

The sympathetic Boyd sat down again on the rocks and briefly told Matilda his purpose in visiting Carlisle. Her eyes lit up at this opportunity to escape. She was more than willing, on the condition that Boyd would be her companion. This time his eyes lit up and without even having to think about the proposal, agreed. He lifted her over the hedge with ease, wrapped his cloak around her and they wandered back to the city centre, hand in hand, to try and find the other members of the group.

The remaining two women, Berta and Edith, were recruited somewhat easily as a result of a hard drinking session. It was an extremely hot day and Enar was naturally feeling thirsty, so he decided to sample a little refreshment at a local tavern. He approached the innkeeper and requested a jug of his finest ale.

The innkeeper looked up at Enar and said, "We only have the one. Take it or leave it." Enar paid the two pence.

The tavern was not busy, the tranquillity being broken by two young women laughing loudly. Enar turned to face them, his jaw dropping at the beautiful sight that confronted him. He nearly spilt his drink but fortunately recovered before much was lost. The women looked up and eyed Enar up and down. He was a very confident person and walked over to the two more than slightly tipsy females. He noticed that they had empty vessels and being such a gentleman, offered a refill. Without hesitation, his offer was accepted and over the next hour or so, during which Enar tried to relate his mission, much ale flowed.

Berta by now was sleeping with her head down on the wooden table, Edith's head was propped up in the palms of her hands, however she was still just about able to maintain her bleary-eyed interest and ask questions about the proposal.

She suddenly staggered to her feet, stumbled over to him, looked lovingly into his eyes and said, "I am going to kiss you."

As their lips neared, her head slowly dipped to one side, at which point she promptly passed out, slumping ungraciously across Enar's lap. He picked up each woman in turn and slung them onto his shoulders, then casually strolled out of the tavern.

Alban, on the other hand, was having great difficulty in finding a suitable female. However, he had been approached by two elderly women who were craving more than the attention of the fine figure of a Scottish warrior. He took refuge in a small vacant bakery and managed to sample a few of the products on offer. As soon as he thought it was safe to emerge, he crept stealthily from his hiding place towards the entrance only to find his two female admirers blocking the doorway. He had encountered some scary situations in his battle career, but this was by far the scariest. He looked round for an escape route but unfortunately, one way in and one way out. So, should he submit to their wanton needs or again try to make his escape? The women started moving slowly towards him, forcing him backwards towards a roaring fire. He was getting uncomfortably warm. The women creeping ever closer, Alban getting ever warmer.

Fortunately, the baker returned and yelled. "What is going on, what are you doing here?" The women looked round, and Alban took this as an opportunity to rush past them to safety.

Unfortunately, though, his cloak had caught fire. Quick off the mark, he ran towards the women, dived between them, rolled forward, scrambled to his feet and ran out of the bakery down the main street. This was probably the first example of a flying Scotsman going full pelt in a cloud of smoke. At least he was safe.

After achieving the primary objective, they all made their way back to the barn, accompanied by their new friends. They each introduced themselves, however with Berta and Edith still asleep, this was left to Anna, who slightly knew them, to give a quick character summary.

Mungo thanked them all, again summarised their intentions and asked if there were any questions. Of the four sober females, only Elen questioned how two sworn enemies now seemed to be the best of friends. Mungo explained that it just happened. Both groups were tired of fighting and all they had seen in their lives was bloodshed, destruction and sadness and deep down, the group, almost as one voice, declared a peace. There was no distrust amongst them, just a desire to settle down, away from all the pointless slaughtering. Mungo's speech was so poignant, heartfelt and sincere that everyone was surreptitiously wiping a tear from their eye. At this point Edith woke up, let out a massive belch and threw up over Berta.

It was getting late, so they agreed to adjourn for the day and meet up again early the following morning. Edith and Berta were in no fit state to go anywhere. Nesta and her sister volunteered to try to clean the girls up. They had no idea what was happening and after being made fairly presentable, were just left alone to sleep. Matilda, for obvious reasons was not too thrilled about returning to her home on her own and asked if she could stay overnight in the barn. Boyd's eyes lit up, however Mungo, to Boyd's annoyance, stated that this was probably not a wise idea. Reluctantly Boyd agreed. Elen said that Matilda could stay with her for the night, so the four women were escorted back to the city under cover of darkness. Eventually, after a particularly hectic day, everyone settled down for the night.

So that appeared to be phase one of the mission complete.

Chapter 2

The Dead See Scrolls

The following morning, they all met up again in the barn, Edith and Berta still very much suffering from more than a mild hangover. Enar and Alban had been out very early and found a herd of cows. Alban was raised on a farm and was extremely proficient at milking cows. Gerik had found some iron pots in the barn and had also managed to light a small fire. Enar and Alban returned with a wooden pale almost full of milk and a second full of water from a nearby stream. The milk was warmed over the fire and with the small loaves that Alban had managed to purloin from the bakery the previous day, breakfast was served. Edith and Berta, still suffering from massive hangovers, slowly sipped the warm settling milk.

When everyone had eaten, Mungo outlined his vision for the new home and told how he was so impressed by the sheer magnificence of a Roman designed city. Elen had mentioned in her introduction that her father was a high ranking official, so he thought this an ideal opportunity for her to help in obtaining designs, plans, or anything they could get their hands on, detailing the general infrastructure of the city, to give them a solid foundation on which to create their new settlement.

He was not completely sure that all the women could be trusted, especially as two were still in a state of intoxication. Influencing them might be one thing but a different approach would be needed to obtain such valuable documents. Yes, the mayor's daughter was willing to help, however with her disappearance, plus the disappearance of official documents, things would not be in her favour should she wish to return at some later date. So, another plan had to be quickly formed.

By now, everybody was awake, not necessarily aware of exactly what was going on, but at least awake.

"We need to create a diversion," said Mungo.

"How about an earthquake?" asked Berta quite innocently.

"Good idea," said Edith.

"Oh No!" thought the exasperated Viking, "What have we got here?" Having quickly dismissed this option, Asmund's proposal of a fire was next considered.

This plan involved using Elen has a hostage, stealing the documents, torching the place then escaping, leaving some of Elen's clothing and jewellery scattered on a recently deceased female corpse, within the collapsed remains, as though she had lost her life trying to stop the theft. No chance of her returning, but then at least she would have 'died' a heroine. This was dismissed when Anna pointed out that it would be impossible for any of the men to return to Carlisle at some later stage, should the need arise.

"Apart from that," she continued, "it is not easy to set fire to a stone building."

"Next," said Mungo wearily.

Boyd rose to his feet. He explained how Matilda fell into his clutches and said that several angry local tradesmen would still be interested in seeking retribution. Matilda mentioned that these particular tradesmen were not the most popular characters in the city and trying to frame them for the theft of documents might be an option. Boyd suggested using Matilda as bait, making sure that these tradesmen would overhear a conversation that she would be around the council grounds at a certain time. While at the council, he and another could steal some of the documents, and as Matilda was being pursued out of the building, grab these characters, plant some stolen documents on them, accuse them of theft and have them arrested. In the confusion some items could quite easily disappear.

Matilda was naturally a little concerned about being used as bait, until Boyd assured her that he would be her personal bodyguard and promised that no harm would come to her. She felt a little happier.

Mungo was silent for a few moments before thanking Boyd for his contribution but thought it was over-complicated and relied a great deal on perfect timing, a quality not recognised too highly in the men.

"Anyone else?" asked Mungo.

Gerik stood up and said, "We have managed to obtain the services of six females by being honest with our mission, so could we not try this approach with some of the members of the council?"

"Well, I have no intention of lying with any man!" huffed Asmund.

"That is not quite the idea," replied Gerik. "It is more to appeal to their sense of ambition and adventure in being able to design and build a new village from the beginning."

This idea met with initial approval. "There are many people who work for my father," said Elen, "and I am quite sure we may be able to influence one or two of them."

"We need the right people," said Mungo, asking Elen if she could think of any potential targets. He continued, "Gerik is right. The simplest approach is the best. We only have two days left before we must return home but please Alban, no more poems." Alban smiled.

By now it was late afternoon and there was not enough time left in the day to put this plan into action, so food was next on the agenda. Around forty chickens were roaming around the barn and fortunately quite a large quantity of eggs had been laid. Water was boiled over the fire and the group tucked into hard boiled eggs and some bread left over from breakfast. They talked a while, each describing how they saw their perfect home and what visions they had for their future. At times, the thoughts were of sadness, as some mentioned how they had lost close relatives through hostilities, disease, famine and family feuds. It was a moment of reflection for everyone, but the exercise served to create a strong bond within the group and for a solid friendship and understanding in times to come. They eventually decided to call it a day and the women were escorted, in silence, back to the city, this time with Edith and Berta.

The final day was upon them. The women arrived at the barn quite early, bringing with them some fruit and barley bread which they all heartily enjoyed. Mungo went through the plan again with Gerik, Nesta and Elen who had managed to identify four possible candidates.

Asmund thought it wise, while the four were putting their plan into action, to accompany them into the city along with Alban and Anna and purchase provisions for the return journey, So the seven made their way into the city, leaving Enar, Boyd, Matilda, Edith and Berta in the barn.

On their way to the city centre, the group passed the seventh century Ponderton Cathedral Priory. Elen thought that a disguise might be appropriate. Who would suspect a group of religious men wandering through the city? The cathedral was deserted and so the two men helped themselves to a few cowls. They discretely hid an additional four outfits in the grounds as they could possibly come in useful later. They split up before they arrived at the city centre, four heading towards the chambers and three towards the market.

Nesta lagged behind a little as the other three went further into the chambers. The first person they met was Elen's father, William.

"Why are you here and who are these people?" he asked rather concerned. Elen was temporarily lost for words at having unexpectedly bumped into her father.

"Erm, erm, erm," she muttered.

Elen now had to think quickly. "I was finishing my chores for the day father and on my way home, when these holy men approached me." She pointed to Gerik and Mungo saying, "They said they were on their way to Ribblehead but took the wrong road and ended up here."

"Ribblehead is a Viking farmstead," said her father. "Brothers, from where have you travelled?"

"From the north sir," said Gerik. "Travelling to see our fellow brethren."

Instead of keeping quiet, for some reason Gerik continued. "I have heard of plans for a Viking raid and need to warn them."

"How did you learn of these plans?" asked William.

"I am from Aalborg sir…"

"He is a holy man and does not like violence and came here to warn people of what might happen," interrupted Elen, who seemed quite pleased by her own quick reply.

This response made William a bit less suspicious, but still he persevered in his questioning. "How many of you came across the water?"

"Five others," replied Gerik. Mungo looked annoyingly at Gerik thinking why he could not have said just one other.

"He likes our city," Elen quickly continued, "and I think they would like to help us."

"You seem to know quite a lot about your new friends even though you have only just met them," commented her father. "Where are the rest of your brethren?" he asked.

"Very close sir, they rested while we came into the city," replied Gerik.

"I would like to meet them," continued William, "Please bring them to me."

After hearing the conversation between Gerik, Elen and her father, Nesta, who had remained out of sight, made a hasty retreat and headed back out of the city to the barn to tell the others what had happened and to prepare them for a possible official introduction.

Passing a local tavern, she noticed Asmund, Alban and Anna who had decided to sample a few ales prior to their shopping trip. She quickly explained the problem, so drinks were finished promptly, and they left slightly worse for wear. On the way back, they picked up the four cowls hidden at the priory before returning to the barn.

Meanwhile, back at the barn in Ponderton, Boyd and Matilda had decided to have a wander round the area, hand in hand, leaving Ensar, Berta and Edith to wait for the others. Enar was having a scout round the barn and came across several highly decorative amphorae, clay sealed, stored high in the loft. Hoping for the best, he removed the stopper and to his great delight the fumes from a well-fermented wine emanated. Each amphora held the equivalent of around six gallons. Enar called to Edith and Berta. He found a length of strong cord, tied it securely around the handles and guided by the two girls, carefully lowered one of the containers to the ground. He then climbed down from the loft carrying three small tankards he had found near the amphorae. Temptation was too much for them. No time was wasted in filling the tankards and sampling the contents, several times.

Eventually they all met up in the barn. Gerik and Mungo were absolutely furious, particularly with Asmund, Alban and Enar. Now the problem was how to quickly sober up three drunken men and three drunken women, and then getting them to understand what was happening and make them presentable as holy men, in order to meet some of the city's more respected citizens.

Nesta had the foresight to guess what was needed to quickly sober up the drunks. An effective remedy for both an excess of alcohol and hangovers was either carrot or apple juice and milk, however, this mixture tended to have a few unpleasant side effects. On the way back to the barn, she managed to collect a few unfortunately not exactly ripe apples. The medication was duly prepared and administered. The three men were then cleaned and made acceptedly respectable in their new outfits, leaving any evidence of warrior attire safely concealed, so they were ready to be presented to the mayor. The newly ordained monks were briefed as far as possible, on the work of the missions in Scandinavia and how they should act, and they then practised the art of walking round like holy men, heads bowed and muttering some unintelligible chants.

With the exception of Nesta and Matilda, they all returned to the city. Elen led Gerik and Mungo into the chambers where they met William.

"Where are the others?" he asked.

"They are having a few moments of private prayer at the priory and will be joining us shortly," replied Mungo.

William continued to ask about how they came across the plans for a Viking raid.

"Before we left our country, we saw a few longships moored in our home port and heard talk of plans to sail here." William looked extremely concerned.

"Please bring the others to me," he requested. "I would like to speak to them."

Off went Gerik and returned shortly, not only with the other four men but also with Edith, Berta and Anna who were still suffering from the effects of alcohol. They all entered the chambers and met up with William.

"How and when did you all get here?" he asked.

"By boat, four days ago," came the reply.

William looked at each one of them in turn as they introduced themselves.

"Gerik, Keeper of the Book."

"Boyd, Keeper of the Chant."

"Mungo, Keeper of the Night."

William looked somewhat puzzled by this last position. "Keeper of the Night?" he asked.

"It's about keeping men safe at night," was the reply.

"You seem to have a Scottish accent," William said quizzically.

"I do sir," he replied. "We have brethren from all over the world." William frowned. He then looked at the next monk.

"Asmund, Keeper of the Book."

"I thought he was Keeper of the Book?" asked William, pointing to Gerik.

"It is a big book," replied Asmund.

William smiled.

"Alban, Keeper of the Gate."

He then looked at Enar. "And you are?" he asked.

"Enar, Keeper of the Holy Water."

"That is more like wine I smell on you?" said William.

"Incense," replied Enar abruptly. "We are disciples of Anger," continued Enar, emitting a loud belch.

"Ansgar," whispered Gerik

"Ansgar," repeated Enar. "The Opposal of the North," "Apostles of the North," again whispered Gerik. "Apostles of the North," echoed Enar.

William next turned to the women. "I recognise you three. What is your purpose in being here?" he asked.

Anna, who was the least intoxicated, slurringly replied, "We have listened to their teachings and hope to understand more about their faith. We wish to follow them."

William was not quite convinced by this reply. However, he continued to ask Mungo about their knowledge of the Viking raids.

Mungo replied saying, "We are travelling south to our kinsmen to warn them to prepare for a possible raid."

Then the light bulb came on. "The Vikings could be here very soon," said Gerik. "You need to hide important scrolls from them, like the maps of the city."

"All will be lost if they attack and ransack the city," sighed William. "You do not know the value of these scrolls the Romans asked us to keep safe. We were told not to look at some of them until they returned. We must not let them fall into the wrong hands, but we have no place to…"

This response was the answer to their prayers. "We will take care of them," interrupted Mungo who by now had cottoned onto Gerik's sneaky idea.

"It is a sign from God. You were truly sent to save our city," said William.

"We will return to the north and if we meet any Vikings, we will tell them that there is a plague in the city and not to come near," chirped Mungo not very convincingly.

"What will befall your kinsmen in Ribblehead?" asked William.

"We will send one of our brethren to forewarn them," answered Mungo. "We must depart immediately."

"Father," said Elen. "I would like to learn their ways. You and mother have taught me to fear God and try to follow his path. I will never get another chance to learn from these monks and I wish to go with them to their monastery."

"My dear," answered her father, "it will be a long and dangerous journey. You will be alone without your friends. No one of your own age to talk to."

"No father, I have spoken to Edith, Matilda, Anna, Nesta and Berta. They too would like to seek new worlds, new teachings and learn about our history and lands far away. These men of God are here to bring peace."

Addressing the other female members, William asked, "Do you want to travel with these men?"

Almost as one they answered a resounding, "Yes."

"Let me speak to their families," continued Elen's father. "We will meet again in the morning. These guests are welcome to sleep in the priory." At that point Berta let out an enormous fart. "Too much incense I suppose?" said William with a wry smile on his face.

"With the greatest respect sir," said Mungo, "we all need to leave immediately."

"I cannot allow these women to accompany you until I have spoken to their parents," replied William. "We will meet again in the morning. I will summon their parents to the council chambers where we will discuss the matter and you have satisfactorily answered any questions or concerns, they may have. That is my final word."

"I must send one of our brethren onward to Ribblehead to warn them," said Mungo.

"I agree. We will meet again in the morning," repeated William. He turned to his daughter saying, "Your daily chores still need doing," he said.

He left with Elen and bid them all a good day.

Back in the priory, Mungo, exasperated at William's words, asked who would be willing to make the return journey home alone to tell the others what was happening. and said that the main group plus their acquisitions would be a day or so late.

As Alban had been a little delinquent earlier, he had no hesitation in volunteering to make the trip. Mungo thanked him and added laughingly.

"Do not think you are completely forgiven. I will still have my eyes on you." Alban smiled, and then he and Boyd returned to the barn. Alban discarded his cowl, saddled up a horse and collected any morsels of food that were left.

"Travel to the south first and then round to the north so as not to raise any suspicion," said Boyd. Alban nodded and departed on his journey. Boyd collected Matilda and Nesta and brought them to the priory.

They were all extremely disheartened, especially after all the planning and hard work, as it now seemed quite improbable that any of the women would be allowed to travel back home with them, as the suggestion of an imminent hypothetical Viking raid would be a major safety issue.

The rest of the day was taken up with the whole group discussing what to say in the hope of convincing those who needed convincing, that their intentions were assuredly honourable. After some debate, they actually managed to convince themselves that the ruse was a reality. Matilda, Nesta and Anna were escorted home to their parents. Edith and Berta asked to remain in the priory. Boyd asked if there was a problem.

Edith looked at Berta and they both started to cry. "We have nobody," said Edith. "Our parents were murdered in a Viking raid when we were about twelve years old. I still have bad dreams of that day. I will never forget the man who murdered my parents. He was a giant of a man with a long red beard and a bright red patch over his right eye. The men were rounded up in the middle of village, surrounded and then we watched from a hill as they were all slaughtered without mercy. The women were raped then murdered. Children were forced to watch what was happening and then they too were slain. We swore that if we were ever to meet another Viking, we would kill them. Drinking helps us forget."

She looked at Enar and said, "You are not like the others. I see sadness in your eyes." Enar approached the girls, sat down between them and put his arms round them.

He started to cry. "I feel guilt and shame. I cannot change what has happened in the past, but I can promise you a future." Edith pulled a Viking knife from under her tunic and slammed it onto the table.

"This was the knife that pierced my father's heart. It was going to be for you." She put her head on the table and cried uncontrollably. There was a long silence in the room.

Gerik then went over to the two girls and said, "It takes more courage to do what you have just done than to kill a fellow human. You will never again have to do anything against your will. That I promise."

The girls soon fell asleep, however the men sat quietly, vividly remembering the atrocities that they too had committed. It seemed a long time ago since they were involved in battles. Much had happened in the last year, and they would dearly love to forget the past.

Gerik stood up and said authoritatively. "We now take an oath that there will be no more needless bloodshed. We are here to start a new life and we will get what we need from wherever we want peacefully, for the good of our descendants. We will not need to justify ourselves to anybody. We can learn from our history, and we can learn from other countries and civilisations. We are on our own now."

They were about to give Gerik a thunderous show of appreciation when Berta released yet another untimely fart, displaying a satisfied smile on her face. It was definitely time to sleep.

Morning came and they all trooped into the meeting in the council chambers wearing their cowls. They were met by Elen's father who asked Mungo if Brother Alban had departed safely to Ribblehead.

"Who?" inquired Mungo.

"Brother Alban," repeated William.

"Aye, the drunkard got away fine," replied Mungo; not realising what he had said. His mind was totally elsewhere. William smiled.

As they entered an extremely ornately decorated room, they saw four very official looking gentlemen sitting facing them behind a large wooden desk on a raised platform; two on either side of a grand mayoral chair.

Already in there were Matilda, Anna and Nesta with their parents. Edith and Berta entered a few steps ahead of the men and sat with Elen, behind the other women. They all rose to their feet and bowed their heads in respect as the monks entered. The greeting was returned and Asmund decided to take this one step further giving a blessing to all attendees.

Boyd had great difficulty in stifling a laugh which was nicely camouflaged by a sudden outburst of coughing. One of the officials brought him a drink of water to which Boyd reacted saying, "Thank you my son." Mungo raised his eyes skyward and shook his head slowly side to side in utter despair.

William climbed up the few steps onto the platform and took his place on the mayoral seat. He thanked everyone for coming at such short notice and after introducing those present, began his opening speech.

"Good friends, we have two problems to discuss today. Firstly, through these devout monks, I have been informed of a possible Viking raid. You are aware that, many centuries ago, not only did the Romans trust us with looking after ancient deeds and documents of our city, but also maps showing secret passages that lead to the vast store of Roman diamonds, gold and jewellery which we have managed to keep safely hidden for many years."

At this point, the monks looked round at each other, jaws dropping at such a bombshell. "We cannot let these plans be taken by our enemies and therefore I propose that such documents be put into the hands of these monks for safe keeping. May I now ask the six young women to stand." They stood up looking a little perplexed. "Now as for you two, I cannot speak for you," pointing to Edith and Berta, "I have had a little time to discuss the matter of your requests to learn more about these holy monks with their parents and we have come to a conclusion."

He turned to one of the officials sitting next to him and asked, "Silas, how far is it to Ribblehead?"

"About seventy miles sir, a good day's journey," he replied.

"In that case," William continued, "as far as the documents are concerned, they should be taken to your retreat in Ribblehead for safe keeping. I do not believe that under the circumstances, it would be wise to take them north." He then looked at Mungo. "What are your intentions after your visit to Ribblehead?"

"We need to head back north sir to our monastery," he replied.

William pondered a while and then whispered something to his colleagues. "We are in agreement," he continued, "once you have returned, in two days' time, if the women still wish to learn more about your teachings, then they will be permitted to accompany you to your monastery.

"I do not believe that your country folk would be prepared to suffer the wrath of the church. I am therefore quite happy to let Elen go with you and the other parents agree in letting their daughters learn the quality of a life of chastity and obedience, however…"

Mungo turned to Gerik and muttered. "I thought it was going a little too easy. Next he is going to tell us to watch over them and keep them pure and innocent and not be led astray by man's wicked desires."

"You must," continued William, "give me your word that you will watch over them and promise to keep them pure and innocent and not be led astray against their will by man's wicked desires."

"Sir," replied Mungo, "we will not force them to do anything against their will." He turned to Gerik and smiled.

"Three of you will go to Ribblehead, the two of you," pointing to Mungo and Gerik, "and Drake," said William, pointing to one of his council members.

"Oh crap," said Mungo quite audibly.

"I am sorry," said William, "I did not quite catch that."

"Oak wrap," repeated Mungo making sure his annunciation was a little clearer. "In the monastery, we wrap all our scrolls in oak leaves for protection against the weather."

He turned to face Gerik with a smug grin on his face, at having, quite masterfully, avoided what could have proved to be an embarrassing situation. Gerik nodded his approval at this quick response.

William continued, "The other three monks will have two days to further instruct not only the women but also their parents as to the role of your mission and how you see that they will benefit from your experiences. Are there any questions?"

Nesta's father stood up. Looking across at Gerik, he asked. "Brother, my name is Thomas. We are allowing our daughters to accompany you to the monastery, and we were wondering exactly where it is?"

Mungo nudged Gerik who had not actually realised the question was addressed to him.

"Iona," replied Gerik hastily, as this was the first place that came into his mind as the only Scottish island with which he was familiar.

The problem here was that around sixty years earlier, a total of sixty-eight monks were slain by the Vikings at Martyrs Bay and by the year 825AD the monastery was virtually abandoned.

At this response, Mungo gave Gerik a really dirty look, as he knew only too well about the non-existence of this monastery. Fortunately, though, nobody else in the room was that familiar with Scottish-Viking history and accepted the response.

"How many days will the journey take?" he asked. Mungo was about to answer when Herman, one of the junior council members piped up.

"Four days sir, about two hundred and thirty miles."

"Just what we need, someone skilled in the art of knowing too much about the wrong thing at the wrong time."

'Why could not the village idiot have been here?' mumbled Mungo.

"If there are no further questions, I will have the scrolls brought up."

He thanked everyone for attending then looked towards the monks. "Brothers," he continued, "It would be my honour to escort you on a tour of the city vaults for you to be aware of the weight of responsibility the Romans placed on our shoulders."

"That would be most kind of you," said Gerik, "however…" Before he could finish his sentence, Mungo gave him a short sharp jab on his ankle. Gerik grimaced.

"However," continued Mungo, "what my fellow brother was about to say was, how do you find the time to run such a large city so smoothly?"

William smiled and replied, "With great patience."

He stood up, turned to Silas and asked him to accompany them. The other attendees made their exit, seemingly content with the outcome. The women met up outside, did not say much, but smiled at each other. Their expressions said it all.

The four made their way through a door concealed behind a large curtain to the side of the chamber and then down two flights of stone stairs. Torches lit the way through a series of dark, damp passages. They came to a large solid wooden door with the letter 'T' etched in the wood.

"The emperor's initial. You have your key Silas?" asked William.

"I do sir," he replied. Silas unlocked one of the steel padlocks with a key he kept on a belt round his waist and William the other.

"As you see," said William, "no person can enter the vaults alone."

With both padlocks unlocked, two massive wooden bolts were drawn back, and the heavy door slowly opened. Silas took one of the lit torches off the passage wall and handed it to Gerik. He took another for himself. They entered the underground vault and were met by an extremely musty, almost sickening stench.

William looked at them and said with a smile on his face. "You do get used to it."

The room was full of hundreds of rolled-up scrolls neatly stacked on wooden shelves.

"Let me think," said William. "Ah yes, these are the most important ones. They show the maze of underground passages and what is inside each of the vaults. The Romans were very thorough in drawing up accurate and detailed maps as, when they returned, they needed to have a simple way to quickly find exactly what they required. There are so many passages and vaults we have not yet needed to explore and according to the maps, there are other ways into these vaults without having to enter the city. Therefore, you need to understand the importance of these maps and why they must not fall into the hands of our enemies."

Mungo, trying to look serious, even though inwardly his excitement was growing, looked at William and said, "We will guard them with our lives."

"It may now be a good time for you to start your travel," said William. "I have three horses and some food prepared for you. Be careful of Drake, he should not be trusted."

Silas picked up the bundle of scrolls and as they were being ushered out of the vault, Gerik noticed a small, padlocked chest with 'XIX' etched into the lid. "What is that?" he asked.

"It belongs to Drake. That is all I know," replied William. The door was locked, the torches were placed back into the holders and they returned to the chamber, meeting up with the women.

"We must now make our way to Ribblehead," Mungo told them. "But we will be back in two days with Brother Alban and then make our way north to the monastery."

The women smiled and said their farewells. Elen followed them outside and then tapped Mungo on the shoulder.

"Drake is not happy here," she whispered. "His mother is an old friend of my father and is only working here at the council because of something that happened years ago, but I am not sure what." Mungo acknowledged Elen's remark.

They mounted the horses and Silas handed Gerik the scrolls, securely bound in a leather pouch.

"I sincerely trust we will see you back here in two days," said Silas pompously. They rode slowly out of the city.

"We have not been properly introduced," said Mungo. "I am Brother Mungo, and this is Brother Gerik." Drake just grunted in response. He was a lanky individual in his early twenties, with short dark hair and a slight Scottish accent. He would not exactly stand out in a crowd. "It seems like you are not too happy with your task," continued Mungo. Drake did not reply but just muttered something to himself.

After riding for about one hour, Gerik turned to Mungo and jokingly said, "Should we kill him now?"

Drake froze. "What do you mean?" he stammered.

"You have said nothing since we left the city. What is wrong?" asked Mungo.

"Why do I have to do all the jobs that nobody else wants to do? Why does everybody make fun of me? Why am I sent out of the room when the others are discussing important matters, why…?"

"Enough!" yelled Mungo.

"Nothing interesting or exciting ever happens to me. Even when he comes round to see my mother, I have to go outside; and you are not monks," continued Drake. They stopped riding.

"What do you mean?" asked Mungo, "saying that we are not monks?"

"I overheard Nesta and Anna talking about you and thought this would be my chance to escape," Drake said, looked worriedly at Mungo.

"What do you mean, escape?" Drake asked. "I know everything that goes on at the council. I must tidy away after the meetings. They all think I am stupid, but I taught myself to read and write and can remember everything I see. They do not know this and so I do not say anything."

"What exactly have you seen?" asked Mungo.

"Everything," replied Drake. "I know where everything is stored in the underground chambers and how to get there. I know that the Romans left maps and drawings of the places they visited. William told me to draw more of these maps. He does not know but I made maps for myself so I could see what the Romans built. I keep these locked away. I want to help. Please trust me."

"Does William trust you?" asked Gerik.

"No," Drake replied.

"Then why should we?" said Gerik.

"Because I know what goes on behind the closed doors and how William is cheating people. He told me that if I ever say anything to anyone, he will have me killed, but I think that is just to scare me. He dare not do anything to me because of my mother."

"Is William your father?" asked Mungo.

"I wondered about that myself," replied Drake.

"There is a likeness," added Mungo. "What will you do now?" asked Mungo.

"Very simple," replied Drake. "I will shelter somewhere out of the city for two days, maybe in the barn." Gerik looked at Mungo and then turned back to look at Drake.

"The barn?" asked Mungo.

"Yes," replied Drake, "the one you have been using just to the north of the city. You can hide the scrolls with the other monks, if they are really monks, and then circle round and enter the city from the south." His plan could not be faulted.

"What do you see as your future?" asked Mungo.

"I like your idea of how you want to build a new life and a safe future for everyone, and I would hope to be part of it," replied Drake.

"To the barn," hollered Gerik and off they galloped.

Meanwhile, at the priory, Enar, Asmund and Boyd had been further apprising the women and their parents as to the role of their missionary work, what was planned for them and how long they would be away.

Boyd stood up and said, "Ansgar travelled to our country about ten years ago and he preached, peace, goodwill and how we should follow a life of forgiveness to all men. That is how we lead our lives. There are some women in our community who come to us before seeking to further their religious life back in our country. We have all we need in our monastery, carpenters, farmers and everyone is treated the same. We live a life of poverty, chastity, abstinence and obedience and we feel that our lives have benefited over the years by following these simple rules. I was fortunate enough to meet Ansgar while I was training to become a monk. He was an inspiration to us all." He rambled on a little more; not exactly saying much until he noticed one of the parents was almost falling asleep.

Enar looked at Boyd and quietly said to him. "Where did you find that?"

He replied, "I found this note about someone called Augustine, so I changed the name and just read it out. I do not think anybody noticed." He turned to his audience and said, "My blessings on you all. Once our fellow brethren return, we will be leaving this fine city and going back home to our monastery. Please pray for us that we have a safe journey." Everybody bowed their heads. Elen got a fit of the giggles, well disguised by pretending she was crying.

At this point William and one of his councillors entered the priory. "I have decided," began William, "that once your fellow brothers return, to have Herman accompany you to Iona. Once you are safely there, he will return to give us the news."

"Do you think it wise to have someone travel for three days on their own?" asked Boyd.

"Does that present a problem?" asked William.

"Not at all," replied Boyd sarcastically.

"That is settled then, we all need a good night's rest for an early start in the morning." At this point, the audience took this as an opportune moment to leave and followed William out of the building.

When they were alone, Boyd said, "We need to get back to the barn and collect our belongings, weapons and clothing."

Suddenly, there was a knock on the priory door. Boyd looked across at Asmund and Enar, wondering who it could be. He cautiously went to the door, opened it a little, very slowly peeping into the gap. Nesta's mother was outside.

"I know you have taken a vow of abstinence," she said, "but as you have a long journey ahead of you tomorrow, I have brought you a little food." She passed the basket to Boyd who thanked her for the kind gesture, closed and bolted the priory door, then returned to the others. He took the cover off the basket to find healthy portions of chicken, cabbage and carrots plus a generous helping of wine. Nobody complained.

Evening was upon them and under cover of moonlight, suitably nourished, they made their way on foot to the barn. When they arrived, Gerik, Mungo and Drake were already there.

Asmund looked puzzled. "Who is this?" he asked.

"Drake," was the reply. Gerik explained the reason why Drake was with them and why he believed he was trustworthy.

"How did the sermon go?" asked Mungo.

"I think it went well," replied Asmund, "but…"

"I do not like the word 'but'," interrupted Mungo.

"We have been asked to take someone else along with us to Iona to make sure that we arrive safely at the monastery which, as we now know, no longer exists," continued Asmund.

"Who is it?" asked Drake.

"Herman," was the reply. Drake went white.

"From your expression, something's wrong," said Mungo.

"Where do I begin?" Drake asked rhetorically. "Herman has always been one of William's favourites. He cannot do any wrong. If he hears any idle talk that could be used against a person, he goes straight back to tell William. William uses this talk to get money out of people for his own needs. People dare not say anything because William would send his guards round to punish them. I heard he had some people killed."

"We will have to take him with us," said Mungo. "We have two days to think of a plan, but we must warn the others not to say anything they shouldn't." He turned to Drake. "Is there anything you know about Herman we could use against him or anything he does not like?"

"Not really," replied Drake. "He does not say much to anyone except William. He lives on his own."

"There is nothing we can do today," said Gerik.

"We could kill him in his bed tonight," said Drake.

"Maybe later," Gerik replied laughing.

"Tell me more of what you know about these maps," asked Mungo.

"I have heard William and Herman talking about what is in each of the underground chambers," said Drake. "I have also seen large heavy chests being carried out and taken to William's house. Herman also seems to have plenty of money. I know what is going on. The citizens fear William. I think he might tell people that you have stolen the maps and raided the chambers and stolen the Roman gold and jewellery stored there. He will have Herman there as a false witness."

Drake's information caused great consternation within the group. They needed to think of something quickly so that they would not be accused of stealing from the city.

Drake had an idea. "William thinks that you two," pointing to Gerik and Mungo, "are on your way to Ribblehead and will return tomorrow with the chest you sent away. If we could sneak into William's house tonight, take some of the chests and leave them with the maps in Herman's house, it would seem to others that Herman has been stealing gold. I have a script that Herman wrote to me about not doing my duty. I can copy Herman's handwriting and leave a scroll where someone can find it, thanking William for the presents of gold and jewellery. That would show that William has been stealing."

"I think that Anna and Nesta's father would be interested in seeing such a scroll," said Mungo. He smiled, looked at Drake and said, "What other talents do you have?"

"Writing poetry," Drake replied. Mungo laughed.

"Do not tell Alban," he said.

"We need to act quickly," said Boyd.

"Drake, where would William hide the chests?"

"They are kept in his basement, but you do not have to go through the house to get to it, said Drake. There is an outside entrance. The chests are taken there at night so none of his family or friends who are there, see them going through the house."

"You know far too much," said Gerik.

"I can keep quiet," Drake replied. Gerik shook his head and smiled.

"I have parchment, quills and ink at home, the same parchment that is used to write down what is said in council meetings," said Drake. "Bring the city scrolls and maps with you." He added, "I have an idea."

Mungo picked up the pouch containing the scrolls. "Lead the way," he said, "and you told us there is no excitement in your life. You are lucky we did not kill you." He continued laughingly.

"The night is not over!" came Drake's quick reply.

Mungo, Boyd and Asmund followed Drake into the city. Drake went into his house and quickly penned the letter.

My dear friend William,
Your kindness and generosity fill me with joy.
You ask that I keep your presents of Roman gold and jewellery a secret.
This I promise.
Your humble servant
Herman

Drake slipped the parchment into the belt round his tunic then then led them to William's house. Making sure that there was nobody around, he led Boyd and Asmund quietly down ten stone steps while Mungo waited at the top on watch. The door was locked.

Boyd looked at Drake and said, "I do not think we have much chance of getting in." he said.

"Wait," replied Drake. He took a small wooden dowel out of his tunic and played around with the lock. "Opened," said Drake after a few short moments. "All it takes is knowing how to move the ward to get to the lever." Boyd shook his head in disbelief.

"Quiet," whispered Asmund. Fortunately, there was just enough moonlight to make out where the chests were located. The two men carefully lifted a chest and very cautiously carried it up the steps. Drake closed and then, with just a little manipulation, managed to lock the door again.

"Onward to Herman's house," said Drake. Luckily, it was not too far away. They now had to sneak the chest into the house.

"Put the scrolls in the chest," said Drake. Gerik and Mungo looked puzzled.

"Trust me," said Drake. There was a torch light flickering, so Boyd crept up to peer inside where he saw a figure lying flat out on the bed, snoring away. He beckoned to Drake to open the door.

"The door is open if you take the trouble to look," he said indignantly." The two men very carefully carried the chest inside.

At the sound of a creaking board, Herman made a loud grunt, turned over on the bed and continued sleeping. Panic over. The chest was carefully placed under the bed and then the two men sneaked out.

One more job left. Now to the twins' house. "Is there anything you do not know?" inquired Mungo.

"I do not know the answer to that question," replied Drake smartly.

After a few minutes, they arrived at a stunning manor house. High stone walls and a moat surrounded the property. It was almost like a miniature castle. They crossed the stone bridge and walked up to the iron gate. Two Vallhund dogs ran up to them. Drake bent down to stroke them.

As he was crouched down, one of the dogs managed to grab the parchment from his belt and ran off with it. Drake stood up to face Boyd and Mungo and was about to explain what had happened when Thomas appeared carrying a torch, shouting.

"Mungo, where are you? Come here please."

Drake crept stealthily away from the gate. "Mungo?"

Mungo walked towards the gate, Boyd slightly behind. Thomas approached the gate and saw Mungo standing there.

"What are you doing here?" he asked, "I thought you were in Ribblehead."

"I heard you call my name," was the reply.

"I was calling for my dog," said Thomas, "but why are you here?"

"We have just returned from Ribblehead and were out walking when I heard you call my name," replied Mungo.

"I apologise for the misunderstanding."

"I am not offended," said Mungo. At that point, the dog approached and sat next to the twins' father.

"What is that in your mouth Mungo?" Boyd looked at his friend and whispered, "Drop."

The gesture that Mungo gave Boyd was not polite. The dog dropped the slightly chewed parchment, so Thomas bent down to pick it up. He read the note by the torch light and then said, "I must bid you good night," then walked quickly away.

Boyd turned looked back and said, "Come here Mungo, good boy."

Mungo looked very sternly at him and said, "Please do not tell any of the others about this," he said.

Boyd looked at him and replied, "Well, not just yet."

Drake went to his home and the others returned to the barn, with Boyd making the occasional barking sound. When they reached the barn, they told the others what had happened and how lucky they were that everything seemed to run very smoothly but they wondered what the morning would bring.

They put on their armour, sheathed their weaponry and then covered it with their cowls.

It was finally time to head back to the priory with all their belongings. When they arrived, Boyd opened the priory door to let them in and they were greeted by the delicious aroma of food.

Gerik and Mungo looked at the others and Gerik said, "Is there something you need to tell us?"

An embarrassed Boyd looked at them and explained how the good folk of Carlisle had kindly prepared a small, average, well, substantial feast for them.

"There are a few carrots and a drop of wine still left," said Enar, rather sheepishly.

Chapter 3

Time to go Home

Early the following morning, they were all woken by a continuous loud banging on the priory doors. Half awake, Asmund yawned his way to the door. The banging continued. He opened the door to find a number of angry citizens on the doorstep. Thomas was at the head of the group holding the forged parchment in his hand.

"Read this," he said sternly, thrusting it into Asmund's hand.

He looked petrified. The others came up behind Asmund, wondering what the commotion. Was about. Asmund read the note then passed it back to the others. Mungo was the next to read it.

"I do not understand," said Mungo innocently.

"It is a confession," said Thomas. "I found this in my garden last night. It must have blown in during the night. We knew William was cheating us, but we could not prove it. Brethren, what should we do?"

"Come in," said Asmund, "and let us talk."

Ten people rolled in and sat in the pews whilst Asmund and the others walked to the top of the priory onto the altar.

"Please explain what this is about?" asked Gerik.

Thomas stood up. "After I had spoken to you," he said looking at Boyd Mungo. "I went to see a few others to show them what I had found. I or all the others when I say we have all been afraid of William. He wn small army of outlaws he uses to terrorise citizens who do not e wants. We all know of someone who has been injured or 'e dare not do or say anything against him. Our women and been threatened. We saw your visit as a hope for our away from here, but I know the threats and torture will who remain here."

his fellow friends and whispered, "We must help."

"It is not our fight," responded Enar.

Asmund butted in saying, "These citizens have welcomed us, helped us, fed us and trust us with looking after their daughters, we are in their debt."

"What are we," said Gerik, "monks or warriors? We have seen slaughter in our lives and vowed that there will be no more. If we leave without helping these people, there will be more innocent lives lost. We cannot and will not let that happen."

"Are we in agreement then?" asked Mungo. They all nodded their approval. Mungo stood up and said, "How can we help?"

At that point, the priory door creaked open slowly. Everyone turned round worriedly to see who was there. A face peered round the door.

"Grab them!" shouted Thomas.

Four of the men ran to the door and dragged the stranger in, shutting and bolting the door behind them.

"Help! Stop!" yelled the incomer.

They carried him to the altar, forcefully lifted his head and Thomas said, "Look, it is one of William's taletellers."

Boyd stood up and rushed to the base of the altar. "Let him be," he said, recognising the poor individual. The four men dropped their catch to the floor.

He turned over, looked up and smiled. "Greetings," he said in a croaky voice. It was Drake.

Boyd got hold of Drake under the arms and lifted him easily to his feet.

"He has been listening to us. He would have gone back to tell William what he heard if we had not caught him." said Thomas.

"Kill him," shouted one of the groups.

"Why does it seem that everyone wants to kill me?" asked Drake.

"You have that sort of face," said Mungo jokingly.

"He is the one who will help bring William and his followers to justice," said Boyd.

"Am I?" asked Drake.

Boyd frowned at him and laughingly said, "Quiet boy!"

He turned round to look at Mungo and the others and shrugged his shoulders. They all stood and formed a line on the lower sanctuary step. Mungo nodded.

"Good citizens," Boyd began, "please sit down." They all obeyed. "Our intentions are honourable, but we have slightly misled you as to the purpose of our visit. We are not monks; we are fighters who have become sickened by needless slaughter. Many of our friends have been killed in battle. We believe the fighting must stop. We befriended these Viking warriors, who were, I must confess, more than a little intoxicated when we first met them. We seek the same peaceful future and despair at the reigns of terror some wish to inflict on others. We will help bring peace to this city and rid it of people like William. If you are not happy with our intentions then please, feel free to kill Drake."

Drake looked at Boyd, snarled, then sat on the altar step with his head in his hands.

Thomas approached the altar, turned to the other citizens and said, "I trust them. Vikings and Scots have been sworn enemies for many years now, but I see honesty in their faces and believe we should all trust them." He turned to Boyd and asked, "What plan do you have to rid us of William?"

Boyd replied, "Go to William's house and tell him that you have heard we are here to steal the city's riches and you have been threatened with death unless you help us. Tell him to meet you outside the priory at once." Thomas sent two of his friends to William's house. "You must also send three men to Herman's house. Drake will tell you where it is. Fetch the chest you will find under his bed, and you must make sure that you bring Herman with you," replied Boyd. The five men departed.

Thomas looked suspiciously at Boyd who said nothing but just raised his eyebrows and smiled.

"Thomas, you will stay in the priory. The others must wait outside in hiding and once William is here, Drake and two others must make haste to William's house." He turned to Drake and said, "We need another chest." Drake nodded.

When the two men reached William's house they banged loudly on the door.

"Please help," they exclaimed.

William came to the door quickly. "What is happening?" he asked. "Why are you here?"

"It is the monks. They have tricked us. They are here to steal from us. They have Thomas imprisoned and are torturing him." William beckoned to one of his servants and whispered something to him. The servant rushed out of the house brushing past the two men. "Wait here," said William.

The servant returned shortly with six brutal looking thugs. "We have work to do," he said to them. "Follow me." He turned to the two men and said, "You will be rewarded, now go to your homes."

They went back to the priory very quickly. When Drake saw them, he said to two of the men. "Come with me."

They sneaked away and as soon as they were out of sight of the priory, they ran to William's house. Drake unlocked the door and told the men which chest to bring.

Meanwhile, the three men sent to Herman's house had arrived, barged their way in, grabbed him, and secured his hands with a tight cord. Herman looked in horror as the chest was dragged out the from under the bed.

"That is not mine," he protested loudly. There was no reply. He was taken by one of the men very roughly out of the house whilst the other two carried the chest.

The two groups arrived at the priory at the same time. The four men who were hiding outside beckoned to them and quickly told them what had happened.

"William burst into the priory with six of his army and saw Thomas tied up. He threatened to kill them all and said he knew why they were here. We were told that when you got here to take the chests into the priory with Herman still bound. We do not know any more."

The men obeyed taking the heavy chests into the priory leaving Drake outside. William and his soldiers were stunned by the sudden interruption. The men holding Herman threw him to the ground in front of the altar.

Thomas stood up, shaking the loosely bound ties from his hands and said, "You are traitors to the city. You have been stealing these riches for yourselves. Open the chests," he said. "Which one was found at the traitor Herman's house! he shouted.

"This one," came the reply.

"Open it," Thomas yelled. It was opened and inside were the scrolls which Silas had given to Gerik on top of a full chest of gold and silver coins and jewellery. Thomas pulled the parchment from his tunic and read it out loud, then showed it to William. He recognised the handwriting.

"You fools!" he shouted.

Herman by this time was screaming, "It's not mine, it's not mine."

"Quiet," yelled William.

"And that one," said Thomas, "was from your house."

William turned to his thugs and yelled. "Kill them all!"

The monks quickly discarded their cowls to reveal an assortment of weaponry. They drew their swords and on seeing this, realising they were facing a far superior force, William's soldiers quickly surrendered, dropping their swords to the ground.

"I said kill them. Have not I rewarded you enough? Kill them!" screamed William. Nobody moved.

William picked up one of the discarded swords and turned to face the monks, only to see Mungo's dagger fly towards him, just before the cold steal pierced his chest. He reeled backwards, tripped, hitting his head heavily on the open chest found at Herman's house.

His last words were, "You do not understand." His eyes were still open as the city scrolls fell out of the chest and covered his eyes.

One of William's soldiers looked up and said, "Mungo, is that you?"

"Bryce?" replied Mungo. They walked towards each other and embraced. "Why are you here?" asked Mungo.

"I like Roman gold," replied Bryce smiling.

"We were heading south, came to this place and he," pointing to William, "told us he would give us gold if we did what he asked, I did not like him much, so you have saved me from killing him."

"What will you do now?" asked Mungo.

"We like this city and would like to stay but after what we have done here, I do not think the citizens would welcome us."

At this point, Herman stood up and was about to speak when Gerik's fist caught him fully on the jaw and knocked him out cold.

"Just stretching," he said. Nobody bothered.

Thomas faced William's soldiers and said, "We see that you were following William's orders for a reward, and it will take time before you gain the trust of the citizens, but you are known to those who helped us. Carlisle is a growing city, and we will need help in keeping it a place where there is always peace. The Romans did much for us and we need to carry on their good work." He turned to the soldiers and said, "You can choose your punishment, Stay and help us keep the peace or you are banished, never to return."

Bryce looked round to his friends and said, "You do not leave us much choice. We wish to stay."

Mungo turned to Thomas and said sincerely, "You can trust them."

Thomas then turned to the nine citizens and asked, "Do you wish to speak?"

One of them replied, "You are an honourable man, Thomas, we trust in your judgement."

Mungo then addressed everyone saying, "Your mayor is now dead, and you seem to have great faith and trust in Thomas. I believe he is a worthy successor."

Nobody disagreed. At that point, the priory door creaked slowly open. Everyone turned to see who was there. A face peered round the door.

"Is it safe to come in?" asked Drake looking suspicious but relieved.

The following morning, after the chaos from the previous night had been cleared and Herman had been unceremoniously dumped in a cold, dark dungeon, they all met up again, this time in the council chambers. Alan and Silas had already taken their place on the platform on either side of the mayoral seat, the nine citizens, six women, monks, who were now in their more familiar battle gear and William's bodyguards, also in their battle gear had already assembled.

Silas stood up and said, in a rather pompous voice. "We do not allow any weaponry in here, now go before I make trouble for you."

Bryce rose to his feet and a booming voice yelled, "Sit down and be silent!" Silas quickly obeyed.

Thomas and Drake walked in smiling, discussing the events from the previous evening. They climbed the steps to the platform and Thomas took his place in the mayoral chair with Drake sitting next to Silas.

"What is this?" demanded Silas.

"A change of leader," replied Thomas.

"I cannot possibly allow this," said Silas arrogantly.

Again, Bryce stood up and this time, in a polite manner, said, "You will do as you are commanded."

Thomas stood up to address the meeting, "Silas, please make way for Drake."

Silas looked at him and replied, "You have no authority over me." Boyce stood up once more and without hesitation, Silas quickly vacated his seat allowing Drake to sit next to Thomas.

"I would like to thank Drake for calling you all here this morning. Events of late have shown the need for a change of roles and rules in the city. Neither William nor Herman will be tasked with any further matters regarding the running of the city."

Elen sat quiet. She had a good idea what had happened but still sat there motionless and expressionless.

Thomas continued, "I have gratefully accepted the role of mayor and if nobody objects," he looked across at Silas who for once remained silent. "I will outline my wishes. First though, I must thank all those here for the way they brought certain matters to my attention. I wish to address our brethren from the north. I have spoken, at length, to my daughters, Anna and Nesta, and they have explained the true purpose of their visit. I know that they will be well-treated and safe in their new home. I ask only one favour and that is that you will return one day so I may see my daughters' children."

"That I promise," said Mungo.

"Next is to address those who have made us live in fear and who have slaughtered our friends. Peace be upon you. I have thought of a suitable punishment for you. Till the next full moon, you will be at the mercy of any citizen. If they ask you to clean out the pigs or clean the shit off the horse tracks, you will obey. When your term of punishment has passed, you will serve to protect the city from those who would wish to bring harm upon us."

Bryce stood up and replied, "It will be an honour to serve you and the city."

"Silas, Alan," Thomas continued, "I cannot see how you have contributed to the wellbeing of our city and therefore I relieve you of your duties. You may now leave."

"But we have done nothing," said Alan.

"That is what I mean, you have done nothing." The two of them rose from their seats, made their way begrudgingly down the platform steps and out of the building.

"Drake," continued Thomas, "you have a choice. You may stay to advise me in the matters of my duties and responsibilities or you may accompany Mungo, Boyd, Gerik, Enar and Asmund to help them build a new future."

Drake replied, "After being someone who did not feel he was wanted or needed to become someone who now has to make an impossible choice, I now do not know what to do. All my life I have had no excitement but now so much has happened. I love my city, but I want to be happy. I have learnt that there can be so much good here, but I have also seen so much greed and sorrow. I know that with Thomas leading us there will be a great future ahead. I also…"

"Are you going to decide today because we need to go home soon," interrupted Boyd.

Drake smiled and said, "You have been good to me. You trusted me even though you have threatened to kill me more than once."

"I will decide for you," said Boyd. "You know more than anyone else about the city. Thomas, Carlisle needs someone trustworthy. We are only two days' journey away and we promise we will return."

Thomas and Drake stepped off the platform and approached the others. They all stood in the centre of the chamber. They embraced each other in turn. Many a tear was shed as they said their farewells. Outside they were met by what appeared to be the whole population of Carlisle. Men, women and children gave them a thunderous acclamation as they appeared.

Thomas faced Boyd and said, "I have been told that you enjoy chicken, cabbage, carrots, wine and a few barrels of ale so I am sure that this time you will all share the food and drink we have prepared for you. There are two carriages ready for your journey; one for the women to ride in and the other for your clothes, foods, drinks, meats, a few live chickens, cereals and whatever else we could find that will help you in your new home. I think it is time."

The women boarded the carriages. Asmund and Enar were responsible for driving them. Boyd and Gerik mounted their horses. Mungo approached

Drake and firmly embraced him to the extent that Drake needed to tell him to loosen his grip as his breathing was becoming a little difficult.

"Thank you for everything," said Mungo.

Drake was the most tearful as so much had happened to him in the last few days that would now change his future.

"Please take good care of our daughters," said Thomas.

"You have our word as monks," replied Mungo. Thomas laughed.

The return journey north would this time take a good four days, progressing at a rather steady pace, in which time the travellers would get to know their guests a little better. After journeying for about twenty miles, Berta leant out of the carriage and shouted to Asmund.

"I am hungry, and I need to pee."

Asmund called ahead to the others, saying, "We need to stop."

The procession came to a halt, Mungo and Boyd turning their horses to face the carriages. The women alighted and Berta dashed behind a large tree, raised her tunic, and out of sight relieved herself. Apart from the occasional sound of a chirping bird, all that was heard was a long "Aaargh."

She returned to the group with a satisfied smile on her face and sat on the lower carriage step. "I am still hungry," she said. Enar and Asmund went to the provisions carriage and opened the door.

They called for the others to come quickly. They looked inside and under the three large food hampers were two familiar chests. Asmund unloaded the hampers and Boyd reached over to one of the chests and opened it. There was a note inside which simply read, 'Use it wisely' and signed 'Thomas'.

Boyd sat down on a nearby fallen tree staring at the note in his hand. Behind him he heard clinking of jewellery.

Without even looking around he shouted, "Put it back and close the chest please Anna!"

"I was just looking," she said.

"And how did you know it was me?"

"I heard Nesta saying, Anna how about that one." He looked round and smiled at her.

The food hampers were opened. They were packed with poultry, carrots, cheese, nuts plus numerous flasks of wine and ale. As before, nobody complained. Once they had satisfied their appetites, it was time to move on.

To pass the time, they took it in turns to sing a traditional local ballad, obviously with some being far more in tune than others. Evening was soon upon them, so they decided to make camp for the night. It was a cool, quiet evening and sitting round a nice warm fire added to the ambience. Remembering what they were told before embarking on the mission, Mungo reiterated that the women were to be returned untouched.

After another satisfying raid on the hampers, they decided to settle down for the night. The men used the monks' cowls to cover the women. Mungo and Gerik took the first watch while the others slept. They recalled that only a short time ago, the two nations had been at war.

"If you had not been drinking then we would not be here now," said Mungo.

"If Berta and Edith had not been drinking, then they would not be here either," replied Gerik.

"There is much to be said for drinking," replied Mungo with a great big smile on his face." They sat quietly looking up at stars in the clear sky until Mungo broke the silence saying, "Enjoy the peace while it lasts. I can see we will have much ahead of us. This is only the beginning." Gerik nodded.

Morning arrived. Gerik and Mungo had fallen asleep on watch and woke to a loud shout from behind some trees. Enar appeared holding his backside.

"I did not see the thistles," he moaned. "I am sure there must be some spikes still stuck there." He walked up to Gerik, lifted his tunic and stuck his backside almost in Gerik's face. "Look," he said.

Unfortunately, at that moment Anna and Nesta woke. An embarrassed Enar quickly let his tunic fall back into place and shouted, "Thistles." The two women smiled politely.

Asmund and Boyd had been out hunting and returned with a wild boar. A frame was erected over a fire and the beast was spit roasted. Gerik went to see what drinks were left in the hampers and returned carrying a few jugs. Pork and ale for breakfast. There was nowhere to wash, so after everyone had relieved themselves, all were loaded into the carriages, and they continued making their way north.

It was not long until they came across a secluded tarn. It was an ideal opportunity for the women to freshen themselves. Being perfect gentlemen, the men respected the women's wishes and allowed them to bathe in privacy, however it was quite a different story when the men bathed with the women watching from a discreet distance, while remaining well hidden.

One more day's journey left. They had made good progress over the past two days and seemed to be well on schedule to complete the journey within four days. The women were becoming a little apprehensive, wondering what lay ahead. They were used to the comfort and routine of life at home but having to adjust to a completely different lifestyle, at the moment, seemed a little daunting. Also, the prospect of being one of only six women among thirty men now seemed somewhat intimidating.

Matilda saw the nervous smiles on the faces of the others and asked, "Do you think we are doing right?"

Elen was the first to respond. "I have thought about that, but do you remember when we were younger and looked out onto the hills and wondered what it would be like to go beyond them?"

"My father talked to Nesta and myself," began Anna, "and he told us that this would be our only chance to get away from Carlisle and begin a new life. He said that if he had been given the same opportunity when he was our age, he would have taken it. He was sad to see us go but happy for us."

Edith was the next to talk. "I have no one and nor does Berta. I think if we had stayed in that city then nothing would be any different for us. We were not happy. I have no regrets." Berta nodded her agreement.

It was very warm inside the carriage, so Berta decided she needed a little air. Clambering out of the window, onto the carriage roof, she made her way to sit next to Asmund.

"Tell me what it is like in your country," she asked.

"Aalborg is a big settlement. Many of our folk are fishermen. Wood from the forests is floated down the Limfjord for the boat builders to build our longboats. It is very cold and very peaceful."

"Will you take me there one day?" she asked.

"I may," he replied. She smiled and rested her head against Asmund's shoulder.

Soon evening was upon them, so they found a suitable place to set up camp for the night. A fire was lit and again they all sat round enjoying the food that had been prepared for them by the good citizens of Carlisle. Satisfied, they all settled down for the night. Boyd and Asmund were on watch duty first.

After a short time and making sure all the others were asleep, Matilda and Berta rose from their beds and approached the two men.

"We could not sleep," said Matilda as she sat next to Boyd. Berta nestled up to Asmund and he put his arm round her shoulder to keep her warm. "We have grown to know you, but what are the others like?" she asked.

"When we were leaving, they were starting to build more huts for us in the village, but as there was still plenty of ale left for them to enjoy, I am not sure what we will find."

"You will promise to protect us," asked Matilda.

"We promise," replied Boyd. Both women soon fell asleep.

The morning of the fourth day came all too soon. After the calls of nature had been satisfied, they began the last leg of their journey. In a matter of a few hours, they would be beginning a new life. In the distance Mungo spied a lone rider. He signalled for the carriages to move off the track and shelter behind a thickly wooded area. Boyd and Gerik rode on towards the approaching figure.

Getting closer, Mungo recognised the rider. He dismounted and stood in the middle of the track. "Alban!" he boomed.

The rider came closer and while his horse was still moving, jumped off and ran towards Mungo. They embraced. "Welcome, welcome," said Alban, "but where are the others?"

Mungo gave a loud whistle and out from behind the trees came the two carriages with the women straining to look out of the windows.

"You have been busy," said Alban "and you are two days late," he added.

"We have much to tell you. Lead the way home," said Mungo excitedly.

Approaching the settlement, they noticed cattle and sheep grazing in wooden fenced fields, wattle and daub huts and some clay-bricked dwellings, thatched roofing, smoke rising from chimneys, smooth tracks. There were signs of iron, bronze and copper mining. On the way in, they passed numerous buildings still under construction, eventually to be use for storing meat, fruit, cereals and much more. Areas had been allocated and construction had begun, and in some cases, was almost completed, on a place of worship, a medical centre, stables, a forge, a blacksmith's, a carpenter, food storage, clothier's and washrooms among others.

Garmund, Angus and Dougal had perfected a process of obtaining salt from brine so preservation of food would not be a problem. Even a sewer and drainage system had been partially constructed below the surface using small carved stones to line a series of channels, water being diverted from the Tay and then flowing back further downstream.

Many scouting parties had been sent out to locate sources of produce, travelling as far west as the now derelict monastery at Iona. The Columban community were extremely industrious, cultivating orchards, groves and a variety of vines. Seedlings and vines were carefully uprooted and brought back to the settlement and replanted in rich soil. The transformation within such a short time was astounding — a whole new village had sprung up.

Alban led them to the centre of the settlement where Hithin and Alpin were waiting. The men dismounted and were heartily greeted. The women remaining nervously in the carriage.

Mungo looked round, turned back to Alpin and said sarcastically. "I see nothing much has changed since we left. I do not remember bringing sheep and cattle with us."

"I think they must have walked into the field one night, and just like us, set up a new home," replied Alpin. By this time everybody had congregated around the carriages.

"Give them room," shouted Hithin.

"The women need to rest," said Mungo. "They have had four long days."

Hithin climbed up next to Asmund, saying, "We have prepared food and comfortable beds for the women and there is hot water and fresh clothing for them. Tomorrow, they will meet us all." Hithin took the reins and drove the carriage to the far side of the settlement. "Guards will be outside to make sure that nobody enters their dwellings. We have much to talk about." The carriage drew up outside a large timber building. Hithin and Asmund climbed down and opened both carriage doors.

"Do not worry," said Asmund. "This is Hithin. He is a good man."

The women were helped out of the carriage and escorted into their new home. Inside two quite attractive nuns, both in their early thirties, were waiting.

"This is Mildrith, and this is Eangyth. They were at the monastery in Iona when Gillis and Frothi travelled there on a scouting trip and were saddened by how it had been destroyed. They had nowhere to go and so came back here with them. They will look after you. Their huts are just along the path."

The women introduced themselves in turn and the initial apprehension seemed to have diminished.

Nesta looked nervously at Hithin and then unexpectedly threw her arms round him, well halfway round him. She started crying and just kept saying, "Thank you," over and over again.

"Child," said Hithin, "you must rest. We will see you in the morning." The men left and the women sat on the floor with the two nuns.

Mildrith settled them saying, "We have been here a few days but already we see peace and goodwill as never before. Our lives in the convent were religious but here there is a different type of faith. One which is, well, beyond words. You will see for yourselves in the morning what I mean. Now, there is clothing for you, hot baths and food. This is your new home."

The women bathed, ate then retired to bed, falling asleep as soon their heads touched the soft feather pillows.

All the men gathered round a warm fire in the sandy covered clearing. They talked for much of the night about what had happened in the settlement, the journey, the events in Carlisle and to the amusement of the men, how some the women were chosen.

"Our travellers are so happy to be home," said Alpin.

Mungo replied, "I did not recognise where we were. I said to Gerik that I thought we were lost."

Alban was sitting drawing in the ground with a stick when suddenly he shouted, "Stoleware." The others turned to him looking rather confused. "We are lost," said Alban.

"No, we are home," responded Mungo.

"No, we are lost, Stoleware," said Alban again.

Suddenly it clicked. Mungo looked down at what Alban had drawn out in the sand and said, "Yes, yes, that's it, Stoleware. That is where we are, Stoleware." After a little clarification and explanation, everybody agreed. "Stoleware," said Mungo again.

Chapter 4

A New Beginning

A beautiful morning to begin a new era.

The men were very hygienic, washing every morning even though some mornings the water was refreshingly cold to say the least. However, the women did have the luxury of the water being heated before being brought to them. They dressed in clean outfits and prepared themselves to meet the men. Boyd, Alpin, Hithin and Gerik approached the women's huts.

Mildrith came to the door and said, "They are ready."

Hithin looked at the women, smiled and said, "Please do not be afraid. They are all good men here."

The women were led to the clearing where most of the men were sitting in a semi-circle awaiting their arrival. Opposite them, on the other side of the circle, stood Enar, Asmund, Mungo and Alban waiting for the women to emerge into sight.

The women smiled as they saw the familiar faces.

"Come, sit with us," beckoned Boyd. They sat down, nervously looking around at the staring faces. Alpin stood in the centre of the circle ready to address the audience.

"This is it," he began. "There are a few away hunting but they will return soon." Thirty men and eight women." he said.

Eangyth looked at Alpin and laughingly said, "Two of us are here for religious purposes only."

Alpin politely acknowledged their response. "Twenty-six men in the camp, four out hunting, six women and two for religious purposes only. Any questions?" he asked, smiling.

"Today we start a new beginning. No one knows what lies ahead. There will be good and troubled times and there is still the threat of outsiders who wish to make trouble. We need to protect ourselves. We have much to learn.

We are lucky to have among us, some who are wise in healing, some are skilled in hunting, building, sailing and in time, during our travels, we will learn much more. We are fighters but not just fighters in battle, fighters in spirit. We were brought together for a reason. Our religious friends may have an answer to that question."

"Look around and see what we have done in a short time. You have done this," he said to everyone whilst pointing around. "It is your home. I spoke to Mungo and Gerik last evening and they told me about the women. Some have very sad stories to tell. They will not be forced into seeking a husband. Gerik promised them that they will never have to do anything against their will, and I uphold that promise. If I see or hear of any wrongdoing by any of you men, then you will answer to me. We must be true to ourselves."

One of the carriages was on the edge of the clearing. Boyd looked at Mungo and Gerik, nodded and then stood up.

"We have not told Alpin all that happened in Carlisle. We wanted you all gathered together."

Alpin looked puzzled. The three men stood up and beckoned Enar to join them. They approached the carriage, opened the door and brought out the two chests placing them in front of Alpin.

"These are gifts from the citizens of Carlisle for the help we gave. We were told to use them wisely," said Boyd.

Enar and Gerik opened the chests to reveal the contents — gold and silver jewellery and a large number of coins.

The only person to speak was Anna who quietly said to Nesta, "I do like that necklace." Boyd looked at her and smiled.

Everyone stood up and walked towards the chests, amazed at what they saw.

Angus, one of the Scotsmen said, "That is Roman gold. How did you come by it?"

Mungo simply told them it was a gift. "It is many generations since the Romans came to our shores and I do not believe they will return."

"We will use it wisely," said Alpin. He turned to Colban. "You will need to build or find somewhere safe to store the chests." Colban nodded.

"Back to your places," continued Alpin. "It is now time to meet the women." He turned to them saying, "Please stand. They look quiet and shy, so I will have Mungo and Gerik to tell you about them."

Mungo beckoned them to approach, and they stood in a row behind him. He introduced them one by one, the men cheering loudly as each name was called. That greatly amused the women. Edith was the last to be introduced and on her name being mentioned, she took one step forward, curtseyed and then stepped back into line. This action received the loudest cheer. The women then sat down again.

Alpin turned to address them. "In your absence, we held games to find the most suitable amongst us." He briefly explained the nature of these games and some interesting results regarding the finer aspects of etiquette. This caused great amusement. However, some of the men were slightly uncomfortable at being reminded of their activities, but this seemed to put everyone more at ease.

"Please come forward Frothi, Garmund, Donnan, Duff, Ewan and Malcolm. These fine men have shown themselves to be our best."

The six men stood in front of the women looking a little embarrassed, especially as the others were shouting none too complimentary comments. The women huddled together to quietly discuss the candidates standing before them. Elen was elected to speak on their behalf.

After a few moments, she stood up and said to Alpin, "These men may have shown good skills, but a woman should know best what she wants to see in a man, so, we would like to see everybody." Alpin nodded his agreement.

He turned to the six and asked them to return to the others. "I will tell you their names," he said.

"We will never remember what they are called," said Elen.

"I have an idea," sparked Alban. He asked the nuns if he could use some of the paper, quills and ink they had brought from Iona.

Mildrith went to fetch the items. Meanwhile the four men who had been out hunting returned with their quarry. Chickens, geese, a deer, wild boar and a few carp, cod and herring and sat at the back of the circle. Quite a successful outing. The whole compliment of the village was now present.

Alban wrote each number, one to thirty, on a separate slip of paper, handing them out to the men as he did so. Eight of the men declined the invitation so that left twenty-two potential suitors. Even Alpin, albeit reluctantly, accepted an invitation. The women were each handed a slip of paper and a quill to mark down their initial selection. The parade began. Each man stood in front of the women holding their allocated number, introduced themselves and stated what qualities they possess. The whole group were in hysterics as some of the men tried to relate an extremely personal biography in the hope of being chosen.

"I have a large spindle," said one.

"I wash my ears and can sing while standing on one leg," said another.

All of which had the women wiping tears from their eyes with laughter. Even the two nuns could not resist the occasional smile. After all the candidates had filed through, it was now up to the women to make their initial selection. Both Matilda and Berta had written down just one number. Matilda, after her ordeal in Carlisle, had unsurprisingly chosen Boyd and Berta, after having spent plenty of time helping to drive the carriage, chose Asmund.

The ballot papers were given to the nuns, who were obviously impartial, to read out. Numbers were called and Boyd, Asmund, Mungo, Ewan, Alpin, Gillis, Angus, Dougal, Enar and Kyle came forward. As Matilda and Berta had just the one choice, Boyd and Asmund respectively were asked to sit with them. Next it was Nesta's turn to pick just one.

She asked Mungo and Ewan to stand in front of her and looking at Mungo, she asked him, "Why should I choose you?"

Mungo replied, "I am strong, honest and I promised your father I will care for you."

"That is not fair," said Ewan. "You have had the chance to talk to Nesta before now and she knows what you are like and…" Before he could say any more, Nesta interrupted.

"Instead of telling me about you, you began by saying it was not fair of Mungo to bring up about my father, so I choose you Mungo."

Ewan realised his mistake and apologised for being so snappy. "You are right," he said, "I should have told you about me, not said anything wrong about Mungo. You have chosen the better man."

Nesta walked over to Ewan, gave him a kiss on the cheek and said, "You are a good man."

"Thank you."

Eangyth stood and said, "We now have two young women who have chosen the same two men. Anna, Edith you have both chosen Enar and Kyle."

"Let them fight!" yelled one of the Scotsmen.

"I had thought of that," replied the nun, "but I do not think Anna fighting Kyle would be a fair contest." This caused great laughter in the audience.

"Anna," said Eangyth, "which one would you choose first?" Anna walked up to Enar, looked him up and down, walked round him, still casting her vision all over him, then she did the same with Kyle, however when walking behind him she pinched his bottom. He let out an enormous squeal and turned round quickly to see a cheeky smile on Anna's face. She returned to the others.

"Do not say your choice," said Eangyth. Edith copied Anna, even down to pinching Kyle's bottom on the way round.

She approached Anna and the two women walked out of earshot of the others. After a few minutes, they returned and Anna said, "We have chosen." She walked over to Kyle, gave him a peck on the cheek, smiled then moved to take Enar's arm.

Edith then approached Kyle and said, "Will you take me?" Kyle nodded.

One more to go. Elen had four to choose from. Alpin, Gillis, Angus and Dougal. They stood about five paces from her and about an arm's length apart. Alpin was the tallest of the four, standing about six-foot seven inches, clean shaven, well-built, with a slight scar on his left cheek. He had quite a soft voice for such a big man.

"Speak to me," she said.

Alpin was the first to respond. "I am Alpin," he began. "I was born on a farmstead on the Isle of Mull and my parents taught me much about raising sheep and growing crops. I had two older brothers who became monks and were in the monastery at Iona when it was attacked. They were both killed." Gerik rose and walked away, his head down. "Wait," said Alpin. Gerik continued to walk away. Alpin ran to him. "Friend," he said, turning Gerik round, "you cannot take the blame for something that you were not part of."

"I am ashamed," said Gerik. He sank to his knees. Alpin crouched down facing him. "Did I not say that today we start on a new beginning? The past has gone. We cannot change it." Gerik had a tear in his eye as he looked Alpin in the face.

"Let us return. I believe Elen has some more to ask me."

Gerik returned to his place and Alpin stood in front of Elen.

"I have heard all I need. I choose you Alpin," she said.

He looked surprised. "You have not spoken to the others," said Alpin.

Elen continued, "You showed compassion and forgiveness. I have seen more goodwill from you today than I have done for many a time in my life at home. You are a kind man Alpin. I have made my decision."

"Does that mean I do not have the honour of singing to you?" asked Dougal.

Elen looked at him, smiled and said, "Oh yes, please do sing to me."

He began,

"Oh, maiden fair of face and skin,
It is your heart I wish to win,
I am a man who has no fear,
I'll keep you safe from wild deer,
I will fight the man who makes you cry,
I will hit him in the eye.
Please say that you will be mine,
Or I will have to drink much wine."

Elen's expression was one of bemusement. She was totally lost for words.

Eventually, after successfully stifling her laughter, she said, "Dougal, that was beautiful, but I am sorry, Alpin is the one I have chosen."

Dougal smiled and sat down with the others, aware that he had failed the audition.

Alpin rose to his feet. "The women have chosen. I now ask our two sisters Mildrith and Eangyth if they will prepare to join us together."

Mildrith replied, "We will." She stood up and announced. "The weddings of Boyd to Matilda, Asmund to Berta, Mungo to Nesta, Enar to Anna, Kyle to Edith and Alpin to Elen will take place at the fifth hour in two days' time and until then the women will be untouched," and with that the meeting adjourned.

Matilda walked up to Boyd, said nothing but hugged him tightly. She turned, walked backed towards the other women and after a few steps, looked back over her shoulder to give him a loving smile.

Alpin stood up. "Let us feast."

The haul from the morning hunt was roasted, the vegetables brought from Carlisle prepared and ale and wine served. Everyone was enjoying themselves. The men were coming up to the betrothed couples congratulating them. Edith was talking and laughing with some of her new friends.

One of the Vikings, Vogg, came up behind her and tapped her on the shoulder. She turned round quickly, looked up to see who it was and suddenly screamed loudly, dropped her drink, fell to the floor on her back, crawling quickly away. Enar, Kyle and Alpin rushed up to her. Kyle asked her what the matter was.

She was white, hysterical, still screaming and shouting, "No! no!" There was absolute horror in her face.

The whole party fell silent. Edith scrambled to her feet and ran as fast as she could towards her hut. Berta threw her drink to the side and ran after Edith shouting for her to stop. Edith eventually stopped, bent down, hands on knees gasping for breath.

"It is him," she said panting, "It is him." She collapsed to the ground crying uncontrollably. "It is him," she said again. Enar, Kyle and Alpin were approaching but Berta signalled for them to wait back.

"It is who?" asked Berta.

"Him," said Edith still panting heavily.

"Breathe slowly," said Berta, "be calm."

Suddenly it dawned on Berta what Edith meant — a giant of a man with a long red beard and a red patch over his right eye. Berta sank to her knees, her heart beating very quickly.

"We cannot stay here," she said. The three men approached and knelt down next to them.

"What troubles you?" asked Alpin. Edith looked at Berta, neither saying anything at first.

Still trembling, she began. "My parents were slaughtered in a Viking raid many years ago and the man that killed them is here." Alpin closed his eyes and shook his head in disbelief.

"It is Vogg," said Enar, my brother."

Edith burst into tears and threw her arms round Enar's neck. "I did not know." He continued, "I did not know." Nobody said anything for quite a while.

"I cannot go back. I cannot face him knowing he killed our parents," said Edith.

"That was many years ago," said Alpin. "Much has happened in that time. Vogg is one of my most trusted men. He is a gentle giant, but you must face him."

The women nodded knowingly. Enar and Kyle helped them to their feet, and they started walking slowly back to the camp. Alpin went on ahead to talk to Gerik and Hithin. Eventually the other four arrived.

Vogg was sitting on the opposite side of the circle, wondering what had happened. When he saw them returning, he stood up and started making his way towards them. Hithin told him to stop. Asmund went towards Berta, and she put her arms round him but said nothing. Hithin and Alpin went across to speak to Vogg. He collapsed to his knees and put his head in his hands. Eventually, he raised his head, noticed Edith and Berta looking at him, got to his feet, turned and walked out of the camp. Not even a bird could be heard.

"What will become of him?" asked Berta.

"I do not know," replied Hithin, "but for now, leave him be. He needs time to think."

After the earlier celebrations, the mood was far more subdued. Alpin went into the middle of the clearing to speak to everyone.

"There has been sadness and joy when we wished only for joy. It will be difficult to forget the sad times in our lives and forgive those who have wronged us and caused sadness. We all need to be strong and help each of our friends."

Edith walked up to Alpin. "Please find Vogg, she implored."

Alpin signalled to Sholto and Angus to go in search of him.

Edith went up to Hithin and asked, "How do you say, 'My heart is heavy with sadness' in Danish?"

"Mit hjerte er tungt af tristhed," he replied.

Edith kept repeating the words to herself. Everyone was waiting in silence for the three men to return.

Vogg shortly entered the clearing with his head down, being urged along by Sholto and Angus. Edith approached him, tears still in her eyes. She raised her hand to lift his head and still concentrating so hard on the words she had been told, said to him.

"Min hest er tung af tristhed."

He looked at her, giggled and then roared with uncontrollable laughter. She looked so puzzled.

"What is the matter with him?" she asked Hithin. "You have just told him that your horse is heavy with sadness." Edith started to giggle and then she too was holding her stomach with pains of laughter.

To make matters worse Vogg eventually managed to say to her, "You have a very caring horse," before the two of them were again laughing uncontrollably.

Word soon spread round the camp as to the reason for the hilarity and once again the mood lightened. It was quite some time before everyone settled down. Vogg and Edith sat facing each.

"I will never be able to say sorry enough times for what I have done in the past."

Edith looked him in the eyes and said, "If the horse is happy, then I am happy." That did it.

Nobody else heard what was said but just saw the two of them rolling round on the ground, once again in agonising laughter.

Eventually they managed to get to their feet, Vogg totally dwarfing Edith. They walked up to Alpin and Hithin.

"Thank you," said Hithin. "You are a good man, and we need men like you."

Vogg nodded and walked with Edith up to Kyle. "You have a brave woman here," said Vogg. "Take good care of her or you answer to me." Vogg gave Enar a 'friendly' pat on the shoulder almost knocking him over.

"There is still much food and drink!" shouted Alpin. "Let the feast go on. Please come with me to meet the others," he said to the women. "You will know their names in time."

As the women approached, the men stood. Alpin began introducing them individually, moving slowly along the line, each man bidding them welcome.

"Donnan and Ewan are my scouts. They travel far to see what lands lie beyond ours and what dangers we may face. They draw maps of the land, rivers and villages. Malcolm and Dougal make bread and tasty meat and ale and chicken and vegetable pies and cook the food for all of us. Gillis planned our village and he tells Kyle what we need. Kyle, Colban and Asmund cut down the trees and shape the wood and we all help with the making of everything from plates, goblets to building tables, carts, carriages and our huts. Angus is our blacksmith, always working hard with the ores that Enar, Frothi and Kentigern mine from under the ground. As you see he makes our knives and spoons for eating and tools and weapons. If you are ever cold, this is always the warmest place in our village. Fingal is a well-learnt man and with the help of Mildrith and Eangyth, will be looking after both our earthly and spiritual needs. They are wise men and if any matter troubles you, please talk to them. Ulf and Nevin are hunters, Coll is skilled at shoeing horses. These three like to keep their own company at night and we do not ask more. You have met Vogg." Alpin had a great big smile on his face as he introduced Vogg once again. "He is our best hunter." Edith went up to Vogg and hugged him. He leant over and gave her a kiss on the top of her head.

"A few more left. These are Halfred and Sholto," continued Alpin. "They make the clothes and the shoes from the animal skins that Ulf, Nevin and Vogg trap after Malcolm and Dougal have skinned them. In Aalborg, Garmund was a physician and now he treats all from small wounds to bad illnesses. Duff and Ross were farmers in Scotland before they became warriors. They will grow the fruit trees and grape vines brought back from Iona, all our vegetables, tend sheep, pigs, chickens and cows and collect milk and eggs. In time you will know them all. This is Mirren. He is the quietest, but he does much that nobody sees. With Gillis they plan the village and where to build the stores for our food, drink, clothing and much more. Now Gerik, Boyd and Mungo have returned they will all act as a council with me and Hithin and care for us and all that we need to be happy and warm."

The women were overly impressed with how thorough they had all been in designing and building a new village in such a short time. There was still much work to do but the basics were there, and the place was reasonably habitable. Alpin wondered if there was anything else they wanted to know.

Elen asked, "When we are joined with the men we have chosen, where will we sleep?"

Alpin replied, "We have thought of that, and we have six huts made ready for you, away from where the others sleep, for after the ceremony." The women looked quite relieved that there would be a little privacy.

The feasting went on well into the night. The women sat with their men talking about how peaceful it was and such a change in atmosphere compared to the bustle of Carlisle. They were told of the plans for the future of the village and how it was their intention to keep it secret from prying eyes. Eventually, they all fell asleep outside in the warm air, completely satisfied with the most excellent refreshments.

Chapter 5

Far Better or Worse?

The village was to be prepared by the following day for the six weddings. Asmund, Kyle and Colban had to work hard to make sure the church was completed or at least usable for the ceremony. Ulf, Nevin and Coll, being by far the most artistic, took it on themselves to organise proceedings, advising every one of their duties. There were tears and tantrums, but Alpin managed to settle arguments between the three planners before they came to blows.

The women's outfits were the first item to be addressed. The three checked the clothing that the women had brought with them and decided that with a few alterations from Halfred and Sholto, they would be perfectly acceptable. Personal decoration was next. Ulf approached Hithin and Alpin to ask if some of the Roman jewellery, particularly rings, could be used in the service. Alpin agreed but stressed that they were only to be worn by the women. Nevin looked a little disappointed as he had noticed a sparkling necklace which he thought would suit him. The grooms were told to wash their own tunics, either in the nearby stream or the wash tubs for the ceremony. As they were warriors, they would carry the daggers and swords in leather straps around their waist. The others were ordered to make themselves presentable, especially Hithin, who it was agreed, had the dirtiest tunic in the village and needed a good wash himself. Despite protesting, Hithin made his way to the washroom, muttering to himself and thinking it was a bad decision to put those three in charge.

Nevin asked for volunteers to clean the carriages and groom and shoe the horses. Frothi, Enar, Alban and Ewan willingly accepted the first task and Tovi the second, probably because they would not be pestered further for any other more menial duties.

Dougal, Malcolm and Ross were put in charge of the catering. There were some vegetables remaining from the feast, so these were gathered to make soup. Sacks of wheat and flour brought back from Carlisle were used and with the yeast obtained from nearby plant leaves, bread, pies and cakes were made. There were two large ovens constructed from branches of willow, which were bent into a semi-circular shape and covered with clay and turf. When lit, the branches would burn, turning the clay into brick. As the meats would take quite some time, Dougal decided to roast them overnight. The aroma of fresh cooking and baking circulated round the camp, causing sudden bouts of hunger. However, the three cooks ensured there was no pre-ceremony food sampling. Vogg and Enar were sent to the river to catch what they could and with the trappings from the morning's hunt being prepared, it seemed as if another feast would be enjoyed. Plus, there was still an adequate amount of alcoholic refreshment remaining.

Coll's roll was to plan the events starting with the brides being collected from their huts in the morning, the service, celebrations and finally the six couples being returned to their new homes at the end of the day. He and the nuns met in one of the completed buildings to discuss the preparations. The two nuns would help with the order of service at the church and would prepare the vows to be read out during the ceremony.

After outlining his ideas, Mildrith did have one question for him. "Who is going to lead the marriage service?"

"I had not thought of that," Coll replied, looking extremely puzzled. "Who do you think?" he added.

"I was going to suggest Alpin," replied Mildrith, "but as he is getting married, I do not believe he can marry himself, so as Hithin is the leader of the Vikings, then I think he is a good choice."

They agreed. "I think we should tell him soon then he can be prepared. We will go to speak to him." said Eangyth.

Off they went, eventually discovering Hithin still in the washroom, immersed in one of the tubs, merrily singing to himself. Unfortunately, Angus had not quite got round to putting bolts on the door and as Mildrith and Eangyth entered, Hithin had just stood up displaying his full profile to two shocked yet smirking nuns. Quickly re-immersing himself into the water, he peered over the wooden tub, asking the purpose of their unexpected visit. Mildrith explained that, as he was the most senior among the group, it would be right for him to conduct the wedding ceremony.

"But is not Fingal most wise in these matters?" he asked, trying to pass the task on.

"They are learnt in earthly ways, but lack spiritual guidance," she replied.

"Therefore," continued Hithin, still trying to wriggle out of it, "I think you should perform the ceremony."

"In the eyes of God, we cannot," began Eangyth, "but I believe you, as leader do have the rank and authority." Mildrith looked at Eangyth who gave her a sly wink.

"This is so," said Mildrith, "our teachings at the convent made it known that a hersir[1] has the right to marry a droengiar[2]."

"You know much about Viking tradition, so I trust what you tell me," said Hithin. Eangyth looked at Mildrith who returned the wink.

"May I now finish my bathing and then I will join you later?" asked Hithin. The nuns politely bowed, turned and walked out of the washroom.

Outside Mildrith turned to Eangyth, smiled and said, "Not quite as big as Brother Dunstan." The two returned to their meeting with Coll.

With just over half of the contingent allocated tasks, the others were on call to do jobs or errands for any group that was shorthanded — building, carrying, tidying, hunting or any task that needed work. The mood was one of excitement, expectation and general joviality.

Ulf insisted that the church be decorated with flowers and sent out Donnan, Garmund and Duff. There was quite a variety of flowers blooming in early summer and within a circumference of a few miles, the group managed to collect roses, daisies, foxglove, lilies and not exactly suitable for decoration, but of particular interest to Garmund, bunches of lady's mantles. This caused him great excitement as he was aware of the many health benefits in healing wounds, skin problems and treating bites and stings from insects. He was totally in his element telling everybody of his find. All he did that afternoon was stock up on bunches of the flower for future use.

---

[1] Viking military commander
[2] Young Viking warrior

Hithin eventually resumed his meeting with Coll and the nuns, looking a little embarrassed as he walked into one of the huts.

"We have prepared the vows for you to read out at the service," said Mildrith, handing him the paper.

He read the words to himself, distorting his face, stroking his chin and scratching his forehead at fairly regular intervals whilst throwing in the occasional 'Hmm' and 'Erm.' "So, I have to read this out six times?" he asked.

"Yes, that is all you have to do," replied Mildrith.

After a few more 'Hmms' and 'Erms,' strokings and scratchings, he asked, "Are you sure there is no one else who can do this?"

All three replied simultaneously with a resounding "No."

"How about…?"

"No, no, no," interrupted Mildrith, "now go and keep reading the words." Hithin left feeling he had been severely reprimanded.

"For a man who has led large armies into battle and made speeches to kings, he seems to fear speaking in front of thirty people," said Coll.

"Would you do it?" asked Eangyth.

"Only if they were all men," replied Coll, with a twinkle in his eye.

"We must have music at the feast," said Mildrith.

"I never thought about that," replied Coll.

Mildrith continued. "I rescued my cithara from Iona and Eangyth's flute. I know that Ewan has some bagpipes, and I am sure that there will be a few who will sing to us. We can always play some games."

"I believe there is a ball somewhere so we will use that," mentioned Coll.

That seemed to be everything sorted. It was approaching early evening, so the three organisers decided to do the rounds, checking on progress. They first inspected the church and were impressed at how colourful it looked. They praised Ulf for his efforts. Next, they checked on the horses and carriages and were again overwhelmed by the effort put in to prepare them for the big day. Dougal, Malcolm and Ross were on schedule with food preparation. They were also impressed with the work put in by all the men and the grooms, in cleaning their tunics and polishing swords.

They had all been secretly looking forward to the final check, the women's gowns. Nevin had chosen the jewellery but had not, as yet, seen the finished bridal outfits. They politely knocked on the door of the women's huts and were greeted by Mildrith who bid them enter. They were all in their bridal outfits and Halfred and Sholto were with them, making minor alterations.

The jovial atmosphere soon changed when Ulf, Coll and Nevin entered. "That does not look right," said Ulf pointing to Elen's dress. "Far too much bosom on show," he said. "Cover them up," he said rudely walking over to Elen.

"Do not touch me," she said in a slow, stern manner. Ulf was a little taken back by her forthrightness.

"When was the last time you wore a dress?" she boomed. Ulf did not answer but looked a little uncomfortable.

"I think it shows her to the full," said Coll.

"I hope you are not getting any ideas," said Nevin. Coll turned to Nevin and blew him a kiss. It was the twins next. Both had long flowing white gowns, trimmed with fleece round the hem. The three approved. Matilda was the tallest of the women, standing about five foot and eight inches, long dark hair fastened in a ponytail. She had a fuller figure but was by no means overweight. The most noticeable feature of Matilda was a very cheeky smile, as though she was trying to keep secret some wrong, she had done. Her dress was very flowing and bounced as she walked. Berta and Edith were similar in appearance to the twins and slightly taller than Matilda, Berta having long ginger hair and Edith short curly black hair. They had decided on knee length dresses, almost like gypsy outfits.

The women had selected jewelled bracelets and almost matching necklaces and gold rings they wanted their men to give them. An element of jealousy was noticeable between the three planners, Nevin turning to Coll, pointing to Nesta's outfit and saying, "You would look lovely in that." Coll smiled.

Elen entrusted the jewellery to Ulf, making sure he would remember which was which. "Please take these and entrust them to those responsible for their safe keeping," she said.

"I will go now," he replied and with that the three left, happy that the brides were extremely pleased with their outfits. The women changed in something a little more comfortable and then settled down for the night.

The final task for the day was to deliver the rings to those charged with escorting the women up the aisle, after which they sat and relaxed with most of the others by the fire in the clearing, downing the obligatory ale, totally satisfied that all was going to plan. The only one not relaxing was Hithin who was pacing up and down in his room, going over and over his lines and occasionally referring to the paper to nudge his memory but generally all was going well, even though he still appeared a little nervous.

Morning arrived, Ulf, Nevin and Coll were awake about the first hour, around seven in the morning.

"Much to do," said Coll excitedly. "I do not know where to begin," he continued. "Horses and carriages first, no, church, no food, no, grooms, no…"

"Be still," said Ulf, "the more you fret, the less you will do."

"Such a rock," said Coll, "always hard." Ulf smiled.

It was eventually decided, after about an hour, that the congregation should be the first to arrive at the church, then the grooms and finally the brides. Coll went to the stables to make sure preparations were in hand. Each carriage would be hitched up to a pair of beautifully groomed, white horses. Frothi and Alban had been designated as coachmen with Kentigern and Tovi as footmen. The four men looked resplendent in their armour. The carriages looked immaculate inside and out with rose petals scattered on the floors providing a fresh, delicate aroma. Even the four horses looked as though they were enjoying the occasion.

It was now approaching the third hour, so Nevin decided to check on Hithin and see if everything was fine. He went to Hithin's hut and saw the door opened. He entered, shouting for him but there was no response. Nevin searched everywhere but Hithin was nowhere to be found. He ran out of the hut, again calling his name. The shouting attracted the attention of Boyd and Alpin, who were in the process of getting ready. They came running out of their hut, Boyd asking what the matter was.

"I cannot find Hithin. Have you seen him?" asked Nevin.

"Not since yesterday," Boyd replied. "Let me wake the others," he continued. Boyd went back into the hut to wake Asmund, Enar, Kyle and Mungo. "Get dressed," he shouted, "Hithin is missing."

They got up, dressed quickly and went outside. "Fetch Vogg," said Alpin, "If anyone can find Hithin, Vogg can."

Enar rushed off to wake Vogg who fortunately was already up. Enar explained the urgency. Vogg got his Gjallarhorn[3] and summoned the rest of the men together. He quickly explained the problem and men were dispatched in every direction to find Hithin.

"You must be back within the hour," ordered Alpin.

Halfred and Donnan had barely got into the woods when they heard a faint groaning. They stopped, stood silently and looked all around.

"Hithin," said Halfred. Nothing was heard at first but soon there was a faint groaning and rustling of leaves. The two searched through the bushes on the ground, calling for Hithin.

The groaning got a little louder. "Hithin, where are you?" yelled Donnan.

"Here," came the faint reply.

"Where is here?" said an exasperated Donnan.

"Here, in the tree," was the reply. They looked up to find Hithin slung over a branch about twenty feet from the ground, hanging on for dear life.

"What are you doing there and how did you get there?" asked Halfred.

"Get me down," he asked in a very quiet voice.

"I cannot see how he got up there or how we can get him down."

We need a rope," said Halfred and off he dashed back to the camp. Fortunately, Vogg was still there so Halfred asked if he could use the horn to summon everyone back. Vogg smiled and passed the horn to him. Halfred puffed his cheeks out preparing to sound the signal, but nothing came out.

He tried a couple more times then handed it back to Vogg saying, "It is broken."

Vogg got hold of the horn and with one massive effort blew the signal whilst Halfred sat panting on the ground. Soon everyone returned.

"Where is he?" asked Alpin.

Halfred had just about got his breath back and replied, "Up a tree, on the other side of the wood. We need a rope." There were a few startled faces at Halfred's response. Vogg just shrugged his shoulders.

---

[3] Loud Norse horn

A rope was soon found, and they all headed back to where Donnan was waiting, finding him sitting on the grass picking daisies.

"Where is he?" asked Alpin. Donnan just gazed up to the tree.

"How did you...?" Alpin was starting to ask when Hithin replied sternly.

"I do not know and if I did know then I could climb down and would you be a little quieter, my head is very sore." Alpin started with a giggle, then a chortle and soon broke into a raucous laugh.

"There is no way to climb the tree," said a puzzled Alpin. "We need to throw the rope over the branch, pull someone up, tie the rope round Hithin, then lower him down to the ground."

After numerous attempts by a few of the group, the rope was eventually thrown over the branch. Fingal looked about the lightest of the group and was volunteered, not at all against his will, to be hauled up to the precariously balanced Hithin.

He reached Hithin and asked, "Have you been drinking?"

"If I had not been drinking," Hithin began, "how do you think I could have got here? My head hurts."

Fingal tied the rope securely round Hithin's waist and then purposely shouted loudly, "Lower him down." Hithin groaned and put his hand on his forehead.

Unfortunately, he started rolling off the branch the wrong way, so the gently lowering of him to the ground was not exactly needed. Vogg had realised what was about to happen, lurched forwards towards the falling Hithin and caught him about two feet from the ground, then purposely let him roll out of his massive hands.

"Ouch!" groaned a disgruntled Hithin.

"Sorry," said Vogg smiling. "You do smell of drink."

"I was reading my words for the ceremony and having a drink, but I must have had too much, so I went for a walk but cannot tell you how I managed to get up the tree and I cannot quite see straight," replied Hithin slightly slurring his words.

"We need to get you ready for the weddings," said Alpin.

"I hope you have not forgotten about me," shouted Fingal.

"Vogg," said Alpin. Vogg stood under where Fingal was lying on the branch.

Fingal looked down. "No rope?" he asked.

"No rope," replied Vogg. Fingal closed his eyes, rolled off the branch and hoped for the best.

"My turn," said Vogg smiling, looking up to the branch after putting Fingal safely on the ground.

"My head is still sore," moaned Hithin.

He was led back to the camp, the others being hardly sympathetic to his self-inflicted ailments. There was only one hour left before the ceremony, so much haste was now needed in the final preparations; but more importantly, getting Hithin into a fit state to conduct the ceremony. Garmund quickly prepared a remedy of boiled carrot juice and milk but did say that the mixture might well take a little longer than an hour to ease the effects of the hangover and correct the slight blurriness of his vision.

"We will just have to hope," said Alpin.

"Would it help if there was someone to stand aside Hithin in case he cannot read any of the words?" asked Boyd.

"I think that would be most wise," replied Alpin.

"May I suggest one of the nuns?" said Boyd.

"Again, I think that would be most wise," replied Alpin.

Having had to dress quickly in their frantic search for Hithin, the men had not really had time to wash and the stale 'eau de sweat' from the previous night was noticeably lingering in the air. Gillis and Sholto ran to the nearby stream filling four wooden buckets with cold but refreshing water. The grooms barely sprinkled themselves with the water. However, at least it slightly suppressed the overpowering aroma. Viking grooms did not have a particular costume or ornate garment. However it was customary to bring a newly acquired grave-robbing sword during the ceremony and carry a symbol of Thor, such as a hammer or an axe. This represented his mastery and was believed to ensure a fruitful marriage. As no graves had been robbed recently and Angus had, as yet not got round to making symbolic tools, they would have to make do with their polished armour and everyday weaponry.

The fifth hour was rapidly approaching. Frothi, Tovi, Alban and Kentigern went off to the stables to collect the horses and carriages and then make their way to collect the brides and the two nuns. A dozen men were tasked with setting up the tables and seating in the middle of the camp, Hithin was plied with more carrot juice and milk and Ulf told everyone else to make their way to the church.

Nevin and Coll were the first into the church, acting as ushers and trying to maintain a little decorum as everyone was in good spirits. Ewan had brought his bagpipes and was standing at the back of the church entertaining the congregation with what he claimed to be Scottish ballads, while Dougal was threatening to sing one of his own compositions so, all-in-all, it seemed like a very historic festive occasion was about to take place.

The six grooms were pacing around nervously at the altar. Ulf gave them each the jewellery chosen by their women. Along with the two footmen and two coachmen, Gerik and Vogg were to escort the brides up the aisle to the altar. Hithin, still noticeably suffering from the effects of the previous evening, was helped up the aisle by Garmund. As they passed Ewan, he purposely added a little more volume to his playing, to which Hithin gave him a very dirty look.

Soon the clatter of hooves could be heard on the gravel track that ran through the village. The carriages came to a halt outside the church. Frothi and Alban held the horses still, while Tovi and Kentigern jumped down from the rear of the carriage to open the doors. Mildrith, Berta, Anna and Nesta alighted from the first carriage, helped down by Tovi and from the second carriage Eangyth, followed by Edith, Elen and Matilda, helped down by Kentigern.

Once they were all out of the carriages, Halfred and Sholto, with a little help, well more like interference from Coll and Nevin, made sure the bridal outfits looked perfect. Frothi and Alban unhitched the carriages and secured the horses to a nearby hitching rail before returning to the others. Frothi led the procession up the aisle, linking arms with Anna, then Alban with Nesta, Tovi with Berta, Kentigern with Matilda, Gerik with Elen and Vogg with Edith who gave her escort a great big hug.

The two nuns were first into the church, Eangyth staying towards the back while Mildrith walked to the front to the altar, to provide Hithin with moral support, a focusing pair of eyes and an ability to read simple lines coherently. He was having a little trouble staying on his feet, so Gerik asked Fingal to provide some physical support.

The six grooms nervously lined up at the front of the altar facing the congregation. Ulf had arranged the position of the grooms to make life a little simpler when the brides were led to their prospective partners. Enar was on the left then Mungo, Asmund, Boyd, Alpin and finally Kyle. The procession up the short aisle was to more of a military march than a bridal march and the attempt to keep in step with the music proved impossible. As they arrived at the top of the church, the women were led to the respective smiling grooms; and then the escorts moved to sit in the pews. Eangyth made her way to the altar, standing alongside Mildrith.

All was quiet. Hithin stood with his head down still appearing alarmingly unsteady. He looked up a little too quickly and the sudden movement caused him to step back. Fortunately, Fingal was prepared and put a steadying hand on Hithin's back.

Hithin turned to Fingal and tried to say quietly, "I need a piss."

Unfortunately, his quiet whisper was a little more audible than he had hoped and caused a ripple of laughter around the congregation.

Alpin shook his head and said, "We need to let Hithin rest for a short time." At which point Ewan decided to deliver a deafening skirl on the bagpipes, much to Hithin's annoyance but to everyone else's amusement.

Fingal escorted Hithin out of the church round the back of the altar where he was propped up against a wall.

"Now piss," said Fingal, "and let us get on with the weddings."

Hithin yawned, smiled drunkenly at Fingal, hiccupped and then collapsed to the ground in a heap.

Fingal knelt down, lifted Hithin's head and gently tapped him on the cheek to try to wake him.

"Come on, wake," said Fingal. "Wake up," he repeated a little louder. Hithin, friend, wake." Still no response. "Hithin!" screamed Fingal. The shouting was heard inside the church. Asmund was the first out and saw a very white faced Hithin lying motionless in Fingal's arms.

"Garmund," he yelled. Garmund was quickly out, looking extremely concerned as to what he might find. By now, there were about twelve people outside. The women were kept inside for fear of the worst. "Jeg tror, Hithin er død," said Asmund quietly. Garmund put his hand across Hithin's mouth. "Han trækker ikke vejret," he said.

Vogg approached and thumped Hithin firmly, to say the least; on his chest. Hithin began coughing and spluttering, turned onto his side and began to vomit over Fingal's legs.

Fingal looked up at Vogg and said, "You could have warned me."

Vogg smiled and replied, "They usually die when I hit them that hard."

Hithin was conscious enough to understand what Vogg had said. He looked up and said smilingly, "We are on the same side."

Slowly they got Hithin to his feet. "How are you feeling?" asked Garmund.

"Shaking a little, sore head, cannot see straight and a very sore chest," he replied.

"Normal then. We need to get him inside," said Fingal, desperate for Hithin to continue the ceremony, "but I must clean up first, because I do not think the smell on my armour will be welcome."

Off went Fingal to find an alternative outfit whilst the others helped Hithin slowly into the church. There was obvious relief that Hithin was at least alive but both concern and amusement as to his appearance. A chair was found for Hithin as the risk of him trying to stand during the service was too great to be left to chance. He was put down between the two nuns.

Alpin asked for quiet and said, "We need to wait for Fingal to return before we begin, and I also think it may be wise for the pipes to stay silent for now." Ewan looked a little disheartened by this comment but in the interest of peace and Hithin's current condition, he agreed.

Fingal soon returned wearing a monk's habit. "It is all I could find," he said. There were a few chortles as he made his way up to the altar.

"Welcome Brother Fingal," said Eangyth. Fingal turned to her, smiled and with a mischievous glint in his eye said, "Thank you Sister Eangyth. I am sure that after the service we can discuss how the missionaries can unite as one body."

Eangyth giggled and her cheeks turned a very bright shade of red. Fingal took his place behind a seated Hithin just in case there was a further attack of unsteadiness.

Alpin began. "As we are at last all together, I think we should start the service."

No one had any reason to disagree with this proposal and all nodded their approval.

Hithin, turned to Mildrith and said quietly, "I can neither remember what I should say or see what is written and so if you would read out the words, then I will repeat them."

This was an extremely sensible suggestion from someone who was still suffering mentally and physically. The stench from stale ale and a mixture of carrot juice and milk was unpleasantly noticeable and the frequent gurgling sounds emanating from both Hithin's gut and rear end seemed to echo round the church.

Hithin tried to stand, however his imbalance proved a little too faltering, so in the interests of safety it was suggested he remain seated.

Mildrith removed the prepared service sheet from the sleeve of her habit, turned to Hithin and asked, "Are you ready?" He slowly and carefully nodded his agreement. "Please stand," she whispered to Hithin. Hithin stood. "Not you," she continued. "This is what you need to say."

He returned to his seat, apologising to Mildrith. "Please stand," he began. The six couples rose to their feet.

Mildrith slowly whispered the words, "We are standing here in the sight of God." Hithin whispered the words back to her.

"You will have to speak a little louder," she said, "then they can all hear you."

"But my head hurts," he replied.

"May God forgive you," she whispered to which Hithin looked up at the brides and grooms and said in a loud clear voice.

"May God forgive you."

Mildrith was starting to get a little exasperated by Hithin's antics. She turned to him and said, in a rather severe tone. "There are twelve people here waiting to marry and if you do not come to your senses, as God is my witness, I will punch you on the nose with all my strength and under threat of being struck down by the Almighty's thunderbolts, you will sit there and suffer my wrath. I hope I have made myself clear."

"You look very sweet when you are angry," responded Hithin.

That was the catalyst. Mildrith wheeled her arm backwards and with all her strength swung round and landed a punch smack in the middle of Hithin's nose. "I warned you," she said, "now start the ceremony."

Hithin, to say the least, was a little shell-shocked. "That hurt," he said, as a smidgen of blood trickled from his nose. "Shall we get on?"

It is quite surprising how someone can very quickly come to their senses when an unexpected action deals a blow to their person. Mildrith composed herself, took the service sheet in her hands, looked sternly at Hithin and began.

"This day we see a great step forward in the life of our village." Hithin duly repeated the words faultlessly. Mildrith continued, breaking quite regularly so as not to over-exert Hithin's memory cells. "Enemies have become great friends and now, through the marriages of these twelve people standing before us, our village looks forward to new life. Please bring the brides forward to their grooms."

As the women were being escorted to their prospective partners, Hithin looked towards Mildrith, opened his mouth to speak to her, but thought better of it, as she returned an intense frown, so he just put one hand on his forehead and the other on his nose and displayed a sign of anguished pain in his eyes. She smiled at him, looked down at the paper and continued to read.

"I, Hithin Godriksson." At this, Gerik quickly looked up. "Godriksson?" he said inquisitively.

Hithin turned to Mildrith and said, "Read." Mildrith started reading but Gerik interrupted, repeating the name. The others looked perplexed at Gerik's sudden outburst.

"I do not understand," said Garmund.

"I have thought this for a while but have not said anything." started Gerik, "I have heard strange talk in our homeland but only now do I understand."

"Please tell what you know," said Garmund.

"You are a son of Gudfred[4]," stated Gerik.

Hithin looked a little embarrassed, said nothing for a few moments but then stood up, shakily and said, "This is so. I am the brother of Horik, but I left to seek my own life away from all the fighting in my family. I want to be Hithin the hersir and nobody else."

Gerik was aware of the circumstances that prevailed in Denmark around the time that Hithin left and understood the reasoning saying, so, in rather an official yet light-hearted tone he said, "To us, you are Hithin who could have been King but let us not dwell on the past, Your Majesty."

---

[4] Danish king 804-810

Hithin snarled a little at Gerik and then sat down as the unsteadiness had returned.

"Now can we get on with the service, Your Majesty," said Alpin with a big smile on his face. Hithin raised his eyes to Alpin, said nothing, turned to Mildrith and said, "Let us try to finish this without more delay and please do not hit me again because that was not my doing."

Mildrith bowed, smiled and whispered to Hithin, "I Hithin Godriksson."

"I am not saying that again, let us move on." Turning to the men, Hithin continued, echoing Mildrith's words. "Each of you has chosen a partner through whom you hope to live a happy life, prosper and bear children. You are the ones we will depend on for the future of our village. You must promise to support your family in bad times as well as good; teach your children in the ways of our ancestors to be good and loyal and guide them to become respected citizens in what they choose to do. Are you willing to accept this responsibility?" The grooms each nodded in turn.

Turning to Enar, Hithin said, "Anna has agreed to be your wife. Do you accept her?" Enar looked lovingly at Anna and replied, "I do." Turning to Anna, he said, "Anna, Enar has asked you to be his wife. Do you accept him?" Anna excitedly answered, "Yes, I do." "Enar, do you have a gift for Anna?" Frothi stepped forward to give Enar the ring that Anna had chosen and then returned to his seat. Enar smiled.

Mildrith continued, "Repeat after me."

"I am," replied Hithin.

"No," said Mildrith, "this is what you say to Enar."

"Sorry, but I think I may need to go outside for a few moments," he said. Mildrith beckoned to Fingal to help Hithin up and take him outside for a little fresh air.

The humid atmosphere inside the church had not exactly helped with Hithin's physical state and once outside, he quickly lifted his tunic and as the effects of the recent liquids had at last worked their way through his system, proceeded to splatter quite a large area with the contents of his stomach to the sound of a very satisfying "Aaaaahh."

The rate at which Fingal leapt out of range was very impressive.

"That did not help my sore head," scowled Hithin.

"Can we go back inside now please?" asked Fingal.

"You go on and I will follow in a moment," replied Hithin.

Unfortunately, due to his current fragile and forgetful state of mind, Hithin was still holding up his tunic as he entered the church.

It was Alpin who advised Hithin of his oversight saying, "It may be wise to place a cover over the royal standard before we carry on."

Hithin looked a little confused by this comment until Alpin pointed to his lower region. Fortunately, this gesture was quickly understood and an embarrassed Hithin released his grip on the tunic, allowing it to cover his person, and then retook his place between the two nuns who were not overly impressed with the lingering odour, however in the interests of expediency, wisely said nothing.

Mildrith continued to feed Hithin the words despite the noxious fumes having a slightly off-putting effect.

"Enar, will you take Anna as your wife?"

"I will," he replied.

"Anna, will you take Enar as you husband?"

"I will," she replied. "You may now place the ring on her finger."

Enar took Anna's hand and carefully placed the ring on her wedding finger. Anna smiled and gave Enar a quick kiss on the cheek at which point, Coll burst into tears and had to be comforted by Ulf and Nevin.

"You are now husband and wife," said Hithin. Finally, one pair married but five to go.

Next, it was the turn of Mungo and Nesta. Hithin managed to get through this without any unnecessary delays as he did with the next four couples. At last, it was Alpin's turn.

Hithin stood up, walked slowly over to Alpin, put his arms on his shoulders and said, "Alpin. Not long ago I was looking to help conquer this land but if it were not for you, I would be still slaying every Scotsman I saw. You have taught me how two nations can become friends and work together. I owe you so much my friend and today I feel that I am so honoured to be able to marry you and this beautiful woman you have chosen as your wife."

This was far too much for Coll whose further uncontrollable tearful outburst had now caused the same reaction from his two friends.

"This is too much for me," said Coll, who had to sit down and have cold air fanned across his face.

"Alpin," began Hithin, "will you take this beautiful woman as your wife?"

"I will," said Alpin. Elen turned to Alpin and said, "And I will take this man as my husband."

Gerik came forward to give the ring to Alpin who then placed the ring on Elen's finger while looking lovingly into her eyes.

"You too are now husband and wife."

As Hithin finished the words a massive cheer rang round the church causing him to bend over with his hands covering his forehead in the hope that this would ease the throbbing. The service was over.

Nobody paid much attention to Hithin's suffering as they all walked down the aisle towards the church doors and out into the sunshine accompanied by Ewan's gusto performance on the bagpipes.

The two nuns were the last to leave and looked back to see a forlorn figure sitting motionless with his head still in his hands. The nuns looked at each other, shrugged their shoulders and walked out of the church, gently closing the solid wooden doors behind them.

After a short while, the church door slowly opened and in walked Garmund. He approached the still Hithin and asked, "So, far better or worse?"

"I do not know the answer to that," was the reply.

Chapter 6

The Wedding Feats

The service now over, the feasting was to begin. Malcolm, Dougal and Ross went back to the ovens to fetch the food, while Duff and Ross took the horses back to the stables. The soups, meats, pies, cakes were loaded onto wooden carts and safely wheeled to the dining area. The seating arrangement resembled a pillared dome with the newly-weds seated in a semi-circle and four tables, two seating six people and two seating seven, branching out from the main table. Each setting had a spoon, a knife and a drinking vessel already laid out. There was no set place for anyone except the six couples. However, Coll, Ulf and Nevin managed to sit together with Fingal, still wearing his monk's habit, craftily sneaking in between Mildrith and Eangyth. The food, along with the last two barrels of ale and amphorae of wine, was laid on two tables at the side of the dining area.

The six escorts Frothi, Alban, Tovi, Kentigern, Gerik and Vogg acted as waiters serving the top table with food and drink, with Malcolm, Dougal and Ross serving out the food. Once the top table was served, the others lined up in a fairly orderly manner, much like a buffet, to help themselves to the food. Fingal, being the gentleman, willingly brought the first course of vegetable soup for the two nuns. While the first course was being consumed, the second course of roast boar and vegetables was being prepared.

Fingal was ensuring that, despite protests, the nuns had a full goblet of wine each. The waiters were doing a marvellous job of ensuring the smooth running of the feast. No one appeared to notice the empty place setting, as hearty laughter and conversation filled the clearing.

The succulent aroma from the feast filtered through the village, circulating inside the church, where the lone figure sat still holding his head and nose, saying to himself, "I have much to answer for."

Boyd beckoned Alpin over asking, "Do you think we should take some food to Hithin?"

"For now, I think a bowl of soup may help but I do not think we should take him any other food where too much movement of the jaw is needed," replied Alpin.

He called Garmund over and asked if he would deliver the soup and at the same time check on Hithin's wellbeing. Garmund collected a bowl, filled it with the vegetable soup and took it to Hithin. All he could hear as he quietly opened the church door was, in a very nasally tone.

"My poor, poor head."

"Hithin," said Garmund in a very soft tone. No response. "Hithin," said Garmund a little louder. Still no response. "Hithin!" yelled Garmund. Hithin did not look up, just grimaced a little more, holding his forehead tighter whilst gesturing to Garmund to keep the noise down. Garmund approached a very pale looking individual.

"You need to eat," he said. Hithin looked at the bowl of warm soup. His mouth wanted it, but his stomach was not so keen. "It will help. I will leave it here for you," said Garmund. He put the bowl on the floor next to Hithin and made his way out of the church.

All he heard was a very faint but grateful, "Thank you."

Garmund made his way back to the wedding feast and took his place after mentioning to Boyd that Hithin was still suffering but at least fully dressed and quite coherent.

When the second course was over, and the tables cleared. Gerik stood up and asked for quiet. He made sure that everyone's cup was filled with a drop or two of wine and then began.

"Sadly, there are only six women with us in the village."

At which point Fingal piped up. "Are not my two friends women?"

Gerik smiled and said, "I will begin again. There are eight women in the village, but only six who have taken the vows of marriage. These are our future and all of us here will stand by them and help where and when we can. I do not know if I am jealous of the six men who have taken a wife or relieved that I do not have this burden placed upon me, but I wish, not just for these twelve here health and happiness for the future, but I wish the same to all of you here. Please stand and join with me in wishing all our friends here and the one who will be with us later, love, happiness and health." They all stood and raised their cups to toast the wellbeing of all. "It is now time for the games to begin," continued Gerik. "Clear away the tables. Where are the minstrels?"

Ewan's eyes lit up at this and off he quickly trundled to get his pipes. Fingal turned to the nuns and asked, "Where are the instruments you brought?"

"In the carriages," replied Eangyth. "I will fetch them for you."

The carriages were still at the church and as Fingal approached, he saw the church door open, and a head slowly emerge.

"I need help," said Hithin.

"Are you ready to join the others?" asked Fingal.

"I think so, but I would like more soup."

Fingal retrieved the instruments from the carriages and lent a supporting arm to Hithin as they made their way back the short distance to the others.

"I have not been well," said Hithin.

"You cannot put the blame on anyone but yourself," was the reply. Hithin slowly nodded his head in agreement.

Ewan was madly going full blast on the pipes with the newly-weds prancing around like people possessed. The others were clapping in time to the music, shouting and whistling at the carefree exhibitionists. Hithin was sitting down by the food and Fingal served up a further helping of the vegetable soup.

"I will return soon," he said as he took the instruments to the nuns leaving Hithin, for the first time in quite a while, drinking something non-alcoholic. Three bowls later, Hithin seemed to be regaining his senses. It did not matter that the soup was cold, it was perfect.

Fingal handed the cithara to Mildrith and the flute to Eangyth.

"Ladies," he said, "it may be time for some gentle music."

He asked everyone to form a circle and hold hands while the two nuns each played some completely random notes, which could hardly be described as tunes. It did not matter. The group moved slowly round in a circle throwing in the occasional bowing or turn whenever they felt like it.

"Time for the games!" shouted Alpin to a massive cheer. "Bring the ball." The ball was an inflated pig's bladder tightly stitched to seal the opening.

"Men against women!" yelled Ulf, "and we will play for the women." This suggestion was quickly dismissed.

"Scots against Vikings!" yelled Colban to a massive cheer. Hithin shook his head declining the offer to participate.

"Please get to your sides!" yelled Alpin.

The fact that most of the players were still in ceremonial battle dress did not seem to matter. There did not appear to be any rules for kicking or throwing the ball or blatant fouling of an opponent. It was, by now, a chaotic free for all. The women cheering, the nuns still happily playing random tunes and Ulf, Coll and Nevin trying desperately hard to keep out of the mass scrummaging.

After about half an hour, as quite a number of the players were lying around exhausted, the six husbands returned to their wives and spent time with some of the others who just sat around talking and drinking, Alpin decided it was victory for the Scots, which obviously received quite a few boos and derisory comments from the Vikings.

"Now we will have a contest for the women," declared Alpin looking mischievously at Elen.

"I do not think I am going to like this," she said.

"Find a rope," he shouted. "It is time for a tug of war. Viking wives against Scottish wives."

This produced the best cheer of the day. "Come forth ladies," he requested. The women were really up for this. "Anna and Berta, you are over to this side and Edith, Matilda, Nesta and Elen, you are on this other side. As the sides are not quite fair, you may choose one man to help you."

The choice was pretty obvious and after a very short discussion the two women together shouted, "Vogg."

"I had not thought of that," said Alpin, "but I cannot go back on my word." He called over the smiling giant.

Both teams were ready, with the women taking the strain and Vogg sat down as the anchor-man, with a large goblet of ale in one hand and the rope in the other.

"Begin," shouted Alpin.

Cheers went up as the women tugged and strained whilst Vogg just sat there totally unmoved. After he had finished his ale, he put down the goblet, stood up and with one mighty pull gave victory to his side. The women ended up in a crumpled mass similar to a collapsed scrum, unable to move through laughter.

"We win," said Vogg nonchalantly, leaving the women to pick themselves up.

"I believe that is one win to the Vikings and one win to the Scots," declared Alpin.

"Now we see who the best at running is. Will all the women please stand by me," requested Alpin.

Eangyth nudged Mildrith and said, "Ready?" Mildrith smiled, stood up and they both made their way to the start. A jaw dropping expression of disbelief ran round the men. With the brides in long wedding dresses and the nuns in quite tight-fitting habits, this was going to turn out to be quite a race.

Alpin looked at the contestants and said, "All you have to do is run to the church and back." Without Alpin giving them the signal to go, off they ran with the brides holding up their wedding dresses to make running easier.

He was about to call them back when Fingal said, "Let them be." It was less than fifty yards to the church and in that short distance there were three fallers. Elen was the first down, managing to trip up Nesta who superbly tackled Anna as she was being brought down. By the time the remaining five had reached the church, Berta, Edith and Matilda were totally out of breath and gave up but Mildrith and Eangyth were still full of energy. They touched the church door, turned and started the run back. It was remarkably close, but Eangyth won by less than a foot. They fell to their knees exhausted but smiling.

Fingal ran over to them. "I have never seen women run that quickly."

"We had to at times," said a panting Eangyth, "to escape the monks." Fingal did not know whether to believe them or not. He helped them to their feet.

Alpin was at a loss to decide which team the point should go to, until Mildrith shouted, "Victory to the nuns!" There now appeared to be three teams competing in the feats.

"The next event is jumping," declared Alpin. He drew a line in the sand. "You will run up to this line and see how far you can jump. The winner is the one who jumps the farthest." Everyone except Hithin, who was starting to feel a little better, lined up about ten metres from the line.

The six brides went first, again hitching up their wedding dresses to make the competing considerably easier. The longest jump was from Edith who far surpassed any of her rivals and from the men, unsurprisingly the lightest of them all, Fingal. Needless to say, Vogg's jump was interesting. If he had tripped over the line and fallen flat on his face, he would have covered a greater distance. So, the only competitors remaining were the two nuns. Mildrith first. Lifting her habit slightly, off she sprinted producing an absolutely amazing leap, far in excess of Fingal's attempt. Gasps of amazement rang round the spectators.

Finally, Eangyth. The concentration and determination on her face was intense. She hitched up her habit and almost flew down the run up, taking off at a tremendous rate and bicycling her way through the air. Those standing at the end of the jump had to dive for cover as she came hurtling towards them. It seemed an eternity but eventually she landed on her feet, looked round and said, "I believe that is two wins to the nuns!"

"Are you going to tell me that was to get away from the monks as well," quipped Fingal. Eangyth just smiled at him and said nothing.

The next feat was throwing a spear at a mark on a tree and the one who got the closest was the winner. Some of the efforts were, to say the least, extremely dangerous but the good news for any potential prey, was that there was no chance whatsoever of being even remotely grazed by the inaccurate throwing. It came down to a playoff between Vogg, Ulf and Nevin; however this time, the object was a small stone placed on a branch about two metres from the ground. Ulf and Nevin were very close managing to hit the branch, however, Vogg despite just having one eye, was the winner. The score was two to the Vikings, two to the nuns and one to the Scots.

The evening was drawing in but more importantly the reserves of wine and ale were dwindling. The final event was going to be chicken chasing. Malcolm was asked to fetch one of the chickens from the cage. Alpin explained the rule.

"The chicken is released and then I tell you when the contest begins. The one to catch the chicken and bring it back to me alive is the winner." Simple and straightforward.

Malcolm returned and Alpin told him to release the chicken, waited a few moments and shouted, "Go."

Chaos followed. You may remember the carnage caused earlier when the two groups first met and were trying to catch their first meal. This was far, far worse. Rivalry between the groups of friends? Definitely. Pride was at stake. As the two nuns had proved their athletic ability, they were the first to be brought down quite unceremoniously immediately after the start of the race. Not that there were any profanities shouted at their assailants, they were far too religious for that.

Quite blatant irregularities were forthcoming in the final event. Even the chicken looked shit scared as around thirty people tried to catch it. It made its way into the forest managing somehow to evade its captors, doubled back, causing total mayhem as some competitors ran headfirst into each other and then darted, making one hell of a racket towards where Hithin was sitting. He stood up just as the chicken was passing him. The startled bird tripped over his outstretched leg and collided with a table leg.

It was dazed long enough for Hithin to bend down, grab it by the neck, hold the bird aloft and shout, "Victory to the Vikings."

However, what he failed to notice was the group of six charging towards him. He turned, saw the onslaught and in sheer panic, released the bird which madly flapped its wings in the vain hope of escape and somehow managed to glide back into Alpin's hand.

"Victory to the Scots!" he yelled.

This was greeted with great derision, booing and cries of, "Unfair," mainly by the non-Scottish teams, however he did remind everyone that the chicken had to be returned to him alive and as stewards' enquiries were not to be introduced for the next few hundred years, the decision was reluctantly allowed to stand.

Bit of a predicament now. It was a three-way tie, getting darker and nobody could think of any other fair games. Weightlifting was ruled out because there would be an obvious winner. Throwing, running and jumping events had already been decided and so the whole group stood around in silence wondering what they could do. For no apparent reason, Donnan started hopping around in circles.

"I know!" shouted Alpin. "Everybody stand in a circle." There were some rather puzzled looks, but they all obeyed. "You need to stand one arm's length apart." The circle widened to accommodate this request.

"When I say begin. You will all stand on one leg and the winner will be the one who can do this for the longest. If you touch the person next to you, then you are out. Begin."

Thirty-eight people standing quietly on one leg in a circle. If any marauding group had come across this, then they must have thought this was some sacrificial ritual and quickly abandoned any thought of a surprise attack.

Time dragged on... and on... and on.

Eventually there were just three competitors remaining. Halfred and Ross were next to each other and Mildrith on the opposite side of the circle. The title of best group was literally in the balance. There was some tottering and wavering by all three, however very little sign of any of them giving up.

And still time dragged on.

Food and drink does tend to have strange effects on a digestive system and the rumblings emanating from the two men were becoming increasingly audible. Mildrith was standing, eyes closed, looking as if she was seeking divine assistance. It had to happen at some point. Ross was the first to break silence with an outbreak of wind and judging by his expression, a follow-through as well. He was trying to keep all four cheeks tightly closed but to no avail.

Mildrith started to giggle, her upper body quivering. She could not hold the position any longer. Down came her other leg and she burst into laughter. Halfred was not only put off by both the sight of Mildrith's uncontrollable laughing, but also the sounds and smells coming from Ross, and he too was forced to concede. That was it.

"The Scots have won," declared Alpin but due to the current odour surrounding Ross, hoisting aloft the victor was resisted.

There was no prize, just a moral victory.

The wedding feats were over. It was time to call it a night. They all walked back to their huts, some more gingerly than others, reminiscing over the day's events. The newly-weds walking arm in arm to their new homes whilst the others wandered back in various states of sobriety and injury to their quarters.

The clearing looked like a disaster area, but the cleaning could wait till morning.

Chapter 7

The Mourning After

Silence. Absolute silence.

It was around the fourth hour when someone started to stir. Hithin was the first to wake and decided to enjoy the fresh morning air, strolling around the village to clear his system. He walked from the main sleeping area towards the church, passing the debris from the previous evening's celebrations then doubled back heading to the stables and the married quarters. He stopped to look around and noticed a figure running out from the nun's huts. It was Fingal. Hithin hid behind a large tree unnoticed as the figure scurried past him. He thought it wise not to say anything.

It was about another hour before there were further signs of life. People slowly emerged, very slowly. Some were holding their sore heads and some covering their eyes from the bright sunlight.

There was an adequate amount of soup remaining which Dougal warmed and this, with some fairly fresh bread, had to suffice as breakfast until further supplies could be sought. The smell of food attracted people towards the impressive cookhouse. The newly married couples emerged from their huts to a massive cheer. Mildrith was next to arrive shortly, followed by a red-faced Eangyth. They helped themselves to the soup using whatever receptacles were available.

When they were all gathered together, Alpin stood, wished everyone a good morning and spoke.

"I am sure that you all enjoyed yourselves last night and some probably more than others." This was greeted by a thunderous cheer from the men and a little embarrassment on the part of the women. "Our food store is getting low, and we need to clear-up the mess from the feasting. As you all look awake and so well," he paused for a moment after this comment, waiting for the expected and duly delivered 'do not get me involved in anything today' reaction, "we need our hunters to go out and hunt and the others to clean the village from the church to the stables. I am sure that you will allow these newly wedded people to have time to themselves. There is much work to do. You built the village in a few short days and now we must return it to looking as it should."

After breakfast, they all knew what to do. The hunters left armed with bows, arrows, spears and knives, the cooks made their way to the ovens, farmers to the fields for fresh milk, to the chicken runs to collect eggs, woodsmen to collect and repair, as necessary, any broken furniture, Garmund to treat those still suffering, Angus and Tovi to tend to the horses and the others to make the village presentable.

The atmosphere was superb. The new wives did not want to be left out and happily joined in with the tidying operation, insisting that their men help.

"Already being told what to do?" said Donnan to Boyd. Boyd acknowledged Donnan's comment, looked towards his new wife, smiled but wisely remained silent.

The day passed peacefully and gradually everything got back to normal. After eating freshly made meat pies and drinking warm milk, they all gathered in the torch-lit church. Hithin and Alpin stood on the altar step facing the others. Hithin began. "It is now time to seek out other lands. We know how the Romans not only conquered these lands but also helped in building them up again to be much stronger and safer. We need to build boats, travel to other lands and see what we can learn from them and bring back new skills and whatever else they can teach us." He suggested that there would still be some deserted Viking langskips[5] at Oban, as some of the Viking fleet sailed north, a possibility of a few at Glencoe.

Boyd mentioned that Drake had told him it was forty-five miles to Glencoe and then thirty miles down the river to Oban. Alpin took over from Hithin.

"That will be a day's journey. From there it is no less than four days to the Viking's homeland, but we also need to explore other lands further away and those who go on this journey will be away from us for many weeks."

---

[5] Viking warships

It was Hithin's turn to speak. "Donnan and Ewan have explored lands around here and drawn maps, but we need to travel further in this land. We still need to keep our friends here safe from attacks." He looked at Alpin and said to the men, "As leaders of the group we look to you for your help. We would like you all to talk about this and tomorrow we will meet back here then you can tell me your answer."

They were thanked for listening and as the men made their way out of the church, discussions had already started. Hithin turned to Alpin who were both still at the top of the church and said, "Are we doing right?"

Alpin looked at him and replied, "I hope so."

There was much discussion that night between the whole group, men and women. It was an exceedingly difficult decision for the new husbands to make as their particular skills could be called upon in determining the future direction. There were great periods of silence, deep thought and concentration. Kentigern eventually spoke.

"Why are we here," he asked, not really expecting an answer.

Gillis responded, "Because we are. We had a choice and I believe we are right in what we are doing. Does anyone here want to go back to fighting and killing? Are we happy here? We should do whatever it takes. Some of us will be gone for a time but look what we will return to." This short speech rallied the group.

Matilda turned to Boyd and said lovingly, "I will miss you."

The meeting reconvened around midday. Alpin and Hithin expected a subdued mood, but they were greeted with everyone in high spirits, laughing as they made their way into the church. They all sat down but before either of the two men had chance to speak, Boyd stood up and said, pointing to them in turn.

"Gerik, Enar, Angus, Nevin, Asmund, Mirren, Ross, Sholto and I will be sailing across the water to new lands. Frothi, Donnan, Ewan, Ulf, Alban, Colban and Malcolm will travel across this land and the others will remain here to look after the village."

Hithin and Alpin were dumbstruck. "Who agreed to that?" asked Alpin.

"We all did," replied Boyd. He continued, "Tovi and Coll will use the horses and carriages to take us to Glencoe and from there we will make our way to Oban and on their return after a day's rest, the horses will be ready to take these," pointing to the other group, "round this land. There will be fourteen men staying here to work on and guard the village. We leave in two days' time. We have asked Tovi and Coll to return to Glencoe by the thirteenth day." Boyd took his seat totally satisfied with his presentation.

There was no answer to this.

"There is nothing we can add to this. We see you have chosen well, taking people with different skills on the two journeys. Are you all in agreement?"

As one, they gave a resounding. "Yes."

Fingal looked across at Eangyth and winked. The embarrassment was rather evident on her face.

Hithin said, "You need time to gather together whatever you are taking, and we are all here to help with anything you may need." He turned to Halfred and Sholto and said, "We need to make some fine tunics for those travelling over the seas. I know there is not much time but with what we have and using some of the fine cloth from the women's clothing, can you quickly make something for the men?"

"We will work hard to make sure there are enough fine garments for the men," replied Sholto.

Elen chirped up, saying, "Use what you need, and we will help you make them."

Hithin continued, "Take some of the gold, jewellery and coins with you and tell those you meet that this is what our city has to offer in exchange, but say you are from Greenland and are known to Erik the Red." This was met with some amusement.

The meeting was adjourned amid both excitement and apprehension as to what they might discover on their travels.

That day and the following day were taken up by preparations, checking and double checking what would be needed. Tovi checked the horseshoes, equipment and carriages, Boyd, Gerik and Mirren went over the routes with Tovi and Coll. The women were contemplative but also very supportive and proud of their husbands for volunteering for such a mission.

The early morning departure for the inland group soon arrived. The carriages were loaded with the necessary equipment and clothing, the men said their goodbyes, boarded and rode west out of the village to both cheers and tearful waves. When they were out of sight, everyone stood there in silence for a few moments, more in disbelief that this was actually happening.

The twenty-two remaining had their work cut out for them. There was still much to do in the development of the village — construction of other buildings, cultivation of plants, vegetables, mining for materials, clothing, wellbeing and security. Boyd had been extremely thorough with his selection of people to travel and those who would stay at home ensuring, where possible, that all areas of expertise had been covered.

Hithin and Alpin had ideas for how they saw the village developing and with the information brought back about Carlisle by Gerik, Boyd firstly considered ways of protecting the village. Coll and Vogg had experience of setting traps to catch animals but needed to develop their skills and methods in the detection and deterrent of unwelcome guests. Tovi and Coll would be back in about two days, so those travelling inland could help with some preliminary research. Frothi and Kentigern were to continue with the mining exploration while Gillis, Colban and Kyle would look at ways of improving the huts, with furniture and even help with devising a more efficient oven and food storage facility. Garmund had been out on his rounds collecting various plants, leaves and vegetable roots; aware of both the medicinal benefits and also the nourishing aspects of drinks. Nettle tea was to become quite popular, mainly because there was an abundance of the weed. So basically, there was plenty to keep everybody occupied for at least the next few months.

The first group made their way, quite incident free, across dirt tracks, fields and occasional precariously steep mountain sides and reached Glencoe by the evening. Approaching the river, they saw what looked like an abandoned birlinn[6] with the mast still raised, moored by a makeshift jetty.

Boyd smiled, looked round at the others and said, "Let us hope there is no one aboard." He beckoned to Gerik and Nevin to join him, telling the others to remain quiet and moved slowly and quietly on foot towards the vessel. "What do you think?" he asked. They moved closer.

"There are no tracks," said Nevin. They crept closer until they were almost up to the boat; still no sign of life.

---

[6] Scottish inland wooden vessel propelled by sail or oar

The sun was slowly going down, casting eerie shapes and shadows on the hoisted mast. The three were now lying flat, edging their way stealthily along. Apart from the odd few creakings of the timbers, there was no other sound. They remained motionless for a while, slowly stood and then clambered aboard, gently rocking the boat as they did so. The timbers creaked a little more and a gentle breeze now caused the wooden mast to sing. The deck was perfectly dry, and nothing appeared out of place. They walked from bow to stern slightly uneasy at every creak. At the bow of the ship lay another mast, sprawled out over the width of the boat and up to around two metres from the end, covering a variety of objects. They looked nervously at each other wondering what the mast was hiding.

Nevin and Gerik got hold of the mast from each side of the boat and carefully started drawing it back. Nothing at first, but then a pair of women's feet were uncovered. An expression of horror crossed their faces.

"I cannot," said Gerik.

"We must," replied Boyd.

The mast was slowly moved further back revealing bare legs. They were bordering on physical sickness at this point. Boyd looked up at the others and just nodded. The covering was drawn completely back exposing the naked body of a badly mutilated young woman. Gerik collapsed to his knees and both Boyd and Nevin ran to the side of the ship and vomited into the calm water before sitting on the deck, shocked at what they had just found.

It was quite a while before anyone moved. "Get the others!" yelled Boyd eventually. Nevin jumped onto the jetty and ran to fetch them. They returned armed and unsure as to the urgency.

Enar approached the body. "She has not been dead very long," he said. "Sadly, I can see who has done this. I have seen bodies cut like this before. It is the work of pirate Moors. This girl is a Spanish Christian, she is wearing a crucifix. I do not understand why they are here. There will be other bodies under the mast."

Slowly the mast was moved back to reveal another seven bodies, all of whom had been badly mutilated. Spears and knives had been left scattered by the bodies.

"They were killed for their faith," continued Enar. "We must be careful. Tovi, Coll, you must go back now and warn the others of what you have seen. Stay in the moonlight but go now." The two men hurried away. The sound of hooves disappeared into the distance, leaving the nine men on the boat.

"We must go quickly. Cut the mooring rope," ordered Gerik.

The breeze was strong enough to gently float the boat downstream. They all stayed low so as not to be seen. They felt the boat tilt a little to port and heard faint talk from over the side. The men moved across to the starboard side of the boat, staying within the shadows. Four heads popped up over the side. The nine stayed flat on the deck waiting for the intruders to come on board, but nobody appeared. They vanished quietly into the water. The men stayed low for quite a while as the boat continued floating smoothly towards their destination. It seemed for the moment that they were safe. Sunrise could not come soon enough.

Tovi and Coll drove the horses as fast as possible for a few miles continually looking over their shoulders. They were hardened soldiers, but after seeing the mutilated bodies and realising that they were less than a day's journey from the settlement, there was fear in their hearts.

The small craft drifted slowly along in a steady breeze at about four knots, so the journey to Oban should take between six and seven hours. The silence was at times unbearable. The crew could not stay flat on the deck for the whole journey. The smooth flow of the water was disturbed only by the occasional goose breaking the surface, the flapping of the wings sounding like someone struggling to stay afloat. The boat had to be searched underneath, bow to stern. Nevin was a strong swimmer and volunteered to carry out the check. He slowly crept to the bow of the boat. Boyd tied a rope round Nevin's waist and gently lowered him into the water.

By now, the other members of the crew had spread out along the ten-metre length watching over both sides. Boyd guided Nevin round, watching him disappear under the water to check each side of the keel. It seemed to take ages but at last Nevin had completed a round check. He approached the stern from the port side, being helped up by Boyd. Nevin was about to climb back onto the deck when he suddenly let out an agonising and unearthly scream. Boyd looked over the side just in time to see a goose release its grip on Nevin's backside. Unfortunately, Boyd laughed so much that he let go of the rope, watching Nevin fall back, inelegantly, into the water. The others rushed to the front of the boat as the goose returned to the water with an indignant expression on its face.

Eventually Nevin was brought back on board, gently rubbing his backside. All Gerik could say was, "All clear then?" Nevin just suffered in silence. It was not exactly the first time he had felt something a little rough on his rear.

The rest of the journey to Oban was relatively uneventful apart from Nevin complaining every few minutes. It was light by now and as they approached the destination, to their absolute amazement there were two knarrs[7] and a longship. Each knarr had the capacity to hold about twenty crew and the longship around forty so there were potentially eighty Vikings in the area. The nine men would just be able to sail the knarr across the ocean, but the longship was definitely out.

They were about one hundred metres from the vessels and as they neared, they could see life on one of the cargo ships.

Gerik said to Enar, "We will have to moor against them and find out why they are here." He turned to the Scotsmen and said, "Let us talk, you must keep quiet."

They pulled alongside one of the cargo ships. A Norse voice shouted, "Throw the rope!" Gerik duly obliged. The boats were secured. The voice again shouted, "Come aboard!" Warily they climbed aboard, Gerik leading the way. A fearsome looking Viking soldier faced them.

Gerik looked up. "Maarku?"

"Gerik?" was the reply.

"Maarku?" repeated Gerik slightly louder. "Maarku!" yelled Gerik, embracing his friend, "Why are you here and why do you still carry that oyster shell around your neck?"

"There were rare pearls in the oyster, so I keep the shell round my neck and the pearls in my pouch and it brings me luck. I was hurt in battle and could not go with the others, so I stayed here to watch the boats. My leg was injured," he continued, as he raised his tunic to reveal a wooden splint round his knee. "The others have been gone many days. I have heard strange cries of pain and torturing from around these riverbanks and I now fear they will not come back but why are you here?"

"So being injured is lucky and it is a very long story," replied Gerik.

---

[7] Viking cargo ship

Maarku smiled at the response, looked around and said, "I am in no rush."

The others climbed aboard. Gerik introduced his friends in turn. Maarku was puzzled at the Scottish accent of some of the men.

Gerik looked at him and said, "I will explain." They all sat on deck, Gerik quickly ran through the events of the past few weeks, Maarku, at times, seeming even more puzzled, as the recent history unfolded. He related what they found on the birlinn and believed it wise to tow the boat out to the open sea and carry out a ship burial when they were out of sight of land. Under the circumstances and so as not to attract the attention of possible nearby hostiles, this was agreed.

"I was told that there were Moors here but did not believe they had come this far south. We must leave."

"So now we are all going to sail to where?" asked Maarku.

"We?" inquired Gerik.

"Yes, we," was the answer. "I cannot fight, I cannot hunt, I cannot walk at times, you are not leaving me here, so what do you think I should do?" he asked.

"Does that mean he will be with us?" asked Mirren.

Maarku looked up at Gerik and with a most ridiculously pleading and innocently smiling expression on his face, stared at his rescuer.

"Only if you promise to do as you are told," said Gerik. "Let us set sail. We have a long journey ahead of us to."

"Where are we going?" asked Maarku.

"To our homeland," Gerik replied.

"Why?" inquired Maarku. "We need to go to other countries. Let us sail to Frisia." It was everyone else's turn to look puzzled.

"I think that is where we should go," agreed Gerik. "Set sail." The mast was hoisted, mooring rope untied and after a few manoeuvres to point the boat in the correct direction, off they sailed.

Ross went up to Gerik and asked, "Does he know where he is going and where is Frisia?"

Gerik replied, "South, I think. He was the skipper of the Viking fleet, so I trust him to know where we are going."

"But can we trust him?" continued Ross.

"We can," replied Gerik.

The aim was to cover around three hundred miles per day, so assuming good conditions and a favourable tailwind, which would mean the journey to Frisia would take around four days. Maarku, was a highly experienced skipper with excellent navigational skills. He had travelled far from his homeland in Iceland, west to Greenland and North America, south to Francia and Spain and across to Italy, visiting Frisia once or twice on his expeditions and east as far as Iran, so he was the ideal person to guide them. Their route would take them through the Irish Sea, along the English Channel and then north to Frisia and from there, anywhere could be possible.

They waited till they were about ten miles off the south coast of England, then using a piece of carbon steel on flint, they ignited some dry straw they had collected and placed it in several areas of the birlinn before letting it drift. The knarr sailed on, leaving the burning boat-grave idling in the sea. The crew stood in silence at the stern of the knarr, in mourning, after the recent tragic and inhumane events.

Chapter 8

Schlock[8], Aleing and Watermelon

The crew made good progress and with the help of a very favourable tailwind, reached the warm Frisian coast by the morning of the fourth day, landing at Dorestad. There were a number of boats of all shapes and sizes already moored at the impressive jetty. The township was established at the base of the former Roman fortress of Levefanum in the seventh century. Under the Frankish rulers, coins were minted, and it established itself as a central meeting point for traders from numerous other countries. There had been frequent Viking raids; and treasures, mainly consisting of silver, were buried in this area and neighbouring Belgium and Luxembourg. It was an ideal first stop to acquire information about potential trading, well, one-sided trading.

Even though some Vikings had already established a settlement near Wieringen, the locals were still somewhat apprehensive of the Scandinavian visitors, no matter how small the group. In fact, the locals were suspicious of virtually every traveller despite the quite regular markets attracting large numbers of visitors from various parts of the globe. The men needed to learn as much as possible about commodities, trade routes, alliances, hostilities; in fact even overhearing the local gossip might come in useful.

About fifty metres inland, close to a thriving tavern, a market was in full swing. There was a large campsite not far from the market, for the use of both traders and visitors and there must have been at least fifty stalls spread out over quite a fair-sized area. Spices, perfumes, gold jewellery, leather goods, animal skins, silks and other materials, exotic fruits, herbs, wines and a variety of other items from around the globe were on offer.

---

[8] Cheap, inferior goods, trash

The group split into pairs, tasked with visiting the stalls and keeping their ears and eyes open. Each member of the group was given samples of the Roman gold and jewellery with strict orders only to show the items as an incentive for prospective trade. They were told to only use the coins for food and lodgings. They arranged to meet up at the tavern, surprisingly, after about four hours; and hopefully by then, having had ample opportunity to examine the goods on offer they would be able to discuss possible trading.

Gerik and Maarku began looking at the various materials laid out on one of the stalls.

"Where is this from?" Maarku asked the stallholder pointing to a large roll of material.

"This is the finest cotton in all of India and this," he continued, "is the softest silk in all of the world. We trade with China and then trade the silk and the cotton with many other countries."

Maarku was not only extremely impressed with the quality and intricate patterns dyed into the material, but also intrigued with the already established trade routes between east and west. Gerik, however, was still admiring the material and asked how they managed to get such bright colours on the cotton.

"Plant roots, tree barks, spices, onion skins and nut shells."

What are you trading?" asked Abhay.

"We mine gold," replied Gerik.

Maarku's jaw dropped at Gerik's quick, but not exactly honest response.

"I will show you," he continued, producing gold jewellery from a pouch inside his tunic. Maarku's jaw dropped even further.

"That looks like Roman gold," said Abhay.

The quick-thinking Gerik replied, "The Romans must get their gold from somewhere and as there are no gold mines in Rome, we send the gold and the jewellery across the water to them." Amazingly, the Indian tradesman seemed convinced by this lie.

"Where are you from?" asked Abhay.

"Brattahlið in Greenland," replied Gerik, hoping the Indian had never heard of the place.

so, am from Hampi, and it would be a great honour to seek trade with you," said Abhay, whose eyes were still alight at the sight of the precious Roman gold and now, or so he thought, he was aware of its source.

Gerik then said, "I would be most pleased if you would allow us to purchase some of this fine cotton and take it back to our home to show our country's leaders and then, when we meet again, we will look forward to more trade with yourself. We hope this will be the start of a good friendship between our two cities."

"The market will end tomorrow. Come here to me then and we will exchange our goods," said Abhay; and with that, the pair moved on.

Considering there was a wine market and based on a previous experience, one of the least wise pairings was Enar and Asmund however, by fate or a pure fluke, these two chanced across a stall, laden with, as each stallholder would state, 'some of the finest Spanish wines', directly next to a stall displaying 'some of the finest French wines', which was directly next to a stall displaying 'some of the finest Italian wines'. However, their attention was suddenly drawn to a different liquid display from where emanated an extremely interesting and distinctive aroma.

They approached and were greeted by a friendly Turkish gentleman, looking resplendent in a very brightly coloured abaya, decorated with fine strands of gold. With a great big smile on his face, he cheerfully greeted his new friends.

"My name is Hakan. Please try our drink."

They were each passed a small goblet, smelled the contents and tentatively took a small sip. The pair were unaccustomed to such strong alcoholic beverages.

"Fire water!" screamed Enar. "What is this?"

"We take grains of barley, corn, wheat and rye, mix them and boil them in water, then let them cool until we have this. We call it Grain Ale."

"We need this," said Asmund in a very hoarse voice after his first sample.

"What do you trade?" asked Hakan.

"In our country we mine precious metals, diamonds." Enar had a few samples of diamonds extracted from some of the Roman jewellery. "Here," he said, "these are from our country."

"Where is your country?" asked Hakan.

"Cambria," replied Asmund, "a city called Luentinum."

"I have not heard of that," said Hakan.

"It is a very busy city," continued Asmund, "built by the Romans, who settled there to mine gold and diamonds. We would like to take some of your grain water back to our country's ruler and when we meet again, we will look forward to more trade with yourself. We hope this will be the start of a good friendship between our two cities."

"The market will end tomorrow. Come here to me then and we will exchange our goods," said Hakan. And with that, they moved on.

Mirren and Boyd were intrigued by one particular display which was set up a little distance from the main stalls. It was in a large open area and small spherical devices were being lit, thrown a short distance and then exploded. There was quite a large crowd watching as a variety of new weaponry was demonstrated. Two Chinese gentlemen, Tian and Zhuo, with perfect command of English, Frankish and Spanish, were explaining the purpose of the devices.

"This powder," Tian began, "has been used in China for many hundreds of years. It can be used in war and in peace." He lit a small firework, threw it into the air where it made a loud bang then sparkled in a rainbow of colours. He then lit an arrow and shot it into a wooden frame where it completely demolished the target. "This powder has the power to kill, destroy or amuse. It is up to you how you use it."

Mirren turned to Boyd and quietly said, "We need to know how to make this. Try to get some of the powder to take back to Garmund."

The demonstration was repeated, a firework was lit and thrown into the air. Unfortunately, an impromptu breeze caught the firework, extinguishing the fuse and the firework fell, landing next to Boyd. He quickly, yet extremely innocently, put his foot over it, hoping no one would notice.

"We will try again," said Zhuo. As the demonstration went ahead and the spectators marvelled at the colourful display.

Boyd took the opportunity to pick up the dud firework. Mirren turned to Boyd and simply said, "I did not think it would just fall out of the sky into our hand." And with that the pair moved on.

The quantity and variety of goods from China and India were quite amazing. The stallholders travelled the world displaying their wares at established markets. Nevin and Sholto were attracted to a very colourful and extremely deliciously smelling display of exotic herbs and spices. The first plant they noticed was an approximately one metre high plant with small pink bell-shaped flowers. The two stallholders, Abbas, an extremely tall Indian and a Chinese salesman named Fuling approached them.

Fuling said, "Very fine flower, grown only in the Himalayas."

Abbas, leant over the smaller Chinese tradesman and interrupted. "He means to say the Indian part of the mountains."

Fuling looked annoyingly at his colleague, and they started arguing in a mixture of Chinese and Indian both appearing to understand each other perfectly.

After a short while the Indian looked at Nevin and calmly asked, "How can we help?"

"What is this?" inquired Nevin.

"Nard." Was the reply. "It is used to flavour wine, as a perfume and to help coughing and aching bones. Very old plant, used to anoint Christ."

"It has many uses I see," said Sholto.

"What do you trade?" asked Abbas. Sholto pulled out some of the Roman jewellery from the pouch and one piece fell to the ground. He was bending down to pick it up when a brooch he had pinned to his tunic was exposed.

Abbas stared intensely. "Where did you get that?" he asked.

"From my village," he replied.

"Where is your village?" asked the Indian abruptly.

"Devana in Scotland," replied Nevin.

"Please may I see the brooch?" asked Abbas. Sholto unpinned it from his tunic but held onto the brooch as the Indian carefully examined it.

The roughly twelve-centimetre diameter silver brooch was made in Ireland in about the year 700, mounted with gold, silver and amber decoration. It was exquisitely decorated with animals in gold wire and granules. In the centre of the brooch was a cross, flanking a golden 'Glory' representing the risen Christ. The Indian tradesman was apparently aware of such a brooch and asked Sholto to turn it over. The inscription read 'ᛘᚨᛚBRIXᚭF ᛉPᛏᚻ THIᚻ BRᛟᛟ<Hʼ[9] which when translated from the original Old Norse Runic, read 'Mælbriɡða owns this brooch.'

---

[9] Reference to the Hunterston Brooch

The two tradesmen talked feverishly between themselves, regularly glancing and pointing to the item.

Eventually the Indian said, "I will give you all this," pointing to the goods on the stall, "for the brooch."

The smart thinking Sholto replied, "This was my father's and on his death bed he told me never let it into the hands of another. I must respect his wishes." The two tradesman talked amongst themselves once again.

"Next time we meet," began the Chinese gentleman, "I will bring very rare spices only found in my country and then we will talk again. The market will end tomorrow. Come here to me then and we will give you some more of our eastern herbs and spices as a goodwill." And with that, the pair moved on.

Angus and Ross were intrigued by one particular stall massed with black-centred, bright red flowers having an alluring citrusy scent.

"What are these?" asked Ross.

"Poppies," replied Merulf, the Frisian tradesman. "Very good for pain and bad coughs."

"Do you eat the plants?" asked Angus.

Merulf replied by describing the two methods of preparing the petals to make either a syrup with the fresh petals and the dried petals for an infusion.

"I think Garmund will be most interested in this," Ross said to Angus. "Can we trade some of these poppies for gold?" inquired Angus.

"No need to trade," replied Merulf. "These poppies grow wild in the fields just over those hills. Help yourselves to as many as you need."

"But why do you give them away?" asked Angus.

"We also have special poppies," replied the tradesman.

"Special poppies?" asked a puzzled Ross.

"These special poppies help you to relax. Come back tonight when the market closes and I will let you try them for yourselves." And with that, an intrigued Angus and Ross left the stall and continued looking round the market.

Enar and Asmund, each still clutching a bottle of Italian wine, had spent a considerable amount of time sampling the various refreshments on offer and as expected, were a little worse for wear. However, being extremely conscientious about their duties, they continued blearily onwards. They literally stumbled into a stall displaying brightly coloured novelties which, on the face of it, appeared to serve no purpose whatsoever. The pair were intrigued by the variety of wares, some of which made strange squeaky noises and others which just felt warm and fluffy.

"What are these?" slurred Enar.

Observing that the two potential customers were slightly, well more than slightly inebriated, Barnabas, the English stallholder, decided to take advantage of this situation and answered.

"These rare and delicate goods are carefully made by craftsmen using traditional skills handed down through generations and shows the history of not only our people but also, when each of these fine pieces are placed together in the right order, they will show the history of the world and how life began, millions of years ago."

Enar and Asmund were left speechless by this total bullshit but being in their current state of mind, unquestionably believed all they were told.

"And over here," continued Barnabas, "we have musical toys to amuse your friends."

Quite simply it was a blown-up sheep or pig's bladder with a double cane reed stitched into a small opening and covered in strands of dyed fleece.

"I will show you," said Barnabas as he picked up one of the items and squeezed it between his hands. The resulting noise highly amused Enar and Asmund.

"We must have these," giggled Asmund. "How many of these do you have?" he asked.

"We have five hundred in different colours and many more items which are of little or no use" replied Barnabas.

"We will take all you have," said Enar, totally missing the relevance what Barnabas had just stated.

Barnabas's expression was one of joyful disbelief. He conveniently failed to mention that the squeaky toy could work once before it needed to be blown-up using a hollow reed.

"What do you have to trade?" asked the stallholder.

"Lots of gold we took from the Romans," replied Asmund, taking a quick swig from the bottle. He fumbled inside his tunic and produced a handful of gold coins. Some slipped out of his hand and in trying to catch them, fell clumsily onto his backside. On landing, all the coins fell from his grasp, He tried to stand, but as balance and co-ordination were sadly lacking, he sat down again and continued to taste the wine. Enar wasn't much help either, still giggling as he tested a number of other toys getting more and more frustrated that despite almost crushing the toy, he could only get one squeak out of it, until he was unceremoniously forced to sit down on a stool from which he promptly fell and to his great relief, managed not to spill one drop of wine.

All he could mutter was, "They fart," and with that he passed out.

Barnabas took this opportunity to collect the gold coins scattered on the ground, pack the remaining stock into large sacks which he stacked next to Asmund, close his stall and wander off overjoyed by the day's trading and the handsome profit in his possession. Strangely he was nowhere to be found for the remainder of the day. It would be a few hours before Enar and Asmund would be able to reflect and ashamedly regret their recent purchases.

Gerik and Maarku continued wandering around the market when their attention was drawn to a large stall displaying a wide variety of colourful fruit and vegetables, some of which appeared alien to the pair. Two extremely attractive African women, in their thirties, were very vocally trying to attract customers, shouting, "Exotic fruits and vegetables all the way from Africa. Come for a taste, come and quench your thirst!" It was an offer the two gentlemen could not refuse.

"What are these?" asked Gerik.

"Watermelons," said Lesedi. Anika expertly sliced the watermelon offering each a generous segment. They took a bite and were overwhelmed by the succulent flavour. Lesedi continued, "You must eat them when they are fresh, when they are sweet and smell pleasant. Bad watermelons are sour. How far have you travelled?"

"The journey took six days," lied Gerik.

"You must keep all the fruits cold, or they will go rotten," said Anika. She continued, "Some, like these strawberries, we cut up and put them in one of these clay jars and cover them with honey then seal the jar with hot wax. Watermelon, quince, medlar we wrap in banana leaves to keep them fresh. Maarku was familiar with most of the fruits but Gerik not so.

"What is that?" he asked, pointing to the medlar.

"Try one," suggested Lesedi.

Gerik had an expression of disgust on his face and the mere thought of tasting one based solely on its appearance was enough to put him off. Maarku had no hesitation in sampling one.

"Very sweet," he said. He continued to be more adventurous in sampling all the fruits on display. Gerik, on the other hand was still enjoying slices of watermelon.

"We will take all the watermelon and just a small amount of the other fruits," he said.

"What do you offer as payment?" asked Anika.

"We offer gold jewellery," replied Gerik, showing the women some of the gold items on offer. The women's eyes lit up on seeing the intricate and delicate adornments. They were suitably impressed by the items on offer.

"I have only once before seen gold like that," said a suspicious Lesedi. "Come and see the other vegetables we have," she added "and then we will talk about what you can do for us."

She led them to a second larger stall displaying a wide variety of plants and vegetables. Roses, lilies, madder and juniper plus onions, parsnips, fennel, cabbage, carrots and various beans to name but a few.

"You have not told us where you have travelled from," said Anika.

"From Birka in Sweden," replied Maarku.

"That will take you three weeks to get home," continued Anika. Maarku just nodded. "One day I would like to travel to your country." Lesedi approached. "I would like to go too," she said. "My grandfather was from Paviken and my grandmother from Aoudaghost and I have seen the value of two cultures."

"My grandfather was from Amalfi and my grandmother was also from Aoudaghost, and I lived in Italy when I was much younger, and I remember my father telling me he worked advising Pope Gregory. He took me round the Vatican one day and showed me gold and treasures which were hundreds of years old. I know this gold is not from your country so how did you find it?"

There was a long pause before Gerik answered. "Many years ago," he began, "my grandfather crossed the seas and visited Italy where he was taken prisoner by the Romans. He escaped torture and imprisonment and fled for his life back to his homeland taking chests of gold with him."

"Where in Italy was, he imprisoned?" asked Lesedi.

"Lombardy," replied Gerik.

"And that is where he took this gold?" inquired Lesedi.

"I believe that to be true," was the reply.

"Now tell me the truth," said an extremely sceptical Lesedi.

"What do you mean?" said Gerik nervously.

"What you have told me is not true as this gold is from the south of Italy." It had crossed Maarku's mind that Lesedi might be bluffing so he interjected.

"How do you know so much about the origin of the gold?"

"My father's brother owned gold mines in Italy, and he showed me the two types of gold. That is from the south."

Maarku looked at Gerik. "Please be seated," said Gerik politely. And so began an edited version of the history of events from the original meeting of the two groups to why they travelled to Frisia.

The women sat riveted to every fascinating word and after a lengthy pause, Anika said, "We are travelling with you to your home. We will bring the seeds for all these fruits and vegetables and help you build your village. Please take us with you."

The two men did not waste much time in agreeing to the women's proposal, believing that their village would benefit considerably from the expertise of the women and hence a definite "Yes" was firmly stated.

On hearing this, the two excited and relieved women, each gave Gerik and Maarku a massive hug, tears coming from their eyes as they thought of the exciting life which might lie ahead.

"Please do not go without us," pleaded Anika.

"I promise we will help you and you have my word that we will not go without you," replied a sincere Gerik. "You must help us pack our stall tomorrow," said Lesedi.

Maarku looked a little worried. "What is the matter?" she asked. "How many watermelons do you have?" he asked.

"About one thousand," was the response.

Gerik's expression said it all. "You promised," said Anika with a big grin on her face.

"We did," replied Gerik. And with that, the two men bid their farewells, having unintentionally acquired a large quantity of fruit and vegetables and two more members for their community.

The light was fading and as requested, Angus and Ross returned to the poppy stall. There were ten people already gathered. Merulf appeared. He was quite fluent in several languages and addressed the guests, in turn, in their own tongue.

"You have seen the poppies which are good for helping pains and coughs and now I have a different type of poppy which will help you keep calm. He produced a handful of small soft chunks of reddish-brown crystals which he offered around to the group.

"You will need these," he said handing out a hollow bamboo pipe, around twenty inches long, to which was attached a small piece of crudely carved-out semi-spherical bone, roughly one inch in diameter. "Please sit down," requested Merulf. They all obliged, sitting in a circle around a warm open fire. In front of each of the guests was a small Herodian lamp containing burning olive oil. "I have invited you here as friends, to relax after a long hard day and enjoy the calming effects of what I am about to offer you." He explained at what stage of the plant's cycle the substance should be extracted and how to do so. He continued. "Put a small piece into the bowl and gently warm it above the lamp." He demonstrated as he was talking. A few of the guests were quite familiar with the procedure and willingly assisted the novices.

After a short while and with a sour odour settling around the area, the atmosphere became friendly and even though there was six different nationalities and the same number of languages, conversation was flowing affably.

As the drug started to take effect, Merulf thought this an appropriate time to discuss business. "If you wish to trade, I will accept gold. I have prepared bundles of these poppies." As he was speaking, two of his helpers brought out fourteen well-packed hessian type sacks. "If you wish to take these, I need payment now," he continued.

Each guest produced a small pouch of gold coins which they threw towards Merulf who examined them in turn. When he was satisfied with the payment, he showed how to extract the sap from the pod and again explained the procedure for preparing the drug,

Angus tried to stand to thank Merulf for his assistance but still being light-headed, only managed to achieve an unintentional performance of an elegant three hundred and sixty degree turn before falling flat on his face.

Ross sat there with a pathetic smile on his face, occasionally giggling and pointing to the heavens, repeatedly saying, "Look, this finger is on the wrong hand."

Other guests were making equally insane and irrelevant comments, but nobody bothered. Merulf took this timely opportunity to collect the purses and sneak off with his helpers into the fading light. There was further irrational bidding on who should become the owner of the two spare sacks. A bid of four banana trees and three goats was declared the winner, outbidding the previous offer of two camels, a Roman toga and a thorn bush.

Eventually, after further sampling and many more incoherent and nonsensical discussions, the group fell asleep totally unaware of Merulf's secretive departure.

Gerik, Maarku, Mirren, Boyd and a still groggy Enar and Asmund finally met up at the tavern. Gerik's expression was one of disgust at Enar and Asmund. He could see that their contribution to the day's mission was less than fruitful and suggested they sleep off the effects in the stables next to the tavern.

Maarku quietly said to Gerik, "Did you not ask the innkeeper for a room for the evening?"

Gerik turned to Maarku and with a grin on his face. "Angus and Ross must have found a place to sleep, and I must have overlooked saying anything to these two about a bed for the night. I now think it is time we rested because we have another long day ahead of us tomorrow before we return home."

Enar and Asmund, assuming they were all spending the night in the stables, made their way there ahead of the others and once their heads touched the warm straw, they promptly fell asleep. The remaining four then made their way back to the tavern and after brief summaries about the day's achievements, including the unplanned and generally approved recruitment, enjoyed the luxury of a nice comfortable bed in a warm and pleasant environment.

Chapter 9

The Taming of the Shrewd

The four woke at approximately the same time and after the normal routine morning ablutions in a large, extremely offensive smelling shack attached to the tavern, enjoyed a filling breakfast of frumenty[10].

It was a nice fresh day, with a gentle breeze and a warming sun. Outside, they saw Asmund and Enar sitting on a wooden bench, slumped over a table, still half asleep. Gerik walked quietly over to them and in booming voice shouted.

"Morning!"

Enar stirred slowly, gently lifting his head, still with his eyes closed and said, "I am sorry."

Gerik sat down next to him and replied, "What have you done now?"

Enar explained that, in their enthusiasm to sample the extensive variety of wines on offer, obviously for the benefit of the community at home, they had not only managed to lose all the gold that was given to them but also, regrettably and unwillingly, bought all the useless, yet colourful toys that made a funny noise.

Angus and Ross soon appeared, each carrying one of the large sacks given to them the previous night. Maarku noticed the dilated pupils and quickly realised what they had being doing.

"What is in the sacks?" he asked.

Ross, memory still a little hazy, explained, as far as he could remember, the previous evening's events.

Maarku opened one of the sacks, took out a poppy, looked at Ross and yelled. "What is this!"

---

[10] Hot cereal porridge made of wheat and cooked in milk

Angus explained its uses. Maarku shook his head. "You have been fooled," he said. "This is a field poppy. You cannot get opium from this." Enar and Asmund suddenly came to life. "

How much did you give?" demanded Gerik.

"Everything," replied a white faced Angus.

"So, between you two and those drunken half-wits you have given away nearly half our gold!"

Maarku turned to Gerik and said, "We need to find the two thieves that took our money." Angus and Enar both said that the stallholders were not around when they woke. "That does not surprise me," said Gerik sarcastically.

"We will find a way of luring the two and I think if we use my pearls, we will get our gold back and much more," said Maarku. "Angus, Gerik told me you are a blacksmith." Angus looked puzzled. "Enar, you are a miner," said Maarku. Enar looked even more puzzled. "We need to find shells or pebbles by the shore, the same size as these pearls. We may need you to shape the stones. Sholto, you are good at dyeing, and we will need your help in getting the shells the same colour as these pearls."

Sholto said, "I cannot do what you ask. I have nothing here to dye the shells, I do not know what I can use, I do not…"

Maarku interrupted. "I am sure you will find something. I have great trust in you. They think they are wise and cunning, but we will not be fooled by anyone. If we do nothing, then we are the fools. We must try."

"What do you need?" asked Asmund. Maarku smiled as he outlined his plan for revenge.

He turned to Gerik and said, "We must set sail as soon as we can after night falls. We cannot wait till the market closes to finish our business with the traders, so we must collect what we have bought, trade as we agreed and then return to the ship, ready to set sail."

Angus, Sholto and Asmund scoured the shore making sure they kept well out of sight as they searched for appropriate stones and pebbles. Maarku, Ross and Enar returned to the market, the latter two keeping their cloak hoods up to safeguard being recognised. Enar led them to Barnabas's stall. Maarku told Enar to stay back out of sight and he went with Ross to the stall. Barnabas greeted the pair enthusiastically.

"Good morning," he said. "May I welcome you to my fine stall." He proceeded to deliver the same speech about the rare and delicate goods being hand-crafted and so on, and the two listened patiently.

Maarku then said, "I have heard that there is great power in these goods. The Viking God Sina believed he could control the world with these effigies and when they were brought together, he created life in heaven and the underworld." Maarku continued to prattle on for a while and Barnabas was drawn to his every word no matter how ridiculous it seemed.

"I need to buy all you have," said Maarku. "Would you accept these as payment?" he continued, discretely lifting out the two pearls, so no one else could see them.

Barnabas's eyes lit up and after a really long pause he said, "I have heard that such perfect pearls exist but in my sixty years, I have never seen them, and I have travelled to many countries."

Maarku continued. "I think even one of these rare pearls is more than enough to buy all your goods. What else can you offer in trade?"

"Wait here," said Barnabas. "I will return soon." And with that, off he scampered.

Ross turned to Maarku and said, "You almost had me believing your story."

"Very strange," replied Maarku, "because I almost believed it myself."

Barnabas returned out of breath, carrying two full jingling pouches.

"Here," he said, "I offer this gold which belonged to my family. Please take it in exchange for a pearl."

Maarku shook his head and said, "I do not think it safe to trade here where we can be seen. Others may be watching. I will return when the sun goes down. It will be safer then." Barnabas agreed and with that, they parted company.

One down, one to go.

The pair returned to Enar who asked Maarku, "Did you get our gold." Maarku just smiled at him and then turned to Ross and said, "Now, to the next stall."

As they approached, Ross became worried, nervously looking round. "What is the matter?" asked Maarku.

"The stall has gone," he replied. Their hearts sunk at the thought of losing the gold.

"Think," said Maarku, "can you remember anything that he said about the poppies?"

Ross thought for a while and replied, "When I asked Merulf about the poppies on his stall, he did say that there were fields full of them over those hills and we could take them without payment."

"To the fields then," said Maarku.

The trip to the top of the hill took ten minutes.

"Down," said Maarku. They wriggled forward to the summit and looking down over the hill, saw nine people about fifty metres away busily cutting down the field poppies and putting them into sacks.

"That is Merulf with the long white tunic," said Ross.

Maarku replied, "I do not think he will go back to his stall. I think he is getting the poppies ready to take to his next market and I think he will take them by boat. He knows people will be trying to find him. We need to go to the boats and wait for him. Ross, you must not be seen. Go back to the tavern and wait for us. Enar, come with me." They both obeyed.

"All we have to do now," began Maarku, "is find the most likely boat. He has to move the sacks quickly so I think he will have a small rowing boat near the shore and his sailing boat will have dropped anchor a distance out at sea. His helpers will load the sacks onto the boat, and he will not want to be seen so he will exchange tunics with one of his helpers."

"How do you know all this?" asked Enar.

"I have done this myself to escape," replied Maarku, with a big grin on his face.

As the two men made their way down to the shore, they found a solitary rowing boat which was about the right size for four sets of oars and space to hold a good number of sacks. Maarku told Enar to keep out of sight by hiding behind some trees about thirty metres from the shore. Maarku sat waiting on a rock by the water's edge. It was not long before he heard the sound of footsteps on the pebble beach. He reached into his tunic and brought out the two pearls. He was studying them intensely as the group approached. As anticipated, Merulf, who had now donned a long black cloak, came up to Maarku and said in a threatening tone.

"What are you doing?" Maarku stood and turned to face Merulf whose tone dramatically changed when he saw the size of the man opposite him.

Maarku made certain that the two pearls were visible and watched as Merulf's eyes focussed on them. He returned them to the pouch in his tunic.

"Are they real pearls?" asked Merulf.

"I do not know what you mean," Maarku replied.

"You have pearls," said Merulf. "Where did you find them?" Maarku said nothing. "Let me see," said Merulf.

"Walk with me," said Maarku. Merulf turned to his helpers and gestured for them to put the sacks in the boat.

"You are leaving?" asked Maarku.

"I need to travel to Málaga. Now show me the pearls," demanded an impatient Merulf.

"What do you have to trade?" asked Maarku.

"Gold and silver," replied Merulf.

"Show me," said Maarku.

"I do not have any with me, but if you let me have the pearls, I will bring you payment later." Maarku shook his head, turned and started walking away.

"Wait," shouted Merulf. He pointed out to the open sea. "Come to my boat later and I will trade with you."

"No. I will meet you and you alone outside the tavern near the market at nightfall," replied Maarku firmly. Merulf reluctantly agreed.

Maarku, Ross and Enar made their way back to the tavern and met up with the others in the room Gerik had reserved.

"Nice room," said Enar sarcastically. "I wonder who slept here last night."

Angus, Sholto and Asmund had collected a good variety of stones and pebbles from the shore, and they spread them out on one of the beds. Gerik suggested that apart from himself, Maarku, Sholto and Angus, and the others should go back to the stalls where they had each agreed to trade, think of some excuse as to why they needed to leave before the end of the market, pay a fair price and return with the goods. "You may need to find two large carts," he added, "and do not forget the two women, I did promise to help them, and I will not go back on my word." The six men left, puzzled as to why two large carts would be needed.

The remaining four, slowly and carefully scrutinised the collection. "It is for you to make these stones white," Gerik said to Sholto.

"I can do this," he replied. "I need some yeast and hot water."

"The innkeeper makes his own ale," said Gerik and with that he left the room.

Maarku lifted out the pearls from his tunic. "We need to find four pebbles the same size and weight as these pearls and if Sholto can make them the same in colour, my plan will work."

Maarku explained that, as the light would be fading, it would be quite difficult for either Barnabas or Merulf to distinguish between the real pearls and the fake ones, especially as neither of them had seen any for many years and would not be familiar with the exact texture, weight or colour.

"And you thought Barnabas and Merulf were cunning and clever," he added. "You are quite evil," said Sholto.

"Thank you," replied Maarku.

Gerik returned with a handful of yeast and a small clay pot full of boiling water.

"I need to mix the yeast in the water," said Sholto. Maarku slightly raised his tunic and removed the wooden splint from his leg.

"It was nearly healed," he said with a smile on his face.

Sholto prepared the mixture. There were six suitable, slightly off-white, round pebbles which he dropped into the mixture. He stirred the pot slowly with the others looking on speechless, as though something miraculous was about to happen. The three sat on the floor, staring into a small three-inch diameter pot, while the magician performed his trick.

Sholto retrieved one of the pebbles smartly from the hot water to gasps of amazement from the spectators. He dried and polished the pebble on his tunic and raised it to eye level. He moved the pebble round in his fingers as the onlookers followed every twist and turn, seemingly in some hypnotic trance. He stood and went towards the window for better light, the others following like sheep. "Well?" said Sholto.

Maarku lifted out one of the real pearls and took the fake from Sholto. "They feel the same and in the dark I think they will look the same."

"Now for the other pebbles," said Sholto. They turned out just as good and in a fading light could easily be mistaken for the real thing.

"Thank you," said Maarku, "and now we get our gold back."

Meanwhile Ross, Enar, Asmund, Mirren, Boyd and Nevin had been to all the stallholders they had previously seen, explained their predicament in having to leave earlier than planned, completed their business and collected the wares, thanking the stallholders for their help and vowing to meet again at the next market. They still wondered why they needed two large carts. The wines, spices and materials easily stacked onto one of the carts.

Their final call was to Lesedi and Anika. Mirren went up to the two women to tell them that they needed to leave early.

"That will be fine," said Lesedi. "All you need to do is take all you can see on this stall…"

Before she could finish her sentence, Mirren interrupted, "There seems little to take so…"

Lesedi continued, "And all you see on the other stall and what is under the tables."

Mirren lifted the white cloths covering the tables to see a very large reserve of watermelons. "Oh," he exclaimed, "Now I know why we needed two large carts. Bring the carts" he said gesturing to the others. Anika and Lesedi left to collect their belongings from their nearby tent.

The women soon returned with their personal possessions but stayed a little distance from their stall, watching and admiring the effort put in by the six, by now, exhausted helpers. When the loading was almost complete, they casually walked up to the stall and looked around.

"What about that one over there?" asked Anika, pointing to one which had fallen off the cart.

Boyd glared at her and said smiling, "I think it is nearer to you than it is to me." Anika obliged. "And now to the boat," exclaimed Boyd.

Three men to each cart, one pulling and two pushing with the two women following, discussing the merits of Mirren and Boyd's physique.

The other four were already by the boat. "We must hurry," said Gerik, "the light is starting to fade, and we need to have the boats loaded and ready to set sail before Maarku sees Barnabas and Merulf."

They all helped in the loading. Maarku said, it is time and then made his way to Barnabas's stall.

Barnabas was smiling widely as he saw Maarku approach. "Do you have the pearls?" he asked, nervously looking round.

"Do you have the gold?" asked Maarku.

"Yes, yes," he replied as he handed Maarku three large pouches. Maarku checked the contents and looked up at Barnabas a little puzzled.

"The pearls are much better than I could ever wish for. I want to keep my stock and I offer you all I have been given by traders wanting to buy my wares."

Maarku was not going to dispute this offer. "Please let me see the pearls again." Maarku removed the real pearls from the pouch, showing them to Barnabas. "Can I touch them?" asked Barnabas.

Maarku paused, looked round and replied, "I will hold them, but you can feel the quality."

Barnabas found it difficult to control his excitement. "They are perfect," he said.

Maarku put the pearls back into the pouch and as he passed them across to Barnabas, he dropped them. Barnabas gasped in horror. Maarku bent down to pick them up, slyly switching the pouch with one containing two fake pearls. At that point, Mirren and Boyd walked by.

"Quickly," said Maarku, "hide them inside your tunic. I do not think it will be safe to look at them again until there is no one around." Barnabas agreed. They bid each other farewell and went their separate ways.

Mirren and Boyd caught up with a smug looking Maarku who complemented them on their perfect timing. "We are nearly there," he said.

They all went back toward the tavern. Maarku sat alone enjoying a tankard of ale when Merulf and two of his helpers approached, hoods covering their heads. Merulf sat down opposite Maarku, his helpers standing a few paces back.

"I told you to come alone," said Maarku.

"You cannot trust anyone," Merulf replied.

"Is that why you are ready to set sail?" asked Maarku.

Merulf looked menacingly at Maarku. "Show me the pearls," he said sternly.

"I do not like the way you talk to me," replied Maarku.

"I do not care," said Merulf. "I am here to trade, not to talk idly. The pearls."

"The gold," demanded Maarku. Merulf raised his hand and one of his helpers walked forwards, leant over and Merulf whispered something to him. The two helpers then left.

"Where are they going?" asked Maarku.

"I needed to be certain you were on your own before I brought the gold."

It was quite some time before the two helpers returned, hoods still covering their heads.

"You were gone a while," said Merulf. The helpers said nothing but one of them placed a single pouch of the Roman gold on the table.

Maarku opened the pouch, looked up at Merulf and said, "You insult me. I am no fool. You think yourself cunning by offering me this meagre sum." Maarku stood to walk away.

"I did not wish to offend you," said an apologetic Merulf. He beckoned to his other helper who approached and placed two large pouches onto the table.

Maarku checked the contents and then handed over the real pearls. Impatiently, Merulf took them out of the pouch, studied them, smiled, replaced them into the pouch and tossed them to one of his helpers saying, "Just so you do not cheat me." He then got up from the table, went up to the helpers who handed him back the pouch. He then walked off towards the market and the two helpers towards the rowing boat.

When Merulf was out of sight, Maarku picked up the three pouches, walked towards the two helpers and said, "I hope you left them somewhere safe and did not hurt them."

The two men took their hoods down, turned to Maarku and said, "They are sleeping. How did you know he would send his helpers back to get the gold?"

"It is what I would have done," he replied.

Boyd, Mirren and Maarku then made their way to the jetty, boarded the ship and sailed off into the darkness to start the long journey home.

Chapter 10

From Wags to Witches

While waiting for Tovi and Coll to return with the horses, Elen, Anna and Nesta had been extremely helpful in briefing the inland travellers on suitable places to visit. Elen's father had told her about the large towns and cities as he himself had done much travelling, going as far south as London. However, such a journey was ruled out as being somewhat impractical.

It was decided that for now, a trip as far south as York would be sufficient. The three-hundred-and-fifty-odd mile outward trip would take around seven and a half days, not pushing the horses too much. They hoped to be able to swap the horses once or twice at some point in the journey if the opportunities arose.

So off they went. Frothi, Donnan, Ewan, Ulf, Alban, Colban and Malcolm, eager to explore and hopefully return with a greater understanding of what Scotland and England had to offer. The first quick refreshment point was a Culdee monastery at Dunkeld, about thirty-five miles from Stoleware. Here they were welcomed by a handful of monks who provided them with a little nourishment and also food and water for the horses before a comparatively shorter trip, just fourteen miles to St. John's ton.

Due to its strategic position on the River Tay, St John's ton was starting to become a major town, effectively at that time, being the unofficial capital of Scotland, also due to its frequent holding of a royal court. Apart from a few aristocracies and those who tried to seek favour with the well-to-do, the area had attracted numerous farmers and craftsmen and had secured a regular extensive trade with Francia, particularly in wines, precious metals, ceramics and glass. In return, exported goods included unprocessed raw materials, wool, hides, salt, fish, animals and coal.

Towards evening the seven travellers rolled in. They were impressed by the dwellings; well-maintained daub and wattle homes on the outskirts of the town and as they rode towards the centre, brick and stone cottages all very grand. The town was quiet, most residents being home for the evening after a hard day at work and a few locals out for an evening stroll. They approached the interestingly named 'Le Grand Coq', presumably influenced by some French farmer. The front of the tavern was decorated with at least twenty small 'The Cross of St Andrew' flags.

They entered and approached the innkeeper. "We would like a room for the evening," said Donnan. The innkeeper looked at them and said in a belligerent tone, "I do not want any trouble." They were taken back by this response. "The last guest who stayed here is buried in the church yard," added the innkeeper.

"What happened?" asked Ewan nervously.

"He died," replied the innkeeper.

"How?" asked Ewan.

"Stopped breathing," replied the straight-faced innkeeper.

"Why?" pressed Ewan.

"I think somebody choked him while he was sleeping," came the reply, at which point the innkeeper let out a raucous and extremely annoying laugh.

The group did not know whether to laugh or run until he said in a far more friendly manner, "Welcome my friends, my name is Alfred. What brings you here?"

"Horses," replied Ulf with a smile on his face. At this response, Alfred burst into hysterical laughter.

"I thought I was the only joker round here. Now what can I do for you?"

"Seven tankards of ale," requested Alban.

"Where are you from?" asked Alfred whilst drawing the ale.

"We have travelled from Iona," replied Donnan, "making our way south."

"Are you traders?" asked Alfred.

"We would like to trade and are seeking goods to take back home."

"There are many craftsmen here in St John's ton and I am certain you will find much to please you. For the ale and a room for the night, that will be two schillings. I only have one room free for all of you as there is a royal visit here in the morning and the rooms are being used by knights and nobles from other towns," said Alfred.

Donnan paid the money, turned to Malcom and said, Well Sir Malcolm, we may see some of your old friends again." With that Malcolm's jaw dropped. "We will be happy with the one room," continued Donnan.

"Sir Malcolm?" said a surprised Alfred.

"Yes," replied Donnan, "This is gold merchant and explorer Sir Malcolm of Hithin. We are travelling as traders so as not to be noticed."

Alfred was a little taken back by this, as was Malcolm.

"Sir Malcolm," he began, "I beg your forgiveness in not knowing who you are. May I lead you to your room."

Alfred replied, saying, "We will find our way, but I thank you for your kindness."

When they entered the room, Malcolm glared at Donnan saying, "Sir Malcolm?"

"It will be a way of being introduced to the other knights who will be here," replied Donnan.

Malcolm thought a moment then reluctantly nodded his approval at Donnan's foresight. Unfortunately, there were only two beds, however Malcolm, now being Sir Malcolm, thought it only befitting that someone of his status should automatically qualify for one of the beds. This idea was unanimously rejected, so the only fair way to decide who would have a bed was to flip a coin. It was agreed that when two out of the seven coins matched as either cross or pile, these would be the lucky winners. Well, that took ages — sore thumbs, lost coins, accusations of cheating, but finally Frothi and Ulf came through victorious.

"Now to more important matters," began Ewan. "We need to find out more about who is coming, where they are from and why they are visiting. Alban, Ulf, I think you should go and ask the innkeeper to prepare some food for us and also find out as much as you can."

The two agreed and went down the rickety wooden stairs to see Alfred.

"May I help?" he asked.

"We have travelled a long way and are hungry. Would there be a little food?" asked Ulf.

"I have pottage warming on the fire. Roasted beef with carrots, cabbage and onions. I will prepare the food for you all."

"That is most kind of you," said Alban. "Who will be here in the morning?" he asked.

"I have heard it is Kenneth MacAlpin, the King and his royal party, travelling to Dùn Èideann. I am sure he would like to meet Sir Malcolm."

"And I am sure Sir Malcolm will be pleased to meet his grace," replied Alban.

Alban and Ulf then returned to the room, told them what he had said and learnt. With Malcolm now feeling a little apprehensive, they all proceeded to the dining area where steaming bowls of inviting food and tankards of refreshing ale awaited them. After feasting, they adjourned to their room for the evening.

They were all awake bright and early the next morning. The priority was to find Malcolm suitable attire if they were to meet the King. The group had not planned for such a regal encounter and were discussing what outfit they could put together. They exchanged clothing, dressing Malcolm in the cleanest and least malodorous outfit available. At least he looked presentable, and now for breakfast.

Alfred was looking quite resplendent in his clean white cotton tunic, dark woollen trousers, short black leather tabard and polished black leather boots. He started singing an uncomplimentary song about the queen.

'Her Grace has a face like strands of lace,
Tied in knots and covered in spots,
She waddles like a duck through a pile of muck.
And her rear is the size of a flagon of beer'.

His annoying laugh returned. "I am such a wag," he said, amusing nobody except himself. "I have food for you." Rye bread, cheese and a hot drink resembling the liquid drained from the previous evening's meal were on offer. Nobody complained too loudly. By now, the whole population and the pseudo-aristocrats had lined the road into the town as a strange multitude of characters began descending on the quaint, normally quiet community.

Extravagant figures in fancy dress — jesters, acrobats, musicians, magicians and many more colourful personalities, were singing and dancing as the... what only could be described as a circus, made its spectacular entrance. The seven friends, sat outside the inn, enjoying yet another tankard of ale, dumfounded at the unnecessarily extravagant parade. Finally, after what seemed to be the whole world had passed by, there appeared in a white open carriage decorated with gold trimmings, drawn by four magnificent white horses and escorted by a guard of honour, the man himself, Kenneth I, King of the Picts, accompanied by his wife who actually looked quite bored with the whole pageantry.

The carriage came to a halt outside Le Grand Coq. The King and his wife were helped down by a couple of effeminate-looking male aides who then skipped away holding hands. The royal party made their way to the entrance.

Alban looked up at the King and said, in a loud voice. "Alpin?"

The King stopped, turned round slowly and looked disapprovingly at Alban.

Alban stood up and again said, "Alpin?"

The King approached and said, quite pompously, "My name is Kenneth MacAlpin. I am the King. Why do you call me by that name?"

Malcolm now stood up and said, "You are Alpin." The crowd fell silent.

"I do not understand," said the King. Malcolm and Alban approached the King, stared at him for a while and then Malcolm said, "I am sorry if I have offended you, your grace, but you have a very strange likeness to someone we know."

It was the King's turn to look a little perplexed. "The name of this person?" asked the King.

"We know him as Alpin."

"Is he a warrior?" asked the King.

"A warrior and a good friend," replied Malcolm. The King continued to ask penetrating and personal questions about Alpin, how and where they all met, how the group came together, in fact almost all about Alpin's life story but was diverted from receiving a direct answer to the question of where he could now be found.

"Why do you ask so much about Alpin?" asked Alban. There was a prolonged silence until the King gave a long sigh and eventually replied, "I do know this man." The King raised his eyes to the sky and eventually, convinced that it was the same person admitted, "He is my half-brother."

It was the group's turn to display a stunned silence. The King continued to explain how Alpin, whose real name was Donald MacAlpin, believed the regal life was not for him, and left the family home when he was sixteen years of age.

"I thought about him and wondered where he was and what he was doing or if he was still alive, and now I am happy knowing he has such trustworthy friends," he said, looking round at the seven. "If there is anything I can do for you, I will, but you must promise me to tell Donald we met." They promised they would.

So, while the King continued to chat heartedly to his new found friends, the accompanying entourage made the best of their free time, entertaining the locals, laughing and joking with the children and generally enjoying the impromptu festivities while the queen stood around looking even more bored; with the hangers-on trying desperately hard to get involved in the King's conversation only to be told, in no uncertain terms, to go and find someone else to pester as he was tired of their persistent annoying behaviour and their ability to contribute absolutely nothing. He concluded by describing them as snivelling, two-faced, skamelars[11].

That did the trick. Off they scurried, sulking. The King turned to Malcolm and with a big grin on his face said, "I have been wanting to say that for a good time, but today I felt the courage. I must talk to the queen in that manner soon, but do not warn her," he whispered.

"My palace is in Forteviot, no more than a day's journey from here and you would be most welcome. I have battled with the Picts and Viking invaders," turning to Frothi and Ulf, "but if you are friends with my brother, then you are my friends too."

This brought a tear to Ulf's eye who unthinkingly said, "Thank you Kenneth."

The King glared at him, giggled and then broke out into thunderous laughter, attracting the attention of the whole town.

After calming down, he said, "Not even my wife calls me by that name. Today, I met seven of the kindest people ever. I will call you, my friends. It is now with regret I must meet the rest of the peasants." He stood up from the bench, picked up Malcolm's full tankard of beer, downed it in one and then gave each of them a royal hug. As he came to Malcolm he said, "Nice

---

[11] Scrounger, parasite

outfit." He moved back extending his arms and once again said, "Thank you," before bowing and then making his way across the path to greet the other townsfolk.

The group, satisfyingly pleased with the meeting, shouted as one, "Thanks Ken." The King half turned back, shook his head, then continued on, chuckling to himself.

They sat back down discussing future possibilities and how the King might be able to introduce them not only to reputable nobles and traders in Scotland but also, through his acquaintances, potential alliances, both in England and abroad. They also thought it wise to return at a later date to scrutinise the variety of crafts operating within the town more closely.

It was now time to move on. They bade farewell to Alfred and began the journey south, clearly inspired by the friendliness and benevolence of such a fascinating monarch. Their next planned stop was to be Dùn Èideann, a forty-five-mile journey, after crossing the Firth of Forth at Cas Chaolas. Elen's father had mentioned to her about an old Roman boat bridge across the river and they were hoping that there was still such a crossing, as this would save them a day's travel.

The journey was thankfully uneventful, passing through a few small hamlets and they reached Dunfermelitane by the middle of the afternoon, where they rested for a short time next to the shaded remains of a few Neolithic dwellings. Over the next six miles to the bank of the river, each wondered if some form of crossing was still possible, but nothing much was said. Every time one of them tried to start a conversation, it was met with a few incoherent responses. Their thoughts were solely on the crossing.

One mile to go; the coast came into view. They each stretched their necks in the vain hope of being able to get a better view. The gait quickened. From a walk, a trot, a canter, to a full gallop. It seemed a pointless race was on. Colban was the first to arrive at the coast, closely followed by the others. There was no sign of the boat bridge. Disappointment followed.

They heard a voice screaming in the distance. Racing towards the sound, they saw a man in the water, madly flapping his arms up and down. Again, Colban was the first to arrive, jumping off his horse, running towards the man in the water and dragging him to safety on the shore. The man got to his feet, slapped Colban across the face and ran off still flapping his arms and screaming wildly. They could not believe what they had just witnessed.

A voice behind them calmly said, "Do not worry, he is mad. He is trying to fly. He has been watching and listening to the birds and thinks if he can make a sound like the birds and flap his arms like a bird, he will fly."

"Good day sirs," said the stranger, "my name is Noah, may I help you?"

"We are seeking to cross to the far bank on our way to Dùn Èideann," said Ewan. There were some wrecks of small boats scattered by the shore and one relatively seaworthy craft.

"I can take you across for two pence. That is my boat, 'Shark'," he replied. It had to be mentioned. "Noah's Shark," said Ewan.

The seven looked at each other, trying not to laugh, but the laughter could not be contained. Noah stood there puzzled, having no idea what they meant.

They led the horses onto the boat, making the occasional reference to two by two and why the blind bats never made it onto the Ark, but again Noah did not get it. There was an ingenious cable pulley system which required a reasonable amount of effort in manually pulling a rope of connected water reed fibres across the mile and a half stretch of water. Fortunately, there was only a gentle breeze as Noah started drawing effortlessly on the rope, the passengers looking on, feeling rather guilty as he was doing all the hard work. Colban and Frothi held onto the horses as the others sat in a line behind Noah, grabbing the rope and working in perfect harmony to drag the craft smartly across the bay.

Once they arrived at the makeshift jetty, the horses were led off and they thanked Noah for his help.

"Will you return this way?" he asked.

"We do not know," replied Malcolm, "but we will meet again." Just then a pure white dove flew overhead. "Looks like the water level is dropping," remarked Ewan as they rode away smiling.

The remaining eleven miles were covered in a couple of hours. The sight of a small fort on a towering rock was extremely impressive; a perfect vantage point for marauding armies. As the group approached, they became aware of numerous pairs of suspicious eyes following their every step. They tried to acknowledge the locals as they rode towards the centre of town, but were generally ignored. Their priority was to find a room for the night.

The first inn they tried looked quite impressive from the outside. However appearances can be deceptive. Donnan and Ulf entered only to find a few customers asleep on the floor snoring quite loudly.

The innkeeper, a short, extremely fat person wearing baggy yellow braies and an equally ill-fitting tunic asked, "Whit dae ye want?"

"A room for seven," replied Donnan.

"We are fou," came the reply. The relieved pair made a hasty retreat.

"Friend of yours?" asked Ulf. Donnan treated the remark with the contempt it deserved.

The second port of call, a little way down the street, was 'The Sheep Heid Inn', again pleasant from the outside and this time very clean on the inside. They approached the bar and heard a woman's voice call from below the bar,

"Give me a moment." After a few moments, an extremely attractive womanin in her mid-twenties, with long blonde hair and a fine figure stood up. "Good day sirs," she said, "my name is Madelaine, can I help you."

The pair were stuck for words and just stared at her until Ulf eventually stuttering said, "Do you have a room for the night?"

Madelaine smiled and replied seductively, "Is it for you two fine men?" The embarrassment on their faces was clearly evident.

"There are seven of us," he answered.

"Seven! Are they all as fair as you?" she asked pouting.

Before they could answer, a very well-built male came into the bar. "I see you have met my wife," said the man. "Madelaine, prepare a little food for our guests." Off she went looking back very alluringly. "Seven of you. That will be three shillings. There is a stable round the back for your horses." Donnan paid the innkeeper, then went out to tell the others while Ulf remained inside talking.

"Where are you from?" asked the man.

"Iona," replied Ulf.

"I have been to the monastery on Iona. Is that where you travelled from?" he asked.

Ulf hesitated in his response but was fortunately saved from answering any further awkward questions by the timely entrance of the others. They sat down at the wooden table. As the man went into the kitchen, Madelaine appeared wearing an extremely short frock and a very low-cut top carrying four meat pies.

She stretched across the table serving the food and displaying quite an ample bosom. "I hope you like what I have."

"They look very nice," replied Colban, "I cannot wait to taste them."

As Madelaine returned to the kitchen, her husband came out and said bluntly. "If you would like to lay with my wife, it will be one shilling." Stunned by this comment, nobody was prepared to speak first.

Madelaine's husband returned to the kitchen as she came out, carrying three more pies and sat next to Ulf, putting her hand on his thigh.

He turned to her and said, "I am not for you, but I will lay with your husband."

She was speechless at his reaction. Colban decided to chance his luck. "Will you be with me?" Madelaine thought for a few moments before agreeing. She called for her husband and put Ulf's proposal to him.

At first, he was horrified at the thought of being desecrated by a large hairy Viking but then said, "I will for two shillings," Ulf smiled.

After an interesting evening it was time to move on to Jedworð, a near fifty-mile trip south-east. Nobody commented on the previous evening's events but both Ulf and Colban had a pleasantly satisfied expression. They had travelled about twenty miles when Alban's horse was forced to stop. Colban stayed back to help while the others rode on slowly. Alban dismounted to check the horse's hoof and found a stone lodged between the hoof and the shoe. This was easily prised off with a small knife and just as Alban was about to remount, a group of four men appeared from out of the hedgerow.

"We want your horses," said one of them. Alban ignored them and continued to mount his horse. "We want your horses," repeated the man in a much more severe manner at the same time drawing his sword. The four men then moved to cut off the escape path.

"Out of our way!" shouted Alban very loudly.

"Your horses, or we slay you."

Alban and Colban sat on their horses facing the four and Alban again shouted even louder. "Out of our way!"

The four moved towards the two horsemen raising their swords and at that moment a dagger pierced the back of the neck of one of the bandits. He slumped to the ground. They turned round to see five angry warriors standing behind them, swords drawn and prepared for a kill. The three dropped their swords without hesitation.

"Your clothing," said Ulf. The three bandits stood motionless. "We want your clothing," said Ulf again. The three started stripping.

Frothi turned to Ulf and said, "One last night and three this morning." Ulf smiled.

"Now go and take your friend with you," he said. They picked up the lifeless body and started walking away. Ewan cut the clothing into pieces, scattered it around collected their swords and said, "We stay together." On they rode.

They reached Jedworð by early evening and found a very pleasant place to stay; nothing too grand, just a nice simple large fired-clay brick building with superbly shaped Roman glass windows, solid oak doors adorned with decorative iron studs, smoke coming from the chimney and the distinct aroma of chicken being cooked.

It was a case of being in the right place at the right time. As they were riding past, two beautiful white-haired spaniels ran from the house, being chased by two distraught young twin girls.

"Bo, Hardy, come here!" they shouted.

The dogs ran full speed past the travellers. Donnan and Ewan turned their horses around and chased after them. Donnan managed to get ahead of the dogs, dismounted and knelt down. The dogs came up to him, tails wagging, and he started playing with them. They just took to Donnan. He stood up, told the dogs to sit, which they duly obeyed, then they followed him as he led the way back to the house. The children were amazed at how a total stranger could control their dogs so well.

As they approached, the children's parents emerged looking relieved that the dogs were back safely. Donnan walked up to them and again told the dogs to sit.

"Thank you. I wish they would obey us like that," said the father.

"You need to show them who is the master," replied Donnan. He knelt down and said, "Bo, Hardy, come." They came up to him wagging their tails and he started playing with them. The dogs were loving it, rolling over, jumping up at him and having a great time. "Go," he said pointing to the open door. The dogs immediately obeyed, trotting into the house.

Henry, the girls' father and Isabella, their mother, were amazed. "Do you think you could get the dogs to help milk the cows?" she asked.

"I can try," replied a smiling Donnan.

By now, the other six had gathered round the front of the house. The two daughters, Emma and Alice brought the dogs back out; but this time they were restrained by leather collars and rope leads.

Introductions were made and Henry asked. "What brings you to this village?"

Malcolm replied, "We have travelled from Dùn Èideann on our way to Jorvik seeking trade; and we want to see what is happening in different towns and villages and how we can learn from what we find. From here we wish to travel to Monkchester but are looking for a place to rest for the evening,"

"You are welcome to stay here. We have many rooms, and it is the least we can do for you," said Henry.

Malcolm turned to Ulf and Colban and said quietly, "We sleep on our own tonight." They acknowledged his quip and just smiled.

"What is your trade?" asked Alban.

"By trade I am a farmer, but I have over two hundred acres of land which I rent out to other farmers, some growing fruits, vegetables, barley, oats, wheat and rye. Some breed horses, some keep sheep for the meat and the wool, some keep cows for the meat and the leather. I have blacksmiths and swordsmiths, butchers and bakers and three vineyards."

"I do not believe we will need to complete our journey as it seems everything we are looking for is here," said an amazed Alban.

"You are most welcome to stay for a while," said Henry.

"We would like to stay for one night and then we will move on, but we thank you for your kindness and one day we will return," said Malcolm.

Henry called for two of the servants to take the horses to the stables and make sure they settled.

That evening they ate and drank well and talked late into the night, being quite open and now honest about where they actually lived and their ideas for the future. Isabella commented that the two villages were very similar in their outlook but a little different in the way they began as it was only a few years ago that Bishop Ecgred of Lindisfarne founded a church at

Jedworð which soon attracted many settlers, unlike a village that was founded by a mixed group of battle-weary drunken warriors having the courage to forego the evils of war and build on their own initiative.

"I admire what you have done," she said.

The couple were intrigued and amused by the events in Stoleware and asked if they could visit in the future and hopefully learn from each other. Malcolm said that he would like that. That night they slept soundly in exquisitely comfortable beds.

They woke to the delightful smell of bacon being cooked. They washed, dressed and came down to the kitchen.

"Come in and sit down," said Isabella. Henry and the children were already there enjoying a breakfast of eggs, bacon and brown bread. "Help yourself to a hot drink," she said. "There are mugs on the table."

"What is this?" asked Frothi.

"Nettle tea," was the reply. "Nettles boiled in water with sugar and honey."

"Sugar?" queried Alban.

"Yes," replied Henry. "In exchange for wool and leather, we receive sugar and spices from India. I send some of my trusted workers to the fayres in Frisia and they trade for me."

Isabella's expression was one of dismay and disbelief as her husband continued to drone on about how influential he was.

Donnan noticed Isabella's demeanour. but thought it wise to say nothing.

After a most enjoyable and filling breakfast, it was time to leave. Malcolm thanked the family for their most generous hospitality and bid them farewell.

"We will return." He looked at the two girls and said, "Look after those dogs."

"We will," they replied. A day's trip to Monkchester now lay ahead.

From the end of the seventh century, the area of Northumbria was recognised as a centre of excellence and learning in Europe, based chiefly on its Christian culture. It was greatly influenced by the Venerable Bede and contained many treasures in its numerous monasteries. There were many settlements along the River Tyne, established by the Romans in the early fifth century, and due to its diversities, it seemed like a good place to explore.

Up to now, the group had had no problem understanding the accents and dialects of those they met. however this would be quite a challenge for most of them. Fortunately, Frothi and Ulf had come across the accent around three years ago when they were part of a scouting expedition, spending some time visiting the area around Schleswig, and they had become somewhat familiar with the Angle dialect. The greeting was completely different to the wary and unnerving one they had received when they entered Dùn Èideann. It seemed that the locals here were particularly pleased to see the visitors. They were led down narrow stoned-cottage streets which opened out onto a quite magnificent manor house, surrounded by a wide moat. As they approached the house, a flamboyantly dressed gentleman emerged.

"Welcum, follaa wor," he said with extreme exuberance. "Wuh hev been watin fo' yee."

The group was mystified but did as they were asked. They were escorted to the back of the house where a jeering crowd of at least a hundred were standing in a circle. In the centre of the circle was a young woman tied to a stake. There were seven empty seats facing the woman and a very animated figure stood next to her pointing at her but addressing the crowd.

"This bord is a witch. She hez cured deed people. Wuh canna let hor live. She will brin a devil tuh wor village. Wuh will be corsed." He then turned to the group and said, "Yee canny an' just men must decide ha she shud die, that is why yas heor."

They decided to play along with this for the time being. Ulf stood and suddenly everyone went quiet. He was a formidable figure at the best of times and his large presence had an instantaneous effect on the crowd.

"Hvat hafþessir víf done?" he yelled, believing it appropriate to speak in his native tongue for now.

One of the crowd jumped up and shouted. "He is speaking to the woman in devil language. Satan is here."

The crowd now started shouting until the man in the middle raised his arms, signalling for calm. Eventually the crowd responded.

The man in the middle said, "He is speaking Norse," at which point another member of the crowd leapt up and shouted.

"He is calling on the Gods." Eventually, calm was again restored.

Frothi stood up and said, "He wants to know what the woman has done."

The man in the middle approached them and said, "My name is Edmund. I am Burgomaster. We have been waiting a few days for you to come and see if this woman is a witch. We were told that seven men would come and try the witch."

"What has she done?" asked Donnan. "She browt a blurk back tuh life. He had been deed fo' a day. She used hor sorcarry."

"Take me to the man," said Frothi. Frothi had a little knowledge of medicine having travelled and worked with Garmund for some time. Edmund led Frothi to a small cottage. They entered to find a man in his thirties swaying in front of a warm fire.

"This blurk is heor tuh lyeuk at yee," said Edmund.

"Ah wes deed," said the man.

Frothi noticed a very strong smell of alcohol and went round the back of the cottage to investigate. He found a very large cask capable of holding around a tun[12]. He tapped the cask and noticed a hollow sound.

He returned and said to Edmund. "This man was drunk." He looked round the cottage and found a jar of small eels and traces of ground almonds scattered by the jars. "The woman is not a witch," said Frothi. "She is a healer. She saved this man's life. He had drunk too much."

Edmund nodded his head and said, "Ah gan see neeo. The' want tuh born hor as a witch. Yee must tek her awa. Ah divvent want a death on me hands."

"We will," said Frothi.

They returned to the crowd. Edmund and Frothi went towards the woman. Edmund waited for calm and then said, "These men will tek hor yeut iv wor toon see nar na harm will befaal wor. The' will deal wi' hor."

Frothi turned to the woman and said, "Do not worry, you are safe with us, but I must keep your hands tied until we leave." The woman smiled and nodded but remained silent. He turned to Edmund and said, "We need a place to stay for the night."

---

[12] Cask containing 252 gallons

Edmund summoned one of his servants and asked them to follow him. They were led to a stable on the outskirts of the town and told that they could sleep there for the night, but they should keep watch in case any of the townsfolk wanted to kill the witch.

When they were alone, Frothi cut the ropes binding the woman's hands and said, "We will have to leave very early because we have been mistaken for those sent to try you as a witch." He told her that she was very lucky they arrived first because the outcome may well have been very different. "What is your name?" he asked.

"Meaghan," she replied nervously. Frothi again reminded her that she was safe and at that point she broke down more out of relief that her ordeal was over.

"Sleep," he said. "You can tell your story in the morning."

Malcolm and Ewan were the first to keep watch. The only person to sleep that night was Meaghan, being totally exhausted from the traumatic events of the day.

They rose just as the sun was rising and started their journey towards Mydilsburgh. Meaghan rode with Donnan, simply because there was no space for her on any of the other horses, but she insisted on riding alongside her liberator. Frothi and Donnan told her all about their home, how they happened to be passing Monkchester and their plans for the next few days. Meaghan told them that she had been treating the sick there for about a year but after some of the locals heard about someone being brought back from the dead, things changed dramatically. The man was simply in a drunken coma. She thought she was going to be burnt alive as a witch. Now she had hope but no plans for her future and seemed enthusiastic at the prospect of staying with the group, a request they could not ignore.

They had hoped to spend a little more productive time in Monkchester, however circumstances dictated that they should continue their journey. As they had not had the opportunity to eat that evening, food was a priority. After journeying for around ten miles, they found a safe and secluded place to rest. Malcolm and Ewan scouted round for food while Colban prepared a fire in the hope of cooking whatever prey could be found. It wasn't long before the hunters returned with a brace of rabbits. Malcom skinned them before spit-roasting them over the fire and to wash it down they had to make do with water from a nearby stream.

During breakfast, Meaghan told them all about her and her elder sister's upbringing in Bangor, North Wales. She explained that her parents, who were both royal physicians to Merfyn Frych, were aware of the fierce rivalry between the Welsh and the line of Cunedda and fearing for their safety, fled to Monkchester.

"My parents taught me all they knew about medicines and healing. One morning I woke to be told they had gone without saying anything. I was suddenly left alone in Monkchester. I was so sad. I was only nineteen and since they left, over five years ago, I have had to make a living for myself as a physician until I was accused of being a witch. I would be dead by now if it were not for you," she said with tears in her eyes.

She went up to Frothi and gave him a very long loving hug. He was quite overcome with this gesture and put his giant arms around her.

"Where is your sister now?" he asked.

"She travelled across the sea to the County of Flanders when I fled to Monkchester and that is the last I heard about her."

"We will find her one day," said Frothi.

"I do hope so," replied Meaghan.

Breakfast finished; it was time to move on.

"Have you visited Mydilsburgh before?" Malcolm asked Meaghan.

"Never," she replied. "Why do you ask?"

"Just in case," he replied with a smile on his face.

Chapter 11

Poetic Injustice

Northumbria and Mercia had become powerful kingdoms despite frequent raids by the Vikings. However, the persistence of such raids eventually led to the demise of the Angles and a change of rule towards Danelaw. There had been many disagreements between Hithin as Hersir and other Viking commanders, so he had enemies not only among those he had vanquished but also with his kinsmen.

Hithin was a very fair man and resented pointless slaughter. This philosophy had filtered down to some of the men in his charge but was resented by the staunch warmongers. Frothi and Ulf were of the same mind as Hithin.

The group decided to take a pleasant, scenic route down the east coast to Mydilsburgh. There was not much activity in Mydilsburgh when they arrived; no carnivals, fayres or witch trials, just a few monastic cells and a small farming community. It was intended as a timely stop before the last leg of the outward journey to Eoforwic.

They approached to find two farmers fighting with scythes. Even as they neared, the two men were totally oblivious to the presence of the group and continued with their fighting and arguing.

"That is my pig," said one.

"It is mine," said the other.

"No, it is mine," said the first.

This went on for a while and the group just sat watching until matters got a little more serious when one of the farmers swung his scythe and drew blood from the top of the arm of his opponent. The scythes were dropped and the two started punching each other. It was time to stop the fight.

Ulf dismounted, and managed to separate the two, holding them at arm's length. It seemed quite amusing watching the two trying to swing at each other and missing by a short distance as Ulf held them apart.

Malcolm now jumped down from his horse and went up to them. He looked at Ulf who was growing a little tired of the futile attempts of the two farmers to strike at the other, however they were not giving up. As the air boxing was in full swing, Malcolm gestured to Ulf to release the two, which he did with immense pleasure, only to see them crash headlong into each other with a disturbingly loud smack. Even the group grimaced at the sound of the clash of heads, feeling their pain. The two collapsed onto the ground rubbing their heads.

"Ouch," said one. "Why did you do that?"

"My arms were getting tired," replied Ulf.

Malcolm then asked what the argument was about.

"That is my pig," said one.

"No, it is mine," said the second.

"It is mine," repeated the first.

The second farmer was about to speak when Ulf shouted, "Stop!" Even the little piglet sat there quietly, totally bemused by the whole altercation.

Malcolm looked at one of the farmers and said, "Tell me why the pig is yours."

The farmer explained that while he was cutting down the grain, he saw the pig running towards him and thought it had escaped from his pig pen and as he went to chase it, he saw the other farmer running towards him, waving a scythe and shouting to him to catch the pig, so as it was on his land, it was his pig. The other farmer's story was quite similar apart from saying that the pig escaped from his land.

Malcolm thought for a moment and then said, "Alban, you are a farmer. What would you do?"

Alban came up to Malcolm and said, "We take the piglet to the first farm and if it goes to its mother then we know where it should be. Then we take it to the second farm and if it does not know where to go, we take it back to the first farm."

Malcolm then whispered to Alban, "What if it goes to a sow?"

"Then we ask Meaghan to use her powers," Alban replied with a smile on his face.

Fortunately, it all worked out well and the matter was quickly and agreeably resolved.

"Thank you," said the second farmer, "but what if this happens again?"

Alban explained how to make dyes using various plants, wood bark and woad and then mark an 'X' in one of the colours on the hide of the animals. "Please do not use the same colour and do not fight over who uses which colour. Now we must be on our way." Off they rode; exasperated and yet amused by the incident.

They passed through a few small villages, Orm, Steinn and Malti and were surprised at the number of Viking settlers who were already established there. At the last village they visited, they saw a young woman sitting and crying, nursing a young baby.

Frothi, noticing she was of Norse origin approached her and asked, "Hvat er matterrinn?"

She replied, "Minn kind er sick."

Frothi beckoned to Meaghan. She came to look at the child. Through translated conversations Frothi was having with the woman, Meaghan realised the child was suffering from typhoid.

"I cannot cure her," she said in a distraught manner.

"Tell the woman to give the child only cooled boiled water and cooked vegetables, nothing raw." Meaghan wanted to stay but Frothi told her there was nothing more she could do.

On they rode with Meaghan, often looking back until they were out of sight.

"I know what I have said will help but I fear for the child," she told Donnan. "No one else could have helped. You might have saved that child's life but without your help she would have died. We could have found another road to Mydilsburgh, but we came along the coast. You were sent to heal that child. We saved you so you could save the child," he replied. This made Meaghan feel a little better.

They camped for the night about five miles outside Mydilsburgh, and as expected, the trusty pair of hunters, Malcolm and Ewan, scouted for food while Colban prepared the fire. Coincidentally they found a stray pig. Making sure there was nobody around waving a scythe, the meal was prepared and thoroughly enjoyed. Meaghan and Frothi decided to take first watch, the couple talking and laughing until she decided to fall asleep in his arms. He wasn't complaining.

Eoforwic beckoned. There were a few scraps left over from the previous evening for breakfast, just enough to keep hunger at bay for a while. Eoforwic was another good day's journey, almost forty-five miles away, so after the morning toilet visit, more discreet than usual as now they had female company, a quick dip in the local stream was in order. Five days travelling had taken its toll on their unsavoury body odour. The men bathed first and as they dried off out of view of the stream, Meaghan too decided to have an invigorating dip in the cool water.

Frothi, surprisingly, stood guard to ensure that there were no prying eyes, with his back to the stream, well most of the time. Refreshed, they returned to the saddle and continued the journey.

By the eighth century Eoforwic was an industrious trading centre with established links to other areas of England, northern Francia, Frisia and the Rhineland. The Vikings were well aware of the city's potential having studied it closely from Roman times. The Romans themselves were protective of Eoforwic, having built the first wall around the city in 71AD, mainly to keep out the Scots and the Roman influence and style were plainly evident. The city was an important royal, ecclesiastical and learning centre under Northumbrian rule and because of its advancements, was clearly a haven for Viking spies already resident in the city.

The crumbling walls must have looked mightily impressive when they were first erected almost seven hundred and seventy years ago, but time and the elements had taken their toll. Dismounting, they led their horses inside the walls. Despite it being quite late in the day, the city was still active. There were narrow cobblestone streets, crammed with shops, some still open. The Starre Inne looked appealing. It was a good-sized tavern offering rooms and stables at the back of the premises.

Frothi and Malcolm went inside to talk to the innkeeper.

"Good afternoon," said a very friendly voice. "My name is Richard; how can I help?"

Malcolm replied, "There are seven men and one woman, and we would like a little food, rooms for the night and to stable our horses."

Richard nodded and said, "I have two rooms for the men and one for the woman, food for you and the horses. That will be five shillings."

Malcolm paid the innkeeper and went back to tell the others. Alban and Colban led the horses to the stables and then returned to meet up inside.

Sitting in a dark corner of the tavern was the solitary figure of a man looking thoughtfully out of the window.

"Who is that man?" asked Frothi.

"He is a writer," replied Richard. "He sits in the window most of the day watching. Then he walks to the fortress near the river and sits for hours writing. He does not speak, just watches and listens."

Frothi summoned Ulf across and asked him. "Do you know that man?"

Ulf stared for a short while and then said, "I do."

At that moment, the stranger turned and looked directly towards Ulf. A horrified expression appeared on his face.

He suddenly rose from his seat, walked towards Frothi and Ulf and said, "Kommitr mér."

The two followed the stranger out of the tavern, Ulf turned towards the others saying, "Wait here."

They followed the stranger through several winding streets to a quiet area.

"Why are you here?" he asked.

"We are travelling," replied Frothi. "Why are you here?"

"I am writing poems and stories about Eoforwic before I return home to Buskerud."

"Your days of fighting are finished?" asked Ulf.

"They are," was the reply. "I now believe Hithin was right and there should be no fighting. Please do not tell people who I am. I am here for my writing."

There was an element of insincerity in the stranger's voice but the two did not pry further. They all returned to the tavern leaving the stranger to sit back in the window as Frothi and Ulf went to see the others. When they were all in one room, Frothi explained what had happened.

"The man we saw was Ragnar Lodbrok. We fought with him, and he helped plot the Viking raids on this country with his brothers. I do not trust him. He tells me he is writing but I think he is looking round and making plans, then going back home to return with an army when he has found out the strength of the army and the weaknesses in Eoforwic."

"We must tell someone," Ewan said.

"If we are mistaken, then we could put Ragnar's life in danger," replied Ulf. "What can we do?"

"I will speak to him," said Frothi.

He went down to talk to Ragnar, but the window seat was empty. Richard was standing at the bar.

"Where did he go?" asked Frothi. "He went to his room, picked up his belongings and left in a hurry," replied Richard.

"Did you know him?"

"I thought I knew him well, but I was mistaken," said Frothi.

Quite a dilemma. The group discussed the way forward.

"If we tell people and are wrong, then we are the fiends and will be hunted. If we say nothing and he does return with an army, then the fate of this city will be on us," said Malcolm.

"There is an answer," interjected Meaghan. They looked at her in astonishment. "My parents saw the horrors of war and they had to tend to the dying and the wounded. I saw how armies were not ready for war. They were not strong, not enough weapons and no leader. Alban, Colban, when we eat, you need to speak so the innkeeper will hear. Talk about how you were not ready when the Vikings invaded Scotland and how you see that an army should always be ready if the Vikings attack again. Talk of how you lost your friends."

They sat in amazement listening to the wise words of a young woman, totally inexperienced, or so they thought, in the aspects of war.

"Why did you not think of that?" Colban asked Alban.

"For the same reason you did not think of it," replied Alban.

Over the evening meal, they made sure that Richard was listening, emphasising how essential it is to have a strong, well-trained army presence in the city. Now the onus was on someone else to determine the future of Eoforwic.

Chapter 12

The Grapes of Ralph

Everywhere the travellers went, the monks had been before and Gainford was no exception. It was at the centre of an estate supporting houses, barns, farmlands and an extensive forest dominated by a grand manor house, built near an Anglo-Saxon monastery established by Bishop Ecgred of Lindisfarne, after he had fortunately fled the havoc caused by the Vikings in 793 AD.

The village, with all its farmlands, freshwater streams, grazing areas and stables, seemed the ideal place to look for fresh horses. There were around twenty palfreys[13] roaming free in a field. Their horses had served them well for over half the journey but after the near three-hundred-and-fifty-mile trip round to Gainford, it was time to change them. They were still in fine form and had not been pushed, but eight days without a break had taken a toll on them.

The group rode up to a farm. Three men came out of a barn, each menacingly branding a pitchfork.

"What have you come for?" asked one of the men.

Malcolm explained that they had travelled from Hamm tun and had another two hundred miles to travel to return home to Dùn Èideann, so they needed fresh horses.

The three farmers did not seem too keen on helping until Donnan and Meaghan rode forward. Meaghan peered round Donnan's shoulder, dismounted and approached the men.

---

[13] Riding horses

"We have been riding for many days sir. No one in Eoforwic would sell us horses and I fear we will not be able to see my sister's wedding if we do not have fresh animals."

One of the men examined the horses. "These are strong destriers[14] and with a little rest they will be fine. I will trade with you," he said. He turned to discuss the matter with the other two.

Malcolm turned to Meaghan and said, "You can be very sly. We have much to learn from you." Meaghan smiled.

One of the men approached Malcolm and said, "You will need eight of our horses. These horses are rested, but yours will need care." He thought a while, talked to the other two then said, "We will trade for thirty pounds."

Before anyone else was able to speak, Meaghan jumped in saying, "Ten pounds. These are trusty war horses."

One of the men answered saying, "They need care. They have been ridden for eight days and will need new shoes. Twenty pounds."

Before agreeing, Meaghan asked, "Where are these horses from?"

"They are from Amiens in Francia," was the reply.

Malcolm came up to Meaghan and said to her, "Well your grace, have you agreed on a price?"

Meaghan played along with this, trying desperately not to laugh. The three men were taken back by such a formal address.

"If that pleases your grace then we will settle for twenty pounds," said one of the men and with that, the transaction was complete.

Meaghan turned to Malcolm and said, "You learn quickly."

"Is there a place we can rest for the night?" asked Malcolm.

"The monastery," replied one of the men. The horses were saddled, and Malcolm thanked the men for their kindness and bade them farewell.

The monastery was only a few minutes away. They approached the large wooden door and banged loudly using the black cast iron door knocker.

Eventually, a small spyhole opened, and a voice asked, "How can I help?"

Ewan, being closest to the door replied, "We are travelling to Carlisle and have been sent here, hoping you can give us food and shelter for the night."

---

[14] Knight's warhorse

The spyhole closed and there was no immediate response to their request. The group stood outside the doors wondering what to do. After a short while, they heard the sound of the door being unlocked. It creaked open to reveal a small, bald-headed monk.

"Welcome to Saint Cuthbert's," he said. "I am Brother Sebastian. Please come in." The heavy doors were opened, and the group led their horses inside.

The eight introduced themselves one by one as they entered, looking round the courtyard at the magnificent stone buildings. The monk called across to two other monks and asked them if they would take the horses to the stables.

"Follow me," said Brother Sebastian as he led them through the main hall, up and around numerous passages and to what seemed like the furthest point from the entrance. "Here are your cells," he said. "Brother Aidan is preparing food for us, and we will summon you when it is ready. If you wish to look round the monastery and the grounds, you will be most welcome."

There was still two hours light left, so after leaving some of their belongings in the cells, they wandered back down and eventually made their way outside where they found an extremely large aviary populated by a wide variety of colourful and exotic birds. Walking further out they noticed a sweet but earthy smell. Following their noses, they came across an impressive vineyard stretching well into the distance. They just stood and stared.

"Welcome," said a very friendly voice. "I am Brother Peter. This is Brother Ralph's vineyard. He planted the first vines over ten years ago and now you can see how it has flourished. He is here every day carefully tending to the vines and only when he says to pick the grapes will we do so."

"How many monks are here?" asked Colban.

"Around eighty," he replied, "so when Brother Ralph tells us the grapes are ready, then we all help to pick them and make the wine."

"What about the birds?" asked Meaghan.

"These birds are from all over the world, brought here by monks who knew of Saint Cuthbert's love of these small creatures. The sanctuary is home to over one thousand different birds. Brother Andrew looks after them and it can be awfully hard work at times. Brother John looks after the vegetable gardens on the other side of the aviary, so we are busy all day."

"Where do you trade the wine?" asked Ewan.

"When ready, we store the wine in clay amphorae. The lord of the manor collects the jars and takes them to market to sell for us," replied Brother Peter. "I should not tell you this," he continued, "but Brother Ralph does have a temper if we do not do as he tells us."

At that moment, Brother Sebastian approached. "Please follow me, the food is ready," he said. Fresh fish and vegetables and of course a goblet of wine. "All this is from Gainford," said Sebastian. We must wait for Brother Benedict. He is the abbot and will say gratiarum[15] actio.

They were about to start eating when a monk rushed up and sat next to Malcolm.

"Good wine, good wine," he said. "It is my good wine," and then he left.

"That was Brother Ralph. I did not tell you, but he is quite mad. Too much wine, I think. We have found grapes in very strange places on his body," said Sebastian.

The meal and the hospitality were excellent. With not having had too many visitors, the monks were engrossed by the tales of the traveller's escapades and kept asking questions. With eighty monks straining to listen, the atmosphere became a little claustrophobic, yet it was the most excitement and fun the monks had experienced in years.

Malcolm picked up on something Brother Peter had said earlier. "You said there were monks here from all over the world?" he asked.

"Yes," replied Brother Peter. "The monks here at Saint Cuthbert's have a good knowledge of towns and cities in many other countries from news brought by messengers who travel great distances. Pope Gregory has messengers sent out from Rome to all parts of the world and we hear much about what is happening. We know where to visit and where to seek trade and where not to go."

"Brothers," said Malcolm, "we have a long journey ahead of us in the morning and we need rest."

The abbot said, "Yes, we have talked far too long. I will get two of the brethren to take you to your cells."

---

[15] Thanksgiving

They bid everyone goodnight, which seemed to take forever, and then they were escorted to their rooms.

Malcolm called the group together and told them about what Brother Peter had said. "We need to visit here again. The monks know what is happening in other countries so we can learn from them, which places to visit and seek accord and which places are not safe." It was sneaky but very useful.

At that moment Brother Ralph ran past, totally naked shouting, "The grapes are mine," and with that, they all retired for the night.

Chapter 13

Ducks and Drake

The group were looking forward to the next leg of their journey to Carlisle. They remembered the events and people they had met on the first trip and were quite looking forward to meeting up with those who Gerik and Mungo had talked so much about and finding out what had changed in the city since their visit.

They were woken by the sound of the courtyard bell being rung. Sebastian knocked on each door to tell the guests it was time to rise. The sun itself had hardly risen, but as their hosts had been so benevolent, they reluctantly left the comfort of their beds, washed using the water in the basins in their cells, dressed, then were shown the lavatorium, which was thoughtfully and completely vacated for Meaghan's use and when they were all ready, they were escorted to the main hall.

All the brothers had assembled. Brother Benedict came up to Malcolm and said, "Your horses are saddled and ready but before you leave, I hope you will join us for morning prayer."

How could they refuse? After matins, which seemed to last an eternity, Benedict said, "We have prepared a little food for you to take with you and we wish you a safe journey to Carlisle. Please come back and visit us again."

"Thank you for your kindness and we will return," answered Malcolm. Benedict gave each of them a blessing as they said goodbye.

They mounted the horses and rode out through the main gates, turning to acknowledge the good wishes shouted by the monks. As they rode on, they heard the sound of the two wooden gates being closed and an iron bar being slid into position across the gates. The only sound they could hear now was that of the birds singing their morning songs.

"Is that the birds having morning prayer?" asked Alban.

Even though there were around another two hundred and seventy miles to travel, for the first time in many a day, it actually felt like they were going home. Carlisle was roughly seventy miles away and taking it steady, having been forced to set off at some ungodly hour, they expected to arrive there around the middle of the day.

As they rode along at a gentle pace, Donnan and Frothi, with a few interjections from the others, enlightened Meaghan with some of the less gruesome events of their first visit to Carlisle. She began to realise what sort of people she had become involved with and was starting to feel far more at ease but was still a little apprehensive about meeting the rest of the village population.

The journey passed without incident and before long they could see the outskirts of the city. Two guards were patrolling and ordered the travellers to stop as they approached.

"It is Bryce!" yelled Ulf, leaping from his horse.

"Has Mungo sent his spies to see if we are still being good?" asked Bryce as he embraced Ulf.

"How can we help?" he asked. Ulf summarised where they had been and what they had achieved.

Bryce was quite impressed with this. "I must tell everyone you are here. Come with me."

He led them to the council chambers where Drake would be working. Before they entered, Alban mentioned to Bryce about what Gerik and Mungo had jokingly said to Drake.

"Wait here and I will signal to you when to enter." Bryce engrossed Drake in conversation with their backs towards the door and at a convenient moment, signalled for the group to enter. Frothi sneaked up, Bryce trying desperately not to laugh.

"Shall we kill him now?" said Frothi in a loud voice.

Drake froze for a moment then, recognising the accent, turned round and with a great big smile on his face said, "Why do you still want to kill me?"

"Gerik and Mungo must have told you." Frothi smiled.

Drake was overjoyed to meet these new friends. The rest of the group followed; Drake welcomed all of them with a comradely hug.

"After a long journey I think you may need a little drink. Would you please take my friends to the main chambers and ask the servants to bring food and wine and I will fetch Thomas." Bryce nodded. Off scampered a thrilled Drake.

"Thomas! Thomas!" he shouted, "please come quickly!"

Without saying anything, Thomas got up from behind a large wooden desk and followed Drake. They burst into the chambers to see the six men standing in a line.

Thomas looked puzzled for a moment until Bryce said, "These are friends of Mungo's." That was enough. Thomas greeted them enthusiastically.

"Where are Mungo and Gerik and the others?" he asked.

"At home, resting," replied Malcolm. "You are most welcome. I did wonder what the matter was when Drake rushed in. I thought that something terrible had happened."

"It nearly did," said Drake, clenching his lower cheeks.

The servants had brought in a large plateful of bread and a bowlful of costard apples and the almost obligatory goblets of wine.

"Tell me everything," said an excited Thomas.

The group described all that had happened since their first visit to Carlisle.

Thomas turned to Meaghan and asked, "Have you, my dear, agreed to join this group in the hope of starting a new life?"

"I had not planned this, but they did stop me from being burnt alive as a witch."

Based on what had happened in the past, neither Thomas, Drake nor Bryce seemed unduly surprised.

"That does make sense," said a thoughtful Thomas.

"What has happened here?" asked Colban.

Drake explained how much had changed since Thomas became mayor. "The citizens are happy. There is no sign of trouble, and it is a growing city. News must have travelled around because we have so many new people here. Bryce and his men make sure we are all safe. We are so pleased that he decided to stay."

"How long will you be in the city?" asked Thomas.

"Tomorrow, we travel to Dub Glais and from there to Cathures and three days after that we should be back home," replied Malcolm.

"You are most welcome to stay," said Thomas. He summoned a servant and told him to find rooms for the night for the travellers. "You will have a meal with us later." Thomas told them. He then asked another of his servants to make sure that there would be enough food for another twenty guests. "Once my servant returns, he will take you to the rooms he has found and there you can rest, refresh and prepare for dinner. We will forever be grateful for what you did for us, and you will always be welcome here." A beautiful sentiment from grateful people.

The meal, consisting of cooked chicken, stuffed with herbs and various spices and a selection of vegetables was served in the banqueting hall. Parents and close friends of the six women taken to Stoleware plus Bryce and his five assistants were invited to attend and just like the interest and enthusiasm shown by the monks of Saint Cuthbert's at Gainford, the group was bombarded with questions. It had been another tiring, yet most enjoyable evening. Later, they were shown to their rooms at a nearby tavern and within minutes of lying down, fell asleep.

Having endured an early rise the previous morning, a late lie-in was more than welcome. Up, washed, dressed and breakfasted, it was time, once again, to move on. Thomas and Drake were waiting by the already saddled horses as the group emerged from the tavern.

Drake approached Malcolm and said, "Boyd gave me a choice when he was here. He told me that as I knew all about the city, it was wise for me to stay and help Thomas with council matters. Thomas is a good man and runs the city on his own. I am there if he needs help, but there are other good men on the council who have learnt from us, and I think I can now step down from my duties here and help you."

Thomas overheard his conversation and said to Drake. "You made the right choice last time and I think you are making the right choice now, but it is for Malcolm to decide."

Malcolm thought for a while. He realised how much the city had changed since Gerik, Boyd and the others first visited and saw how it had benefited from good leadership. Within a fairly short time, the city had changed from one with a despotic mayor to a place where people trusted the officials and were confident that they were safe.

Malcolm turned to Drake and said, "The choice must still be yours."

"I will get my horse and my work," he replied excitedly.

"Bring a horse for Meaghan!" shouted Thomas.

Malcolm was surprised to see Drake return with six leather satchels crammed with various sized scrolls and the wooden chest with the 'XIX' etched into the lid.

"What is this?" asked Malcolm.

"My work," replied Drake indifferently.

The peace in Carlisle was to remain for another thirty-six years until sadly, the Danes destroyed all the good work instigated by a few honest men.

Another seventy miles took them to the next planned stop at the village of Dub Glais. Meaghan told them that she remembered passing through the village first about four years before; having travelled with her family in a royal party on a visit to Cathures. She continued. "The King, his young son Rhodri and his late wife's father Cyngen ap Cadell travelled there many times. We were always asked to travel with them because the King was a very superstitious man who was worried about his wellbeing. I remember the people in the village had come from Francia and Frisia and nearby countries and the King always spoke to them. He was a very kind man."

They arrived at Dub Glais in the late afternoon. It was a small village, and as Meaghan had said, very friendly, with quite a diverse populace. They were welcomed by an elderly woman who looked at Meaghan as she rode passed.

"Angharad," said the woman.

"Stop!" Meaghan shouted. She jumped off her horse, went up to the woman and said, "You called me Angharad."

The woman replied, "I heard you had left for Cathures two days ago."

"Please tell me about this girl, Angharad. What does she look like?" said an agitated Meaghan. There was much excitement on Meaghan's face. The woman described the girl, her height, hair, eyes and how she spoke with a strange accent. "It is my sister!" she shouted. "We must go to Cathures."

"We will," said Donnan, "but we cannot travel further today. The horses need to rest. If this is your sister, we know where she lives. There is only one road to Cathures so we may pass her on our journey or find her in the city."

The others were wondering why Meaghan was so animated. Donnan explained what had happened. Meaghan was impatiently pacing up and down, muttering to herself. "It is Angharad," she kept repeating.

Malcolm approached Meaghan, put his hands on her shoulders and said, "It is only half a day's journey to Cathures, and we will leave early in the morning."

The elderly woman went up to Meaghan and said, "You are Angharad's sister. You look the same, sound the same and act the same. Your friends are telling you to rest tonight. They are wise in what they say. You can stay at my home and use your sister's room, but your friends will have to sleep in the barn. There is no other place for them." They all seemed more than satisfied with this arrangement.

Meaghan could not eat that night and hardly slept through excitement. She sat on Angharad's bed all night looking out of the window, occasionally nodding off for a short time and could not wait for the sun to rise. The other eight made do with the few scraps of food that still remained from what the monks had given them at Gainford.

Morning eventually came, very early morning in fact. Meaghan was at the barn kneeling next to Frothi as he woke up. The dawn chorus of bodily turbulence was something Meaghan was not used to, but under the circumstances she was prepared to overlook this. Frothi's eyes opened to a surprising and very pleasant sight. He smiled, put his arms up lovingly to hug Meaghan who looked at him, returned his smile and said loudly.

"Come on, wake up, it is time to leave."

'It would probably have been a little quieter to have a cock crow in your ear,' he thought.

The impromptu alarm worked. They all slowly woke, apologising to Meaghan for the involuntary sounds. At least she had the decency to vacate the barn as they performed their morning rituals. Just over thirty miles to Cathures and at a steady trot, the journey should take half a day to complete.

All Meaghan talked about, to whoever she was riding next to, was her sister; what they did when they were young, where they went, the good times, the bad times and much more. The eight seemed to know everything about Angharad before they had even met her.

The path took them along the River Clyde just north of Rutherglen. It was a cool, refreshing day. Hundreds of ducks were enjoying a refreshing paddle in the slow flowing river, minding their own business, content with their pleasant calming environment. Suddenly something spooked the ducks, and they took off, flapping their wings madly, heading directly for the group. The travellers were forced to take cover, quickly dismounting and seeking sanctuary next to the horses. For some reason, the ducks had taken a great dislike to Drake, quacking insanely as they dive-bombed towards him. Fearing for his life, he left the relative safety of his horse, running as fast as he could, being chased by the skein, occasionally looking over his shoulder. Just as suddenly as they had started the attack, the ducks veered off and returned to resume their relaxed paddling. The others caught up to an exhausted Drake.

Panting heavily, he mustered enough composure to say, "Even the ducks want to kill me. Why always me?"

"You do have that sort of face," replied a laughing Ewan.

"What were they?" asked Drake.

"Mallards," replied Ewan, "trying to catch a flying Scotsman."

With more than one set of fur ruffled, it was time to resume the journey. They had travelled about five miles when they saw a group of four riders coming towards them. Meaghan's heart began to race as she spotted a young woman with long blonde hair. They got closer.

"Angharad," she shouted, almost deafening Frothi. "Angharad," she shouted again even louder.

"Meaghan?" came the response. The gait changed from a trot to a quick gallop as the two riders neared. They dismounted and the women ran to each other embracing as they met, tears in their eyes. Everyone was sitting motionless, watching as the sisters just hugged each other for a long time, saying nothing. Even Ulf shed a little tear.

"Crying, are you?" asked Alban.

"No, I have a little dirt in my eye," he replied, whilst trying to disguise a sniffle.

It was an extremely emotional reunion as they had not seen each other for over five years — so many questions and answers. As the two sisters spoke, the others dismounted introducing themselves. One of the riders accompanying Angharad, explained that they were returning from Cathures having visited her brother.

"Her brother?" queried Malcolm. "Meaghan never said anything about a brother."

The rider explained. "When their parents were forced to flee, their daughters were not told the real reason. They were told it was because of a rivalry between Merfyn Frych and the descendants of the House of Cunedda, but that was not true. Their mother was asked to help one of the very sick court elders who was a trusted adviser to the King. The man did not recover from his sickness and the King was told by another adviser, who envied the closeness of their parents with the King, that their mother had poisoned him because he had threatened her husband.

"The King was enraged and swore vengeance on the parents. Only after they fled did the King find out the truth and the treacherous adviser was beheaded for his deviousness. The King sent out messengers to try and find the parents but failed. At the time they fled, their mother was pregnant but because of the worry and fear, their mother died in childbirth. Their father settled in Cathures where he brought up the child. He named him Crispin. Angharad somehow found out and travelled often to see them."

Frothi looked across at Meaghan to see her sobbing her heart out. Angharad was sitting opposite Meaghan holding her hands as she told her sister the same story. Frothi walked across to sit with Meaghan and put his arm round her shoulders. She turned to him and rested her head on his chest.

After a long silence, Meaghan eventually said, "I have a baby brother."

"And a father," added Frothi.

Meaghan now had to sort out a dilemma. She had the choice of returning to Dub Glais with Angharad, the sister she had not seen in five years, continuing to Cathures to be with her father and brother she had never met, or continue going north for about another one hundred and forty miles with the man who had saved her life.

"Walk with me," Meaghan said to her sister. "What should I do?" she asked.

Angharad replied, "If it were not for Frothi, you would not be here. You know where you can find me, and I visit our father and brother every two months and stay with them for one or two days. If you are with Frothi, then it is no more than a two days' journey for you, so we can all be together every two months. Next time we meet, and we will meet again, I can travel back with you to your home. The next part of your journey will take you to Cathures so you can see your father and brother. I will tell you where to find them. I see the way you look at Frothi and how he looks at you. There is both love and joy in your faces. I know you will be happy with him."

Meaghan thought for a few moments and then asked, "Is that what you would like me to do?"

"You will have a sister, a father and a brother and someone who will keep you safe," replied Angharad. Meaghan looked back towards Frothi. He was looking at her. She looked at her sister, smiled and then ran towards Frothi putting her arms round his neck.

"I have to thank you for my life, but I need to be with my sister." Frothi was rendered absolutely distraught by her decision. "I will come and see you," she said.

"I do not think you will," replied Frothi.

He stood up, turned away from her and walked back to the others. Meaghan called his name, but he ignored her and carried on walking. Angharad came up to Meaghan and asked, "What have you done?"

"You left me once and I do not want that to happen again," said Meaghan. She held on tight to her sister, crying.

Frothi approached the others and said, "It is time to move on." They could all see Frothi's sadness, so nobody asked about Meaghan. They mounted their horses and after subdued farewells continued their journey.

They carried on following the River Clyde northwards towards Cathures. In the distance they could hear an eerie squawking. Approaching cautiously, they could see a great commotion in the river. Many hundreds of ducks had now gathered. Drake's face turned white.

"Hide me," he said, visibly shaking.

Chapter 14

The Birds and the Bees

Despite the unplanned delay, they reached their destination by the middle of the day.

From humble beginnings, Cathures, founded in the sixth century by the Christian missionary Saint Mungo, developed into quite an industrious city whilst still maintaining its religious heritage. The Clyde, running through Cathures, had an abundance of salmon and herring and this commodity attracted trade from all over Europe.

There was much evidence of Roman influence in the construction of the outposts, some of which were occasionally manned, however the chance of being invaded by Caledonians was, after all these years, remarkably slim.

As luck would have it, the outpost they approached was manned, however the two guards on duty had clearly been a little over enthusiastic imbibing in a most enjoyable, yet quite intoxicating refreshment and probably did not even notice as the eight-rode past. There was not much chance of getting any sense whatsoever from the two guards.

Ewan turned to Alban and said, "I remember those days." Alban smiled and nodded.

Up to now, the group had not really managed to establish any firm trade contacts, just potential outlets and vague promises. However, their knowledge of the geography of at least some of the north of England had certainly improved. First impressions of the city were favourable. A friendly atmosphere and the vast variety of businesses in extremely pleasant surroundings, were more than they could wish for. They were hoping for a hassle-free visit.

Riding down the main street, it was very difficult to overlook the fact that the dwellings and businesses were all daubed in either a dark blue limewash across the entrances or a very bright red limewash. Even the clothing reflected this colouring. There was an obvious yet convivial rivalry.

One of the citizens, covered in the red limewash, walked in front of the group's horses, held his hands up for them to stop and said, "Wha urr ye fur?" They all looked puzzled. "Urr ye blue or rid?" The second question did not really clarify anything.

"I do not know what you want," said Malcolm. The man looked at them with an expression of despair, shook his head and walked off. A little further along, a man daubed with a blue dye approached them to ask the same questions, getting the same responses.

"What is this?" wondered Ulf. No one could give an answer.

Men, women and children started walking towards the outskirts of the city to a nearby field, roughly one hundred metres in width and length. The red crowd gathered on one side of the field and the blues the opposite side; the two ends being left empty. The group remained in the saddle to get a better view but stayed back a little, wondering if they were safe and also what was about to happen. Then there was absolute silence. Two teams of around fifty people each then rode onto the field to a massive cheer from the crowd.

Each player had a one metre-long wooden stick with a wedge shape on one end. In the middle of the field stood a solitary figure holding a spherical wooden object. He looked to his left, then to his right, threw the object high into the air then ran like hell to get off the field. At that moment, the opposing sides set off at full gallop towards each other. There was absolute chaos as the two sides met. Riders falling off their horses, sticks flying into the air and numerous shouts of pain. Out of the pandemonium appeared a lone blue rider galloping furiously into the opponent's half, hitting the wooden sphere along the ground with his stick, giving it a massive whack and chasing after it. One final hit and the object flew well out of sight. The blue crowd let out a joyous cheer. Those players still on horseback dismounted and congratulations and commiserations were bestowed as appropriate. The crowd dispersed, returning to the city.

The eight looked at each other, wondering what all the fuss was about for such a short event.

"A' dane till neist year," said one of the crowd as he passed by the group. "That wis guid. Better than lest year.

"Ah dae nae think a'body wis murdurred," said another. And that really inspired the travellers with confidence about staying in the area.

As the crowds filed past, one of the locals daubed in blue, looked up at them and said, "Urr ye wanting tae bade or juist passing thro'."

"We would like a room for the night," replied Donnan.

"Follow me," said the stranger. They dismounted and followed their guide to a small house. "Uou kin a' kip 'ere th' nicht. A'm aff tae th' tavern. Piut yer horses in th' field ower thare. Th' y wull be braw. Thare is plenty o' fairn in th' pot," and with that, the stranger left them.

There was a small, enclosed field next to the dwelling with plenty of roughage, straw and hay strewn around. The horses were led to the field, looking quite excited due to the foods scattered around. The men had the run of the house for the night as all the supporters had stopped off at the many taverns lining the main street to the extent that the area around the centre was totally deserted; almost a ghost town. Accepting the hospitality, they helped themselves to the food and enjoyed a good night's sleep.

That morning all was still. Outside they saw bodies lying in various contorted positions all over the place. One particular individual daubed in red, was leaning against a tree at a very precarious angle, muttering to himself, "I cannot move."

Frothi went up to him and gently helped him to the vertical position. Noticing his lack of indigenous accent, Frothi said, "You are not from here."

"I am not," replied the man. "I am from Wales." The man quickly came to his senses and said, "I do not remember where I left my son."

"We will help you find him," said Frothi. "Tell us what he is like."

"His name is Crispin. He is five years old, nearly four feet tall and has blond hair."

Frothi thought for a moment then asked the man, "Is Crispin your only child?"

"He is," was the reply. Frothi's heart sunk for the second time in a short while.

Malcolm came up to Frothi and said, "Do you honestly want to find them?"

"I do not know," he replied.

"Let us help this man find his son then."

Frothi agreed.

It was not long before the boy returned.

"Where have you been?" asked his father.

"Feeding the ducks while you were sleeping on that tree," he replied.

"Not more ducks," said Drake. "We are leaving now."

Malcolm asked Crispin's father what happened the previous day. He explained that, once a year, the people who settled here from other countries, daubed themselves in a red limewash and those from Scotland, daubed themselves blue and the aim was to hit the wood over their opponent's line. The side that lost has to buy the ale all night for the side that won.

"As you see, we can find ourselves sleeping in very odd places, not knowing how we got here. They have won for the last four years but this year nobody was killed. On a bad year, we may have to bury eight people."

"Why do you do this?" asked Malcolm.

"Some of the men were in the Scottish cavalry and helped force the English out of Cathures, so every year we celebrate this. One year we will win. I think there are more of them than there are of us. Next year we will have to cheat."

With the matter now clarified, the eight waited for the owner of the house to return and by the middle of the morning a familiar blue figure staggered towards them.

Reaching his home, he stopped and promptly collapsed onto his backside saying, "We won. Ah hud a bawherr dram lest nicht."

"We know," replied Alban.

"Dae ye lik' mah wee hoose. A'm needin' tae staun up noo," he said. Alban helped him to his feet. "Whit urr ye doiing in Cathures," the man asked.

"On our way to Striveling," replied Alban.

"Ye dae nae wantae gang thare," said the man.

"We are travelling home and will pass through there," said Alban.

"Thare is ainlie a fayre thare. Na fin," he replied. They helped the man inside, sat him down, where he promptly fell asleep, and then left him in peace.

There still wasn't much sign of life as they collected their horses and made their way out of the city. Malcolm had left five shillings which, based on previous stopovers, he thought was adequate.

The next twenty-odd miles to Striveling were covered in half a day. The prospect of a fayre seemed promising and after all these miles, they hoped it would finally produce something tangible instead of a visitor's guide to a fourteen-day round trip.

Having Drake in the party, particularly with his awareness of Roman developments, methods and culture would be of great benefit. At times he was like a mobile encyclopaedia, advising the group on what they should expect to find at the different places visited. However, impromptu games were a surprise to him too.

The River Forth meanders its way to Striveling from the Septentrionalis Oceanus, or Northern Ocean making it an ideal site for tradesmen from the east, particularly Frisia; while unfortunately being equally susceptible to raiding parties from Denmark, a fact known all too well by Frothi and Ulf.

They arrived in the market town amid Drake's informative lectures on both traditional Roman settlements, games and races in this area from AD70 and on why they built Hadrian's Wall fifty years later and the Antonine Wall some seventy years later.

"What did they do in the twenty years between building the two walls?" asked Ewan with a sarcastic smile on his face. "Do you know any Romans? Where did the Romans go when they finished building the walls? Is that a Roman wall," continued Ewan as they passed a wall with no more than twenty small stones in it.

Drake ignored Ewan's facetious questions and continued with the history lessons until he eventually realised that nobody was paying any attention and so he decided to keep quiet.

After a couple of minutes silence, Ewan said, "Tell us more. I was almost asleep."

Drake decided it was time to get his own back. "The Romans brewed a good strong ale here in Striveling and there should still be some here." That was it. He suddenly captured their attention.

"Will there?" asked Donnan. "Where?"

"If I remember from the maps, it was in the middle of one of these fields. They dug a deep hole in the middle of the field and threw in peat, barley, apples, wild nettles and wheat bread then mixed it with some cold stream water, covered it with dry earth then left it for many months. When the ale was ready, they put long hollow reeds, a little higher than those," pointing to some by the side of the path, "into the earth and drew the ale. They sent this ale all across the Roman Empire, even to the Emperors Hadrian and Antoninus."

"Where is the field?" asked Ewan excitedly.

"It is a field with the long reeds growing by the side of it. That one," replied Drake, pointing to his right.

"Tell us what to do?" said an impatient Ewan.

Drake told them, "You must cut the reed, take it to the middle of the field and put it into the earth as deep as it will go, then draw the ale up through the reed."

Ewan, Donnan and Colban could not wait to sample the ale. They quickly dismounted, hacked down a few reeds then ran into the centre of the field, forcing the reeds into the soft earth, sitting down and drawing, as hard as they could, on the hollow reeds.

Malcolm turned to Drake and said, "You can be very evil at times."

"That may be so, but it is amusing," replied Drake.

"It is," said Malcolm, "but I would not like to be you when they return."

The three eventually returned disheartened and quite out of breath. "There was no ale," said a dejected Donnan.

"That is very odd. I think the Romans must have drunk it all in those twenty years between building the two walls," replied Drake.

Ewan, knowing he had been deservedly duped, looked at Drake and said, "I will be watching you."

As they approached, the market was in full swing. There were more than just the locals present. Judging by the clothing there were visitors and traders from many different countries offering a great variety of wares and at the numerous sideshows, jugglers, acrobats and musicians; were keeping both adults and children entertained. Ulf volunteered to look after the horses, allowing the others the opportunity to have a good look round at the goods on offer.

"Did you know," began Drake, "that the first Roman chariot races were over one thousand five hundred years ago, and the first Roman gladiator games were held over one thousand years ago when Decimus Junius Brutus Scaeva had six gladiators fight to the death and the Circus Maximus was started by Lucius Tarquinius Priscus over three hundred years ago?"

"How do you know all this?" asked Malcolm.

"I hear people talking and I remember what I have heard," replied Drake.

There were handicrafts, perfumes, wood carvings, furs, fruits, spices, flour and wines from abroad and in exchange local home-grown fish and cattle were offered. They noticed a familiar figure by a large aviary.

"Brother Andrew," said Malcolm, "Why are you here?"

"Hail my good fellows. I travel here each year to see new birds I can put in my aviary at the monastery. What is the purpose of your visit?" he asked.

"We are wanting to see what wares are on offer and we seek trade with other countries," said Malcolm.

"Where is your home?" asked Brother Andrew.

Not wanting to lie to a man of God, but at the same time disguise the truth from potential visitors, Malcolm replied, "From Gainford, we travelled to Carlisle but heard of the fayre in Striveling, so we rode on to see what was here before returning home."

Fortunately, this answer satisfied Brother Andrew, but Malcolm had to remember to tell the others about his slight deception so they would all be keeping to the same story.

As the group circulated round the stalls, they could not help noticing an extremely sweet florally smell. Following their noses, they found a stall stacked with many earthenware pots containing honey. As Malcolm and Colban approached the stallholder, the others veered off to visit other areas. Colban approached the middle-aged, almost six-foot, slightly stocky stallholder asking if he could sample the product.

"Divine," he said. "I have tasted honey before, but never anything as sweet as this. Where is this made?" he asked.

"In Dunkeld," was the reply.

"That is not far from where we… will be passing on our way home to the Isle of Skye," interrupted Malcolm, giving Colban a rather stern look.

"We have many hives in Dunkeld and two here with us to show how to keep bees and collect the honey. Are you trading?"

"We are here with the monks from Gainford, wishing to trade wine."

"I have heard about the wine from Saint Cuthbert's monastery and have been told it is very satisfying; but you are not monks," said the stallholder.

"No but we are here to help. Brother Andrew is looking at the birds and will be with us soon."

"I have spoken to Brother Andrew before, but I did not know they were selling their wine. I hope Brother Ralph is not here. I believe he is quite mad."

By now, Malcolm was digging himself deeper into the proverbial and trying desperately to think of a way to claw himself out.

"I will see if Brother Andrew is still looking at the birds," said Malcolm, as he quickly exited.

"Why did you say that?" Colban asked Malcolm.

"I just opened my mouth, and the words came out," he replied.

"We should find Brother Andrew and think of how we can make good on what we told the stallholder."

"We?" asked Colban. "I believe you were the one who talked to the stallholder, and you were the one who wanted to trade wine that is not ours to trade."

"I thought we were together," said Malcolm.

"We are. We will be behind you when you tell the stallholder you have no wine to trade," Colban replied.

Malcolm's expression of non-gratitude was clearly evident in his face.

The two returned to the aviaries, leaving the rest of the group to wander round.

"Please take care with what you say. Brother Ralph's wine is not for trade," Colban said to the others as they parted, smirking at Malcolm.

They found an excited Brother Andrew. "Look," he said to them. "It is the honey buzzard from Persia. and see that red bird and the purple one and over there that small green bird with blue below its beak. I have not seen those before. I must have them. Where is the man who has these birds? I must find him." Off he scampered, asking everyone in sight if they knew the whereabouts of the bird keeper.

One of the nearby stalls was displaying an assortment of oils, ranging from mined oils to walnut and hazelnut oil and plant oils. The stallholder was demonstrating the versatility of the various oils from medicinal purposes to how to make smoke bombs; the latter drawing much attention. He mixed a little light oil with some tinder and a handful of slightly damp grass. This was placed in a coconut which had small holes punctured at the top and the bottom. The fire was lit by striking a piece of iron on a small chunk of flint.

Unfortunately, and completely unintentionally, there was quite a large cloud of smoke generated and the slight breeze blew the smoke towards the two beehives around, fifty metres away. Bees tend to get a little agitated when there is smoke around and to make matters worse, the aviculturist, who was totally unaware of the smoke display, overreacted to the smell of the smoke, and started shouting, "Fire." He rushed back to the aviaries to make sure his rare birds were unharmed.

In his haste, on reaching the cages, he was distracted by Brother Andrew shouting, "Where is the bird keeper?" He tripped, fell against the cage door bolt, and accidentally managed to unlock it whereupon the cage door flew open, and the birds made extremely fast progress towards the panicking bees.

It was only a matter of a few short minutes before total destruction replaced well-presented displays. People were shouting, running in all directions, hiding or doing anything they could to keep away from the swarming bees which were attempting to avoid the hungry birds snacking on any of the bees they caught, which in turn were being pursued by the only person heading towards the chaos, Brother Andrew. He was running, waving his large silk net madly around in the air trying desperately to snare one of the rare birds to add to his collection and yelling a few choice words which do not normally appear in a monk's vocabulary.

Meanwhile, during the commotion, the group returned to meet up with Ulf. They stood for a while, saying nothing, but just watching people darting in all directions in an attempt to avoid confrontation with anything harmful. As the smoke started to clear, they noticed a familiar figure. Sitting on a large stone, having suffered one or two bee stings, was a smiling Brother Andrew, staring into his net, more than satisfied at catching the Persian honey buzzard. He stood, looked around and then surreptitiously made his way to the stables, emerging after a few minutes, on horseback with his prize possession, safely secured in the net. In three to four days' time, he would be proudly displaying the bird in his prized collection.

"I do not think it wise to find the beekeeper and ask him about keeping bees. We should leave that till we reach Dunkeld," said Colban.

"At least we did not have to trade Brother's Ralph's wine," replied Malcolm.

They thought it probably improvident to remain in the area for the evening for a number of reasons, and they agreed to look for a safe, secluded area where a little hunting might well be in order; to which Drake added, "Anywhere away from ducks, bees, smoke and monks."

Chapter 15

The Honey Trap

Next stop Dunkeld. After the morning rituals and having eaten nothing for breakfast, they rode on hoping to find some friendly farmer along the route who might offer them a little light sustenance.

It was Drake's turn again to enlighten the group as to the historical significance of Dunkeld. "There is a fort here built for Caustantin by the Picts on King's Seat and a Culdee monastery which I do not think has any monks who like birds, grapes or wine."

"It would be nice to have a quiet stay," remarked Colban.

They neared the monastery in the late afternoon, stopping by the entrance to admire a massive stone slab, twelve feet high and almost six feet in perimeter. It was beautifully carved, depicting twelve figures, one beheaded, beasts and some very intricate patterns. This prominent feature has been completely overlooked by the first group who visited the monastery, their interest lying totally in a little sustenance.

Malcolm turned to Drake and asked, "What is this?"

Drake replied, "It is the Apostles Stone, but I do not know if it is meant to show the first apostles."

At the monastery door, they saw a Celtic hand bell. The group stopped, looked at each other, patiently waiting for someone to offer to ring the bell for attention. After a few moments, Drake reluctantly volunteered.

The monastery doors slowly opened and out popped a familiar figure.

He looked directly at Malcolm and said, "I see you were not stung by any of the bees. You did not expect to see me. Are you here for the honey?" asked the monk.

"I did not know you were a monk," Malcolm answered.

The monk continued, "I am Brother Martin. I do not wear a habit at the fayres as the bees can fly into places I do not want them to fly. I did not talk to Brother Andrew after the bees escaped and I do hope he returned safely to Saint Cuthbert's. I saw him ride away from the fayre with a smile on his face. I wished to speak to him about the wine, but I am sure I will see him again. Please enter. Do not worry, the bees are quite safe. There is no smoke here," he said smiling.

Brother Martin invited the men in and asked fellow monks to take the horses to the stables.

"May I offer you a little food?" he asked.

"We have not eaten since we left the fayre and a little food would be most welcome," replied Malcolm.

"Once you have eaten, I will show you round the grounds. There are two women here who come to collect the honey we gather. You may see them as you walk round," said the monk.

After a little bread and water, Brother Martin took them first to the hives.

"These hives are made from beechwood, cut from our own trees. They are one and a half feet wide and three feet long. We cover them with a mixture of ash and cow dung so they will not rot. There are small holes bored into them so that the wind will keep them dry and cool. If you wish to take a hive, we will gently cover it in skins to protect both the hive and the bees. It is better that you take them at night and then put them in place by first light."

"Where are the bees from the fayre?" asked Donnan.

"They returned here to their home, aside from the ones eaten by the birds Brother Andrew sought." He went to explain how to harvest the honey from the hives and how to store it. "Look round," he said, "then when you are ready, I will come back."

The group split up and started to wander around the extensive grounds. After a few minutes, Alban came rushing back, his face white as if he had seen a ghost.

"We must leave," he said to Malcolm.

"What is the matter?" Malcolm asked.

"Do you remember in Carlisle I was trapped in a bakery by two women?"

"Mungo told me that you ran out of the bakery with your tunic on fire?" replied Malcolm laughing.

"They are here. The women are here," said Alban.

"They have found you," said Malcolm.

"You must hide me," pleaded Alban.

"Why?" continued Malcolm.

"They want my body," said Alban.

"Two women at the same time? I would," replied Malcolm.

"But they are old and their bosoms sag to their knees," said a despondent Alban.

"They are women who have seen life and know what to do with a man," added Ewan.

"I would prefer having a bee sting on my spindle than to place it into a hag's honeypot," came the reply.

"I do believe in time to come, you will look back on this day and rue not wanting to enjoy the delights of two fair-aged women together," said Malcolm who was enjoying ribbing Alban.

"When that day comes, I pledge that I will devour whatever you put in front of me," replied Alban.

"I hold you to that pledge," said Malcolm.

There was plenty to keep the group occupied as they wandered round the grounds. The most novel feature they found was a maze with hedges that were about ten feet high. At the entrance was a map carved into a stone of how to reach the centre.

"There are eight of us, so I think it will be fair if we were to go in twos."

This was about the only time the group was in total agreement, simultaneously shouting that they each wanted to be paired with Drake. Drake was quite embarrassed at being so popular all of a sudden. He then offered a solution.

"I think we should draw lots. We take twenty leaves from the hedge. Lay them on the ground, two piles with four leaves, two with three, two with two and two piles with one leaf. Malcolm, Colban, Frothi and Ewan take a pile, Ulf, Alban, Donnan and me will not watch and then we take one of the piles. When we have all drawn, we see who has the same number of leaves and those two will be together." No one could argue with the fairness of the draw. Airing his knowledge, he continued. "The first maze was made in Egypt in the fifth century B.C."

"Did the Egyptians take twenty years to build that?" asked Ewan sarcastically. Drake just smiled with a suitably derisory expression.

Malcolm was drawn with Alban, Colban with Donnan, Frothi with Ulf and Ewan with Drake, who now outlined the rules.

"Take a look at the map, then we will go in, but not together. After the first two enter, count to ten and then the next two may enter."

As Malcolm and Alban entered the maze, Brother Martin approached the others.

"Tell me the truth," he said, "Where are you from? I know you are not from the Isle of Skye."

The remaining six looked at each other, reluctant to speak first. They all looked at Drake, hoping he would help them out of the predicament and Drake's offering was to say to Ewan.

"It is time we began," and off they went into the maze.

That left two Vikings and two Scotsman. Frothi was next to respond saying, "We are of Denmark and English good not," slyly winking at a nodding Ulf and at that point they too entered the maze.

That left just Colban and Donnan. "I do not know what you are saying," said an innocent looking Colban.

Brother Martin replied, "Skye is not a large island and I know the people who live there. Do not worry, I will not say a word."

Colban looked at Donnan; and Colban began to relate the story of how the group was formed.

"Come, tell me more as we walk through the maze. I know secret passages where we will not be seen," said the monk.

Off they went, explaining to Brother Martin how they all met, what the group and the other group travelling abroad were doing and what they hoped to achieve.

"I would like to help," he said.

Colban and Donnan were somewhat surprised by this response. "I feel that I have been doing what needed to be done for many years. It is now time I moved on and if I can be of spiritual help, I would like you to take me with you."

"Will your spiritual guidance help us find the middle of the maze?" asked Donnan.

"That and my lead will," replied the monk.

"We will speak to the others later," said Colban.

Brother Martin smiled and said "I thank you. God will guide you."

"If he is on your side, then I do not believe we have a choice," replied Donnan.

"Follow me but if we see any of the others I will hide until they have passed," said the monk.

With the exception of Drake and Ewan, who under Drake's expert guidance and an excellent memory, found their way quite easily to the centre of the maze, the others seemed more than a little lost, retracing their steps many times and bumping into others going in the opposite direction. Colban and Donnan, with divine guidance, were second to arrive, having parted company with Brother Martin just prior to their arrival. They told Drake and Ewan about the monk's request and the two seemed quite in favour of it. As they were talking, Ulf's head appeared over a hedge.

"I can see the centre," he said to Frothi.

"Get off my shoulders then," came the reply. It was not too long before they joined the others, so, then the only two who were missing were Malcolm and Alban.

They heard two unfamiliar women's voices not far away.

"Quiet, it could be the women that Alban wishes to meet," said Ewan.

"I do not think it fair for us to call to the women," he continued.

"Fair for the women or fair for Alban?" asked Colban.

Although nothing irreverent was being planned, Drake's suggestion of inadvertently guiding the women to the centre was not dismissed.

"Do you think you could find them?" asked Ewan.

"Are you asking if I think I can find them or asking if I am going to find them?" asked Drake laughingly.

"If you were finding your way back to the start and just happened to have sight of the women, then no one would be any the wiser," said Ewan.

Drake replied, "If I lose my way back to the start and find myself here with the two lost women just as Malcolm and Alban find themselves here, then I am not to blame."

"You are wise, yet frighteningly sly," said Ewan and with that, off went Drake in his bid to find the two women and make sure neither he nor the women were seen until the appropriate time at the appropriate place by the appropriate people.

It was not long before Drake found the two women and having seen them face to face completely understood Alban's reluctance to meet up with them again.

"Are you lost?" he asked innocently.

"That we are," croaked one of the women.

"Follow me, I will lead you to the centre of the maze," he replied.

Drake led and the two women followed, muttering to each other, out of Drake's earshot about certain parts of his anatomy and what they would like to do. Drake had an uneasy feeling at the tone of the women's unnerving giggling and began to sympathise even more with Alban but not to the extent of denying Alban this opportunity.

As they turned the penultimate hedge, Drake saw Malcolm and Alban find their way to the centre amid the cheers of the others and thought this a suitable time to lead in the women. Drake's pace quickened to try not to make the deception too obvious, and before anyone had a chance to say anything, the two women entered. Their eyes lit up at seeing Alban.

"It is the man from the bakery. Quick Mabel!" yelled Agnes.

"I am coming Agnes."

Alban was horrified. The two women discarded their tunics shouting, "Take me!"

There was only one opening to and from the centre of the maze, however in his eagerness and desperation to flee, Alban turned and managed to scramble his way through a once beautifully spruced hedge, now silhouetting a panic-stricken figure, closely followed by two naked women still shouting, "Come here, take me."

Malcolm turned to Drake and asked, "Do you have anything to do with this?"

Drake replied, "I am as innocent as the day I was born."

"If that be so, then I think we should make our way back to the entrance. Lead on Drake," said Malcolm.

They did not see Alban or the two women as they made their way out of the maze but did hear a few screams of anguish and the odd cry of, "Help!"

With Drake's expert guidance, the remaining members of the group reached the entrance to the maze in a very short time, still hearing in the distance the vain cries for help.

They met a puzzled looking Brother Martin at the entrance who asked, "Has one of you lost his way?"

"Not just in the maze," replied Malcolm, "but with guidance from Saint Agnes and Saint Mabel, I am sure he will join us as soon as he has found both spiritual and physical relief."

"I will pray for him," said the monk, who now understood Alban's predicament.

"I am sure that will help him," said Ewan.

The light was fading, and Brother Martin suggested that they join him for the evening meal, an offer which they were not going to refuse. He sat with them as they enjoyed a warm chicken stew. The monk was persistent in his questioning about where the group lived and almost pleaded with Malcolm to take him with them.

"I will bring one of the hives with me, but we must leave while it is dark, and the bees are resting."

"What will you say to the other monks?" asked Malcolm.

"I will tell them that I am helping you put one of the hives in place and will return when my work is finished. I am not telling them an untruth, but it may take time to finish my work with you," he replied.

"Who will care for the bees when you are away?" asked Colban.

"Brother James helps me, and he will be quite happy to carry on my work," replied the monk.

"We will help you," said Malcolm.

"Please tell the abbot what you wish to do."

"I will," said Brother Martin. Off he went and soon returned saying he had the abbot's blessing for a safe journey.

"We must get one of the hives and make our way," said Brother Martin. "Your horses will be ready when we return from the hives. I have the skins to cover the hive and a cart to carry it to their new home. What about your friend Alban?"

"I am sure he will find his way," replied Malcolm.

They got up from the table and thanked the other monks for their kindness and generosity. Colban and Ewan went to collect the horses but left Alban's horse in the stable just in case he managed to evade being desecrated and make his way to freedom while Donnan and Ulf went with Brother Martin to collect the cart and then a hive. They were careful not to disturb the unpredictable bees.

Darkness was drawing in. Fortunately, Brother Martin had travelled the road a number of times and under a full bright moon guided the group north on the final leg of their journey. The monk rode in the cart alongside Colban. He was anxious, apprehensive and yet pleasantly intrigued as to what lay ahead. Colban tried to put his mind at ease, describing each one of the groups as best he could.

"We have two nuns that Gillis and Frothi brought back after their monastery on Iona was destroyed, Sister Mildrith and Sister Eangyth."

"Oh!" said a surprised Brother Martin, turning a little red in the face. "Does one of them play a cithara?" he asked.

"I believe Sister Mildrith does," replied Colban.

"Oh!" repeated Brother Martin, now with a more intense colour in his cheeks. Colban wisely decided to say no more and wait for events to unfold when they returned home.

Brother Martin who had a good sense of humour, related numerous tales of totally inappropriate monasterial activities but refused to divulge whether or not he was involved in the more colourful episodes. However, from his detailed recollections, an obvious conclusion could be drawn.

In the distance, they saw wisps of smoke rising above the trees. They all appeared a little emotional about coming home after nearly fourteen days. It seemed like it was only a couple of days ago that they had left on their journey but after six hundred miles in the saddle they were feeling a little sore.

About half a mile from home they heard a most peculiar and quite unnerving sound. They stealthily approached. Suddenly a row of branches sprung up in front of them, blocking their passage into the encampment. Within seconds. Vogg, Duff, Fingal, Hithin and Kentigern were on the other side of the six-foot barrier armed with bows and arrows, spears and swords.

"Is this how you greet your friends?" asked Malcolm.

Coll whistled a signal and the barrier dropped.

"Where have you been?" asked Hithin, "Alban was been home for some time with a contented smile on his face but did not say much."

"That is a long story," replied Malcolm.

Drake and the monk remained on their horses as the others dismounted and greeted the welcoming committee.

"I see you have been planting quick growing trees," said Colban.

"I had thought that you would be returning with some wares to show for your journey, unless those two you have brought here are hiding something under their tunics," said Hithin. Malcolm introduced the two additions.

"This is Brother Martin from the Culdee monastery at Dunkeld. He has brought with him a hive so we can enjoy the honey, and this is Drake."

"Please just call me Martin," he said.

Hithin turned to Drake and said, "I have heard much about you. You are both most welcome to join our little group."

"Have the others returned?" asked Donnan.

"Tovi and Coll have taken the carriages to Glencoe and should be back by sunset," replied Hithin.

"I thought we had the horses," said Donnan.

"We have been busy while you were away," said Hithin.

"I see that. Like the surprise attack with the branches?" asked Ewan.

"I will tell all in good time," replied Hithin. "Now, let us join the others."

At that moment, Alban walked up to them with a smile on his face and said, "I got stung," and with that, turned and walked away leaving no one any the wiser as to what transpired in the grounds of the monastery at Dunkeld.

Chapter 16

All Together Now

The travellers were quite amazed at the changes there had been at home in such a short space of time; into what could only now be described as a little village.

Everyone emerged from their huts to heartily welcome the first of the returning parties. Martin was still apprehensively looking around as he was introduced to each person.

"Is something worrying you?" asked Hithin.

"No, no, nothing," replied the monk nervously.

"Come then, Dougal and Duff will prepare food for us. You must be hungry. You have much to tell us."

"I will need to put the hive in place before the sun gets any higher," said Martin.

Frothi and Halfred led the horses to the stables while Colban, Gillis and the monk found a suitable place, a fair distance from the centre of the village, to set the hive. The skins were slowly and carefully removed, while Colban and Gillis took quite a few steps backwards as Martin unveiled the hive.

The whole village was now gathered outside in the warm early morning air. The introductions took quite a time. The monk's mind still seemed to be elsewhere as he was answering questions.

"Is something troubling you?" asked Alpin.

"No, not at all, I was looking round at what you have done here. It looks like heaven. We did not talk much at the monastery, so this is a great change for me with so many people and so much to do. I hope I will be happy here."

"You will," said Alpin sincerely.

"Please sit down," said Hithin.

A healthy portion of frumenty was served. As Martin was about to eat, he looked up and saw the two nuns directly in front of him. With his mouth wide open and a wooden spoon almost up to his mouth, he froze.

"Good morning brother," said Mildrith.

He stood and replied, "Good morning sisters."

"It is quite some time since we saw you," said Mildrith.

"It is," replied Martin. "I hope you are both in good health. Please sit."

"We are both well, thank you," replied Mildrith. The awkward manner of conversation puzzled Eangyth a little.

"When was the last time you met?" she asked.

Martin hesitantly replied, "I think it is nearly a year."

"And where was that?" asked Eangyth.

"I do not quite remember. Where was it sister?"

Mildrith was now on the spot. "Was it in Oban or was it at the monastery?"

"When did you go to Oban or the monastery?" asked Eangyth.

"I do not remember where or when it was," replied Mildrith.

"Not a time or place to remember then," commented Eangyth. Neither Martin nor Mildrith replied but a little colouring of the cheeks was plainly obvious. "I think we should eat," said Eangyth, being very diplomatic.

Malcolm, Donnan and Ewan sat with Alpin and Hithin as they related the events of the last fourteen days, from the unscrupulous traders, saving witches from being burnt alive, to the interesting events at St. Cuthbert's monastery, to re-uniting a family and Frothi's misfortune. They saved the best two parts till the end.

"Do you remember Ragnar Lodbrok?" asked Malcolm.

"Where did you find him?" asked Hithin.

"He was in a tavern in Eoforwic. Frothi and Ulf spoke to him for a short while but when they sought him later, he had left."

"I do not trust him," said Hithin. "We must warm the citizens of Eoforwic to be on their guard."

"We thought of that, and we made sure that the city would be well guarded."

"Very wise," replied Hithin.

"We met a King who told us of a man he once knew who did not like being of royal blood and left his kin at a young age."

Alpin stared directly at Malcolm and asked, "By chance was his name Kenneth?"

"Yes Donald, it was," replied Malcolm.

Hithin looked very puzzled at this response and said, "I do not understand. Who is Donald?"

Malcolm related the conversation they had with the King.

"Is this true?" asked Hithin.

"It is," replied Alpin. "I am the half-brother to Kenneth MacAlpin but let this go no further. Let me just be Alpin."

"You are the son of a King," said Malcolm pointing to Hithin, "and you are the half-brother of a King," he said pointing to Alpin.

Hithin stood, faced Alpin, bowed low and said, "Your grace," forcing the same response from Alpin.

"Do we have a queen?" asked Malcolm.

"Would Elen be a princess?" asked Donnan.

Before Ewan could contribute, Alpin said, "We should say no more about this."

They all agreed, however Hithin had the last word saying, "We will obey, Your Grace," which was greeted with the contempt it deserved.

Having restored a little decorum, Hithin then summarised the outcome of the expedition.

"So, you met a King, a man trying to fly, a mad monk, men riding into each other, a farmer, you know how to make a smoke bomb and where to get sugar, wheat, rye and horses and you brought back one beehive." Neither Malcolm, Donnan nor Ewan could think of any mitigating circumstances to justify their lack of wares.

"I hope the others have a little more to show when they return," said Alpin, "but I do think my half-brother will help when we are looking for places here and across the seas to begin lasting treaties. Forteviot is no more than a day's journey so I will visit him."

Donnan and Ewan were confused but very interested in the trees that had sprung up in front of them as they approached the village.

"I will have Gillis and Kyle tell you," said Alpin. He went to find them.

As he left, Hithin turned to them and said, "He is happy that you have returned safely, and he knows that what you have done is for the good of us all. I think you have done well." This inspired a little more encouragement than the speech Alpin gave. They were quite satisfied.

Soon Gillis and Kyle came over.

"It is our way to keep out those for who we do not care," said Gillis.

They were led to the barrier and Kyle explained that all round the area there was an intricate system of underground ropes which when something or somebody either stood on or pulled one, it would trigger an alarm in the village. He took them out further, about half a mile from the village, along the path the group rode in on.

"It is like a catapult. We knew you were coming before you reached the village, so were waiting for you."

"Then each time someone enters the village, the barrier will rise?" asked Ewan.

"When the first rope is moved, a bell rings in the village. There are guards in huts all-round the village and they can see who is coming in and from whence they came. If it is an enemy then they wake others and if it is people we know, they are able to stop the fence from rising."

"We thought we would leave it to come up for you."

"That is most kind," replied Malcolm.

"You have more to show in the village than we have from our travels," said Donnan.

"When you wish, I will show you what we have done, what we have made and all we have found," said Kyle.

"It is most odd how so many horses, sheep, chickens, goats and pigs have found their way onto this land," said Gillis, with a smile on his face.

"We did bring back about twenty thousand bees and a monk," said Ewan.

They made their way back to the centre of the village where the others, with the exception of Alban, who seemed to have disappeared, were waiting.

"What did happen with Alban?" asked Gillis.

Donnan shook his head. "I do not think we will ever know."

Gillis and Kyle gave the others a conducted tour of the village showing them the improvements that had been made to the beautifully finished traditional daub and wattle homes. Kyle explained that Gillis had used kilns to make bricks with red clay dug up from nearby fields and dirt banks and

Vogg, Duff and Kentigern had managed to excavate a good quantity of stones near Glencoe which they brought back to the village.

He continued, "Garmund, Fingal and Dougal found other stones and ores and Garmund has made glass, using them. He has been very quiet, working in his hut and is not letting anyone know what he is doing. I am sure the bees will be useful," he added sarcastically.

Suddenly, they heard an alarm call from the village.

"Someone is coming. Quick hide!" said Gillis.

The group took cover behind the trees. They then heard a different sound.

"It is Tovi and Coll back with the others. Let us go back."

They arrived in the centre of the village where everyone had now gathered, just as three carriages pulled up.

"Three carriages," said Alpin. "I remember only two leaving,"

"It is nice to be home," said Gerik.

Tovi and Coll were at the reins of the first two carriages and Ross was at the reins of the third. As the carriages stopped Angus, Boyd, Lesedi and Sholto climbed down from the first, Maarku, Asmund, Ross and Nevin from the second and Mirren and Anika from just one door on the third.

"The others brought back two more and you have brought back three more. Is there anything you have to show from your journey?" asked Hithin.

Gerik opened the other door on the third carriage and an endless cascade of watermelons fell out.

"Anything else?" asked Alpin.

"Seeds for strawberries, onions, parsnips, fennel, cabbage, carrots, beans and peppers," replied Anika.

"And poppy seeds," added Ross.

"And more gold," added Boyd. "And we know how to make fireworks."

"And with the same powder, weapons," added Mirren.

"Do not forget about the carriage," said Alpin.

"Nobody was using it when we found it," replied Ewan looking up to the sky.

"Is that it?" asked Alpin.

"I know Maarku," said Hithin, "but who are these two women you have brought back to us?"

Gerik introduced Lesedi and Anika and explained why they were brought to the village.

"You are most welcome, and I am sure that you will be of great help to us. Now come and join us for some food. You must be tired and hungry after your long journey," said Alpin.

Tovi and Coll unhitched the horses, and then led them to the stables for them to enjoy a well-deserved feed. Not surprisingly, another feast had already started with nourishing food and a little ale freely flowing and the growing population of forty-three people getting to know each other. Nobody was left out. Even to the newcomers, the air of friendship and hospitality was clearly apparent.

The wives were extremely pleased to see their husbands. Ulf elaborated on his exploits to Coll and Nevin, Martin was deep in conversation with Mildrith and Fingal was engrossed in conversation with Eangyth and Anika and Lesedi had fallen asleep on the wooden tables, no doubt extremely relieved to have found a new home.

Hithin stood with Alpin and Elen looking at the gathering. He smiled and said, "Time, love, hope, life." That summed up everything beautifully.

Chapter 17

Sauces and Sources

The following morning, Hithin and Alpin called together all those who had been on the travels. He also invited Drake to make notes of the events for future reference.

He first thanked them all for their efforts and then asked Gerik and Malcolm in turn to detail their exploits, giving Drake time to document their tales. However, he diplomatically omitted some of the more personal events, well at least not penning them in too much detail.

They listed the priorities in building relationships with towns in other countries, where it would be made difficult for foreigners to trace the exact location of their village; although it wasn't that vague or misleading, directions would be given intentionally. The fireworks were of particular interest to Garmund, who suddenly had either a moment of insanity or a moment of inspiration wondering if the fireworks could be used as a diversion while the group armed themselves.

"Why would you want to show where we are by setting off fireworks?" asked Alpin.

"It would distract an enemy watching the fireworks, so we could then ambush them," he replied.

His suggestion caused both amusement and disbelief until Lesedi stood up and said, "I know how to make people weep using peppers."

There was respectful silence as she explained how to make a type of tear gas.

"How do you know this?" asked Gerik.

"I was trying to make a sauce with red peppers, rice and grapes and when it was done it did not taste nice, but the smell made me cry."

Garmund thought for a moment and then asked, "If we mix this with the fireworks and throw them into the sky then what falls to the ground could get into the eyes of the enemy and slow them down. I think we should try. Could you make more?" Lesedi nodded.

"Is there anything else you could make?" asked Hithin.

"I will help Lesedi and whatever sauce we cannot eat we will use against intruders," said Garmund.

Lesedi did not know whether to take this as a compliment or an insult but with this being her first day, she politely said nothing.

The meeting went on for a while with Hithin eventually summarising the way forward.

"I do not think we need to travel to places as far away as India and China for the silks and cottons as we will find these in Frisia or Francia when those goods are taken there as trade. I think we can make the wines that Enar and Asmund tasted here, but I do not want them tasting what we make. Garmund has the powder Boyd brought back and will see if he can make more."

"I can help Garmund," said Drake. "I know how to make the powder. The Romans started to make it when they were in Carlisle, and I wrote down what they used."

"Can you cook?" asked Malcolm sarcastically.

Drake was about to answer when Alpin said, "Malcolm was just thinking that if you were able to help him, it would be useful, but we will come back to that as I think Anika and Lesedi might help."

"I think Henry in Jedworð would be helpful. It is a three-day journey but as he has been trading with other countries, he will know which lands we can safely visit," said Hithin. "

We should travel to my half-brother first," said Alpin, "for him to tell us where he believes we could go and who to see."

"We can always say we are here on behalf of the King when we go to these other towns," said Gerik; cunning but practical.

"I can see that the next journey will be to Francia," said Maarku.

"And from there to Germania, Italy and Al-Andalus," added Drake.

Alpin turned to Drake and said, "You will be of great help to us, and I am so pleased you are here." Drake embarrassingly acknowledged the sentiment.

Alpin then turned to Maarku and said, "With all you know of other lands and the many people you have met, you too will be of great help to us."

"I have dreamt of a place like this and never thought my dreams would come true. I will be happy here," replied Maarku.

"Does anyone want to say any more?" asked Hithin.

Anika whispered something to Lesedi. Boyd looked at the women and asked, "Is there something you wish to say?"

Anika nodded to Lesedi and began. "I lived in Amalfi in Italy when I was younger, and I know places to go, and I know the language. When I lived in Aoudaghost in Africa, we made a mix from rotting fruit and vegetables to give us heat and light."

Garmund was intrigued by this, so with Drake's knowledge on producing fireworks and gunpowder and Lesedi's knowledge on producing a source of heat and light, he immediately suggested that the two work with him. A little tear ran down Lesedi's cheek.

"What is the matter?" asked Gerik.

"I have never in my life felt so welcome and so happy. I will always have you in my heart. I thank you."

Gerik went up to Lesedi, put his arm round her shoulders and said, "It is us who should be thanking you, but Malcolm will be preparing most of the food."

"My sauces are sometimes very good," replied Lesedi.

"It is the other times that we will have to worry about," said Gerik.

Alpin said to the group, "We will sit down again in two days to plan who will go and where to go, but for now return to your friends and again, I thank you all for that you have done."

As they made their way back, Alpin said to Hithin, "I blame you for all this, for being drunk when we first met and offering to share."

Hithin replied, "and I blame you for accepting."

After a couple of days' rest and recuperation, Alpin and Hithin invited Gerik, Maarku, Garmund, Enar, Halfred, Malcolm, Coll, Angus, Lesedi and Drake to talk about the way forward. Each had a particular skill and combining their talents would give greater benefit.

Alpin's proposal of a trip to his half-brother was deemed to be the first step, with a second trip to Henry in Jedworð as a good follow up. For the first trip, as Malcolm had previously met the King, Alpin believed it sensible to take him along, plus Maarku who was a highly experienced traveller and might know the towns abroad. The King had suggested using Kentigern for his expertise in mining, Duff for his farming skills and Gillis for his work in planning and architecture. That would also give those who had not been on any ventures the opportunity to travel. The roughly fifty-four-mile trip to Forteviot could easily be managed in one day.

"We leave in the morning," said Alpin.

"Have you told Elen?" asked Hithin.

"Not yet," replied Alpin, "but I think it may help if we took her with us."

"How long have you been planning this?" asked Malcolm.

"Last night I told her about my past and she did say that she would like to meet my brother."

"When were you going to tell us that you wanted her with you?" asked Hithin.

"Now," replied Alpin hesitantly.

Hithin thought for a moment then said, "I do think that would be good. I am sure the King would be happy to meet your wife. He may grant you a castle or some land as a wedding present." Alpin's dismissive expression said it all.

By mid-morning, Tovi and Angus had readied the horses. At a steady canter, the group anticipated reaching the castle at Forteviot in about three hours.

"When will you return?" asked Hithin.

"I do not think we will be more than three days," replied Alpin. And off they rode.

They passed through the small, scattered settlement at Amulree at which point Malcolm pointed out the church dedicated to Saint Maelubha.

"Has someone been learning from Drake?" asked Maarku.

"Not at all," replied Malcolm/

"I happen to know all about this place."

"We all believe you," quipped Alpin.

They eventually reached the castle at Forteviot to be greeted by two guards who blocked the way, crossing their spears.

"Stop!" one of them ordered. "Who do you seek?"

Alpin edged forward and was about to speak when the guard said, "Your Grace, please forgive your humble servant. I did not see you."

What crossed Alpin's mind was whether to come clean and say who he really was or play on the guard's inability to recognise his King. As it would seem a little time consuming to go into great detail and explanation, he decided to go with the latter.

"You have my forgiveness," he said and rode with the party across the drawbridge into the courtyard.

They were greeted by seven stable hands who held the reins as the group dismounted. One of the King's servants approached the group and so, as not to confuse anyone else and with Alpin shielding his face, it was Malcolm who said, "We are here to see the King."

The servant asked, "Who should I announce?"

Malcolm replied, "Tell his grace, Donald wishes to speak to him." The servant politely bowed and ran off.

In a short time, the King, in all his splendour, ran through the courtyard, brushing aside a number of his servants in the process, straight up to Alpin and threw his arms round him. Needless to say, the numerous onlookers were dumbfounded by the King's actions.

"Welcome brother," he said. "Welcome. I did not think I would see you so soon."

Alpin introduced the others to the King, starting with Elen, at which point the King said, "I am the more handsome brother," and then moved onto the rest of the party.

On greeting the King, Malcolm said, "Ulf has asked me to pass on a message to you. He says, 'Good day Kenneth,' and I believe you owe me a tankard of ale."

"That I do. Now come with me," replied the King.

He led them into the main dining hall, ordering his servants to bring food and wine. He had so much to ask Alpin to the extent that the others were left to talk amongst themselves. Even Elen found herself with the others as the half-brothers were engrossed in conversation. All of a sudden, one of the servants announced the arrival of the queen. She seemed confused at the impromptu activity and made her way towards the King.

"Who are these people?" she asked with an air of indignity.

The King at first ignored her until she repeated the question in a significantly louder and far more indignant tone.

The King turned to her and said, "This is my brother, now please leave us."

She turned, saw the other six guests and walked up to them.

"I am Queen Nadbroicc." They greeted her in turn, bowing out of respect. "Who is that with the King? He said it is his brother."

"It is Donald MacAlpin, his half-brother, your grace," replied Malcolm.

"And who are you?" she asked Elen, looking her up and down in a most derisory manner.

"I am Donald's wife, so that means we are related by marriage, your grace," she replied, stressing the words, 'Your Grace,' to imply an equally condescending tone. The queen said nothing, just sniffled, turned and walked out of the hall to the relief of all present.

The King beckoned them over and said, "I see you have met the dragon. Where is Saint George when you need him? Now let us eat and drink."

It was like a get together of long-lost friends. The King was in his element, talking and laughing with all of the group, making sure that not one of them was left out of the conversation.

"It is too late in the day to talk about what you have come for and I am having a little problem staying still when I stand. Servant!" he yelled, "bring me a piss pot."

A servant duly obliged. As the King relieved himself, he asked, "Is there anyone who would care to join me?"

Well, there was quite a rush, however most of the guests missed the target and ended up decorating the walls. The multitude of servants were desperately trying not to laugh, but when one started, the others could not help but join in and soon the hall was in total uproar.

"I can fart too," said the King.

To which Alpin replied, "So can Elen."

That did it. Stomachs were being held in case they burst, tears were rolling down cheeks and limbs had just lost their rigidity.

Everybody sat on the floor by now, in various stages of inebriety. The King called for more ale and ordered his servants to join in the party. At first, they were reluctant to obey, however under threat of being sent to the queen, they duly obliged.

By morning, there were around thirty people asleep on the dining hall floor. The King was one of the first to wake, bitterly complaining about the state of his head and threatening to behead anyone who spoke too loudly. After eventually managing to focus, the King, who was lying next to Alpin, prodded him until he woke.

"Have you woken?" whispered the King loudly.

"Not yet," replied Alpin, still feeling extremely groggy.

"I will not wake you then," said the King, who then slowly managed to prop himself up against a cold stone pillar, his head swaying from side to side as he said, "I command you all to stop moving." Nobody stirred. "Bring food!" yelled the King, quickly regretting yelling. "That hurt," he added.

Amid the moans and groans, the rest of the attendees began to cautiously rise. The servants slowly and quietly made the way back to their quarters, keeping their eyes covered due to the intensity of the light. As they left, a band of finely liveried servants made their grand entrance carrying copious amounts of bread, fruits, oats and jugs of wine.

"Eat," said the King in a wavering voice.

Each slowly crawled, was dragged or staggered their way to the tables, slumping down and randomly reaching forward in a vain attempt to attract some food into their outstretched hands. The co-ordination of hand to mouth proved extremely difficult, a number of those present bursting into fits of giggles at seeing chunks of bread being thrust towards ears or foreheads.

It was quite some time before some semblance of sanity was established, expedited by both dunking heads into basins of freezing cold water and Queen Nadbroicc's insistence that she needed the dining area cleared urgently as it was time for the local jugglers, acrobats and singers to entertain her, something akin to a ninth century Forteviot's Got Talent.

The revellers slowly and reluctantly made their way into the grounds at the rear of the castle, each still complaining about their current state of mind and body.

The King eventually rallied sufficient brain cells together to coherently say to Alpin. "I cannot remember why you are here."

Alpin drew a deep breath to try to clear his head and succinctly replied, "We wish to visit different lands and learn what they have to offer and from there reach out to lands further away. We seek guidance from yourself in knowing where we should first travel."

The King pondered for a moment and then asked, "You have not told me where you have built your village. If you wish to seek goods from other countries, will you tell them about your village and what you have to trade? You were always the cunning one of the family, wanting to get your own way by not telling anyone what you were thinking or what you were doing."

"But I did not hurt anyone," replied Alpin.

"You were skilled in learning many languages, your counsel was of great help to us. You were very wise for someone so young, and I know that what and who you seek will be of help to you in building your village but do not make enemies of people. I believe you will not hurt anyone. You are too careful. I will help, but you must not say it is I who helped you."

"I promise that I would never betray you. You are my brother," said Alpin.

So, with the ground rules firmly established, the list of places, people and products were penned.

The King then asked Alpin. "Do you know of any person near who can help?"

"We met a man called Henry when we went to Jedworð," replied Malcolm.

"Henry and Isabella?" asked the King.

"Yes," said Malcolm.

"Do you know who he is?" asked the King.

"A farmer with much land," replied Malcolm.

"He is the Earl of Roxburgh, and his wife Isabella is from the Clan Douglas, a well-respected family from the Scottish Lowlands. They have much land in Scotland, Francia and Sweden and for you, they are good people to know. How did you meet him?" asked the King.

"We stopped the dogs from running away," replied Malcolm.

"You will have a good friend in Henry, but he can be a little strange at times. When you see him, please tell him I send my good wishes."

"I will," said Malcolm.

The group spent the day enjoying the hospitality laid on by the King, the servants acting as guides to the rest of the group, apparently relieved to be outside the castle walls and not having to bear the incessant demands of the queen, as Alpin, Elen and the King walked, talked, laughed and cried as they reminisced about their youth and events over the last ten years.

They all assembled late afternoon to enjoy a feast of stuffed chicken covered in pomegranate seeds, cabbage, carrots and a very tasty sauce of wine, vinegar and verjuice, spiced with ginger and cinnamon. After the previous evening's events, the King thought it most prudent to limit the amount of alcohol just to that used in the sauce. There were no complaints.

"We must tell Lesedi about this sauce," Alpin said to Malcolm.

"How to make it or how to use it against an enemy?" he replied. Malcolm just smiled.

The King looked puzzled by this comment until Malcolm explained Lesedi's interesting culinary skills. He summoned one of his servants to fetch the cook, who explained that the recipes he used are found in the fifth century collection by the Roman Apicius.

"I will have a scribe write them out," said the cook.

"That is most kind of you," said Malcolm, the King also expressing his gratitude.

The group spent a luxurious night in the resplendency of a warm, well-maintained castle, enjoying a peaceful night in a comfortable bed.

Morning came; however, no one was too eager to rise until nature had its evil way of forcing the vacating of comfort to necessitate the vacating of discomfort.

After a hearty breakfast of eggs, oats and warm nettle tea and now armed with a list of contacts and recipes, it was time for the group to make its way home. The King insisted that they visit again in the not-too-distant future and demanded that an invitation to the village should be forthcoming.

And so began the journey home, the group appearing extremely satisfied with the outcome of their trip, now having a better initial idea which towns abroad they could relate to and hopefully build a one-sided relationship with.

The next step would be to get Henry and Isabella on their side and establish additional contacts across the Frisian Sea. Their plans were ambitious, but the rewards were potentially significant and the anonymity, imperative.

Chapter 18

Hooray Henry

Out of the original thirty, just nine had not been on any of the expeditions and Alpin and Hithin always believed it only fair to allow everyone the opportunity to become involved in every aspect of the development of the village.

Hithin summoned Coll, Dougal, Fingal, Garmund, Halfred, Mungo, Tovi and Vogg to discover who was interested in journeying to Jedworð, once the Forteviot trip had returned. Neither Garmund, Vogg, Fingal nor Mungo were particularly bothered about going on what would be an overall seven- or eight-day trip, so the remaining five, plus someone who had already been to Jedworð, possibly Donnan, as the saviour of the dogs, should make up the party. They all seemed satisfied with this arrangement, so it was just a case of waiting for the travellers to return, confirming the group and then deciding when to go.

The travellers returned in the early evening, Tovi and Angus stabled the horses while the party made their way to the church where everyone else had assembled. Dougal, Lesedi and Anika were proud to show off their skills having prepared a buffet of bread, chicken, salmon, sausages and a variety of fruits including an abundance of watermelons. As they were about to tuck in, Brother Martin stood, cleared his throat and ad-libbed his way through a prayer of thanksgiving.

Alpin turned to Hithin and said, "We have only been away for a few days and now we have a beekeeper in charge."

Hithin surreptitiously managed to hide his outburst of laughter and replied, "He is also wishing for us to confess our sins, so I believe he will be quite active in the village."

"Who does he confess to?" asked Alpin.

"I believe he is seeking forgiveness from Sister Mildrith, but his penance seems to be rather loud at times with Sister Mildrith calling for God."

For the morning meeting, Drake was again tasked with emphasising the salient points of the debrief and suggested creating a journal on the blank parchments he had brought back from Carlisle, so everyone was made aware of what was happening and could reference them whenever they wished. After the events at Forteviot had been recorded, Hithin put his Jedworð proposal forward and with Donnan agreeing to accompany them, all was set for the next mission which was to commence the following day.

Drake himself raised an interesting point. "We are in the year 842, but I do believe that we should know the day and the month to enter into this book." Nobody had actually considered this but acknowledged his suggestion. The problem now was to either try to calculate the date based on the sun and the stars, guess or try to find someone who knew.

Fortunately, Brother Martin came to the rescue and said, "In the monastery, we kept note of the day. I left the monastery on Moon's Day, and this is my seventh day, so it is again Moon's Day, and we are in the month of June." He thought for a moment, looked up and started counting aloud on his fingers. After a few moments came the confident declaration, "It is the fifth of June." Drake nodded his agreement and entered this date in the journal.

Hithin then said, "Drake, I wish you to note all that has happened from the time our two groups first met. You will have to speak with all of us and I know that this will take much of your time, but for our children and their children and for time to come, to be able to know how this all began, I do believe this to be of foremost importance."

"I will," said Drake.

The following day was taken up with further improvements in the village. Coll and Vogg were out hunting, using more sophisticated methods. Based on the intricate system of the defence barrier, Kyle and Coll had developed a similar box trap. However, for the prey more fleet of hoof, the trusty bow and arrow still prevailed. In his recent mining excavations, halfway between Stoleware and Glencoe, Kentigern had discovered rich veins of gold and silver and Duff, Halfred, Anna and Nesta went out to try to encourage a few more cows, goats, pigs, sheep and chickens to come into the confines of the village. Coll and Gillis continued their building work while Malcolm and Dougal were joined by Lesedi and Anika and the latest edition of the Apicius Recipe Book, to increase the choices on the menu. However, the number of dishes using watermelons was, needless to say, limited. The women helped in the fields, assisted Halfred in the design and creation of fashion and ensured the cleanliness and tidiness of the village, often berating the men for their lack of hygiene but more importantly, ensuring that Coll and Nevin limited their tantrums.

The morning came when Hithin, Coll, Dougal, Halfred, Tovi and Donnan set off on their three-day journey, first to Dunkeld then on to Perth, Dùn Èideann and finally to Jedworð, hoping to stop at places used by the first group. They found the same hospitality at the Culdee monastery, the same old jokes from Alfred at Le Grand Coq, Noah's flying friend at Queensferry and the seductive Madelaine at the Sheep Heid Inn. However, on recognising Donnan, Madelaine's husband, for some strange reason, decided to keep out of sight.

They reached Jedworð by early afternoon on the third day, Donnan leading the way to Henry's stately home. The dogs, Bo and Hardy were playing in the garden and when they caught Donnan's scent, they ran towards the gates, barking excitedly with tails wagging madly. The two girls wondered what the commotion was, then noticed Donnan at the gates.

"Mother, it is the man who saved the dogs." Isabella came running to the gates. "Come in," she cried, opening the large iron-barred gates.

"There are six here," said Donnan.

"Please, you are all welcome," she replied. Donnan introduced them as they filed in. They led the horses through the gates, Isabella directing them to the stables.

She then led them inside the house and asked, "What brings you here again?"

Hithin introduced himself and replied, "We are here to see your husband. When we last visited, your husband told us that he had much land, many working for him and knew of people in Frisia and as far away as India."

Isabella shook her head. "He has no money," she replied. "It is I who own all the land. This is my house. Henry tended my parent's gardens, so they were displeased when I told them I wanted Henry as my husband, but please do not say this while he is here. He has the title granted to him by the King to save face, but it is I who seeks trade with other countries. He is not the wisest of men and he does like to tell people he has wealth, but all this is from my family."

That left the group a little lost for words. Hithin then explained that they had seen the King and he had given them names and places and they were hoping that Henry would further enlighten them.

"I will help you," said Isabella. "Now please, follow me. Eggs, bacon and nettle tea?" she asked.

"Malcolm did tell us how much they enjoyed the food here," said Hithin. They all sat in the kitchen, Bo and Hardy not leaving Donnan's side.

Henry returned a little after they had finished eating. "Welcome friends." He turned to Donnan and said, "It is good to see you again. Who are these people?" Henry seemed uninterested as Donnan introduced them all. "I have been with the Earl of Aberdeen, Lord Peebles and the Earl of Fife, playing dice. I won one hundred pounds but gave it all away to the poor and then I drank two bottles of wine and went to see the King. Now I am going to bathe in the lake," and off he went.

Isabella sighed and said, "He has been into the town wearing his fine clothes and making the townsfolk believe he has wealth. He likes to boast so he can enter into the company of those who really do have wealth. He tells them that I am from a poor peasant family, and he owns the land. I want to leave him, but I fear he will lose all I have."

Hithin thought for a moment and then asked Isabella. "What would your children say if your husband were to leave?"

"He does not care for them, so I do not think they will miss him," she replied.

Hithin turned to the other five and quietly said, "Angus and Ross were led astray by Merulf in Frisia. Do you think we may be able to tempt Henry to find Merulf?" "But Merulf is a charlatan," said Donnan.

"He is," replied Hithin.

"I see your plan," said Dougal.

Hithin then turned to Isabella and briefly explained Merulf's greed and deceptive practice.

"Perfect," she said. "When can Henry leave?"

"When Henry returns, we will begin the ruse," said Hithin. He turned to Isabella and asked, "Is this what you want?"

"It is," she replied, heaving a sigh of relief.

It was not long before Henry returned to overhear the group discussing poppies, pearls, gold and silver. They purposely stopped talking when Henry entered the room.

"What is this I hear? Pearls?"

"You are mistaken," said Hithin.

"You were speaking of pearls," said Henry, raising his voice.

Hithin mumbled gibberish to the others and then said," We will be travelling to Frisia as we have heard of a man whose name is Merulf, who fishes for pearls off the Frisian coast. He does this alone and will not tell anyone when he fishes but we have found out and we want to fish for these rare pearls. He is very rich and powerful."

Henry's eyes lit up. "Tell me more," he said.

"He travels many miles along the coast to find the right places to fish. It takes time, but when he fishes in the right place, he finds many pearls," said Hithin.

"He travelled west across the vast seas to find these pearls," added Donnan.

Henry thought for a few moments and then said, "I must find this man and we can fish for pearls together. Isabella, I must go. I know this will hurt you, but this is my dream. I will have more wealth than all the kings and then you will respect me."

Isabella, very dramatically replied, "It is for you to decide, but if you must go, then I understand."

"I leave in the morning," he said adamantly, walking out of the room to pack clothing and other essentials for his trip. Isabella was dumfounded as to how simple it was to play on a man's gullibility.

"He trusts you," she said smiling.

"That is what concerns me," replied Donnan.

"If he finds Merulf, then I am sure he will soon be acquainted with the joys of smoking poppies," said Hithin. He again said to Isabella, "Are you sure this is what you want?"

"I am sure," she replied.

The two girls came in and asked their mother, "Where is father going?"

"He is going away for a time," she replied.

The two girls looked at each other, then asked their mother, "Can we have another dog then?" Isabella smiled and nodded her agreement. The girls ran back outside to play, unable to hide their joy.

The five stayed in the house overnight, greatly disturbed by Henry's clattering around as he tried to decide on what he should take, every few moments asking his wife if she thought he needed to pack totally unnecessary items like chamber pots or glass vases.

Morning came and Henry was nowhere to be found. "I have been trying to get rid of him for nearly twelve years, you managed it in less than one day," Isabella said to Hithin. "Do you think he will come back?" she asked.

"I do not think he will return," he replied.

There was an expression of delight, tinged with a touch of sadness on Isabella's face, however that did not last long.

"Now," she began, "you would like the names of people and places."

Hithin nodded then asked her, "What will you do now?"

"Begin life again now that I feel free," she said.

She looked at Donnan and said, "After you left, the children would not stop speaking about you and how good you were with the dogs. They liked you. Would you like to stay here for a while?"

Donnan was flattered by her invitation and replied, "Your husband has just left, and you wish me to stay?"

"He left me many years ago," she replied.

Donnan looked at the others for inspiration, but the only words of not particularly useful advice were from Hithin who said, "It is up to you."

The girls, who had been secretly listening, ran into the room, looked at Donnan with puppy-dog eyes and said, "Please stay. After you left, I heard mother say to the dogs that she would like to show you something, but she did not say what." Isabella blushed but said nothing.

Changing the subject smartly, Dougal said. "You are three days journey away and I know you will be of help to Isabella in what she does. You will meet new people in many places."

"I will stay," said Donnan. The two girls went up to Donnan and put their arms round him, one of them asking, "Are you our new father?" He just smiled.

"I have what you came for," said Isabella, as she handed Hithin a parchment with names, places and trades neatly written out.

"Be careful with Donnan," said Halfred, "he is young and innocent to the ways of the world."

"I will," she replied with a lustful glint in her eye.

Time to start the journey home. It was a poignant moment as this was the first member of the original group to leave. The uneventful trip retraced the outward journey, staying overnight at the same places and Madelaine's husband still being unavailable when the five stopped at the Sheep Heid Inn at Dùn Èideann.

At last, they arrived home, Alpin looking quite mystified as only five returned.

"The others managed to return with more bodies, you have managed to lose one," he said.

"I will tell all, but first my backside is sore from being in the saddle for too long," said Hithin.

Ross and Angus stabled the horses, then joined the others in the cool shade of the centre of the village to listen to the results of the trip to Jedworð.

"We will all miss Donnan. He is a good scout, and I am sure we will see him again," said Alpin.

With the people and places supplied by both the King and Isabella, the group had their work cut out for the next few years at least.

Chapter 19

Twinning

It was all very well knowing which places to visit and who to see but having either something tangible to trade or being able to identify similarities with targeted places, might prove a little more difficult.

It was time for yet another get together to try to find a simple solution. Alpin asked the assembly if, during the visits, especially to towns overseas, anyone had come across anything unusual or anything which might relate to Stoleware. Sholto mentioned a strange encounter he had in Frisia with Abbas, the Indian tradesman, who took a particular interest in the brooch he was wearing.

"Let me see," requested Gerik. He looked at the inscription on the back of the brooch and asked, "Who was Mælbrigða?"

Drake suddenly came to life. "Mælbrigða is a woman's name which means 'Devotee of Bridgit'. The brooch was made in Hybernia about one hundred and fifty years ago, but the inscription is Scandinavian."

"How do you know this?" asked Hithin.

Drake replied, "William talked about this brooch. Many people in the world have heard of its existence, but very few have seen it. It is said that whoever rightfully owns the brooch has great wealth and power."

Sholto just shrugged his shoulders and said, "I wish."

"Where did you find it?" asked Hithin.

"My mother gave it to me, passed down from her mother. My mother told me that my ancestor's name was Bridgit," he replied. "No harm has befallen me but nor have I seen the power the brooch possesses."

Hithin continued, "Drake tells us that the brooch is a sign of great power and wealth, and this is the only one. Angus, could you make this?"

Angus looked at the brooch very carefully, turning it slowly over and over in his hands. "It will take time," he said, "but I can make one. Why do you ask?"

"If we make more, then we can use them to trade, but we must tell those we trade with not to say to others they own it, for fear of it being taken and they then losing the power of the brooch. They will believe they have the only one."

Angus appeared a little concerned at what was coming next. "You asked if I could make one," he said.

"I am with Hithin," said Alpin. "We should make more."

"You will be telling me you want me to make nineteen," said Angus jokingly.

"Yes," replied Alpin, "that should be fine," and before Angus had time to respond, Drake had already added, 'Angus to make nineteen brooches' into the daily journal, saying each word deliberately as it was entered.

"They can be placed in the chest I brought from Carlisle. I will let you have the key," said Drake.

Hithin reminded Angus to make a minute change to the detail on the copies to distinguish them from the original.

"I had thought of that," said Angus. "I will need help," he added.

"I can help," said Tovi

"And I," said Enar.

"When they are finished, we will use them to trade with when we visit the places described to us by the King and Isabella. If you wish to embark on this journey, tell Drake," said Alpin.

Elen stood and said, "It may serve us well if some of the women went on this journey with our men."

Alpin thought for a moment and said, "You are right. To have the charms of a woman to affirm the accord with those of high rank in towns and cities will justify our intentions. I leave it to you all to decide who should make the journey."

The meeting adjourned to much excitement at the prospect of an association with other places and people, while maintaining the anonymity of the village.

Work progressed in the village, with new and intriguing ideas arising virtually each day to improve the efficiency. There were some ingenious inventions. Garmund's secret project was soon revealed. Quite accidentally, he had noticed that when he shaped the glass and made into a semi-circle, objects looked at through the glass appeared larger than normal and with a different thickness and shape of glass, smaller than normal. Playing around with various shapes and sizes of glass, inserted into a hollow bamboo shoot, he eventually constructed a simple yet effective telescope. He had also, much to his amazement and embarrassment, inadvertently discovered how to set fire to his tunic, having left a shaped glass on his lap, directly in line with the sun.

Kyle, Duff and Gillis, with the help of an over-worked Angus, were creating new tools to aid in the cutting down of trees and the ploughing of fields to sow seeds. Anika, Lesedi, Berta and Matilda were harvesting plants and with Frothi's help, looking at innovative remedies for both ailments and the interesting flavouring of teas, some being more tasteful than others. Everyone was active and most importantly, enjoying their new life. Vogg, Dougal and Malcolm were experimenting with various mixtures of barley, hops, yeast and fruits, intending to brew their own ale, however with strict orders not to let Enar and Asmund anywhere nearby. Alban and Duff had planted numerous fruit and vegetable seeds, wheat, barley, oats, bulbs and vines brought back from Frisia by Anika and Lesedi. No one was unoccupied. Everyone was in good spirits, particularly the brewing team, as on the odd occasions, they needed to sample the goods.

The dubious acquisition of a large number of cattle, pigs, sheep, goats and chickens, meant the farming work was very demanding, not only in the upkeep of the animals but also in the maintenance of the penned areas to ensure that unscrupulous rustlers were kept away. Alban and Ross were primarily in charge of the farming side of the community with valuable assistance from Anna, Nesta and Elen. Edith had the job of ensuring the tidy appearance of every resident, using a crude but effective pair of scissors and a very sharp razor, delicately forged by Angus. Brother Martin, ably assisted by Sister Mildrith, cared for the bees whilst Sister Eangyth busied herself with the general tidiness and cleanliness of the living quarters. No one was inactive.

The villagers were given plenty of time to discuss between themselves who would be the best candidates to promote the village without; firstly getting drunk, secondly, giving too much away about the village, thirdly not being tempted by trivialities and finally holding onto any gold and silver entrusted to them. Fairly quickly, a number of unsuitable candidates were ruled out. A short-list was drawn up consisting of Hithin, Frothi, Dougal, Ross, Boyd, Matilda, Kyle, Edith, Mungo, Nesta, Lesedi and Maarku. Quite unnoticed, Maarku had been spending some time with Lesedi and the two of them had grown quite fond of each other. They had much in common from both their travel and backgrounds and seemed relaxed in each other's company.

Alpin, Hithin, Boyd, Gerik and Maarku, together with Drake and his summarised list of recommended places, met to discuss the itinerary.

Alpin began. "Your journey will take over two months. Do those who have put their names forward know this?"

"They do," replied Hithin. "Maarku, you are much travelled. Do you have a plan?"

"I have talked to Drake, and we have mapped out a journey through eighteen towns in seven countries," he replied.

Maarku added, "I do not think it wise to take twelve horses. We will take two carriages and four horses across the water and buy fresh horses when we need them. We will travel to Dùn Dèagh and from there, I know we will find a boat to take us across the sea to Frisia and then across land to Germania, Osterrîche, Vitalia, Helvitia, Francia and Belgica. I have travelled to some of these countries before."

"As have I," said Frothi.

"I too and I know the languages," added Lesedi.

Maarku continued, "Drake learnt much from the charts left by the Romans and gave us a lesson about Anaximander and the Imago Mundi. We may make fun of him, but for someone of his years, he knows a lot. We will do well to have him here with us." Drake, while embarrassed, welcomed this adulation.

Luckily there were additional funds available, kindly donated by the unscrupulous Merulf and together with the fake brooches, entrusted to Hithin, a reasonable allowance of Roman gold and silver coins and jewellery, it was deemed sufficient to serve their purposes. In order to avoid any suspicions, only one brooch was to be used at each major stopping point.

Their brief was to find out as much as they could about the resources in each place visited, spend very little and tempt the higher ranking individuals, by whatever means necessary, into giving up a few local secrets. The group had to keep to one story. Unsurprisingly, it was Drake who came up with the idea that the brooches were from a small but thriving community, rich in veins of gold, copper and iron, on Haudonia Isle, one of the islands in Orcades or Orkneyjar.

"How did you think of that name?" asked Alpin.

"I used the last letter of the names of those who were travelling and turned them round. It does sound real," replied Drake, saying 'Haudonia Isle' slowly and deliberately, with a self-satisfied smug expression on his face.

Alpin said, "Angus will finish making the brooches in about five days, so that will be when you leave. Does anyone have anything to ask?"

They were all quite satisfied with the arrangements and so ended the briefing.

Alpin and Hithin were the last to leave and as they made their way outside, Alpin turned to Hithin and said quietly, "Something is going on with Drake which I do not understand."

"I have that feeling too," replied Hithin.

In the few days before departure, the twelve readied their luggage, ordered provisions from Ulf, Nevin and Malcolm, checked with Tovi about the state of the horses and Colban about the carriages and finally confirmed with Alpin and Drake the route they hoped to travel. By the fourth day, the fake brooches were finished and to the untrained eye, were extremely difficult to distinguish from the original, which Sholto now guarded with his life, after asking an exasperated Angus, on many occasions.

"Are you sure this is the real brooch?"

The day arrived and everybody gathered outside to wish the party a safe passage. With necessities packed, it was time to leave. Boyd and Matilda took the reins of the first carriage and Maarku and Lesedi the second, whilst the remaining eight enjoyed the comparative luxury of being chauffeured.

The first part of the journey to Dùn Dèagh was estimated to take around one and a half days, hopefully stopping again at the delightful Culdee monastery in Dunkeld and then would come a trip, which none of them were particularly relishing, of over four hundred miles, across the Frisian Sea to Amestelle.

They arrived at Dunkeld, by now a regular stopping place, at around mid-afternoon, just as six monks were approaching the gates from a walk outside the monastery.

One of the monks recognised Mungo from the first trip to Carlisle and asked, "How is your friend Alban? Did he find enlightenment from the two women when he last visited us?"

"He did not say," replied Mungo.

"Then neither will I," said the monk with an innocent smile on his face. "You will be wanting a little sustenance and cells for the night before you journey on to wherever you are going," continued the monk.

"There are twelve of us on our way to Dùn Dèagh and we will be happy to sleep anywhere we can," replied Hithin.

"We will find six cells for you," said the monk, for which Hithin expressed his gratitude.

The group had a fairly comfortable night and after being summoned to the exceedingly early morning prayer, enjoyed a little cereal breakfast before moving on. They were hoping that Maarku's mention of a suitable craft being at hand was justified and a little under four hours later, as they neared the port, they saw three cogs idling in the calm water. Two of the vessels were being loaded and a boat named 'Fjölnir'[16] was being unloaded.

Boyd approached one of the crewmen and asked, "Where is that boat bound?"

"Nowhere," was the reply. "Where are you looking to journey?"

"Amestelle," answered Boyd.

The man sat there and slowly nodded, looking deep in thought and then asked, "Where is that?"

"Are you a sailor?" asked Boyd.

"No," said the man very slowly, "I just like looking at boats."

"Where can I find the captain of that boat?" asked Boyd pointing to the Fjölnir.

"He will be in The Bell," came the reply.

"Where is that?" asked Boyd.

---

[16] Single masted trade ships

"Well, it is not out there," replied the man pointing across the sea." Boyd gave up.

"Hithin, Mungo," he said, "let us find the tavern." He turned to the others and said, "We will return soon."

The tavern was a short walk from the docks. The three entered to a rowdy reception. Not too many of the drinkers looked or sounded particularly sober; however they realised that this might be an ideal opportunity to negotiate a good rate for passage to Amestelle.

While Hithin and Mungo waited, Boyd approached a man sitting quietly alone and asked him if he knew the captain of the 'Fjölnir'.

"I do," he replied.

Boyd paused for a moment hoping the man would volunteer further information, but his hopes were in vain.

"Where is he?" asked Boyd politely.

"In front of you," came an indignant reply. "What do you want?" he snapped.

"I wish to travel to Amestelle with eleven others, four horses and two carriages."

The man's attitude suddenly changed. "I have to be careful because I do not know what people want," he said.

"I am here in good faith," said Boyd.

"Come with me," said the captain.

The four of them walked the short distance back to the boat. Only then did Hithin notice the name of the boat and said to the captain, "That is a strange name for a boat."

"It means 'four' in Norse. I have four sons, who were born in Denmark, so I named the boat 'Fjölnir'."

Hithin looked at Boyd and Mungo and discreetly said, "Fjölnir was a legendary King in Norse mythology, said to have drowned in a vat of mead, while visiting a King in Zealand. Fjórir is the Norse word for four, but I do not think it wise to tell him."

"So, we are going to sail on a boat named after someone who drowned?" asked Mungo.

"I do not see any other empty boats in the port and at least Fjölnir would have died happy," said Boyd.

It was time to negotiate a price. The captain thought for a few moments then said, "The voyage will take nearly two days and if you are willing to help, it will be forty pounds."

Hithin replied, "Maarku has crossed many seas and knows how to sail a boat and I have sailed with him many times. We will all help in the voyage to Amestelle. I will give you twenty pounds now and twenty pounds when we get there."

The captain agreed. "We set sail in the morning," he said.

The two carriages were loaded onto the boat by hand and fastened to the deck with ropes and the four horses were led into individual compartments and secured in slings for safe transport across the sea.

Fortunately, there were calm waters on the outward journey and by early evening on the fourth day, the small fishing port of Amestelle was in sight. Everything was safely unloaded, no worse for wear. Hithin paid the captain the remaining twenty pounds.

"Will you be wanting passage back to Dùn Dèagh?" asked the captain.

"We will need a boat to take us back to Scotland," replied Boyd, "but it will not be from here. We will be travelling from Antwerp in about seventy days."

"I will be there," he replied.

"We do not know your name," said Maarku.

"I am Captain Teach," he replied, "and my family have been sailing these seas for many generations."

The journey had been long and very few had slept much, either through boredom, excitement or other more intimate reasons, so an overnight stop in Amestelle seemed appropriate. The first lodgings they came across was named 'De Waterherberg'. First Maarku and Lesedi approached the innkeeper and she asked, "Heb je zes kamers voor de nicht?"

The innkeeper suspiciously surveyed the twelve travellers before replying, with a smile on his face, "You want six rooms for your niece?"

Lesedi looked puzzled until the innkeeper explained, "Night is nacht." Lesedi acknowledged the correction. "Six rooms. That will be six shillings."

"Will you take this as payment?" asked Hithin showing the gold coins.

"Four gold coin," said the innkeeper.

"Two," replied Lesedi abruptly "and that is for feeding and stabling the horses too."

Begrudgingly the innkeeper accepted, knowing full well the value of the gold. "Bring the horses to the back and I will get one of my sons to stable them. There are six rooms up the stairs for you."

Maarku thanked the innkeeper. Dougal and Ross led the horses round the back while the others ordered a little refreshment.

After eating and resting for a while, they retired to their rooms.

When Maarku and Lesedi got to their room, he asked her, "How did you know the worth of a gold coin?"

"He looked a little greedy when he saw the gold, so I said half of what he asked," she replied.

Maarku was impressed by her astuteness. "We will be good together," he said. Lesedi smiled lovingly.

There was nothing much to see in Amestelle, apart from a large number of canals and a few small fishing vessels, so the twelve made the sixty-mile trip south-east to Arneym. Plenty of fields, trees and streams but not much of significant interest. The leisurely pace meant that they arrived late in the evening, and as they did not wish to disturb any of the locals, they camped in a clearing just outside the village, enjoying some of the food prepared at home. It was not the freshest food they had eaten but it satisfied a need. The four women slept in the carriages that night and the men remaining outside in the cool night air.

Dougal and Ross woke early that morning to hunt for local cuisine, returning with a few rabbits which Dougal promptly roasted over the campfire.

After nearly seven days, the group was becoming tired with just travelling and looked forward to the prospect of meeting some of the people suggested by both King Kenneth and Isabella at the first major trading place in Throtmanni, which unfortunately was another two days journey.

The trip was pleasant enough, roles being swapped at fairly regular intervals to allow those who had been at the reins the comparative comfort of carriage travel. When they arrived, they found Throtmanni itself not one of the most industrious towns, however much trade passed through from Belgica to Čzechy and further west to the Byzantine Empire, so there was a possibility that some sort of trade fayre might be in progress; thus giving them the opportunity of building 'official' relationships with even more places.

As luck would have it, there was a fayre. Numerous tents had been pitched for both stallholders and visitors, so renting one for six pence for a night under cover seemed practical. Kyle and Edith remained in the tent with the belongings. The horses were tethered nearby and the carriages just outside, while the others ambled round the fayre.

Boyd and Ross remembered some of the tradesmen from the earlier Frisian visit. Ross had recollections of the stall displaying herbs and spices from India and Sholto's close encounter with Abbas, the Indian gentleman. Boyd mentioned to Hithin that this could be a good opportunity to use one of the brooches, to which Hithin agreed. He went to fetch one from a locked box concealed inside one of the carriages. He asked Ross to tie one of them onto a long strand of thin tunic thread and place it round his neck. While the others made their way round the displays, Boyd and Ross approached the targeted stall and as hoped, Abbas caught sight of the brooch and again his eyes lit up.

"Welcome," he said giving Ross a slightly puzzled look.

Before Abbas had time to say anything else, Ross said, "I have the good fortune of seeing you again. I did say I would return."

Abbas's previous fixation on the brooch as opposed to his inability to recognise someone of different nationality, countenance and build, worked well in Ross's favour.

"Tell me where in India you are from," asked Boyd.

"I am from a small village called Katyur in the Himalayas," replied Abbas. "I will tell you about my stall. The nard flowers grow high in the mountains. The oil is for perfume, incense and medicine. It is very rare. I will give you all this for the brooch," he said pointing to the stall.

"The brooch is worth more than what you have to offer," said Boyd. Abbas then turned to Fuling and muttered something. Fuling nodded.

"Come back when the fair has ended for the day. We will have a gift for you," said Abbas.

The two continued looking round the fair intrigued as to what Abbas and Fuling had on offer to warrant a clandestine meeting.

Early that evening, they all met in the tent to relate the day's events, Boyd recapping his meeting with Abbas. The others too had a little luck managing to build friendships with towns in Belgica and Francia, not yet having visited the places but saying they would do so, later in their travels. Unsurprisingly nobody had heard of Haudonia Isle, but there was keen interest in the rich veins of gold, copper and iron.

When all was quiet, Boyd and Ross returned to meet Abbas and Fuling who were very excited to see them.

Fuling began, "Lao Tzu taught us how to exist in harmony with the universe and through meditation we can use the power of nature to become one with ourselves."

Not being very philosophical, neither Boyd nor Ross quite understood this.

Fuling continued, "I knew you would be here. I have a gift for you." He disappeared into the tent pitched next to the stall and emerged carrying a beautiful, delicately patterned kaolin vase. "This is from the Shang Dynasty," he said. "It is two thousand years old."

Both Boyd and Ross felt a little guilty knowing they were exchanging this rare piece of pottery for a fake brooch.

"Please show me the brooch," requested Abbas. Ross removed it from around his neck and passed it across. The two studied the brooch talking very excitedly, the smiles becoming wider and wider as they carefully scrutinised it.

"It is perfect," said Abbas. "Please tell no one about this. No one must ever know we have this."

"You have my word," replied a relieved Boyd.

Abbas held the brooch in his two hands, looked up to the skies, then closed his eyes and said a short incantation. There seemed to be a small flash of light appear above the brooch, startling Boyd and Ross.

Fuling saw this reaction and said, "This has the power of nature." Boyd now wondered if the brooch did have mystical powers and they had given the real one away, a concern that would be with him for the next sixty days.

"Did you see that?" Ross said to Boyd as they walked back to the others.

"I do not understand," replied Boyd.

"I wish Drake was here." Boyd was awake all night, mulling over the events while Matilda was a little disappointed at not getting the attention she would have enjoyed.

It was quite amazing how one of the rented tents managed to magically fold up and find its way into one of the carriages. A two-and-a-half-day journey to Frankenfort lay ahead, passing, after half a day's travel, through the small settlement at Lüdenscheid and then on towards Sigena, where they camped for the night.

As the others began pitching the tent, Kyle and Edith scouted the area nearby and came across a very pleasant farmstead. A few chickens and cows grazed in a small field. They approached the farmhouse and the door was already opened. Kyle knocked. The door opened a little further.

He shouted, "Hail, good fellows!" There was no response.

Edith stayed close behind Kyle, holding tightly onto his tunic. They went further inside. Kyle shouted again. Still no response. Edith's heart was beating a little quicker. They entered a small room at the back of the farmstead, Kyle looking to his right. Edith entered behind him looking to her left. Kyle turned to see a man and a woman, hanging by a noose from a wooden beam. They quickly ran towards the door, only to be confronted by three men blocking their path.

"Take the woman," said one of the men. The two grabbed Edith and took her out of the room. Kyle tried to fight them off, but they were too strong for him.

"Now you will hang," said the first man at which point he heard a loud banging on the front door.

"Alban, Godric!" he yelled. No answer. "Alban, Godric!" he yelled again. Edith's piercing scream was heard. The first man ran outside to see his two friends with daggers to their throats and Edith in Hithin's arms. Kyle quickly followed him out, wrestling him to the ground.

"Edith," said Hithin, "it is for you to choose."

Edith's recollections of her parent's savage slaughter came back to her. She forgave Vogg but she was not prepared to forgive these three for the senseless murders.

Hithin said to Nesta, "It is for you to choose." Without hesitation, she signalled for them to be hanged.

The farmer and his wife were carefully taken down from the beam and reverentially carried out the back of the home.

The ordeal was too much for Nesta and she broke down as the three aggressors were led to the back room, pleading for their lives and trembling as they contemplated their imminent fate. Shortly thereafter, Boyd, Maarku and Mungo returned. It is right that we bury the farmer and his wife. The three dug a grave at the back of the farmstead where they laid the two, side by side, to rest in peace.

After a short prayer, Hithin said, "I do not think they would mind if we took a few eggs."

"I am pleased you said that," said Frothi, "as I do not believe we have room for a cow in a carriage."

Back at the camp site, the tent being fully erected, they enjoyed a healthy portion of both boiled and poached eggs.

Hithin came up to Kyle and Edith and said, "We are always close. No harm will befall any of you." Edith soon fell asleep in Kyle's arms.

From Frankefort to Stuotgarten they went, and then on to Munichen. The stopover in Stuotgarten was purposely brief, mainly due to the prospect of Ungarian invasions, so they went back on the road for another three days. From there, the group travelled to Osterrîche stopping at Salzburg and then on to Italy, calling at Uillach, Venice, Verona, Milan and finally Turin, before progressing through Helvitia.

In Venice, Hithin decided to take one of the brooches along with him. When he opened the locked box, he noticed a small scorch mark on the inside of the lid. He asked if anyone had been near the box, but nobody had. He thought no more about it.

Venice was developing into a powerful maritime empire under the guidance of the doge Pietro Tradonico, and Boyd, Hithin and Maarku found him to be a well-educated man who inspired confidence in his leadership. Pietro impressed the three of them and in exchange for fostering a long-term relationship with the two places, one of the brooches was bestowed upon him. Again, he had heard of the legend and promised to uphold the honour of the brooch.

Many friendships were struck but only a few merited the high accolade of being awarded what, on the face of it, was a worthless piece of hastily copied jewellery. The legend of the brooch had spread far and wide and those deserving enough to have been given one of the brooches, swore to keep its existence secret. None wanted to share the prospect of power and wealth.

After Geneva, it was to Francia, the towns of Dijon, Auxerre, Paris then Lille, before a return visit to Belgica where they hoped Captain Teach would be waiting.

On the final leg of the journey to Antwerp, they were discussing the advancements in architecture, farming, weaponry, materials and medicines they had come across and how the relationships they had built up would serve, at least Stoleware, in the future. They had only used four of the nineteen brooches, however there were still many places to visit throughout the world. The group had made good progress by cutting short their time in both Salzburg and Geneva, as they found nothing of particular use or interest on this visit.

Antwerp proved to be an interesting town. "I have been here before," said Frothi.

"I have too," said Hithin.

"The fortress," said Maarku.

"Het Steen," said Hithin. Their expressions changed to one of sadness.

"Why are you sad?" asked Lesedi.

"I have bad memories," said Maarku.

There was a long silence as the three Vikings closed their eyes, mentally reliving the brutal incursions into Antwerp.

"Will we ever have forgiveness?" asked Frothi.

Matilda approached Frothi and said, "Do you forgive those who have wronged you?"

Frothi thought for a while and answered, "Boyd said that Fuling told him of the teachings of Lao Tzu, that we must live in harmony with the universe."

Boyd then added, "Lao Tzu was a very wise man. I remember what else Fuling said about his teachings. He said, 'Being deeply loved by someone gives you strength, while loving someone deeply gives you courage'." Boyd looked at the tears in Lesedi's eyes and said, "She can see guilt, but she can also see love and forgiveness. Let us move on."

After the lesson in philosophy, they moved into the centre of Antwerp. Kyle and Edith tended the horses while the others looked round a busy market.

Boyd, Matilda, Nesta and Mungo were amazed at the intricate patterns on the exquisitely delicate glass figurines. Nesta pointed to the glass statuettes and asked, "How do you make these?"

"I will show you," said the owner. He took them round the back of the market stall to where two men were sitting near a hot furnace. The owner explained how the molten glass was shaped using long blowpipes and various tools and how the glass was coloured.

"We make these for monasteries in many countries. These are for the Culdee monastery in Dunkeld," he said, pointing to some exquisite six-foot tall stained-glass windows. "Where are you from?"

Boyd replied, "Haudonia Isle, an island in the Orcades."

"I know the Orcades, but I do not know that isle, but there are many small islands there."

Changing the subject very quickly, Boyd asked if the women could try the art of glass blowing.

The owner smiled and said, "It will be an honour for a beautiful woman to try." He sat Matilda down and gave her a long pipe with a small blob of molten glass on the end. "Blow gently," he said. Matilda blew gently watching the glass slowly expand.

Unfortunately, she blew a little too hard and a small bubble appeared on one side of the glass. She started laughing and said, "It looks like it is with child, just like me."

Everything went quiet, jaws dropping. Then a great big smile appeared on Boyd's face. "I am to be a father?" he asked.

"You are," replied Matilda. Even the owner of the shop had a little tear in his eye.

"I did not know you could conceive a child blowing glass," said Maarku.

Matilda stood and after the congratulations, she was presented with her first glass blowing effort.

"It is my gift to you," said the owner.

"What is your name?" she asked.

"It is Farraj. It means joyous in Arabic."

"I will not forget," she said.

They left the stall happy and excited and returned to the others where Matilda gave them the good news.

Edith came over to Matilda and whispered in her ear, "So am I, but I have not yet told Kyle."

"When will you tell him?" asked Matilda quietly.

"I am afraid," said Edith.

"What is there to be afraid of," asked Matilda.

"My mother lost four children at birth, and I am afraid I may lose our child."

"Kyle will understand. You need to tell him."

"I will," said Edith.

"Now," replied Matilda, quite forcibly.

Edith went up to Kyle blushing. He put his arm round her and said, "I did wonder when you were going to tell me."

"How did you know?" she asked.

"You told Berta, Berta told Asmund and Asmund told me." Edith explained her worries to Kyle who simply told her to rest for the next few months.

"There are many people at home who are there to help you. All will be well," he said. That made her feel a little easier.

Besides having a renowned glass industry, Antwerp was a recognised centre in the production of pottery, based on the Carolingian art of the Frankish Empire. No one dare venture a request to throw pottery after the interesting events of the glass blowing session. However, Dougal and Ross took great interest in the precision, design and colouring of the finished stoneware.

Dougal turned to Ross and asked, "Are you thinking what I am thinking?"

"I think we could make this," replied Ross.

One of the potters approached the two men and said, "My name is Tigaerd. Are you looking for some of our fine pottery?"

"We are. Where do you get the clay?" asked Dougal.

"From the banks of the River Scheldt. It is soft clay and good for what we make. Come with me," said Tigaerd.

He showed them many finished items from large vases to small thimble-sized novelties and as they were walked round, how the clay was prepared, shaped, fired, glazed, trimmed and then painted and decorated.

Tigaerd asked, "Where are you from?"

"Haudonia Isle," replied Ross.

"Are you traders?" asked Tigaerd.

"We are here for a royal person," replied Ross.

"May I ask who the royal person is?" responded Tigaerd.

Hithin just happened to join them as Dougal replied, "It is Princess Mælbrigða of Ribe."

"Mælbrigða?" asked Tigaerd.

Hithin's expression was one of, 'why could he have not thought of a different name?'

Tigaerd looked up at Hithin and asked, "Who are you?"

"I am with these two," he replied.

"You are here for Princess Mælbrigða? I did not think she was still living," replied Tigaerd sceptically.

"It is a descendant who has kept the name in memory of her ancestors," answered Hithin.

"I have heard of a brooch. Is this true?" continued Tigaerd.

"I too have heard of this brooch, but I have not had the good fortune to see it," lied Hithin, in an attempt to dig them all out of a hole.

Tigaerd thought for a few moments, and not that the prospect of power and wealth influenced him in the slightest, he replied, "I am the burgermeister in Antwerp and I do believe that if I had sight of this brooch, then we could enjoy a lasting friendship between our two towns."

The dilemma was establishing an accord with a centre of excellence in glass and pottery for a fake brooch, which, as Tigaerd seemed to be an expert in adornment, might prove a little awkward, or otherwise continue down the innocent, 'what brooch?' route.

"If what is said about the brooch is true, how would you use it?" asked Hithin.

Tigaerd's mind was working overtime. "I would use my power and wealth to guide others," he replied.

"Only those who use the brooch for the good of everyone are worthy," said Hithin.

"I know you have the brooch," said Tigaerd.

"If you seek all for yourself, then the brooch will not bring you the power and wealth you seek," replied Hithin.

He was feeling quite proud with himself thinking that he may be able to establish a relationship with Antwerp and yet provide Tigaerd with an element of doubt as to his worthiness.

"If you are not true to your word, then the brooch will not bring you all you desire."

"I will prove I am worthy," said Tigaerd.

Hithin, being the nominated custodian of the brooches, took one out from inside his tunic.

"Remember," he began, "it is now for you to prove yourself. It will take time and you must not say you have this for fear of it being taken and used for evil."

"I promise," said Tigaerd excitedly. He took the brooch, carefully examined it and said, "It is as I believed. Now I have a gift for you."

He disappeared for a few moments returning with a magnificent, highly decorated handled jug about twelve inches in diameter and eighteen inches tall. Numerous hand-painted animals were depicted round the jug.

"This was made for King Lothair of Italy, but he did not wait for the decoration to be finished. Now you must have it."

Hithin gratefully accepted the gift and then said to Tigaerd, "We must leave. Our boat is about to set sail. We will visit again soon."

The group assembled and made their way to the port where Captain Teach was ready to take them back home.

"It is good to see you again," said Hithin.

"I kept my word," replied the captain.

All loaded and secured, the near six-hundred-mile journey north was underway. In three to four days, with a fair wind, they should be home in Stoleware.

Chapter 20

The Power and the Glory

It was early morning when they landed at Dùn Dèagh, carefully unloading the expectant women, horses, carriages and precious gifts.

"I have a feeling I will see you again," said the captain as he was paid his forty pounds.

"That you will," replied Hithin as they rode away from the port.

Twenty-eight miles later they arrived at what seems to have been designated as their second home; the Culdee monastery at Dunkeld. A friendly face appeared at the entrance.

"Six rooms for the night?" said the monk as he opened the two large wooden doors, allowing the carriages to enter adding, "You seem to arrive just as we are about to eat. You are most welcome to join us."

Evening meal, overnight accommodation, early morning prayer, breakfast then back on the road. Forty miles to go. They could almost smell the village.

Familiar landmarks appeared; familiar faces greeted them as they rode into the village. Alpin was at the front of the welcoming committee, closely followed by the rest of the village. After two months, both the village and the vegetation had blossomed into an extravagance of colour as had Alpin's bright pink tunic.

"It is not as you would be unseen by outsiders," said Boyd as he and Matilda climbed down from the carriage box seat.

"Anika was trying a dye from the madder plant, and I believe she used a little too much. If I lose my way, I will be easy to find," said Alpin in his defence.

The carriages were vacated, everyone wanting to know how the trip had gone.

Alpin said, "Tomorrow, when you have all rested, you can tell all of your journey."

He held Hithin back and out of earshot of the others, and said to him, "I must speak to you alone about Drake."

"What is the matter?" asked Hithin.

"About ten days after you left, he was with Sholto, when a spark of light came from the brooch Sholto was wearing hit Drake. Drake went into a deep sleep for two days. When he woke, he was not the same man. Garmund and Frothi do not understand."

Hithin thought. "I was in Throtmanni at that time with a man named Abbas. He was holding a brooch and said an incantation when a spark of light came from it. The next time I opened the box of brooches, I saw a burn mark on the inside of the box."

"What does this mean?" asked a worried looking Alpin.

"Is Sholto hurt?" asked Hithin.

"No, only Drake," was the reply.

"We must watch him," said Hithin.

"How many have a brooch?" asked Alpin.

Hithin thought, "Five. Abbas in Throtmanni, Pietro, the doge in Venice, Paganello, a man of high stature in the royal circle in Milan, Bastien, a merchant in Geneva and Tigaerd, the man in Antwerp who gave us a fine stoneware vase."

"I do not know what we should do," said Alpin.

"Let us watch Drake for a few more days, but do not say much to the others," said Hithin. Alpin agreed.

The following morning, with everyone refreshed, the whole village met in the church. Surprisingly, Drake was there, looking as though nothing had happened. Alpin opened the meeting by thanking the travellers for their efforts in securing friendships with the towns and cities they had visited and then turned his attention to the small matter of Matilda and Edith. There was a thunderous cheer from the group. Berta then stood up and announced that she too was expecting, which resulted in another thunderous cheer. Sister Eangyth shuffled in her seat looking a little more radiant than normal.

Hithin summarised the events, showing off to the assembly the numerous prized acquisitions brought back by the travellers. The majority of places visited had shown interest in developing a lasting bond with Haudonia Isle, intrigued by how such a small territory could sustain an endless supply of precious raw materials, but as these places had not previously been approached by overseas visitors offering such goodwill gestures, any scepticisms were withheld. As Boyd and Hithin, with interjections from the others, summarised events in each place visited, Drake listed them in the journal. Alpin, who was sitting next to Drake, noticed that even on the two days that Drake was unconscious, entries were made in the journal in Drake's handwriting.

"Does anyone have anything else to say?" asked Alpin.

Drake stood. By now, everyone knew of Drake's outage and as he stood, the whole hall fell silent. He began. "I have talked to many people in the village and made entries in our journal. We need to keep safe all we have; from the day you first came here to what you have now brought from other countries and what you will bring back in time to come. There is no place to hide all this above the ground, so I ask that we build a vault under the ground where no one can see it. We may forget where these gifts came from, so I will place a scroll by them showing from where and when they came."

"Can this be done?" asked Alpin.

Enar responded, "Kyle, Nevin, Frothi, Asmund, you have helped in the building of the village above the ground, can we build what Drake is asking for under the ground?"

"This will take much thought," replied Asmund, "but it may well be so."

"It is for you to see. When you five have spoken, we will decide," said Alpin.

"It may be wise to put the brooches that remain, inside the chamber," added Drake. This comment caused a little consternation within the assembly. "I must leave now," said Drake. He rose and walked out of the church. Alpin signalled for Coll to follow him but to keep out of sight.

Coll returned about two hours later and found Alpin. Coll look quite puzzled.

"Tell me, where did he go?" asked Alpin.

"To the stream. He was watching the fish jump out of the water and did not move at all until he walked back to the camp. He did not see me. What do you want me to do?"

Alpin thought for quite a while and then replied, "Do nothing. Say not a word to anyone but keep a watch on him."

"I will," said Coll.

The next day, Alpin, Hithin, Enar, Kyle, Gillis, Nevin, Frothi, Asmund, Duff and Drake, met to discuss the underground chamber proposal. Drake had already drawn his plan for the chamber, showing the nine his idea.

He began. "We will build the chamber one hundred and sixty feet long and one hundred and sixty feet wide, twenty feet deep and four feet below the ground. There will be one way in. Holes will be put in for air and the sides of the chamber are to be lined with wood and covered in pitch so no water will enter the chamber." Drake was very thorough and precise in his specifications, answering questions about the excavations and materials as he went along.

The plan was carefully studied by all, as Drake sat motionless, appearing to be in another deep sleep.

"This will take many months," said Gillis.

"Are you going anywhere?" asked Drake, suddenly coming to life. There was no answer. Drake continued. "Here is what you will need." He presented them with his calculations on the amount of wood needed to fully line the chamber and how much tar would need to be extracted from burnt wood. He had also planned for where the excavated earth would be taken, slightly changing the landscape surrounding the village but helping to reinforce its integrity and secrecy.

He was also inspired by some of the inventions the group had learnt about on their travels and how he could employ them in the village. He was particularly interested in using the mechanisms of water mills, adapting them to generate a sustainable source of air inside the chamber.

Some of what Drake showed them was far in advance of anything they had ever seen before and despite the fact that they found it difficult to understand, they could not fault his reasoning and decided to proceed with his proposals, but still remained a little sceptical about his ambitious innovations.

While the group of twelve were away, Drake had talked about using mirrors to light up the chamber and what materials would be needed. Garmund was aware, from his previous incursions into Scotland, of the high density of copper and silver ores around Glencoe and obsidian from ancient volcanic activity on the Isle of Eigg. Enar, Asmund, Coll and Colban volunteered to make the explorative seven day, nearly a hundred- and seventy-mile round trip to the Isle of Eigg, crossing the water at Glencoe and Glenuig. The latter combined a wild and rocky landscape with thriving fishing and craftwork industries, stimulating ideas for additional activities at home.

Slowly but surely, the plans came together. Those, who at first were unconvinced about the viability of Drake's chamber, became increasingly enthusiastic as the building progressed. Garmund had created large circular mirrors using the materials brought back from Glencoe and Eigg, and these would be carefully positioned inside the chamber to provide light, at least when the sun was shining. Producing a safe and natural light at other times of the day, was on the list of things to do.

Matilda and Edith were nervously excited at the prospect of impending motherhood. However, Sister Eangyth was appreciably a little less than enthusiastic, as she was trying desperately hard, but unsuccessfully, to conceal her fuller figure. It was not long before Anna, Berta, Elen and Nesta too, announced their good news. Six planned additions and one inhabitual exposition.

Elen came up with the idea of using a relay of messengers to keep in contact with the people and places previously visited but it seemed unfair to ask members of the village to perform this task, as it would mean many of them would be away for quite a long time. Malcolm had remembered that on the first visit to the Culdee monastery at Dunkeld, where it was mentioned how the monks got messages from the Lateran Palace in Rome and how these messages were disseminated across the world. The best person to assist, unless he was a little preoccupied with his frequent confessions, was Brother Martin. Fingal was sent to fetch Martin and escort him to the church.

"What is this about?" asked the monk.

"I have heard that it is something you did at the monastery," replied Fingal. At that moment, Sister Mildrith walked by, as visions of interesting associations came flooding back into Martin's mind. "I do not understand," said Brother Martin.

"Where are you going?" asked Mildrith.

"Alpin and Hithin wish to see me about something I did at the monastery." Mildrith blushed a little and quickly went on her way.

"Sister Mildrith looked a little warm," said Fingal as Martin adjusted the collar on his habit in a vain attempt to cool his glowing cheeks.

When they arrived at the church, Hithin said to Martin. "How did you do it in the monastery?" Martin felt a little uncomfortable at this question.

"Were there many monks who did this?" asked Hithin.

Martin decided that it was probably better to come clean about the whole affair and replied, "There were few nuns at the monastery, so we had to share."

"I did not believe that the nuns would do this," said Hithin.

"Not all of them did this and they were very careful about watching to ensure that no one was around," replied Martin.

"So, they rode to other monasteries?" asked Hithin. Martin looked extremely puzzled by this apparently unrelated question.

"I do not think they did," replied Martin.

"How did you get word from Rome?" asked Hithin. "You said to Malcolm when he came to the monastery, you know what is happening to your brothers around the world."

Martin now realised what they were talking about and gave a great sigh of relief. "We have many monasteries in the world and the brothers journey between them. We can send word to our brothers, but it will take time."

"You are wanting to send word to those you met on your travels?" asked Martin.

"We are," replied Hithin. "Would the monks help?"

Before Martin could answer, Alpin said, "My brother will have messengers."

"I do not think we can trust all the King's messengers. We have passed many monasteries on our journeys but few kings; and if the monks would help, we can send word to those with whom we have traded," said Hithin.

"I think the monks will help," agreed Martin. "Now please tell me what this is with sharing the nuns," requested Alpin.

"I meant sharing the work at the monastery," replied Martin. Alpin gave a nod, however obviously he was unconvinced by Martin's response.

Hithin continued. "We have many to send word to, from Amestelle to Geneva to affirm our bonds. In time to come, we hope to seek bonds with countries further away, Rus, Song, Dali, Jin and Xia. We will learn of how these towns and cities develop and use their knowledge so we can improve our village, but no one must know where we are. We must make Haudonia Isle real, but how?"

Alpin and Martin looked at each other and shrugged their shoulders, not expecting such a question. Hithin looked at each of them in turn, hoping for some sort of response but nothing was forthcoming.

He continued, "I will speak to Drake in the morning, and we will speak again soon." Alpin and Martin rose and left the church, leaving Hithin alone with his thoughts.

The following morning, Hithin gathered together, Alpin, Martin, Drake, Boyd and Maarku. He again asked the question. "How can we make Haudonia Isle a real place?"

Drake, who was sitting nodding his head from side to side with his two index fingers raised by the side of his head, said, "We need to put the island on a map."

"Without seeming to be a little simple, how can we do that?" asked Maarku.

"Draw it on a map," replied Drake with an expression of exasperation at what he deemed to be a stupid question. Maarku then repeated his previous question. Drake looked at him and said, "There is a respected man who has made maps, and these are used by men across the world."

"We must see this man."

"Where is he?" asked Alpin.

"Baghdad," replied Drake. "He is known by Muḥammad ibn Mūsā al-Khwārizmī."

"We were hoping he might be a little closer," said Boyd.

"If we have the island drawn on his map and this is put onto more maps he draws, then those who have his maps will make more maps that will show the island," said Drake.

"I do like what you say," said Hithin, "but that does mean we have to journey to Baghdad."

Drake turned to Maarku and said, "I have heard that, not so long ago, Vikings sailed down the Volga, making their way south and followed the trade routes of central Asia across the Caspian Sea to Baghdad."

"Is this so?" asked Alpin.

"I have heard this to be true," replied Maarku.

"Then that is what we must do," said Boyd.

Drake said, "The journey will be to Dùn Dèagh then across the sea to Beirut, then by land to Baghdad. It will take more than thirty days to get there."

"Is there any other way we can have the island on a map and how do you know his name?" asked Alpin.

"Muḥammad ibn Mūsā al-Khwārizmī was well-known by the emperors of Rome, and he was well trusted. I said that if we have the island of Haudonia drawn on his map, then it will be on all maps. I heard of him from scrolls the Romans left in Carlisle," replied Drake.

"There is no other way we want the island to be known," sighed Alpin.

Drake added, "It will be wise to take one of the brooches. He is a very wise man and will know of this brooch."

"We now have to decide who will go on this journey."

"I will," said Drake immediately. "If I can see what he has, I will commit all to memory."

Bearing in mind Drake's recent comatose state, Alpin was a little reluctant at first, to allow Drake to embark on this long journey.

"I know what is in your mind," said Drake, "but you do not have to concern yourself. No evil can befall me."

"I do not understand," said Hithin.

"I am a descendant of Mælbrigða. I have the power and the glory," replied Drake with an eerie air of authority.

The room suddenly went cold.

Chapter 21

The Power and the Gory

Alpin, Hithin, Boyd and Maarku met up in the church hall. Garmund, Vogg and Fingal had not yet travelled on behalf of the village. Garmund, being an expert physician and Vogg, being an intimidating, yet gentle giant, who was thought to be essential as the village bodyguard, were excused from this duty. That left Fingal who, as yet, had not been too forthcoming about his relationship with a certain nun, even though it was commonly known that he was guilty of being the cause of her current predicament. Therefore, it did not seem particularly appropriate to send any of these men on such a mission.

Alpin began. "We must find someone who is willing to make this journey, but at the same time a top priority for our community should surely be to make certain that the island will be put on a map."

At that moment in walked Drake carrying a rolled-up scroll. "I have this," he said, opening the scroll to reveal the seventy islands of the Orcades. This is where we are." He pointed to an island just north of Hrossey. "The island is there on the map."

"Where did you get this?" asked Alpin.

"The Romans drew many maps. I brought this from Carlisle. It is my work," replied Drake.

"Do we need to travel to Baghdad if the island is on a map?" asked Boyd.

Drake thought for a moment then said, "I wish to give a brooch to Muḥammad ibn Mūsā al-Khwārizmī then I will discover what he is about."

"I do not see how that will help," said Hithin.

"But I do," snapped Drake. "I will take it to him," upon which he stormed out of the meeting.

Hithin shook his head. "Does anyone understand this?"

Maarku looked up from the open maps and said, "I do." Alpin, Hithin and Boyd were more than a little surprised at Maarku's response. "Many years ago, I was in Beirut and chanced upon a man named Alam. He had a facial likeness to Drake, in what he said and did. I have not said anything as I was not certain, but now I can see that Drake could be a getwinn[17]. The name Alam is Arabic for world, and he spoke strangely about knowing all there is to know. At times he was dark, and I felt frightened by him."

"Does Drake know of this man?" asked Alpin.

"He may well do which is why he is eager to take the journey, but not to see the man who makes the maps. He must not go," stated Maarku forcibly.

"The only man who knew the truth was William, but Mungo's dagger silenced him," said Boyd.

"Did we slay the right person?" asked Alpin.

Boyd suggested. "We must return to Carlisle and speak with those who knew Drake. I will go with Mungo and Gerik. The journey will take three or four days. We hope to return within nine days."

"You must leave soon," said Alpin, "but do not tell anyone where you are going."

"I will need to tell Nesta that I will be away," said Mungo.

"Tell her you are going to visit my brother at Forteviot. It is better that few people know where you are going. You will leave in the morning, I will ask Tovi to ready three horses for you," said Alpin.

While most of the village slept; just as Alpin was ready to see Boyd, Gerik and Mungo off to Carlisle, Coll came running up to them.

"Drake has gone," he said.

"Check the horses," said Boyd.

Coll ran to the stables, and returned shortly, saying, "One is missing."

"You must make haste to Carlisle. I will send one of us to Dùn Dèagh,"

"I will go," said Coll. He saddled his horse and the four set off south, first towards Kenmore, from where Coll would then ride on to Dunkeld, while the others would divert to Carlisle, not wishing to stop longer in one place than was absolutely necessary.

Slowly, the rest of the village came to life, for the moment unaware of the current emergency. The most popular venue was the ever-expanding

---

[17] twin

brewery, where the endless stream of visitors, complaining of their thirst after a hard day's work, kept Vogg, Dougal and Malcolm fully occupied.

As they made their way out to the fields, Anna asked her twin sister Nesta. "Where is Mungo this morning? Does he not walk you to your work?"

"He is to visit Alpin's brother in Forteviot with Boyd and Mungo. He will be gone for no more than nine days."

"Sister Eangyth is putting on a little weight," said Anna with a wry smile on her face.

"I have also heard that Sister Mildrith has been stung and not by one of the bees," replied Nesta with an equally wry smile on her face.

Despite the jibes, the atmosphere for now, was extremely convivial. No one had any reason to worry. The village was developing, above and below ground and early warning systems were in place just in case someone inadvertently strayed into risky territory. In fact, nothing could be better.

The search party was having no luck trying to find any trace of Drake. They stopped at the numerous small hamlets and farmsteads along the route, but no one had seen him. At Kenmore, the group split, with Coll heading towards Dùn Dèagh while the others made their way south to Carlisle. Five miles further on, Coll felt that, as he had no joy from people he passed on his journey, it was time to return home. It was just past midday so hopefully he would be back in the village early in the evening.

The others were conscious of the importance and urgency of their trip and spent as much time as possible on the road. Luckily, there were numerous ranches along the route where they sought fresh horses for a relatively small outlay, promising to return the horses on the journey back. In under three days, they arrived in Carlisle and went straight to the council chamber.

They were surprised to see an extremely distraught Thomas looking very dazed.

"What is the matter?" asked Gerik.

Thomas felt his head then looked at his hand. It was covered in blood.

"What happened?" asked Boyd.

"I do not know," replied Thomas. "I was in the council and heard footsteps behind me. Before I could turn round, I felt a heavy blow on my head. I do not remember any more until I woke."

Suddenly three women came running towards then from different directions, covered in blood, screaming in horror.

"What is this?" asked a concerned Thomas.

The first woman, panting heavily said, "Silas is dead."

The second woman collapsed onto the ground barely able to speak. "Herman is dead," she eventually said.

They looked at the third woman, tears coming from her eyes, "Someone has slit Silas's throat," she said.

Boyd, Gerik and Mungo looked at each other all thinking the same.

"It cannot be," said Mungo.

"What do you mean?" asked Thomas.

"Drake," said Gerik.

"Drake?" asked Thomas.

Bryce and his guards appeared. Thomas explained what had happened and the guards quickly ran to see the victims.

They soon returned, one of them saying, "They have all had their throats cut."

"Do you remember William's dying words?" asked Boyd.

"He said, 'You do not understand'," replied Mungo.

"I am beginning to understand," sighed Boyd.

By now, many people had gathered, trying to comfort the three grief-stricken women. Boyd, Gerik and Mungo took Thomas, Bryce and his guards inside the council chambers and explained his fears.

"Where is Drake's mother?" asked Gerik.

"I do not know," replied Thomas. "When Drake left, his mother went away but no one knows where. Why do you ask?"

"Not many people knew Drake and those who knew him the most are now either dead or have left," replied Gerik

"We need to return home," said Mungo.

"You cannot travel tonight. You must stay and tell me all that worries you," said Thomas.

As the three women were being comforted, Thomas led the group inside the council chambers where Boyd related the events that had happened from the time Drake was struck by a light from the brooch.

"There is something we do not know," said Gerik.

"Elen!" shouted Boyd suddenly.

"Elen?" queried Mungo.

"She is William's daughter," replied Boyd. "She is now the only one left who may know Drake."

Mungo then told them of a question he had asked Drake when they first met. He asked if William was his father.

"If that is so," he said, "then Elen would be his sister. We must go now," he added. Their hearts sunk as they feared the worst.

Bryce said to one of his guards, "Quick, fresh horses. I will come with you."

Quickly, the horses were saddled and the four started the journey back to Stoleware, very apprehensive as to what they might find. The one hundred- and seventy-five-mile trip seemed an eternity away. They rode hard and fast, only stopping to change their horses at the farms they had previously used, causing some annoyance by waking up the occupants at highly inconvenient hours. Again no one they met had seen a lone horseman.

They arrived very early in the morning of the third day. Vogg and Ulf were on guard and Boyd asked Vogg to blow his Gjallarhorn to waken the village. Bleary-eyed people came out to see what the commotion was about. Boyd looked round trying to find Alpin and Elen. There was no sign of them.

"They are not here!" he shouted.

Boyd and Mungo barged their way through the villagers and ran towards Alpin's home. They burst in, finding them both lying on the bed with their throats cut. They collapsed in tears. Hithin was the next to arrive. He looked on in horror at the sickening sight that confronted him.

The three slowly walked out into the open; everyone asking what the matter was. Slowly, news filtered through to everyone. There was disbelief on their faces.

Gerik said to Hithin, "Please check the brooches."

Hithin returned shortly, "One is missing and Drake is gone. He must have had a key for himself," he said.

"Who has done this?" they all asked.

Hithin started to address the people. "There is a person who we took in and this is what he has done to us. If you see Drake, you must kill him, cut him into pieces and then burn his body."

No one slept. They all sat outside holding lighted candles keeping vigil out of respect for their departed friends.

Chapter 22

Little Feet

When morning broke, they all gathered in the church. Hithin and Boyd tried to explain what had happened and how they were all taken in by Drake.

"Those who were brutally slain may have been aware of Drake. Elen was the daughter of the mayor of Carlisle and Drake could not take the chance that she, or anyone else, knew something about him, nor could he chance that she had not told Alpin. I do not believe he will return," said Hithin.

"Why did he want the chamber under the ground?" asked Coll.

"I do not know yet," replied Hithin, "but I am certain we will know in time."

"How did Drake return from Carlisle so fast and how did he get into our village without being seen?" asked Gillis.

"I do not have answers for you yet. We must improve our guard," said Hithin. "Drake knows how we stay safe. There will be more on watch from tonight. Garmund, you have made looking glasses. We need to use them to look out for those who try to come into our village. Lesedi, Garmund, you spoke of making tears from peppers. You must do that."

Angus rose, saying, "I can use a fire in the mirrors to light the village."

Hithin then said, "We need a strong lock on the door of the chamber. There will be no more journeys until we feel safe in the village. We all have much to do."

Brother Martin then stood. "We are here to mourn the loss of our dear friends. Please stand. This brutal slaying will not go unpunished. God will never forgive him and if I get to him before God does, I will slit his throat. I am a man of God, but I believe in justice on earth. God can do with him what he wants but not until I have finished with him and then Satan can have him. May they rest in peace."

The villagers stood astounded by the tone of Brother Martin's words considering, as up to now, he had been perceived as a mild mannered, if not extremely randy monk.

Hithin then asked Asmund and Colban if they would make two coffins. "There is flat land near where we are building the chamber. Frothi, Alban, will you dig the graves? One of us will need to ride to Forteviot to tell the King."

"I will go," said Kentigern.

"Upon your return we will lay the two to rest. Be on your guard, we must be watchful."

They all left the church in silence. Kentigern rode off to Forteviot while preparations were made for the funerals. Not much work was done that day. An air of apprehension and sadness filled the village, with people looking nervously over their shoulders at the slightest unrecognised sound.

Kentigern arrived at Forteviot late in the day and after telling the guards the purpose of his visit, he was shown to the King.

"Welcome. Why have you come alone?" the King asked.

Kentigern began to tell the King the terrible news. The King walked towards the window and looked out, but his vacant expression showed that he was not seeing anything. He shouted for a servant. "I need to journey in the morning, and I want all my personal guards with me." The servant bowed and left the room.

"Who is this, Drake?" asked the King. Kentigern briefly explained where they had initially found him, and how he had changed after being hit by a light from a brooch, but before he could continue, the King interrupted saying, "What brooch?" Kentigern told how Sholto had an old brooch with an inscription on the back. The King's expression was now one of sheer panic and disbelief.

"Do you know of such a brooch?" asked Kentigern.

"I will tell what I know tomorrow when we are all together," the King replied.

The King, Kentigern and around twenty guards set off early the next morning. "Why have you brought all these guards?" asked Kentigern.

"I will tell all later," replied the King. The journey was made at a fair pace, and they arrived at Stoleware by the middle of the afternoon. The village had never seen so many visitors, Sister Eangyth was already panicking about the cleanliness of the village and Nevin and Coll were in a flutter about where they would all sleep, and they all got rather excited at seeing the guards' shining armour.

Hithin and Malcom greeted them. "Please take me to my brother," said the King. "Follow me, your grace," replied Malcolm. "This is no time for a ceremony," said the King. "My name is Kenneth." Malcolm chuckled to himself.

The King was led to the church where Alpin and Elen were lying in open coffins. "Please leave me," he said.

Outside, the guards were welcomed by the villagers and appeared mightily impressed by the secluded hideaway.

Dougal approached the platoon commander, introduced himself and said, "You must be hungry and thirsty. I did not expect so many, but we can prepare food for you."

The commander thanked him and told the soldiers to dismount. "We have not been told why you are in such haste. Why was the King so eager to come here?" he asked.

Dougal explained. "I do remember seven men seeing the King, but I did not know that the King had a brother."

"It is a sad day," said the commander. Dougal led them towards the cookhouse, where Anika, Lesedi, Anna and Nesta were helping with the preparation of food. "I can offer you a little bread and wine," said Dougal.

"Bread and water will be fine," replied the commander. He looked round, extremely impressed by the sight of such a flourishing community. "Do you have room for one more?" he asked.

"I do not believe your King would be too pleased if his trusted commander left his army," replied Dougal.

"Why did you have to think of a good reason?" asked the commander jokingly.

The women had cooked meat pies for the villagers. However, with the unexpected guests arriving, they were quickly and heartily consumed by the guards.

"Are you sure I cannot stay here?" asked the commander again.

"I am sure," replied Dougal.

The King came out of the church with tears in his eyes and sat on the church steps. 'Why?' he asked himself, shaking his head.

Malcom sat next to him. "Tell me about the brooch," said the King.

"I will bring Sholto," replied Malcolm. He returned with Sholto who explained how he came by the brooch. The King listened intently, however when Sholto mentioned that Angus had made a further nineteen and that five of the brooches had been given to people they had met in other countries, the King's expression turned to one of horror.

"You know of the brooch?" asked Sholto.

The King began. "One of my ancestors, Eochaid mac Domangairt, sailed across to Hybernia to see the high King Fínsnechta Fledach. He was told of such a brooch. In the hands of the good, it is said to bring great power and wealth, but those who have greed in their hearts do not fare well. You used a brooch to falsely lure those who knew of it into a bond. You are fortunate that you told those who have one, to keep it safe, but beware that it is not used for evil. Drake has one now and he believes that no harm can befall him. You must either destroy the others or hide them in a safe place where no one can get to them," said the King.

Hithin joined them and told the King about the events in Carlisle and a man named Alam who Maarku had met in Beirut. "I believe Drake has gone to find this man," said Hithin.

"That may well be," said the King, "but only one will survive. You have seen the last of Drake."

Brother Martin approached. "It is time," he said.

"Please fetch my commander," requested the King. "He will know what he should do."

Sholto found the commander who ordered his platoon to ready themselves. They marched in perfect precision to the church and stood to attention outside. The King had already made his way inside where he joined the rest of the villagers. Brother Martin conducted a short service, with the King giving a heartful and tearful eulogy for Alpin and Elen. Martin gestured to Asmund and Colban to close the two coffins.

Four guards carried each coffin to its final resting place, while the others formed a guard of honour along the short route. After the service they all returned to the church to celebrate the life of Alpin and Elen.

The King, unsurprisingly, enjoyed a few tankards of ale, ordering his guards to join in, but not to tell his wife. During the proceedings, he called for quiet, told everyone to sit down.

He was about to start his speech, when Malcolm shouted, "Ken, no one wishes to listen to you, so save your words till we are all sleeping."

The guards looked on in horror until the King burst out laughing, unceremoniously fell onto his backside and promptly fell asleep still holding his tankard.

"Let him be," said Hithin. "There is still more ale," and with that, the drinking continued.

Morning came. Suits of armour were strewn all over the village. Anika and Lesedi had already prepared a fair number of watermelons which she knew would help ease the expected plethora of hangovers.

By mid-morning everyone was awake, however still in various states of inebriation. The silence was disturbed by guards scrambling around searching for their suits of armour, some of which had somehow been carefully concealed by people unknown.

"We must leave now," said the King, "but do not forget where I am and that I am always willing to help. Do you wish me to leave some of my guards here?"

Unsurprisingly, they all volunteered. The King shook his head. "I thought I was a good King," he said laughing, "but my guards would rather stay here. I do not understand why." He looked round and saw four of his guards still completely bereft of any armour.

"You four," he said pointing to them, "as you have already shown that you are not fit to wear the King's armour, you must stay here and try not to look so grateful." The guard's smiles were difficult to hide. "If I hear you have not done as you have been asked, then I will send others in your place, and you will be beheaded."

"We will obey," said one of them.

The King turned to Hithin and said, "I wish we had met again in better times."

Once they had left, Hithin said to the four guards. "It is time to clear out the stables." The guards looked more than a little dejected, assuming they would at least be given time to settle in before they got stuck into the work.

Hithin started laughing. "Do not despair," he said, "that can wait. You must meet the others, but first I need to know your names." They introduced themselves in turn as John, Robert, Ralph and Hugh.

"You will in time remember all the names of the people in the village but do not worry for now. You were the King's guards, but did you have any other duties?" asked Hithin.

John began. "I was a farmer before I joined the guards."

"I helped the sick," said Robert.

"I was a blacksmith," said Ralph.

"I have been a bowman from the age of twelve and I made my own bows," said Hugh.

"You will all fit in here," said Hithin.

During the next few months, life slowly got back to normal, the four new recruits settling in and enjoying their new life. Brother Martin had set up a regular correspondence service through the monastery, with the contacts met on the overseas travels, however no mention of the brooches was ever made. Any request to visit the village received a vague response and complicated directions to its exact location.

Dougal, Ewan and Duff meticulously mapped the local area and then slowly but surely, ventured further out until they had charted around twenty thousand square miles. This proved invaluable to future generations. They also cleverly used the standing stones erected by the Picts, as route maps, having made discreet incisions alongside the symbols. Even the engravings on the Aberlemno Serpent Stone, which were believed to depict battle scenes, contained directions to towns, secret storage areas and lucrative mineral sites.

Garmund, Angus, Ralph and Hugh began to experiment with the abundance and assortment of minerals that Frothi and Enar had unearthed, fashioning new forms of weaponry, tools and more importantly solid construction materials. They soon found and developed gold streams, many of which, especially in the early days, were very productive, resulting in an embarrassingly large stockpile, which proved difficult, but not impossible to exchange.

Daily records were still maintained, Brother Martin being allocated this duty, with of course Sister Mildrith being his ever-faithful assistant, although his handwriting was at times, rather shaky. A trip was made every two weeks, by various members of the village, to the monastery at Dunkeld, where a cell had been permanently allocated for use by the messenger. The monks had taken the liberty of reaching out to Scandinavian countries and the news from back home was eagerly anticipated by the village's Viking contingent.

Details of Viking exploits into other countries filtered through; in particular, foreign cultures, trends and advancements in science were forwarded. For the time being, there seemed to be no need for overseas visits as much was learnt from the correspondence sent by the Scandinavians back home, many of whom were known to the Vikings in the village. They discovered how to make paper from tree bark, hemp and linen, among other enlightenments.

All was progressing well with Matilda, Edith, Anna, Berta, Nesta and the not so celibate Sister Eangyth with Garmund, Frothi, Robert, Lesedi and Anika making the preparations for the forthcoming births. Nevin, Ulf and Coll managed to become involved, even though this only involved arguments over the colour of the nursery in the medical building.

The numerous workplaces, like the six women, were gradually expanding and with techniques learnt from overseas, became more efficient in their operation.

The underground chamber was completed, and the gifts received from overseas were stored there. The remaining thirteen copies of the brooch were sealed in a small vault covered with around twelve inches of clay. The Roman gold and jewellery were safely stored in a locked vault within the chamber.

Defences were improved, with trip wires concealed along an outer perimeter, covering the less visible approaches into the village.

Lookouts were strategically placed, armed with crossbows engineered by Hugh and with a small, simple telescope that Garmund had designed and created, attached to the crossbow, as a sight. Garmund and Lesedi had perfected the tear gas fireworks with unexpected trials taking place at the most inconvenient times. An outdoor morning service, conducted by Brother Martin, seemed at the time, like a good place to carry out an experiment, however the tearful congregation were not too impressed, using terms not generally heard during a service, while Garmund and Lesedi were jumping madly around shouting, "It works!"

The day of deliveries was nigh. Sister Eangyth and Matilda were the first to go into labour. The whole village waited patiently outside the medical building, with Boyd and a slightly embarrassed Fingal pacing frantically around. Robert, Frothi and Garmund seemed to take a back seat as Anika and Lesedi directed proceedings, with Mildrith proving to be an invaluable support.

Garmund justified his lack of expertise in this particular area saying, "Not many men have given birth on the battlefield."

Ulf, Coll and Nevin were panicking far more than any of the soon to be fathers; however they made extremely willing and helpful nurses.

The hours dragged on. The odd few screams of pain and anguish were audible. However, when Nevin was told to sit and take a drink of water, he felt a little better.

Eventually a baby's cry was heard. There was silence outside as they all waited for the news.

Coll burst out of the medical centre, shouting "It's a boy," then promptly fainted.

They all looked at each other, wondering whose child it was and then came another cry. This time a very relaxed Ulf casually emerged, looked down at Coll, shook his head and then announced to a silent crowd.

"Boyd, you have a son, the first born into the village." Ulf's expression turned very serious. "And Fingal, for defiling the celibacy and sanctity of a woman of God and taking advantage of her when she was in a state of drunkenness, you have a goat." Fingal's jaw dropped. "Sorry, I did mean to say, you have a boy."

Great cheers and congratulations were forthcoming.

"I am wanted again," said Ulf and he disappeared back inside. With the two mothers and their new-borns freshened-up, Ulf made another appearance.

He looked at Boyd and said, "Matilda wants to see you."

Boyd's eyes lit up. "I am a father!" he yelled several times, and followed an excited Ulf back inside, who then suddenly reappeared for the second time shouting, "Fingal," and in ran Fingal.

Mothers and sons were fine. The two proud fathers sat by the beds holding the babies' tiny hands.

"What do you want to call him?" asked Boyd.

Without hesitation, Matilda said, "Alpin." Boyd nodded his approval.

"Have you thought of a name?" Fingal asked Eangyth.

She pondered for a while before answering, "I would like to call him after one of the brothers I knew in Iona. I want to call him Dunstan." Fingal knew of no reason to suggest otherwise.

A couple of weeks passed before it was the turn of Anna, Nesta, Edith and Berta, all deciding to go into labour at the same time. Garmund felt a little more confident this time, but still insisted that Anika and Lesedi should take the lead. The previous back-up team was present, with Coll being advised to regulate his breathing to avoid further fainting spells.

As before, everyone except Matilda and Eangyth, who were still enjoying a well-deserved rest, was present. It was the turn of Asmund, Enar, Kyle and Mungo to tread the well-worn path etched by Boyd and Fingal. The babies appeared a little reluctant to make their first appearance and from the initial vociferous encouragement from the assembled crowd, after a good six hours patiently waiting, the animation quietened to a few odd mumblings; so some of those present deciding to find solace at the brewery.

Coll emerged and with all the excitement, promptly fainted again. It was up to Ulf to inform those who were still awake that the births were imminent. The few who had partaken of little refreshment, which unsurprisingly included Enar and Asmund, returned smartly.

After another couple of hours, to the relief of everyone, all four women had given birth. Anna gave birth to twins as did Nesta, both having a girl first and then a boy. It was Edith next who brought a little boy into the world, then finally Berta with her daughter. After the mothers were made comfortable and the babies made presentable, the excited fathers were allowed in to see their children.

Vogg seemed to have one of the widest smiles saying to everyone, "My little brother is a father."

The couples inside the medical centre were discussing names. Enar and Anna were doting over their offspring. Anna looked at them and said, "They look like little bears." That gave Enar an idea.

"We will call them Yrsa and Bjørn," he said.

"I like that," said Anna.

"Yrsa is old Norse for she-bear and Bjørn means bear," said Enar.

Anna smiled. "I like that more now. Yrsa and Bjørn."

Next door, Mungo was reeling off dozens of Scottish names while Nesta was just lying there patiently till he exhausted all the possibilities.

He eventually asked Nesta, "Are there any names you like?"

"My parents were called Cinaed and Merraid," replied Nesta.

Mungo remembered Nesta relating the tragic story about her parents. He smiled. "That will be perfect," he said.

Edith was holding her son lovingly in her arms. "What was your father's name?" she asked Kyle.

"Euan," he replied.

"That is the name we will give him," she said.

Berta was staring into her daughter's eyes. "She looks like a little goddess."

"Then we will call her Åse, which means goddess in old Norse," replied Asmund.

"Welcome little Åse," said Berta.

It was time to leave the women in peace. Each one of the proud fathers emerged with a massive smile on their faces. Sister Mildrith, Ulf, Coll and Nevin volunteered to stay with the women just to make sure that all was fine.

An exhausted Garmund, Anika and Lesedi were last out of the medical centre and after the crowd had given them an appreciative round of applause, Lesedi quietened them down and said, "Let them all rest now," which seemed the perfect excuse for the group to adjourn, once again, to the brewery.

Chapter 23

Big Foot

The four guards recruited from the King proved invaluable as time went by. Not only were they involved in the development of the village, but they were also excellent at babysitting, and unlike Dougal, they could actually sing. Mildrith and Eangyth became proficient at playing soothing lullabies. However, Ewan was banned from playing his bagpipes, most villagers being unconvinced about his musical talent.

It wasn't particularly surprising that the men had little idea on the subject of baby food, Malcolm and Dougal made miniature meat pies for the babies. At least they looked nice.

As the children grew older, Anika and Lesedi were charged with preparing the food. Mashed vegetables, mashed fruit, mashed chicken, scrambled eggs and porridge using the oats harvested from the nearby fields were prepared. As the variety of foods increased, more of the villagers became interested in experimenting with different, foods incorporating the more edible sauces that Lesedi prepared.

Vogg became an expert at hunting and with a variety of bark-coloured camouflages created by Halfred and Sholto, found it easier to stalk his prey without being as noticeable. Vogg's long red beard was a glowing beacon until Edith decided to trim it. However there was not much that could be done about his giant frame. There was plenty of livestock in the nearby fields, but deer and boar had become particular favourites, especially when washed down with a tankard of good quality ale.

Vogg had always been an early riser and preferred hunting on his own. The early sunrises encouraged the villagers to make the most of the day. Angus and Tovi had designed and made a large iron container, continuously topped with water via a water wheel, incorporating an overflow pipe draining back into the stream and heated over an enclosed fire. Thin metal tapped tubes led from the bottom of the container to six cubicles. It wasn't the most efficient shower system, but it worked.

Early morning walks were part of the daily routine, either just for exercise or to check on the animals in the fields. The woman regularly took their children on short walks, but not venturing too far into the woods.

One morning, a terrified Anna and Nesta and their four children came rushing back into the village shouting, "There is a bear in the trees."

Mungo and Gerik were the first to respond. "Quick, find Ulf, Vogg, Coll and Nevin!" yelled Mungo. Ulf, Coll and Nevin came quickly armed with spears, bows and arrows.

"Where is Vogg?" asked Gerik.

"Hunting," replied Coll.

"If you see him, warm him to take care and watch out for the bear," said Gerik. The women and children went back into their houses. By now, all the men in the village had armed themselves and were on guard around the perimeter of the village, just in case the bear should call.

Anna had pointed out where they saw the brown bear, so the three hunters made their way in that direction. It wasn't long before they came across Vogg, wearing one of his light brown camouflage outfits.

"Stay back," he said. They obeyed, crouching down behind him. All they heard was the 'whish' of a spear as it flew through the air and the squeal of a wild boar. "Why are you here?" asked Vogg.

"Anna and Nesta said they saw a bear in the woods, so we are here to warn you and search for it," replied Ulf.

"I have seen nothing," said Vogg. The four continued searching for a while, but as they found nothing, returned to the village, carrying the prey. After Vogg had tidied himself up and Coll had told Gerik that nothing was found, the four hunters went to tell the two women.

"Next time you are walking, take some men along with you," said Nevin.

"We will," they replied.

John, Robert, Ralph and Hugh were tasked with chaperoning the women next time any of them wished to stray outside the village perimeter. However, until they felt that it was safe and that there had been no sightings of the bear, walks were limited to within the confines of the village.

The fortnightly correspondence from the various sources contained a mixture of both general gossip and occasionally inventions and creations from different parts of the world. Spectacles came from contacts in Italy, spinning wheels from India, the astrolabe from Spain, magnets from Greece and compasses from Dali and Xia. Garmund reciprocated by advising the numerous contacts about his telescope, the hot water shower and various efficient farming techniques, with records being kept on who told who what, where, when and how, but still the location of the village was kept quiet.

Many of Garmund's inventions were quite by accident. He had made numerous mirrors of various shapes and sizes. It was a nice warm day, sun shining brightly and Garmund was having a pleasant walk, away from the village, following the stream. He was carrying one of his pocket-sized mirrors which he accidentally dropped it into the stream. It had lodged itself between a couple of rocks about two feet below the surface but out of sight. He was searching in vain and suddenly noticed fish swimming towards him but stopping in just one area of the stream. They circled for quite a while before swimming off back upstream. He sat on the banks for some time confused by what he saw. A little later, the fish reappeared, circled for a while, then swam off again. Rather puzzled, he stepped into the water, searched around and found the mirror. He moved the mirror downstream towards the village, placed it in the water and the same thing happened. This he repeated a few times, occasionally without success, until he realised that the fish would swim downstream if attracted towards the source of light, reflected from the sun. Over the next few days, he set up an intricate system of mirrors, leading the fish into the village. The only problem now was where to store the catch after it had been salted for preservation. An extension to the food store was quickly completed.

Months passed and as there were no further sighting of the bear, it was deemed safe for family walks to venture outside the village, but still with at least one guard. Matilda and Eangyth decided on a stroll along the stream heading out of the village, taking their children to watch the fish as they swam downstream. Ralph accompanied them on their outing. Suddenly Matilda's son, Alpin, froze and pointed to the woods.

"Bear," he said.

The others looked and saw a large creature making its way into the trees. Ralph quickly ushered them back to the village shouting for help. "

Bring the hunters," said Boyd. Ulf, Coll and Nevin rushed out armed with spears and bows. "

Where is Vogg?" asked Coll.

"Hunting," replied Boyd.

Eangyth pointed out where they saw the bear, so the three hunters made their way in that direction. They soon found Vogg wearing his hunting outfit.

"Why are you here?" asked Vogg.

"Matilda said her son had seen a bear in the woods, so we are here to warn you and search for it," replied Ulf.

"I have seen nothing," said Vogg.

They continued searching for a while, but as they again found nothing, they returned to the village. Vogg was still wearing his camouflage as they walked towards the village.

"I will race you back," said Ulf.

They all started running, but Vogg stumbled. He quickly got to his feet and chased after the others. Matilda, Eangyth and Ralph were watching as Ulf, Coll and Nevin came sprinting into the village followed by a large dark figure. Matilda went white as they came into sight.

"B-b-b-bear," she screamed.

By now, there was quite a few gathered watching as the four came into view. Instead of attacking the creature, they all burst out laughing. Matilda was furious at their reaction.

"What is the matter with you? There is a bear," she yelled.

"It is Vogg," said Ulf calmly.

"It is a…" She looked again. "It is Vogg," she said, starting to laugh as the four ran past her. "It does look like a bear from a distance," she said to defend her.

There was now great relief around the village, and thereafter, people were warned when Vogg was going out hunting in his camouflaged outfit. Daily walks ventured further out into the forest. However, the rule of one guard per family remained active. The sight of a man in the distance, clad in brown stalking prey, was quite common now.

All six women were taking their children out one day accompanied by John, Malcolm, Colban, Hugh, Boyd and Ulf.

They had gone a fair way into the woods when Bjørn said, "Look, there is Vogg."

At first, nobody thought anything of it. A little bit further along on the walk Bjørn said, "There, look, Vogg."

A voice from behind the group said, "I was trying to sneak up on you, but you saw me." Bjørn turned round and there behind him was the mighty figure of Vogg.

"You are in the woods," said a puzzled boy. Some of the women who had also seen the figure in the woods were quite aghast at seeing Vogg.

"Who is hunting?" asked Enar.

"No one," replied Vogg.

"What is that?" she asked pointing to a large brown figure in the distance.

"I think we should get back to the village." John, Hugh and Boyd took the women and children back to the village while Malcolm, Colban, Ulf and Vogg decided to follow the creature into the woods.

They tracked the creature deeper into the woods, noticing quite large footprints which did not resemble anything they had ever seen before. The group kept their distance, staying back about a hundred feet. Suddenly it stopped and gave out a very strange cry, something between a lion and a donkey. The four looked at each other puzzled as the strange animal flapped its paws then tried unsuccessfully to climb a tree.

"What is this creature?" asked Ulf.

"I have never seen the like of it before," replied Malcolm.

It then dropped on all fours and began bouncing up and down, then stood up and began beating its chest whilst squawking. Next, it started turning round many times very quickly until it lost its balance and stumbled to the ground. Colban started laughing.

"Quiet," said Ulf who couldn't resist a giggle himself.

It then started to move off, deeper into the forest, and the four followed, still maintaining a safe distance.

Suddenly it vanished.

"Where is it?" asked Malcolm.

"Keep low and stay together," said Vogg, as they edged slowly forward.

They reached the spot where they last saw the creature. There were large animal footprints but no sign of it. They heard a twig snap, turned round quickly and about twenty feet away they saw a hideous looking six-foot creature waving at them. They ran towards it and Vogg punched it across the face.

"Ow," said the creature. That left them even more puzzled.

The four pinned it down to the ground and Colban, who was sitting on its chest, noticed that it was wearing a mask.

He ripped the mask off and said, "Oh no. Please, not you."

The three loosened their grip a little to the extent that its right hand wriggled free and slapped Colban across the face.

Colban got to his feet, the other three still holding down their prisoner. Malcolm and Ulf slowly realised who they had caught.

"How did you get here?" asked Colban.

"I flied here," was the reply.

"You flied here?" questioned Vogg.

"I think the word is flew," said Colban who promptly got an additional slap from Vogg.

"Why did you do that?" asked Colban.

"My English is not as gooder as you speaked and it looked fun when he slapped you," replied Vogg with a big grin on his face.

"Who is this?" asked Vogg as they helped the man to his feet. Malcom explained that, on the journey to Eoforwic, they crossed the water to Dùn Èideann instead of following the coast round.

"We saw a man who we thought was drowning so Colban jumped in to save him. When Colban brought him out of the water, he was slapped across the face by this man who then ran off flapping his arms. It was a mad man who was trying to fly."

"Why did you come here?" asked Colban.

"I flied with the birds," said the man.

"How did you get this?" asked Vogg, grabbing onto the outfit which happened to be one of the suits made by Sholto and Halfred.

"And where did you get those," asked Colban, pointing to the footprint shaped wooden shoes?"

"I did," replied the man.

"We should take him back to the village," said Ulf. Vogg was about to remove the man's suit when he realised that he wasn't wearing anything under it.

"We will find you a tunic to wear," said Vogg.

"I have mine," said the man.

"Do you have a name?" asked Malcolm. The man just looked at him and shrugged his shoulders.

As they led him back to the village, all he said was, "I can fly."

Boyd, Hithin and John were waiting for them as they returned. "This is the bear," said Malcolm.

"I am a bird," said the man. Malcolm explained all about the man. "I do not know what we should do with him," he said.

"Mælbrigða is here," said the man pointing towards the underground bunker.

"There is no Mælbrigða here," replied Hithin. The man thought for a few moments then started counting on his fingers.

After he reached ten, he looked at his open hands and said, "He has ten and more and cannot die."

"What do you mean?" asked Hithin.

"Alam wants to fly like the Drake. Bad Mildrith, poor Alpin, poor Elen," said the man. A cold shiver ran down Hithin's spine.

"Where are you from?" asked Boyd. The man gazed blankly at Boyd then looked up at the birds flying overhead.

"Ducks but no Drake," he said.

"He must be kept somewhere he cannot do harm," said John.

"The chamber?" suggested Boyd.

"Yes, yes, yes, yes, yes, the chamber," replied the man excitedly, "with the ten and more."

"Fetch Brother Martin," said Boyd. Ulf went to find the monk.

"What is the matter?" asked Martin.

Hithin explained as best he could and suggested that they should take the man to Dunkeld, where at least he could be held, under supervision, in a locked cell. Based on what he had been told, Martin had no hesitation in agreeing.

"I will send word to the monks and let them know what they should do. They will understand," he said.

"It is not safe to keep him here," said Hithin. "I will summon the other guards and we will take him to the monastery."

"I know where it is," said John.

"Ulf and Colban will go with you," said Hithin. The horses were readied and the man, after being dressed in a more suitable outfit, was securely restrained and put onto a horse which Hugh led.

"We will go quickly and be back on the morrow," said Colban. They rode off, keeping a tight watch on their prisoner just in case anything untoward should happen.

Boyd, Hithin, Malcolm, Vogg and Martin sat down in the church meeting room, wondering how the stranger had managed to find them, and how he had travelled to the village, knew all about the bunker and the brooches and how he knew of Drake and the other events in the village.

"He will be safe locked away in the monastery," said Martin.

"I hope you are right," answered Hithin.

Hithin found it unbearably difficult to sleep that night, wondering how someone could know so much about the village. He was eagerly anticipating the return of the six from Dunkeld and news that the stranger was securely and safely out of the way.

In the early afternoon, the six returned, looking relieved to be back home.

"What news?" asked Hithin.

Colban replied, "He was muttering to himself about watching fish jump out of the water. That is all he said. I do not know what Brother Martin wrote, but when the monks read it, they took him in great haste to a cell with no light, where he was chained to the floor. Two monks were told to stay outside the cell and never open the door."

"I will find Martin and ask what he wrote," replied Hithin.

He found Brother Martin praying in the church. "What do you know?" asked a suspicious Hithin.

"I do not understand what you are asking," replied Martin.

"Who was that man?" asked Hithin.

"A lost soul," answered the monk, "and that is enough for you to know for now."

Chapter 24

The Look of the Irish

With a ratio of roughly three men to one woman, even allowing for the vulnerability of the two religious sisters and only Anika not being currently attached to anyone, it was decided that another scouting party should be dispatched to a place not too far away, to try and encourage additional females into the village. This time, the recruiting party would include a couple of the wives; in the hope that they would be better able to promote the village through communicating a female perspective.

There was one country, relatively close, that had not yet been visited and that was Hibernia. Boyd and Matilda, Mungo and Nesta, Maarku and Lesedi and Robert and Anika volunteered for the task.

Mungo and Maarku agreed that again, instead of taking eight horses, two carriages should be used; especially considering that there could be additional people on the return journey and that they should share the reins during the roughly twenty-day round trip. Angus, Tovi, Kyle, Halfred and Ralph had designed and made thick leather straps which they attached to the underside of the carriages, thus providing a little extra comfort for the passengers. The box seat was partially enclosed, giving those at the reins a little more protection from the elements. There was now storage space both below the carriage and on the roof. The tent acquired on the visit to Throtmanni was taken just in case there were no rooms free at any of the overnight stops.

Boyd and Maarku described their planned route to Gerik, Hithin and those undertaking the tour.

"We will first journey to our friends at the monastery at Dunkeld, then go on to Striveling, Cathures, Ayr and then an eighty-mile sail across the Inner Sea to Béal Feirsde. From there, we will journey to Dundalgan, Dudh

Linn, then north-west to Sligeach, north-east to Daire Calgaich, across the water to Ilea, Oban and then home by way of Glencoe."

"If only the good captain was around, life would be so much easier," commented Mungo.

During the next couple of days, preparations were made, packing supplies, and limited clothing; especially for the women, despite them insisting that they should take a different outfit for each day. Enough money was allocated for the journey, but it was entrusted to the men; not that the women would be guilty in any way of spending on unnecessary purchases. The hope was to cover between thirty and forty miles per day, depending on the terrain. Boyd, Matilda, Mungo and Nesta took one carriage and Maarku, Lesedi, Robert and Anika the second.

Boyd and Robert were the first to take the reins. They reached the monastery by early evening on the first day, and were met by a familiar figure.

"Welcome. Please come in," said the monk. "Where are you journeying to this time?"

"We are heading towards Hibernia," replied Boyd.

"What of the man that Brother Martin asked you to watch?"

"I do not know of whom you speak," said the monk.

Boyd was about to talk when the monk jumped in saying more firmly, "I do not know of whom you speak, now please come with me." Discretion seemed diplomatic, so no further questions on the subject were tendered.

A filling breakfast of nourishing frumenty compensated for the ungodly hour when the group had been woken.

"Will you be passing by here on your return?" asked the abbot.

"We will not, but I am sure we will see you again. You have been of great help passing on word from those overseas and we have learnt much of what is happening," said Mungo.

"You are most welcome. I wish you a safe journey," said the abbot.

Thanking the monks once again for their hospitality, the group embarked on the next leg of their journey to Striveling. Matilda and Anika decided to take the reins, not that there was any concern whatsoever shown by the others as to the skill or more accurately, lack of skill in driving a carriage. However, the odd term relating to horsemanship and some choice terms not exactly relating to horsemanship were occasionally voiced by the passengers.

Eventually, to everyone's relief, they arrived safely and relatively unscathed, mainly due to the enhancements to the carriage suspension. Just like the last time when they were in Striveling, a trade fayre was in full swing. However, they decided to keep a low profile, bearing in mind the unfortunate events of their last visit. They decided to pitch their tent as far away as possible from the fayre but near the other tents.

As they were about to settle in for the evening, they heard someone say, "I have heard that the pirate, Captain Teach is here."

Boyd looked at Maarku and said, "There cannot be many named Captain Teach. Do you think?"

Maarku replied, "He may remember me."

"Boyd, come with me; we will try to find him. Robert, Mungo, please stay with the women."

They left the tent and followed the sound of the voices, staying out of sight. They saw two men wearing dark cloaks ahead of them, asking around if anyone had seen a man matching the description they gave. At first, no one was able to help but eventually they found someone who told them where to find the captain.

"We must follow," said Boyd. "I do not believe those men are seeking to befriend the captain." The two cloaked figures arrived at a small tent and waited outside, talking quietly between themselves. Maarku and Boyd watched as the two drew their daggers and burst into the tent.

"Quickly," said Maarku. They stayed outside the tent listening to the raised voices.

"You thief," said one of the men. "You stole his gold."

"I do not know what you mean," replied the captain.

"You are a liar and a thief," said the second man. "We trusted you to take the gold to Merulf in Frisia."

"I did as you asked," replied the captain.

"Merulf tells us that he never saw the gold."

"He lies," replied the captain.

"No, you lie," said the first man.

As the argument progressed, Maarku and Boyd slipped quietly into the tent, standing behind the two cloaked figures, opposite the captain who made no acknowledgement of their presence.

"Merulf wants his gold," said one of the men.

"Merulf has his gold," replied the captain in a very determined manner.

"Is this the same Merulf who tried to cheat me out of gold when buying pearls?" asked Maarku.

The two men turned round quickly, recognising Boyd and remembering their last encounter with him. They looked at each other, fully expecting what was to come and soon enough, they were lying unconscious on the ground.

"I see you have met these two before," said the captain.

"We too know of Merulf," said Maarku.

"Where are we going to this time?" asked the captain. Boyd smiled and outlined their plans.

"My boat is moored at a port near Dùn Èideann. I can sail to Ayr within two days. If you wish to travel with me, you are most welcome, said the captain."

"We will travel over land and meet you in Ayr," replied Boyd." While they are sleeping, I may borrow one of their horses," said the captain.

"Why not take both," said Maarku.

"I think I will. We will have left by the time they wake," said the captain.

By early morning they had all left Striveling, travelling their separate ways and hopefully meeting up again in Ayr in a few days. After the interesting experience of the previous day, Mungo and Robert decided to drive the horses, not that there were too many derogatory remarks coming from the women. However, it was incredibly strange how the passengers generally felt a little more relaxed and comfortable.

The twenty-five-mile trip to Cathures was covered at a steady pace, within the day, stopping occasionally for natural breaks. None of the group had visited Cathures before. They had only heard about the place and the interesting events described by Malcolm and Frothi.

All looked normal as they approached; in fact very normal and very quiet. They approached a bridge across the River Clyde, and saw hundreds of people gathered by the banks, dragging fishing nets through the water. Maarku drew his carriage alongside Mungo.

"Can this way of catching fish be as simple as it looks?" asked Maarku.

"At least they have not painted the fish," replied Mungo.

They continued across the wooden bridge, the locals focusing their attention to the matter at hand. There was one man standing alone, watching the events in the water.

"What is this about?" asked Mungo.

The man looked up in disbelief at the question.

"Catchin fish," was the abrupt reply.

Mungo looked a little embarrassed at asking the question, but followed up with, "Why so many people?"

"Because thare a lot of o fish."

Mungo's expression of 'Why did I bother' was clearly evident. They thought it wise to continue to an area away from the activity. Again, not wishing to inconvenience the locals, they pitched the tent in a nice quiet area, Maarku and Lesedi prepared some of the meats brought from Stoleware over a makeshift spit. They all settled down for a peaceful night, the air still thick with the smell of fish.

Nesta and Lesedi's turn to lead the horses. By making a fairly early start, they sought to reach Ayr at a reasonable hour and hopefully meet up with the captain. The two women seemed quite oblivious to the direction of travel, being totally engrossed in conversation, frequently missing obvious signs to their destination. Fortunately, there were helpful and occasional sarcastic suggestions at hand, thereby ensuring that their destination would be reached that day.

Ayr was quite a thriving fishing port, with traces of small Viking settlements but more noticeably, as Robert pointed out, there was an upended Stone Age standing stone suggesting that the place was inhabited largely by sun worshippers.

"Is there anywhere normal in this country?" asked Maarku.

After having spent two nights camping outside, the group felt that a tavern offering homemade food and a comfortable bed for the night, would be most welcome. The Morven Tavern in the centre of the town seemed promising. Boyd and Matilda went inside to talk to the innkeeper. It was very clean and tidy, with a very friendly but very overweight innkeeper.

"They ca' me Morven. Howfur kin ah hulp ye?"

"We would like four rooms for the night and a place to stable the horses and carriages," replied Boyd.

"Whaur urr ye fae?" asked Morven.

"Dunkeld, seeking passage to Ayr," replied Boyd.

"Thare is a boat anchored a bawherr wey oot tae sea, bit na yin haes come ashore," said Morven. "Fur th' rooms 'n' th' horses trhat wull be five shillings. Ah wull prepare ye a bawherr fairn fur twa mair shillings," he added.

"The food will be most welcome. I thank you," replied Boyd, paying Morven seven shillings.

They were told where to stable the horses and securely park the carriages and then returned to the inn, where they were shown to their rooms.

"I did not understand what that man was saying," said Matilda. Boyd smiled.

After a very pleasant meal they retired to their rooms. Anika felt a little uncomfortable sharing a room with Robert, who promised to be a gentleman and sleep in a chair, as she slept in the comfortable bed.

The following morning, as they sat outside the tavern in the warm sunshine, the captain rolled-up looking very thoughtful.

"You seem a little worried," said Boyd.

"I do not know if I should ask, but this has been on my mind all the night."

It was Boyd's turn to look a little worried.

"What troubles you," he asked.

"I have sailed many seas and as you have seen with the thieves sent by Merulf, it is time I settled and what I have seen of the way you live, makes me wish to be part of your village. Will you let me join you?"

Boyd could hardly contain his enthusiasm.

"Captain, we would welcome you but only if you bring your boat."

"That I will," he replied.

"Does that mean that we do not have to pay you this time?" asked Mungo cheekily.

The captain was a little taken back by this question and after a deep sigh said, "Twenty pounds."

Boyd nodded his head.

The captain asked, "there is one thing I do not know. Where is your village and where is the nearest port?"

"There is a port at Glencoe and from there we will take you to our village," replied Boyd. The captain agreed.

"When you are ready, we will sail to Béal Feirsde."

The captain brought the boat into the port and led the horses on board. Carriages were loaded using an ingenious swivelling treadwheel crane, hooking the carriages to an iron hook, raising them, rotating a large horizontal wooden wheel by hand, round to the boat and finally and very carefully lowering the carriages, securely fastening them to the deck.

At a steady ten knots, they completed the sail down the Inner Sea in under half a day. Carriages, horses and passengers were unloaded.

"When will you be in Daire Calgaich?" asked the captain.

"In about twelve days," replied Boyd.

"I will be there," he replied.

"Where are you going to sail to now?" asked Boyd.

"I have provisions on board so I can enjoy a pleasant sail," replied the captain.

By the middle of the day, the captain had set sail and the travellers decided to see what the small settlement had to offer.

The few locals told them about the five-thousand-year-old Giant's Ring and about a number of forts in the surrounding hills; but beyond that, there didn't seem much to get excited about. There was still a good half day's light, so after hitching up the carriages and purchasing a few provisions, they made their way south towards Dundalgan.

Matilda thought it a good idea if the women took one carriage and the men the other, so they could talk a little more easily. The men saw no problem with this, provided they kept up and watched where they were going. Boyd took the leading carriage and Matilda followed at a distance that ensured that their conversations were not overheard.

The first and most pressing question was put to Anika.

"Did you lay with Robert?" asked Nesta.

"I did not," she replied. "He is a nice man but not the one for me."

The three continued to press her on the subject but she was not giving anything away about her choice of men. The women discussed, fairly intimately, the merits of their men, some learning more than others about a variety of fetishes. The outbursts of laughter caused a little concern with the men, who kept turning round, wondering what the cause of the intense amusement was.

After about twenty miles, they came across an abbey and hoped that it would be an ideal place to stay for the night. Mungo rang the large gate bell which was promptly answered by a very jovial monk.

"Welcome to Saint Colman's. I am Brother Fergus. Please make your way in. From where you have come?" he asked.

"Across from a little village near Dunkeld," replied Boyd.

He looked at them in turn and said, "Then you are known to Brother Martin. I have heard everything about you and he holds you in high esteem."

They were quite honoured and astonished as to how word of even their existence had managed to travel to such a remote place.

"I believe Sister Mildrith is with you," said the monk nodding suspiciously.

"She is. How do you know so much about us?" asked Boyd.

"Brother Martin must have told you that we have messengers and thus we know a lot about many places. There is only me here at the abbey. The others have journeyed to other villages. You seek a room for the night?"

"That would be most welcome," replied Boyd.

"Come, join with me in a little food, but you will have to help me prepare some." Lesedi and Nesta followed the monk to the kitchen to help with the food.

"I wonder what Brother Martin has told others about us. Do you think Brother Fergus will know about the man at Dunkeld?" asked Robert.

"I do not think it wise to ask about that," replied Boyd.

A very tasty chicken stew was served up, accompanied by an extremely refreshing and pleasantly potent mead. They all talked for a while, Brother Fergus, after a good few drinks, volunteered some extremely personal information about Brother Martin but no one dared ask about matters which they had been told did not concern them. The small cold cells could only accommodate one person, which judging by the state of most of them, seemed most satisfactory.

There was the odd hangover the following morning but hopefully the fresh air would quickly take away the pain and suffering.

Unfortunately, the weather, unlike the hospitality, was not exactly clement, so battling against the oncoming rain, the uneven surface and the rhythmic beat of a pounding head, proved to be an ordeal. Slowly but surely, both the rain and the pounding ceased as they approached Dundalgan. They were extremely surprised by what they found. The settlement was inhabited by several Norwegian Vikings who made the party most welcome.

"How long have you been here?" asked Maarku.

"Less than a year," replied one of the settlers. "We sailed across to Lothlend, but there was much fighting, so came to settle here. It is quiet."

"Why are you here?" he asked.

Maarku replied, "I have been in this country for two years. I am travelling with these friends from Béal Feirsde to Dubh Linn."

"My name is Leif," said the settler.

"And I am Maarku."

Maarku introduced the others and Leif introduced his family. "You are most welcome to join us," he said.

There were some provisions left over from those bought at Ayr and these were shared with Leif, his wife and their two young children. As there was no suitable tavern, in fact no tavern at all for them to stay in, the tent was pitched, the men complaining about having to erect the tent and the woman complaining about having to sleep on hard ground. At least it was dry.

Next stop Dubh Linn. This time, it was Maarku and Robert at the reins. Again, the Viking presence was evident but on a much larger scale, with the establishment of a fortified base. As the group neared the centre, their concern grew as they saw a large number of men, women and children chained in dirty wooden cages.

Maarku and Robert told their passengers to stay out of sight and keep very quiet. They were approached by not one of the most endearing people they had come across, who said in a gruff voice.

"Have you brought more slaves?"

Maarku was somewhat shocked by this question and replied in his native tongue. "Þar er plague. Vér erum taking þessi away til burn bodrrinn." The only two words recognised by the individual were 'plague' and 'burn'. His expression turned to one of horror. He put his hand over his mouth and yelled, "Go," adding, in a very loud voice, "Out of the way, plague."

It was quite surprising how quickly their path out of the town was cleared, the settlers encouraging the travellers to make haste with their departure.

Once they were well out of sight of the area, they stopped the horses. Robert drew alongside Maarku and said, "Was that what I think it was?"

Maarku replied, "I am certain that there were some Vikings trading slaves."

They explained what they had seen to the others.

"What can we do?" asked Boyd.

"There are too many of them for us to help," said Maarku.

Nesta was resting her chin on the door of her carriage with tears in her eyes.

"Where will they be going?" she asked.

"They may go to Scandinavia or east to Persia."

Nesta said nothing, her expression showing her feelings.

"We should move on," said Maarku.

The next planned stop was a three-day journey away. Most of the terrain was open with the odd small hamlet dotted around. The people were extremely friendly and very interested in why two carriages were travelling so far away from the larger villages. The standard answer given was that they were travelling to see family in Sligeach. There weren't too many people around, especially in the middle of nowhere, however they happened to chance on one such individual, who was sitting by the side of the pathway. Robert, who was driving the leading carriage, stopped his horses. Maarku did not take much notice of the stranger and left it to Robert.

"Are you well, sir?" he shouted.

The man turned. He looked scared. "Who are you?" he asked.

"Travellers," replied Robert.

"To where?" he asked.

"West," was the response. The man stood. He was a lanky individual in his early twenties, with short dark hair and a slight Irish accent. He would not exactly stand out in a crowd.

"May I ask for a ride?" said the stranger.

"To where and why are you out here?" asked Robert.

"To Maynooth. I ran from Dubh Linn. I did not wish to be a slave."

"What is your name?" asked Robert.

"Darek," was the response.

Still a little wary of the stranger and not wanting to worry the passengers, Robert invited him to sit in the box seat.

The night was drawing in and the only alternative was the beloved tent. Boyd and Robert went on a hunting expedition while Anika and Lesedi prepared a fire. Maarku thought the situation a little peculiar and disturbingly convenient that the stranger happened to be travelling along that path, but he did not want to pry too much. Nobody said anything, but the stranger did bear an uncanny resemblance to someone they did not wish to encounter quite so soon. Mungo and Robert returned with a few hares which Anika and Lesedi proceeded to roast. Mungo went to sit next to Darek.

"Where are you from?" he asked.

"My father is from Throtmanni, and my mother is from Cork. My father was a trader in fine cottons he brought from India and came here to trade over twenty years ago."

"Your name is not one I know," said Mungo.

"It is from Germania. It means 'ruler of people'."

After eating, Mungo said to Darek, "You are welcome to sleep in one of the carriages."

"I will," he replied.

Mungo went over to Boyd and told him that he felt uneasy about having this stranger with them and that it seemed too much of a coincidence picking up a familiar figure on a lonely road.

"He will only be with us for a short time tomorrow," said Boyd.

"I hope so," said Mungo.

Boyd stayed awake all night watching the carriage in which Darek slept. To Boyd it felt like an exceedingly long night, but eventually morning came. They were all woken by a large skein of loudly quacking ducks flying low overhead. Mungo went over to the carriage where Darek had slept. He opened the carriage door but there was no sign of anyone. He looked all around then thoroughly checked the second carriage — still nobody there but he found a note on the carriage floor which read, 'Ducks but no Darek'.

He froze. Boyd came across and Mungo showed him the note.

He said, "We must leave now. Did Robert say where we were headed?" he asked.

"Robert told him west."

Everything was stored quickly, and they promptly left, nervously looking round for many miles along the route. The women were told that Darek had gone back to Dubh Linn and as there was a good distance to travel, they wanted to get an early start in case the weather turned bad. It was another eighty-five miles to Sligeach which meant another overnight stop, but hopefully not in the tent.

By early evening they arrived at a small farmstead at Rathowen. The occupant greeted them.

"Good day sir," he said in a soft melodic Irish accent.

Upon hearing this, Anika leant out over the carriage door to see a six-foot, well-built, young, blond farmer. The carriage door flew open, and she sauntered casually towards the farmer.

"Greetings," she said, "I am Anika."

"I am Owen," said the lad.

The other women sat amazed at Anika's boldness.

"Can we trouble you to stay here tonight," said Anika. "You have a nice farm and we have journeyed a great distance. We have money for a little food and shelter. We are on our way to Sligeach. There are eight of us." Anika could not stop talking to Owen.

The others just sat there wondering when or if she would ever shut up.

"Who do you live with?" Anika asked. At long last, she had allowed someone else a chance to speak.

"My father, mother and younger sister. There is no room for you in the house, but you are welcome to use the barn."

"Please show me the barn," said Anika. The lad pointed to an unmissably large building next to the house.

"It is there," he said.

"That is a nice barn," she replied. "Is there room for us? Would you show me?" He led Anika to the barn.

"I think we have found someone for Anika," said Lesedi.

As the two walked off, the rest of the family emerged to see what was happening. Boyd greeted them and explained the reason why they were passing by and where they were heading.

"You have met my son. My name is Éogan, this is my wife, Aideen and my daughter Concessa."

The parents were in their early forties and the daughter was around sixteen years of age. By now the whole group had exited the carriages and were talking to the family. Concessa became engrossed in conversation with the women.

"There is little we can offer you," said Éogan.

Boyd called Robert and Maarku over.

"We need to feast," he said. Off they went.

"You are to return to Lothlend?" asked Éogan.

"We are," replied Boyd.

"There is nothing here for us," said Éogan. "We can barely live. We had to hide when they came here looking for slaves."

Aideen started to weep. "I fear for my family. I do not want anyone to take them from us," she said.

Mungo looked at Boyd and said, "Do we have room in the carriages?"

"I think we do," replied Boyd smiling.

The look on Aideen's face was one of absolute disbelief and the tears changed from tears of sadness to tears of total euphoria. She went over to Mungo and threw her arms round his neck. Even Éogan shed a tear.

"You should collect all you wish to bring with you," said Boyd.

Éogan and Aideen had never moved so quickly and within minutes they had returned with a few clothes bundled up.

Owen and Anika came into the house. Owen looked puzzled seeing the bundle of clothes on the floor. Before he could speak, Éogan said, "We are going to Lothlend."

Owen looked shocked and Anika was overjoyed. She went to tell the other women. Matilda noticed Anika's expression.

"Is that the look of love?" she asked. Anika blushed.

Concessa asked, "We are going where?"

They all enjoyed a good portion of wild boar before the travellers settled down in the barn for the night. At least, it was a little more comfortable than having to sleep on the ground.

It was only another forty miles until they reached civilisation. Belongings stacked, off they moved, Owen and Anika drove one carriage and Boyd the other. Concessa travelled with the women while Éogan and Aideen were with the men. Concessa was excited to learn all about the village, while her parents were quite content to enjoy the journey, knowing that, for the first time in many years, they were safe. They had no regrets about leaving their home.

Chapter 25

The Storm Before the Calm

Éogan and Aideen had done a little travelling in Hibernia before they settled in Rathowen and were aware of the strategic importance of Sligeach, having lived there for a brief time. It was first inhabited some ten thousand years before, and megalithic monuments and great cairns dominated the landscape. Its natural harbour invited many tradesfolk; particularly from Francia and Spain. The two were not thrilled with life in such an expanding multi-cultural and multi-lingual area and so moved to somewhere more remote but then had fallen on hard times.

As with many of the places visited, there was the inevitable monastery, this one founded by the Irish monk Columba in the late sixth century, so Boyd thought this would be an ideal place to head for. Sure enough, they were expected, as Brother Martin had already sent word that a group of travellers from Dunkeld, or thereabouts, might well descend on them.

Again, they were made very welcome, were fed, the animals were catered for, and they spent a comfortable night in warm surroundings. The abbot, Brother Breandan, was told to expect eight people, not twelve.

Boyd explained the reason for the additional four, to which the abbot said, "I have heard that there is a slave trade in Dubh Linn, but I did not think it was as bad as you say. It is so sad that this is happening on the other side of Hibernia." He went over to Éogan and Aideen and said, "You are with good people now."

One more day trip over land and then hopefully, Captain Teach would be waiting for them. Maarku and Lesedi took the reins for the final Hibernian leg of the journey north-east to Daire Calgaich.

Éogan, Aideen, Owen and Concessa, still could not believe this was happening to them and throughout the journey were continually asking questions about this unbelievably idyllic place, while still understandably apprehensive as to what lay ahead for them.

The coast was in sight and there in the harbour was the boat they had been waiting to see for the last twelve days. There was a great sigh of relief all round.

"Is the captain going to be on board or in a tavern?" asked Boyd.

The general consensus of opinion was that the tavern was more likely. The boat was becoming larger, the smell of sea water more distinct. As they approached, they saw a lone figure perched precariously on the figurehead, firmly clasping a rapidly disappearing tankard of ale and merrily singing a raunchy sea shanty. The two carriages stopped side by side on the harbour about twenty feet from the boat.

"You are late," slurred the captain.

"You are drunk," replied Boyd.

"Do you like my friend?" asked the captain, putting his arms round the figurehead.

"She is a good woman. Does not speak and you can slide up and down her when you want."

"Is that the captain?" asked Éogan.

Boyd reluctantly admitted that he was.

"Come aboard!" yelled the captain, letting go of the figurehead and dropping unceremoniously into the water.

"Should we leave him there?" asked Maarku.

The temptation was overwhelming, but as they peered into the harbour, they saw the captain float to the surface.

"Maybe just for a short time, but we did promise to take him back to the village," said Mungo.

Robert and Mungo retrieved the captain using a long wooden pole and then helped load the passengers, horses and carriages on board. Night was closing in, so they made themselves comfortable on the boat, and prepared to set sail for Ilea the following morning.

The captain was not in the best of health when he woke and was certainly not capable of either walking or steering a boat in a straight line, so Maarku became the temporary captain, with the others ably assisting as crew members. It was the first time that Éogan and his family had been on a boat, and they spent much of the voyage firmly grasping the sides and making strange noises as the boat ploughed turbulently through the waves.

They reached Ilea by the middle of the day after a six-hour sail, and moored for a short time, so that those unfamiliar with life at sea could regain a little composure and stability.

The good news, as a now sober captain told the family, was that the sail from Ilea to Oban was shorter than the one from Daire Calgaich to Ilea. However, he did not clarify by how much and he also failed to point out that there would be a third and final sail from Oban to Glencoe.

Around five hours later, the Oban coast was a most welcome sight. Unfortunately, the weather was a little unpredictable and the choppy seas forced the boat to anchor a little way offshore, much to the frustration of several of the travellers who found sleeping impossible. Calm followed and early the next morning the passengers were looking forward to firm land until the captain broke the good news about the final trip by sea. However, as it was not on the open sea, the sail would be a little less rough. This only slightly appeased the family.

The three-hour trip seemed to pass reasonably quickly. At least there was land on both sides of the loch. They reached Glencoe at last, where everything was unloaded. Éogan and his family, all looking a little worse for wear and visibly shaking, needed to be led slowly along the gangplank by two helpers, who could not resist telling, them not to look down at the water. The four sat on the ground a little distance from the water, breathing slowly but all they felt when they closed their eyes, was the sensation of bobbing up and down on an open sea, which again led to a little upsetting of the digestive system.

Forty-five miles left. Even the captain was excited by the prospect of settling down.

"Will my boat be safe here?" he asked.

"It will," replied Boyd confidently, but not exactly honestly adding, "I will make certain it is watched."

After resting or more accurately recovering for a good hour, it was time to leave. Completing the journey by the end of the day was possible but it would mean pushing the horses, so they decided to travel till the light began to fade. They made good progress and covered about twenty-five miles, Matilda and Nesta this time drove the horses and felt much more confident in that there were either hardly any derogatory remarks or such remarks were kept quiet, as everybody was exhausted. Tents were pitched, some provisions which the captain had left over were eagerly devoured and in no time at all, a well-deserved sleep prevailed, with nobody complaining about having to pitch the tent or the hard ground.

It was quite fortuitous that they had all eaten well the previous evening, as there was not even a crumb remaining for breakfast. With half a day to go, everything packed, Boyd and Robert took the reins for the final leg. They were all excited at the prospect of being home. Mungo was sure he saw the captain smile for the first time. It was less than twenty days but seemed like much, much longer with everything that had happened. Concessa was asking the same questions over and over again and Anika was still looking lovingly into Owen's eyes as they entered the village. Having Hithin, Gerik, Frothi and Ulf there to greet them was very welcoming.

As they all stepped out of the carriages, Gerik looked at the number of unattached women brought back. "I count one," he said.

"We will explain," said a tired Boyd. "We have not eaten today."

"Welcome home," said Gerik, as he walked them to the kitchens. "In the morning, we will all meet and then you can talk about your journey and of those you have brought back to us," he added.

The family was escorted to a spare room until something a little more permanent could be arranged and the captain bunked in with the single men, after having been forced to take a long overdue wash. It was good to be home.

That was to be the last trip for quite some time.

After breakfast, the whole village met up in the church hall. Boyd and Mungo formally introduced and welcomed the newcomers and summarised the events of the last few weeks. Two major concerns were raised. Firstly, was the involvement of Norwegian Vikings in a particularly brutal slave trade and secondly who was the mysterious figure that had appeared and then disappeared.

Hithin looked at Brother Martin and said, "Was that another lost soul?" The monk said nothing.

On the first matter, Hithin said, "We have good defences and lookouts and I do think we are safe here. We always have Lesedi's sauces if enemies get too close."

Anika was still totally infatuated with Owen; and now the young Concessa seemed to have a fixation on Frothi which hardly seemed a fair match, based on the vast difference in size between the two.

On the way out of the church, Concessa caught up with Frothi and in a very sweet and innocent voice said, "Will you show me round the village? I feel safe with you." He agreed, not realising how the girl felt about him.

Hithin, Boyd, Gerik and Mungo stayed back in the church.

"Will the village survive?" asked a very pensive Hithin.

"There is much happening around us of which we are not aware. I think Brother Martin knows more than he is telling us. The messengers take word to him after every visit to Dunkeld, but he is not willing to reveal much to us."

"Should we speak to him?" asked Gerik.

"We must speak to Mildrith," replied Hithin. "She may tell us much of what we seek from Martin but for now say nothing. Let us join the others."

Éogan and Aideen were sitting on their own, relaxing and enjoying one of Malcolm's delicious meat and vegetable pies and sampling one of Berta's interestingly blended teas.

"What is this?" asked Aideen.

"Onion, watermelon and lemon tea," replied Berta.

"Do you like it?"

"It is very different," replied a diplomatic Aideen.

"Would you like more?" asked Berta.

"I have not quite finished this one," said Aideen.

Fortunately, Gerik approached and said, "When you are ready, I will show you round the village."

"I think we are ready now," said Aideen hastily.

"We have become used to Berta's teas and try to avoid them when we can. Where are your children?" asked Gerik.

"Owen is with Anika, and Concessa is still following Frothi. We are not seeing much of them this minute, but we know they are safe. I still cannot believe that we are here."

"Boyd did say to me how much you enjoyed sailing," said Gerik.

"I still see water when I close my eyes," replied Aideen shaking her head.

Gerik showed them round and explained that everyone has a role in the village and that it was up to them to discover what they would like to do and where they would fit in.

Owen and Anika, Maarku and Lesedi and Frothi and Concessa were eventually married. Offspring appeared with fair regularity; however Eangyth did not stray again off the beaten track. The children grew, being well taught in many subjects, both academic and practical and with news and information sent by the contacts from overseas, they soon learnt the techniques of profitable one-sidedness.

Captain Teach had now resigned himself to a life on the land, enjoying telling stories of his exploits to the youngsters. However, he did draw the line at being called 'granddad' by one of Matilda's children.

Sadly, age caught up with the original settlers and it became the turn of the second generation to continue the hard work and dedication laid down by a determined group of battle-weary warriors. From necessity, more journeys had to be made overseas and willing volunteers were recruited to ensure the continual existence of the village.

A strange feeling came over the villagers from time to time. They felt as though someone or something was influencing them in their actions; not in a bad way, but mostly in a positive way. Whether it was through the legacy laid down by their ancestors or just a cordial spirit that prevailed within the village, nobody could tell, but it did not detract from their daily life.

All seemed too perfect.

Chapter 26

As Time Went By

During the next four hundred years, towards the beginning of the thirteenth century, Viking raids continued to diminish until the year 1263, after the Battle of Largs, when through the Treaty of Perth, they surrendered all their territory in Scotland, apart from the Orkneys and Shetland for a substantial sum of money, which was quite fortuitous; as it would have meant revealing the non-existent Haudonia Isle.

By the mid-eighteenth century, the villagers had travelled the world, built new alliances and recruited willing souls, while still managing to maintain a relatively one-sided approach to sharing developments, techniques and practices. Neither the size nor the average population of Stoleware greatly changed over the years, but its ability to extract, disseminate and enhance processes from outside sources grew exponentially.

The underground chamber amassed a great deal of treasures over the centuries, from around the globe. Lost masterpieces of art had a way of miraculously manifesting themselves inside the chamber. Developments in preservation techniques ensured the life span of these precious, priceless works.

Villagers came and went, but they always kept in contact with their home, relaying vital snippets of information to assist in the advancement of Stoleware, not that the terms 'industrial espionage' or 'classified information' were ever abused.

Nearly forty generations have passed since the village began, but still meticulously detailed records were maintained. It sometimes felt as if the likes of Alpin, Boyd, Sister Eangyth and all the others were still part of the community. Those who ventured away from the village never divulged its location and those towns and villages overseas still maintained the same affiliation to Stoleware as they had all those years before. Hacking and forgery had been developed and perfected since the introduction of computerisation. However this was never used maliciously; purely out of necessity and convenience.

The village had its unwelcome visitors from time to time. However, they were put off by the twelve-foot retractable barriers and the bright red signs displaying the notice, 'Restricted Area, Schuno Disease Testing Site;' nobody realising that 'schuno' is an anagram of 'No such.' It worked though.

As the years slipped by, villagers sought a more adventurous lifestyle and slowly but surely, despite this idyllic and self-sufficient hideaway, ventured to pastures new, causing the population to decrease quite dramatically until there was almost no one left.

From time to time, the odd inhabitant did return to make sure the village looked presentable, but again this became more of a chore, rather than a pleasure, until only one person religiously took care of the village.

A Little Ending

The vault just outside the village has undergone many changes and I have maintained it with both the latest technology but more frighteningly, from random thoughts in my mind which I do not always fully understand. It sometimes feels like I am possessed.

I am aware of everything that has happened over the last twelve hundred years; how history has been shaped, and how easily people can be influenced or manipulated by greed and false promises, much to my shame, being guilty of the latter on several occasions.

Brother Martin had the inscription 'Cursum Perficio' on his headstone. My journey has still not ended but for now, I sit relaxing in a perfectly secluded, unspoilt clearing in the woods, admiring the calming flow of the nearby stream. Suddenly a fully mature prime salmon leaps majestically, seemingly effortlessly, hardly disturbing the water's surface as it displays a perfect, almost acrobatic arc before returning gracefully to the clear water.

It is so quiet now with no one else around. There is only the slight humming coming from the units controlling the air in the vault, keeping everything stored there at the correct temperature.

There are no more copies of the brooch left. Over the years, they were entrusted to those who were thought to be of good repute and would not be corrupted by power and wealth, but history shows that it is not always possible to be a particularly good judge of character.

Now there is only the one brooch remaining here. It was said that Mælbrigða used to own this brooch, but it now belongs to me.

My name is Alam Briðge, but you know me better as Drake.

The End

Appendix 1

Places referenced with both their original and current name (The year denotes the approximate year the current name was adopted)

UK Towns

Original	Current	Year
Béal Feirsde	Belfast	1611
Cas Chaolas	Queensferry	1068
Cathures	Glasgow	1116
Daire Calgaich	Londonderry	1613
Dub Glais	Douglas	1203
Dubh Linn	Dublin	1368
Dùn Dèagh	Dundee	1200
Striveling	Stirling	1120

Foreign Towns & Villages

Original	Current	Year
Amestelle	Amsterdam	1327
Arneym	Arnhem	1233
Frankenfort	Frankfurt	1850
Munichen	Munich	1158
Juvavum	Salzburg	700
Sigena	Siegen	1224
Stuotgarten	Stuttgart	1220

Countries

Original	Current	Year
Belgica	Belgium	1830
Čzechy	Slovakia	1918
Dali, Jin, Song, Xia	China	1850
Ungai	Hungary	1178

Seas

Original	Current	Year
Frisian Sea	North Sea	1919
Inner Sea	North Channel	1858

Appendix 2

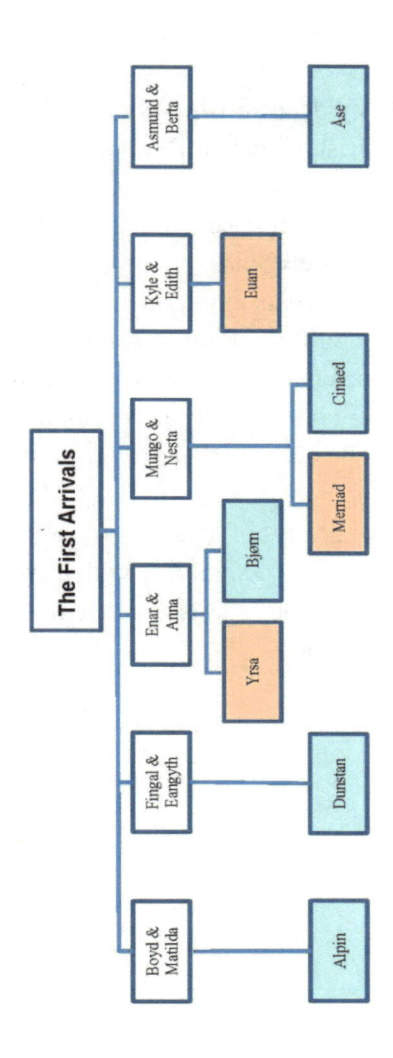

The First Arrivals

- Asmund & Berta
  - Ase
- Kyle & Edith
  - Euan
- Mungo & Nesta
  - Cinaed
  - Merriad
- Enar & Anna
  - Bjorn
  - Yrsa
- Fingal & Eangyth
  - Dunstan
- Boyd & Matilda
  - Alpin

About the Author

Born and raised in Poulton-le-Fylde, near Blackpool in 1955, educated at a local grammar school run by Irish Christian Brothers, then after studying for a degree in Maths and Music at Liverpool, I spent fifteen years as a computer programmer before trying to teach young drivers how to master the art of self-preservation on today's roads.

Now retired, it was time to fulfil an ambition.

I have always been an admirer of the legendary comedian Billy Connolly and how he can create comical situations out of simple everyday events. Coupled with a fascination for the brain as a source of energy, the two topics provide an unlikely combination for inspirational material, however...

This is the tale of how two groups of battle-weary warriors who unite to create and develop a self-sufficient community with all good intentions, but unfortunately, they misjudged the long-term sincerity and potency of individuals destined to shape the future.